The Caretakers
Adrian Chamberlin
ISBN: 978-0-9831603-5-9
Published April 2011 by
Dark Continents Publishing

www.darkcontinents.com

Book design by John Prescott
Cover Illustration by Jethro Lentle

to

Rachel!

THE CARETAKERS

Enjoy the dark side of

Cambridge!

Love and best wishes,

a. Chambers

1.12.11

Happy Birthday!

Oculi omnium in te spirant, Domine, et tu das escam illorum in tempore opportune.

The eyes of all wait upon thee, O Lord, and thou givest them their meat in due season.

- Extract from Grace spoken at High Table, All Souls College, Cambridge

Fail not our feast.

- Shakespeare, *Macbeth* Act III Scene I

PROLOGUE

Durolipons, AD 61

Gaius Suetonius Paulinus was puzzled by the old priest's smile. It was one of relief and satisfaction, as though the druid had witnessed a great victory.

He's witnessed the end of his order, the Roman Governor of Britannia thought. *He knows I'm going to kill him regardless of the promise I made to him on the Isle of Mona. And yet he's content. I'll never understand these people.*

"You do not need to, Roman."

Awen's broken-toothed smile grew wider at the sight of the Governor's stunned expression. "You would not understand." He sighed wistfully, his breath misting in the winter air as he stroked the ground with his bony fingers, ground that had burned with so much heat parts had turned to glass. Shadowy, skeletal figures could be seen beneath the shining surface and it was only now with the rising of the sun that Paulinus realised they were the remains of the priesthood.

Paulinus suppressed a shiver. It would not do to show fear in front of the old druid, but the memory of what he had seen would never leave him. He almost relished the prospect of battle tomorrow with that Iceni bitch. *Odds of twenty three to one*, he mused. *And I'd much rather that than face what I saw last night.*

He pulled his cloak tighter round his shoulders and surveyed the scorched wasteland they stood upon. The closest oak trees in the sacred grove of Durolipons had been incinerated, wiped from the earth by a fire so pure, so fierce, it could only have come from Hell itself. Yet the trees that surrounded it were untouched. No scorch marks showed on the thick trunks. Even the heavy blankets of snow on the twisted branches remained frozen.

The air still stank of smoke, although the fire had extinguished itself last night, dying down with the fierce cold of the winter night.

He inhaled and took in the stink of burnt meat. The stench of cooked human flesh from the druids who had offered themselves.

"She's gone," Awen grinned at Paulinus. "She, and her Children. The world is safe."

Paulinus grunted and spat contemptuously. "Your world, druid? Or Rome's?"

"It matters not, Roman. All things pass. Even gods have their day."

"As have you, Awen." Paulinus smirked as he nodded to a centurion. The soldier advanced, his gladius drawn. But if the Governor of Britannia had hoped to see a trace of fear in the old man's eyes he was to be disappointed.

Awen turned from the holocaust, gave a cursory glance to the approaching swordsman and stared deeply into Paulinus' eyes. The Governor almost started. *Gods, this man's eyes aren't human. That shade of green is unlike anything I have ever seen. And are those flecks of gold in the iris?*

Surely not. It had to be the angle of the sunlight. Perhaps the inferno he had witnessed had temporarily affected his vision. Tiredness, also. He had not sufficiently rested after his cleansing of the priesthood on the Isle of Mona. Weeks of forced marching through the wilds of this accursed land, a march against time to meet Boudicca before she turned any more of Britannia into the smoking ruins that Londinium and Camulodunum had become.

"You think me traitor, Roman? That our Order has banished *Her* from this plane…and thus condemned Boudicca to defeat?" He shook his mane of filthy grey hair and laughed, a cackle of old bones grinding together.

"No. The Iceni queen had no right to invoke Andraste. We beseeched her not to, but she would not listen." A grey-skinned finger jabbed Paulinus' breastplate. "She didn't listen…but who can blame her? After what you bastards did to her and her daughters she was blind with rage. A rage that would burn the world with Andraste by her side…all because you wanted to teach her a lesson in humility!

"Just think how close you came to ending the world. Be glad some of the old priesthood were here, knew what was required...and were willing to pay the price."

A smile broke through Paulinus' sneer. "And you, Awen? What about you?"

Awen shook his head. "Kill me if you wish, Roman. I have done my duty – I came here to bear witness that Andraste is no more. Go now. Go and face Boudicca. You have only human foes to deal with now…*so be grateful!*"

Paulinus nodded to the centurion. He watched the sword slide into the druid's stomach dispassionately, feeling neither remorse nor joy. The priest's hot blood steamed in the dawn air and painted the glassy ground a rich scarlet. The Governor inhaled deeply, and then frowned.

Another scent assailed his nose. A coarse, rich smell. Slightly peppery…

Boar, he realised. *Wild boar.*

He heard a strangled cry from Awen, one of despair rather than pain. He turned.

The old druid lay on his back, his death throes smearing the pool of blood beneath him into a bizarre pattern. His entrails steamed in the fresh morning air, but it was not the prospect of death that had made Awen cry out. The priest raised a shaking hand towards a darker patch of the woods where the sun had yet to shine.

"One survives! Destroy it…or it is all for nothing!"

Paulinus laughed as the beast slowly emerged from the darkened trees. It was huge, one that would easily weigh more than six of his legionaries in full battle dress – and would have presented a fair challenge had it not been in such a state.

It limped on burned limbs that were no more than charred, deformed sticks, scarcely able to support its weight. Paulinus could see ragged holes in its flanks; coils of intestines slipped from its sliced belly and trailed along the leaf litter.

It came closer to what had once been the sacred grove, grunting and wheezing, in obvious pain but determined to reach its destination. It lowered its head on the glassed ground, tilted at an angle with a sigh that sounded almost human.

It then let out a harsh squeal, more akin to the wolves that had haunted Paulinus' nights in Germania than a wild boar. Black blood dripped from its maw onto the scorched, melted earth that had been the sacred grove.

"That? Look at it, druid! It's dying, no threat to us." Perhaps the heat had driven the creatures mad, some gouging and impaling each other as they fought to escape into the woods, away from the conflagration. This was obviously the sole survivor.

The eyes of the boar were glazed. Whatever spirit was in them had departed. And yet…

Was that a red glint in the centre of the eyes? Paulinus blinked and turned away from the creature. The rising sun had reflected in them, that was all.

"No threat at all, druid. So -"

The old priest's eyes were the same opaque black as the eyes of the boar. His hand lay on the blood-soaked ground, as motionless as the rest of his body.

Paulinus looked up to the centurion. "Come. We have a battle to fight. The Iceni bitch needs another lesson…"

His voice died away at the sight of the soldier's shocked expression. He turned on his heel.

The boar had gone.

Impossible! How could it disappear like that? It couldn't have been dead…but how did it get to its feet and lope into the surviving woods so quickly?

Paulinus took a deep breath. The druid's parting gift, an act of sorcery to befuddle his mind and dull his military planning?

No. These druids are rabble rousers and madmen, no more. Put it out of your mind, concentrate on the coming battle.

They made their way out of the blasted grove, through the darkness of the thick oaks to join the road south. But Suetonius Paulinus couldn't stop himself looking at the boar's resting place one last time.

Sunlight reflected off the glassy ground. The blood of the druid and the boar slowly sank into the ground, out of sight.

ONE

Two pieces of bad news were waiting for Andy Hughes when he returned home from the questioning at the police station. The first was a letter from Jen. The second was the person sitting on his sofa reading it.

Combined with what had happened earlier that night at The Porterhouse confirmed the old maxim, *they always come in threes.* He knew something was wrong when he saw Jen's Saxo had gone, replaced with a silver Mercedes that was coated with fresh, powdery snow. That car belonged to only one man.

I don't need this, Andy thought as he rubbed the teeth marks on his forehead. Looking at his fingers he realised there was still a bit of dried blood there. He rubbed it, watched it flake away and fall to the ground. Red flakes lay on top of white flakes, soon obscured by the fresh snow falling to the ground.

He pushed the door open, not surprised to find it unlocked. The house was still warm. Jen had left the central heating on for him, realising that the walk home from the police station - whatever time they released him – would be a cold one.

It was the only warmth in the room. The Christmas tree was sparse and cheerless with the lights switched off. All plans for a quiet Christmas together were well and truly scrubbed now with the presence of the man on the sofa.

Graham Pearce looked up from the letter and smiled warmly. As if he was just an old friend come to pay a social call, embarrassed at having arrived without proper notice. His appearance didn't correspond with his past, or his reputation: a slightly built man who looked more like an accountant than a villain. The elegant, well cut suit and dull grey tie underneath the sober, business-like overcoat added to the illusion. The thinning grey hair was neatly trimmed and combed. The warm grey eyes seemed to smile innocently from behind his owlish, horn-rimmed glasses. His hands were raised as if in supplication.

All an act. When those hands were raised like that someone was going to suffer.

"Hello Andy. I hope you didn't mind me letting myself in." Even the voice gave no clues to his profession. Well spoken, crisp and professional.

"Where's Jen?" Andy already knew the answer. That letter Pearce held had what looked like her handwriting on it. Wherever she had gone, she had gone willingly.

"I think you'd better read this for yourself." Pearce passed the letter and sat back in the sofa, his hands in his lap. He cast an eye towards the overflowing bookcases, eyebrows raised at the contents. World History and the Penguin Classics. Dickens, Hardy, Dostoyevsky, Flaubert. Recent volumes, purchased and read thoroughly. Not old, forgotten course books from a long abandoned academic career. Above the middle bookcase was a framed quotation. Pearce read it and smiled.

"'A room without books is like a body without a soul.' Very nice. Seneca, I believe."

"Cicero."

Pearce grinned. "I see you kept up your learning, then."

Andy didn't reply. He read the letter.

I'm sorry to do it this way, Andy, it began. Handwritten, in blue ink. The ink had run in the latter part of the letter, splodges caused by what could only be tears.

But I think you knew this was coming. I can't go on like this. I know you love me and would never do a thing to hurt me, and God help me I love you too. I think I'll always love you.

But I'm scared, Andy. I'm scared of the darkness in you. The violence. You've never raised a finger towards me, you've never threatened me, never even raised your voice to me during our arguments. But I've seen how easy it is for you to lose control, how much you rage at the world. And it's not just what happened to you in the past. You were born with this rage, Andy. A rage that is one day going to destroy you – and probably everyone who loves you.

When you called from the police station, telling me what you'd done…I realised that the time is coming, and has probably already arrived. And I don't want to be in the fallout zone.

But that's not the only reason I'm leaving you.

I found what you've been hiding. In the attic for God's sake! Why bring that into OUR HOME?

He lowered the letter and groaned. The letter ended with *I'm going away for a while. With Christmas just round the corner I know it's bad timing. But I need some time to think, to work out my options, what I want to do with my life. So I'm going to stay at mum's for a while.*

Please, don't try to get in touch. I'll talk to you when I'm ready.

Jen.

He tried to picture her as she climbed into her car, driving away from the two bedroom house on Didcot's Ladygrove estate, their home for the last three years. Good years, mostly.

Would there have been tears as she closed the door? Or would there have been a smile of relief, a sense of exhilaration, freedom to start afresh? He didn't know. All he knew was the pain the image of her leaving gave him: for the first time in his life a pain he couldn't deal with.

He had suffered physical pain before. He had been beaten, kicked, slashed at with broken beer bottles. It came with the territory. All part of the job. But it was physical pain, felt for mere moments – and then returned twice-fold upon the instigators of the violence. As it had been last night at The Porterhouse.

In his three years of working there his colleagues had accepted and respected him, but also kept their distance. They could see there was something unique about Andy Hughes. He certainly looked the part of a professional doorman, six foot two, solidly built. Shaven head and a hard, appraising stare, a permanent frown on his angular features, but all this could not disguise the fact that Andy Hughes was different.

A difference they could not identify. It wasn't his refined manner of speaking, his command of language. All sorts make a world, and becoming a doorman was not the worst career choice a university dropout could make.

It was partly his eyes. They were a shade of green that few people had ever seen, the shade that Jen had first been drawn to when they'd first met. A luminescent, piercing green with flecks of gold that she said looked like *the sort of glowing jewels for which Indiana Jones would cross continents.*

But that wasn't the sole reason. They sensed something else about him, the darkness Jen had struggled to live with. A darkness that was to be kept at bay, respected. And feared.

No-one feared that darkness more than Andy himself.

Before he'd arrived at the club he had the feeling that something else was going to go wrong. He'd ignored it, pushed the thought away, but all through the evening it kept crawling back, nagging at him. He knew why it wouldn't be suppressed. The genie was going to launch itself from the bottle again.

The previous night's dream of the horses proved that. The stampeding, unearthly white stallions, tearing up the ground and pounding flesh and bones into jelly…

The last time he'd dreamed of the horses was fifteen years ago, when his life had ended.

"A shame." Pearce's smile was far from sympathetic. "I've heard good things about Jennifer. Such a nice young girl, and she's been good for you. Still, nothing lasts forever. Patience runs out, passion fades and dies. Perhaps she felt that she could do better than an ex-con with nothing to offer but a pittance of a doorman's wages... "

Andy was on him in an instant. Pearce's silk tie was clenched in his fist, his whole body raised off the sofa. Pearce's expression changed suddenly. Gone was the smug, self-righteous smirk. It was not replaced with fear, as was so often the case with those who found themselves on the wrong side of Andy's fists. Now there was a look of calm scrutiny, as though Pearce had been testing him, an appraisal of his reaction and reflexes.

"Good, Andy. Very good indeed. Do you know, for a moment I almost felt frightened then?"

Andy's body went limp. His fist unclenched, the tie slipped from his fingers and Pearce relaxed into the sofa. One thing he could never do was attack Graham Pearce. Not if he wanted to continue living.

Pearce straightened his tie fussily, *tut-tutting* at the tightened knot. He indicated the letter. "She's right, though, isn't she? Violence comes too easily to you.

"Look at the facts. It has been an intolerable strain on your relationship with the lovely Jennifer. It has earned you a prison sentence and a criminal record. You probably know that the owner of The Porterhouse didn't want to employ you in the first place…but he owed me a favour." He raised an admonishing finger. "You make people nervous. That club was getting too much attention as it was. The police were keeping a close eye on it, too close for his liking. Now, of course, it is very unlikely that it will keep its licence. That young man is fighting for his life in the John Radcliffe as we speak…"

"No great loss if he doesn't make it," Andy snapped. "Not after what he did. Even the Old Bill said he deserved it – when the interview finished, of course."

"Well, that's the problem." Pearce sighed. "I had to call in a rather large favour to ensure you got away. Didn't you think it odd that they released you when they did? 'Reasonable force' doesn't come into this, Andy. They'll know the SIA licence I got you was a fake. They'll be watching you." *And me as well*, his eyes said.

"Fine. Thanks for the update." Andy said. He looked at the cards Blu-tacked on the walls, realising how many of them were addressed just to Jen. Even the card from her parents made no mention of his name. "I don't need to remind you that the SIA ticket was in return for the favour I did for *you*. Looking after the thing that freaked Jen out – I've been holding it for over a year. When are you going to take it back?"

Pearce laughed. "Relax, Andy. I'll send someone round for it after Christmas. In the meantime, I have a proposition for you."

"Not interested."

"Hear me out, please, Andy." Pearce's face was grave. He steepled his fingers. "I need your help."

Andy frowned. "You need *my* help? What the hell for?"

"A very important job, which I'll make worth your while. Six grand. That'll get you back on your feet again. Think very carefully before you turn it down. It's a lot of money."

"What sort of job?"

"There'll be no violence involved, I promise you. I want you to find an individual for me." He reached into his inside pocket and pulled out a 6 x 4 colour photo. "The address is on the back. Perhaps a break there will do you some good. Where is it Jennifer's mother lives exactly?"

"St Neots," Andy replied, taking the photo.

"Ah yes, St Neots. Cambridgeshire, I believe." Pearce smiled.

Andy frowned. He saw the reason for Pearce's smile when he finally read the name and address on the back of the photo.

"You're joking."

"You see now why I thought of you for this, Andy. You know the city very well."

"That was a long time ago, Pearce." He flipped the photo over and scrutinised the face. "What do you want this guy for, anyway? Has he fucked you over in some way?"

"Not at all. He went missing a year ago. Completely out of character, by all accounts. His parents are not happy with the police investigations, and have approached me to find him. With Christmas in a few days' time, it would be a lovely present for them to know their beloved son is safe and well."

"A year's a long time. How do you know he's still there – or even still alive?"

"Let's just say I'm acting on information received from a reliable source."

Pearce's voice wavered slightly. Andy pondered this.

"Don't suppose you can tell me who this 'source' is? And how much are you charging the parents?"

"That is not your concern, Andy." There was a flash of anger in Pearce's eyes, and Andy knew he'd hit a nerve. Perhaps this source was something that even Pearce was scared of. He mentally filed it away, just in case the situation turned nasty.

"I'm doing his parents a favour," Pearce continued. "I'm doing *you* a favour also. Cambridge is not far from St Neots. Perhaps you could pop over there during your investigations, talk to Jennifer…"

Andy sighed. Just like before, when they were both nearing the end of their sentences, Pearce was pushing the right buttons. Money, to solve his financial problems. Fresh location, an area where his reputation would be if not unknown, at least forgotten. And, of course, Jen.

He'd immediately considered going to St Neots, knowing that Jen wouldn't be receptive to phone calls or emails. Only a face-to-face meeting would give him answers and the hope of winning her back. Now the decision had been made for him.

"When was the last time you went to Cambridge, Andy?" Pearce watched him shrewdly, noted his discomfort at the mention of the city. The memories it had stirred.

The city Andy thought he'd settle down in, the degree he thought he'd finish… and of course, the night it had all ended. His sudden, forced departure from Cambridge.

"You know the answer to that, Pearce." *Fifteen years ago. Never been back.*

"It's still a lovely city. There's a particularly fine hotel I can recommend, a wonderful view of the Backs – "

"No," Andy said. "No hotels. I know someone who can put me up for a while. Old college friend."

"Well, that's up to you, of course," Pearce shrugged. "But please – be discreet."

Andy nodded slowly, miles away. Pearce looked at his watch.

"Goodness me, is that the time?" He pulled out a business card and handed it over. Andy pocketed it without even looking at it, not concerned with the name and identity of whatever front Pearce was now using for his activities.

"Please keep me updated on your progress. There are two very worried parents I have to consider. It may be an idea to leave this morning. The sooner you get started the better. And of course, you can't leave Jennifer for too long…"

No, I guess I can't.

"One other thing. Look under the tree, Andy. I think she's left you a present."

As the door closed behind Pearce, Andy looked around the front room of the house. Didcot burglars wouldn't be interested in his books, the TV and DVD were too cheap to be bothered with…and Jen would've taken all the stuff that mattered to her. She'd left all her DVDs, but the laptop – *her* laptop - had gone.

He sighed as he crouched under the Christmas tree. Only one gift there – he'd been so busy working extra shifts to make ends meet he hadn't had time to get Jen a present.

He frowned as he retrieved the parcel. It wasn't Jen's usual taste in wrapping; the tissue paper was green rather than the expensive foil wrap she normally wrapped his birthday and Christmas gifts in. He smiled faintly as he read the message on the tag.

Merry XXXmas, darling. Enjoy! Jennie.

Odd. Wasn't that the same message she wrote on the tag last year? And she normally signed off with *Pixie Jennie*…

The parcel was circular and felt heavy. The tell-tale noise of popping bubble wrap filled his ears as his fingers tightened on the present. Tears welled in his eyes.

He couldn't bear to open it. They always opened their gifts together, and he was determined this year would be no exception. He placed it on the sofa and went upstairs.

He remembered how her impish face would light up with glee at the opening of his gifts to her. Remembered previous Christmases when she would run downstairs in her nightie, her bobbed hair a complete red shock of uncombed chestnut. Giggling like an over-excited schoolgirl as she opened the final window on the advent calendar and popped the chocolate into Andy's mouth. Then her tongue; then rolling on the floor in passionate abandon, the Christmas presents forgotten.

He shuddered as he passed the open hatch that led to the loft. *How could I have been so bloody stupid?*

He stripped off and headed for the shower. *And to lose control again! Christ, the things she's had to put up with…*

As the hot jets warmed and soothed his strained muscles he thought back to the incident in The Porterhouse.

Barging through the door. The taps on one of the basins were on full, gushing water that overflowed and pooled onto the tiled floor. Handbags were scattered, their contents emptied on the floor. There was a line of three cubicles at the opposite end. Two were open, the swing doors swaying. The middle one was closed, the red engaged sign on. It was from this one that the screams were emanating.

Andy ran forwards, kicked upwards, saw the thin chipboard around the catch crack and fall away as the door swung inwards. The girl twisted her head around and saw Andy. Her eyes were filled with agony, terror and humiliation.

Andy snarled as he lathered body wash over his bruised shoulders. Two memories there. The one opened the locked doorway to the other…

She was in her early twenties. Andy recognised her from earlier on in the evening, a stunning brunette who had politely rebuffed all offers from the drunken blokes on the dance floor. Out of their league, and they knew it, but that had obviously not stopped one of them refusing to take no for an answer.

She was pressed against the end wall of the cubicle, her skirt hitched above her thighs, her torn underwear pushed below her knees. The man holding her had his left hand to her throat, beginning to throttle her. His right hand held the knife tightly, point pressed below her ear. His trousers were around his ankles but not even the sound of splintering wood or the thud of the cubicle door crashing into his naked backside distracted him from his victim.

KELLY! A voice within Andy screamed, fifteen years ago….

Andy stood motionless under the shower water. His body tensed again, and this time the hot jets of the shower did nothing to relax him.

Andy grabbed him by the hair, pulled his head back sharply while simultaneously reaching for the knife hand. His fingers clenched around the tendons in the man's wrist. He applied pressure, digging deeply. A loud screech followed, the knife dropped and Andy was pulling the rapist from his victim and out of the cubicle.

Andy's unnaturally green eyes narrowed, stared into the would-be rapist's eyes with a new sense of revulsion. He took his hand away from the man's scalp, grabbed him by the shirt collar and pulled him up to his own height. The man's feet dangled a full four inches above the tiled floor. The collar of the shirt began to tear.

Andy drew his head back and snapped forwards with devastating accuracy and force. The rapist's nose exploded and Andy felt hot gushing blood coursing down his no-longer white shirt. He didn't even wince in pain as teeth pierced the skin of his forehead. But he smiled at the sound of those teeth cracking and splintering.

The rapist fell to the tiled floor in a crumpled heap but there was no sign of pain or fear in his eyes. There was instead a challenge, aggression. Andy had noted the wide-open stare, the dilated pupils and had drawn his own conclusions. Cocaine and blades, smuggled into the club…someone on the door had been more than fucking sloppy – they'd been paid. Questions would be asked, and someone would have to answer.

But that could wait.

He shaved quickly, ignoring the burning, rage-filled green eyes that glared back at him accusingly.

The rapist got to his feet, a broken-toothed snarl on his blood-drenched face. He tried to step backwards into the cubicle, to get to the knife, but he forgot that his trousers were still around his ankles. He fell backwards and Andy stood motionless. Mentally judged the distance between the man's chest and his foot.

His leg shot out, steel toecaps meeting soft flesh and bone. Andy heard a sharp, satisfying crack and saw that the fractured ribs had pierced a lung because his victim was now spewing blood onto the floor. Now he was in pain, and the coke was no longer an anaesthetic. He writhed on the floor, clutching his chest and howling.

Andy stepped forwards. He was not even exerting himself. Sweat had yet to break out on his body, he was not even breathing heavily. That would come. He hadn't started yet.

The genie broke free. History was repeated and there was nothing he could do to prevent it. Like the stampeding horses of his dreams, crushing and pummelling defenceless flesh beneath their hooves, he was an unstoppable force of nature.

More cracking. More thudding of soft, battered flesh. He saw nothing else, focussed on nothing but the human kick bag in front of him and the work left to do. He wasn't aware of the girl screaming at him, begging him to stop. Wasn't aware of the sounds of approaching footsteps until the policeman's hand was on his shoulder…

He dried off and changed into a pair of jeans and black sweatshirt, comfortable enough travelling wear. Then he began to pack.

After the clothes and toiletries, he remembered the item in the attic that had freaked Jen out. Might be an idea to pack that as well. Pearce had said the job would not involve violence, but Andy was doubtful. Nothing Pearce said was to be trusted. If things got complicated, he might be glad he'd brought it along.

After packing the holdall with Pearce's 'favour' and Jen's present to him he made a phone call to National Rail Enquiries to check times for trains to Cambridge. Surprisingly, the heavy snowfall hadn't affected the lines.

He checked his watch. Half past four in the morning. It was too early to call Rob Benson. Hell, half *eleven* in the morning would be too early to call him. That old boy did like his sleep, had done since his college days.

He'd call later, when he was in Cambridge. No sense disturbing him now.

He thought about getting a taxi, then decided against it. Didcot Parkway wasn't far from here. A walk in the night air would do him good: keep him cold, alert and awake. Would keep the nightmares away.

With his holdall slung over his shoulder, he closed the door and locked it. Through the heavy canvas, the cold steel of Pearce's possession pressed hard into his shoulder as he walked. He ignored the pain and shouldered his burden.

He never looked back.

TWO

Rob Benson knew he was going to have a very bad day. The text message from Andy Hughes proved that.

The Nokia's alarm rang at seven a.m., as it did every morning. And every morning, this one included, he picked it up and threw it on the floor That would be Jasper's signal to jump from the foot of the bed, run over and pick the mobile phone up. Run back, jump onto the bed and drop it on his new and somewhat reluctant master's pillow, dripping with doggy saliva. The combination of *flob* and tail thumping violently on his legs was usually better than any snooze button. Last night, however, on top of the booze Rob Benson had overindulged on some seriously potent dope and had every intention of remaining dead to the world.

Nasty shit, he thought to himself as he rolled over and buried his head in the pillow. *Don't want dreams like that again…*

He shuddered as he turned over. It had to be the skunk. Where Dan and Emma had got it God only knew. All he knew was that he wouldn't be touching that shit again. Dreams like last night's he could do without.

The Nokia was next to his right ear. Jasper prodded it with his nose, pushing it further inwards. The Nokia vibrated with the incoming text. On its lowest setting, it still felt like a pneumatic drill digging into his head.

"Jesus," he croaked as he dragged himself up from the pillow. Jasper sat on his chest expectantly, tongue lolling.

Jasper wasn't a true Border Collie. He was half the size and in Rob's opinion had half the intelligence. There were traces of Alsatian in him, in the strangely thickened forepaws and legs, and the matted, speckled black and white fur of a Springer spaniel. His ears were slightly too large, looking very similar to Gizmo the Mogwai's ears in *Gremlins*, except that the left ear was permanently drooped, always at half-mast. A real Heinz 57.

But one with bags of character. Even Rob, who'd never owned a pet before in his life, had to admit that when Geoff had brought Jasper to the house.

And now Geoff was gone and ownership had passed to Rob. He scratched the top of the dog's head. A bond had formed over the last twelve months. Both looked to each other to fill the hole Geoff Michaels had left.

"Morning, Toto. Got me back to Kansas, did you? Good boy." He picked up the phone and looked at the display. He frowned. It wasn't a number he recognised. He read the message.

ROB. COMING UP TO C U 2DAY. SORRY 4 SHORT NOTICE. ANDY.

"Andy? Andy who…oh, *bollocks*!" He fell back into the pillow, head over his arm.

Never go on Facebook when you're pissed. How often had he been told that? Bad enough leaving messages and comments for friends who suddenly weren't your friends next morning. But to go hunting for people who should have been forgotten, inviting them to be friends…

Andy Hughes. Fuck, what message did he leave for him? Something along the lines of *don't come anywhere near me or my mates in Cambridge you psychotic bastard?* Or perhaps *Andy, mate, ain't see you in donkey's years, how are you? Come up and see me, we'll have a coupla drinks and a catch up.*

The latter would've been worse, Rob decided. It was like inviting a vampire to cross your threshold.

Jasper barked once. *Toilet time.*

"All right, boy."

The cold hit him like a slap in the face. Jasper ran off, oblivious to the temperature, more concerned with going to the bushes and relieving himself. The snow turned yellow before melting.

In the shelter of the kitchen doorway, in just his T-shirt and boxers, Rob lit a cigarette and thought back to Andy's message. Cigarette smoke drifted lazily in the cold breeze, barely distinguishable from his breath misting. He hadn't responded yet. He didn't know what he was going to say.

Andy Hughes had not set foot in Cambridge since 1994, just before he was kicked out of college and imprisoned. Rob shivered at the memory. And the cold.

He shook his thumping head. There had been more snowfall last night, another inch adding to the nasty white shit that was already there. Despite the rising sun the temperature was dropping.

Those roads are gonna be bloody treacherous, he thought as he sucked harder on the Mayfair. The combination of that and a severe hangover…it was not going to be a pleasant day. He thought about phoning in sick but decided against it.

One of the disadvantages of being allowed to take the delivery van home with you was that the firm would still need the vehicle if the driver wasn't coming in. So they'd send round two workers to pick it up, while checking on his physical condition at the same time. He'd been caught out that way on quite a few occasions, phoning in sick with a monumental hangover only to have a knock on the door half hour later and two stern faces – one of them usually being the junior sales rep and professional kiss-arse Terry Harrison– staring at him suspiciously. He'd handed over the keys while trying not to breathe too much alcohol their way, resisting the temptation to smack the smug face of Terry Harrison. Any more time off would be deducted from his wages, and that he couldn't afford. With Geoff gone and no other income coming in he was struggling to meet the mortgage payments as best he could.

Besides, he wanted to stay awake, no matter how painful it was. When he closed his eyes he could see the thing from his dream. *Wickedly sharp tusks emerging from a gaping maw that dripped black blood. Glistening black pools of darkness for eyes that grew dull, opaque, as life slipped from its huge porcine body. Black bristles as sharp as sandpaper on his skin as he touched it, feeling for signs of life.*

He remembered feeling relieved that it wasn't a human being he had run over. That the body which had bounced off the bonnet and spun into the snow-coated oak trees wasn't a person.

Running as the beast came alive. Hiding in the back of the van, closing the doors behind him and sitting in the darkness, huddled in terror as the wild boar crashed into the bodywork. Sharp, ear-splitting squeals as its tusks scraped the metal…a cry of terror from his throat as the beast's tusk pulled the door open and allowed silver moonlight to illuminate its terrifying, dead face. Screaming as it jumped into the cargo hold…

That encounter with the head chef at All Souls on his delivery yesterday had shaken him more than he realised. *I've got boar on the brain*, he thought with a faint smile.

Jasper bounded back into the kitchen, shaking himself. Melted snow flew in all directions and Rob grimaced. Jasper sat down panting, his black and white speckled face split apart by a huge grin. Rob couldn't remember a time when the dog hadn't been smiling. Everything was an amusement to this animal, as if the world and all that passed through it had been created solely for Jasper's amusement.

Even his master's disappearance hadn't seemed to affect him. He'd just taken to Rob straight away. He cocked his head and whined.

"Oh yeah. Breakfast." Rob rummaged through the paper wrappings on the kitchen worktop and found the remnants of last night's kebab. He scraped the dried chilli sauce off and tossed it to the dog.

"Enjoy." Rob turned back and put the kettle on. Odd, he didn't remember buying the kebab last night. But then, there was a lot he didn't remember. *And how the bloody hell did I get home last night, anyway?*

Last night was a little Christmas send-off at Dan and Emma's virtually deserted college bar, a good piss-up with cheap drinks before some of Jamaica's Finest in Emma's room. She was one of those students who was in no rush to go home for the vacations. She'd elected to stay in Cambridge until closer to Christmas, helping out on the trade counter of Granta Office Supplies for some extra pennies.

And that was as much as Rob could remember. A few spliffs in her room at All Souls College, and then - nothing. Did he go online with Emma's laptop? A quick message to Andy Hughes? And then what?

If he'd been that fucked, why didn't he crash there? He obviously hadn't managed to pull her, or perhaps he'd had a massive bust up with her and she'd told him to piss off.

Yeah, that's the likely option, he thought sadly as he tossed his cigarette butt in the sink. As the kettle boiled he looked at the pile of dirty laundry overflowing from the wicker basket. His work fleece lay on top.

Wasn't I wearing that yesterday? It was clean on last night, so why.... He lifted the fleece and saw his jeans. They were clean last night as well. He frowned at the dark stains and bent his aching head closer to inspect them.

Then he recoiled as the stench of blood and rotting meat hit him. Bile filled his throat and he turned to the sink and tried to vomit.

Nothing but watery vomit hit the metal basin. The cigarette stub sizzled. He groaned and wiped the mess from his lips before staring at the blood soaked clothes again. Then he ran through to the hallway and pulled open the front door. Jasper didn't look up from the kebab meat he was demolishing.

The Transit van was parked in its normal place. Outside the house on Thoday Street, behind the Peugeot 306 that belonged to the miserable old bastard next door. Like every other vehicle on this narrow offshoot of Mill Road, they were parked nose to tail, half mounted on the kerb to allow traffic to pass without collision. Parked neatly and tidily, no odd angles to indicate that he had driven home while pissed out of his face. He breathed a sigh of relief.

The street was empty and silent, the small Victorian terraced houses and their tiny front yards devoid of any signs of human activity. Snow and ice seemed to have frozen the life out of them. Rob shivered again, Time to get ready for work, he told himself.

He was about to slam the door shut when something caught his attention. He frowned, leaning over the snow-covered doorstep to avoid putting bare feet on it.

The van seemed okay at first. The logo of the company that employed him was emblazoned on the white bodywork: GRANTA OFFICE SUPPLIES, the script written in an antiquated Gothic font above a stylised depiction of King's College Chapel. Beneath that was the phone number and website address, thoughtfully provided in case anyone wanted to contact the firm and enquire about the products and services on offer. Or complain about Rob's driving.

But something else was there, a small dent just under the wheel arch. He wouldn't have noticed if it hadn't been for the splatters of blood around it. Frosted patterns of dark red that sparkled around the arch and trailed down to the tyre to form a small puddle on the mounted kerb. Ignoring the cold, he stepped onto the path and walked up to the gate, pulled it aside. It shrieked on rusty hinges. Rob ignored it. He didn't even feel the snow on his bare feet. His attention was focussed on the bonnet. Or rather, the dent in it.

This dent was huge. He stepped off the kerb to get a better look.

"Oh, my God," he whispered hoarsely. A huge depression in the centre. Not large enough to damage the engine underneath, but definitely the size a human body would have made when struck. The wheel crunching flesh and bones into a bloody pulp as the Transit ran over the prone body. Blood spraying up, staining the tyre and wheel arch…

Christ, no. Not that. Don't tell me I drove home, pissed up and…and…

The dream didn't seem so wild now. It was part nightmare, part recollection of last night's events.

He *had* driven home from the college last night. Pissed up and completely stoned – and he'd collided with someone.

He doubled over and threw up. Brown-tinged vomit hit the crumpled bonnet.

The trundle of an approaching milk float caught his ears, the whirring of its electric motor and the clinking of bottles in plastic crates at odds with the stillness of the street. He watched it pass, caught the driver's suspicious glance. Rob forced himself up, wiped vomit from his mouth and lifted a hand by way of greeting. *I'm okay, nothing to worry about. Piss off and leave me alone.* Trembling, he headed back for the house.

An hour later, after he'd showered, dressed and scraped the worst of the frozen blood off the Transit, he tried to phone Emma to find out just what the hell had happened last night. It went straight to voicemail.

"Emma. It's Rob." His voice was still croaky. "Give me a bell, will ya? Cheers." He was putting the phone in his jacket pocket when it rang.

"That was quick. Listen, girl, what – oh."

"It's Andy. Did you get my text?"

"Uh…yeah. Look, Andy…what you coming up here for?" Rob tried to keep the nervousness out of his voice, to be nonchalant. It was impossible. The quiet tone of Andy Hughes' voice was enough to make anyone nervous. Rob had never heard Andy shout or raise his voice in any situation. He didn't need to.

That made him even more dangerous to be around.

Andy was silent for a moment. Rob could hear the sound of trains in the background, a P.A. system mumbling out new arrivals.

"I'll explain later. Can you pick me up? I'm at the train station."

"No car?"

Another silence.

"Jen has it."

Rob waited for more information. When none came he sighed.

"Okay, Andy. I'll be there in about twenty minutes. Where are you staying?"

Andy told him. Didn't ask him, *told* him.

"No probs." *Shit.*

He pressed the end call button on his Nokia, caught Jasper's eye and shrugged.

"Well, I'm hardly likely to tell him to piss off, am I?" He pressed the unlock button on the Transit key and motioned for Jasper to jump in. The collie didn't need encouragement. He bounded out of the house and jumped happily into the cab. Rob locked the front door and stared gloomily at the drawn curtains of the first floor bedroom. Drawn and not opened since Geoff Michaels disappeared twelve months ago.

"Besides which, it's not as though we're pushed for space…"

He started the engine and waited for the blower to clear the ice from the windscreen. He lit another cigarette and watched the crumpled bonnet reveal itself through the slowly clearing windscreen. He swallowed thickly. There had been no reports of hit and run incidents on the morning local news reports. But still…

"Guess I'll find out soon enough won't I, shitbag?" He muttered in self-disgust, scratching the collie's ear affectionately. "Find out whose Christmas I've ruined…"

Bright winter sunlight glared from blue skies and reflected off the crisp snow. Rob felt his head pound again. He reached over and took his sunglasses from the dashboard, quickly inspected them for any signs of doggy saliva and put them on.

He drove to the rail station on autopilot; after driving a van for over nine years in the city of Cambridge it was an easy mode to slip into. Especially when hungover.

Today was going to be a real struggle. The Transit mirrored his condition. It felt heavier than normal, was a pig to steer and the suspension wasn't responding well. It was as though the van was fully loaded, and he knew that wasn't the case. Probably down to the road conditions. The extra snow had taken the council by surprise. Cars were sliding all over Perne Road and the Brookfields Roundabout was at a virtual standstill. Rob froze at the sight of a passing police car, wondering if the occupants were on their way to a hit and run scene. If they already had his registration number...

For fuck's sake, don't think like that!

Jasper seemed to respect Rob's condition. He wasn't barking manically at every single car they passed, at every junction they turned into like he normally did.

Rob felt a mixture of emotions when he saw Andy walk from the classical façade of the station, a heavy holdall effortlessly slung over his shoulder. Fear and trepidation, definitely, but as Andy got closer to the van parked in the taxi rank, the sight of him made Rob feel old.

Andy Hughes hadn't changed a bit. The same powerfully built frame, carried with the familiar casual yet confident gait. The shaven head gleamed slightly blue in the winter sunshine, like the polished metal of an artillery shell.

"High explosive coming our way," Rob muttered under his breath. Andy certainly had looked after himself. In a slim-fitting black sweatshirt – no jacket, Rob noticed, in spite of the cold - his midriff hadn't given way to flab, muscles turning to fat, like Rob's had done. There were a few wrinkles around the corners of his unnaturally green eyes, but that was it. Age wise, it was as though the last ten years hadn't happened to Andy Hughes.

Still as intimidating as ever. But there was something else. It wasn't the sheer physical presence of Andy that disturbed Rob – although he knew plenty of people in the past had been terrified by it, particularly when it came hurtling towards them in the darkened corners of a nightclub at lightning speed. It was the realisation that Andy Hughes needed his help.

In spite of his abrupt and somewhat dictatorial communication on the phone earlier, it was obvious that Andy had no one else in Cambridge he could go to. Rob wasn't sure if that thought comforted or disturbed him.

Andy frowned at the crumpled bonnet of the Transit before recognising Rob's eyes. He nodded once, gave a tight smile of recognition.

A middle-aged cabbie, about to give the driver of the Transit a hard time for parking in a taxi rank, suddenly saw Andy's eyes turn in his direction. He halted, his mouth closing so rapidly Rob could see his double chin wobble back and forth.

Seeing Andy open the door of the Transit, Rob took hold of Jasper's collar.

"C'mon, boy. Give our guest some room."

Andy swung himself up into the cab of the Transit. His eyes softened at the sight of the dog grinning at him. Smiling back, he patted Jasper's head while he pushed his holdall into the foot well. Something inside made a heavy, clunking sound.

"Thanks for this, Rob. Sorry to spring myself at you like this."

Rob indicated to pull away. "S'okay, mate. That all the bags you brought with you?"

"That's all," Andy nodded.

Thank Christ for that. Means he won't be here for long.

"And what brings you to the winter wonderland of Cambridge?" he asked as he swung the Transit round, pointing it back to Station Road. He didn't bother asking about the tooth marks on Andy's forehead. He could guess where they had come from.

Andy stroked Jasper. He didn't meet Rob's eyes.

"Family crisis."

"Family crisis, eh? Okay…" *What bloody family?*

The van joined the line of traffic waiting for the lights to change at the junction of Station Road and Hills Road. He frowned. The van still felt heavier than normal. The steering was sluggish and the suspension felt non-existent.

As he turned left into Hills Road Rob felt Andy's gaze turn in his direction and he swallowed nervously. Then he realised that Andy wasn't looking at him but at the war memorial.

The bronze soldier on Robert Tait McKenzie's memorial marched proudly - or thankfully – homewards, a snow covered Lee Enfield rifle slung over his shoulder. A survivor: carrying on, but always looking over his shoulder, unable to tear his gaze from the horrors of his past. Driving on autopilot meant Rob didn't take any notice of the sights and tourist attractions within the city, just accepted them as part of the scenery. But he glanced at it briefly as the van passed, and remembered how it had affected Andy when he first saw it, Fresher's Week so many years ago. What was it Andy had said to him? *The idea of sacrificing yourself for a higher purpose…it's humbling, Rob. It really is. Is that hesitation in the soldier's eyes, a temptation to stay and share the fate of his comrades? Or guilt that he survived? How can he ever be the same man his family had known before he set off for the killing fields of France?* And that faraway look in his eyes as he stared at the soldier…Andy had that same look now.

"Homecoming…" He blinked and Rob saw a visible shudder pass through Andy as the memorial faded in the side mirror.

"So, Roberto. What happened to your van?"

"Bloody good question, Andy. That dent happened last night. I can't remember how it happened, though."

Andy leant over the dashboard and peered at the dent in the bonnet. "You definitely hit something. There's some dried blood down there…" Andy flared his nostrils, smelt the stale alcohol on Rob's breath. He narrowed his eyes in disapproval.

"You were pissed up." A statement, not a question.

"No lectures please, Andy. I don't make a habit of drink-driving, honest." He took a Mayfair from the crumpled pack on the dashboard with shaking hands and lit it.

"Something weird happened last night. I'm waiting for Emma to call me back. She'll know what happened."

"Emma?"

"Emma Robertson, she's a student at All Souls. She helps out in the sales office at work - "

"All Souls." Andy hissed the words. "It happened there then, did it?"

The lighter was ready. Rob took it, applied it to the tip of his cigarette. He frowned as he replaced it.

"All in the past, Andy. It was fifteen years ago – "

"You don't need to remind me, Rob," Andy said with no change in tone or volume, but the tense atmosphere in the cab was strained even further by his words. Even Jasper shrank back from him.

"I don't need reminding."

The rest of the journey to Rob's workplace continued in silence.

THREE

The tortured whisperings faded. Slowly and reluctantly, slithering back to wherever they had come from as smoothly as freshly dug worms burrowing back into disturbed grave soil. Hiding from the light.

Emma Robertson blinked at the bright slivers of sunlight slicing through the gaps in the red curtains of her room, a single bedroom in the Hall of Residence that overlooked the Old Court of All Souls College. They didn't seem quite real, although they had thankfully banished the shadows lurking in the far corners of her small room. She shook her head, which felt dulled and woolly from the sleepless night. She thought she could still detect traces of far off voices whispering to her, but she knew now they were just echoes, grim reminders of her invisible visitors.

What the *hell* had caused all that? She and Rob had enjoyed a few drinks and some weed – correction, she'd had a few, Rob had had a *shitload* – but that shouldn't have created those hideous voices. Then again, there was the absinthe. She saw the bottle now, lying on the beige carpet. Empty, drained.

Oh God. That would explain it. Grabbing her glasses from the bedside cabinet she climbed out of bed and staggered to the window.

She looked at the absinthe bottle again – Rob's little Christmas gift to her - and shivered. She wondered how bad *his* head was this morning.

God, that bloke drank like he didn't want to live. Students overindulged, first years more so. All part of the student experience. Away from the parents for the first time, a new group of friends to mix with, of course you were going to overindulge. But surely you'd outgrow that at some time. Usually after graduation, certainly before you hit your thirties. Not Rob Benson. Hard to believe he had a joint honours degree in English Literature and History.

Not the most useful of subjects, he'd said with a grin the first day they met in the warehouse of Granta Office Supplies back in October. *That's why I drive a van for a living.*

She'd taken to him then. Although he was older and had studied at the 'Tech – or Anglia Ruskin University as it was now called – and she was a first year undergraduate reading English Literature at a prestigious Oxbridge college, they had a lot in common. Not just similar tastes in music and books but a desire to have fun, to poke two fingers up to the pretension and general bullshit they'd both found in Cambridge.

He was a bit of a slob; there was no denying that. Late thirties and he was starting to let himself go. But he was fun to be with, and it was obvious that he'd remained in Cambridge purely to continue living the student lifestyle.

The Eternal Student, she called him. Perhaps he'd still be hanging round in college bars and sneaking into May Balls when he was drawing his pension. The amount of times he had tried to get a guest invite to the bar of All Souls from her – the only one of the thirty two Cambridge College bars he'd never managed to drink at - the amount of times she had said no…

So when she waved a guest pass at him with a conspiratorial smile and a whispered *Merry Christmas* on his return to the warehouse the look on his face was priceless.

Pulling the curtains apart she winced at the piercing bright sunlight reflected from dazzling fresh snow. She blinked, squinted, and then pulled on the catch, pushing the window open. It gave reluctantly, the metal frame held fast with ice, but it was no match for Emma's forceful thrust.

The cold invaded the room and stole what remaining heat it had left. She gasped in the icy, fresh air. It was painful to her chest but welcoming at the same time, revitalising.

From her position on the second floor she could see the vast, perfectly square lawn that dominated Old Court, enclosed on all sides by perfectly formed borders of pebbles which formed an effective barrier between the grass and the ancient grey flagstones of the adjoining courtyard. Now a thick blanket of snow hid the greenery and grey of the lawns and stones. It looked like another inch had fallen last night.

Along the buttresses and lancet windows of the thirteenth century buildings, trickles of water from the leaking drainpipes and dilapidated eaves of the overhanging slate roof had frozen, creating skeletal fingers of ice which clung possessively to the blackened clunch stone and the creeping clusters of ivy that spread moss-like around the lower levels of the Great Hall. The mullioned windows were heavily coated in a thick pane of ice that concealed the rooms and their occupants from casual view.

Not that there were many occupants. All but a few had gone home for the Christmas vac. Those remaining were the die-hard academics, mainly post-grads using the quiet time to put in extra study. Others were committed to staying on in the city and putting in some extra hours at whatever part-time jobs they had, like her. Study was an expensive business when you didn't have rich parents to fall back on.

She considered the view before her. Pristine snow, lit by a fresh winter sun, encasing the ancient and medieval stonework of academia. Still, motionless. As if the snow and ice had frozen not just the buildings but time itself.

She glanced behind her, a heart-stopping moment when she thought the whispers had returned. It was just a gust of the cold air disturbing some of her papers.

Rob hadn't heard them. He'd gone long before it started. She stared at the dried pool of vomit that coated the keyboard of her laptop.

For Christ's sake, Rob! You know how much that cost me?

A giggle and a sheepish grin. *'S alright...Santa'll get you a new one.*

Oh Jesus, I've got my thesis on there! I haven't backed it up...that's it! Get out! OUT!

He'd staggered off with a hurt expression. And come back less than five minutes later. *Dan ain't here. His room's locked. Can I come in...*

No! Fuck off home!

Em, I can't. I'm too pissed to drive.

Bloody well walk home, then!

Shuffled footsteps that faded from hearing. Then the metallic clang of fire extinguishers knocked from their mountings and a repeated thudding noise as he fell down the stairs.

She'd sighed and approached her laptop, her heart sinking at the sight of sparks and the smell of burning plastic. She turned it over and disconnected the battery, grimacing at the rank liquid that dripped onto her jeans.

Emma.

The voice wasn't Rob's. It was a soft, sibilant whisper: like seawater retreating over shingle.

Emma. Hear my song.

More voices joined the first. Whispers that filled her ears with horror.

A choir of disembodied voices spoke to her from all points of the room. She whirled round to face the source of one voice, only to see nothing. Then another would speak to her right, she would turn to face that, and so on. Voices that spoke of things beyond the grave, of decay and putrefaction that destroyed the soul as well as the body. Whispers of violent and agonising acts performed, witnessed and relished. Gleeful voices that murmured descriptions of lives violently taken: bodies shattered and tormented in ways beyond human imagining.

She sank to the floor, hands clasped around her ears, trying in vain to blot out the terrible voices.

They continued singing their gleeful song of destruction, the voices now inside her head. She shook her head violently. *What the hell am I doing to myself? This isn't real! Get a grip!*

She grabbed the empty absinthe bottle. She stood up and drew her arm back…

She'd expected the bottle to shatter as it made contact with the wall. Instead, it hit the wall and bounced back, knocking the ceiling light and smashing the bulb before dropping to the carpet. Light still shone from an anglepoise lamp, but not enough. Shadows were created and the whispering remained. She sat on the bed, dropped her glasses onto the bedside cabinet and buried her head in the pillows. Wrapping herself in the duvet, she repeated the mantra…

"They're not real. *They're. Not. Real.*"

It was a mantra she repeated, shouting it out to the shadows in the room until the sunlight had arrived and the voices faded.

Looking out onto the outside world she was glad that so few college members remained. What would they have made of her cries?

"No more absinthe," she croaked to the winter sun. "Ever."

And no more dates with Rob Benson. She thought of calling him, just to make sure he hadn't driven back in that state. She shuddered, remembering the amount of absinthe he'd knocked back and the weed he'd smoked. God only knew what he might have done in the van, what he might have hit…

She felt goose bumps on her bare arms, their arrival delayed by the numbing effect of the alcohol in her system. Now she could feel the cold. Teeth chattering, she slammed the window shut and looked around the room.

Her mobile was on the bookcase, just beside her textbooks. She grabbed it and looked at the screen.

Voicemail. *Okay, guess I wouldn't have heard the phone going off with that racket.* She pressed a button and held it to her ear.

"Oh my God…" she said in a voice as low as the returned whispering. Her fingers tightened around the handset, inadvertently pressing the Motorola and its hideous voicemail message closer to her ears.

A new voice spoke this time, a fresh addition to the choir of hate. A young woman's. The most terrifying of all. Speaking not only of atrocities already witnessed, it told of horrors yet to come: horrors involving Emma, listing them with a poetic flourish, filled with sadistic anticipation. Emma knew the voice but had never heard it say such terrible things before: not Stacey, the sister she loved more than anyone else on Earth.

The sister who had been in her grave for the last two years.

Emma Robertson threw the mobile away in disgust. It hit the wall, the back cover flew off and the battery slipped from the connections. But still the voice could be heard.

She grabbed the absinthe bottle and brought it down hard on the exposed innards of the handset. Twice, three times, until the Motorola was smashed to ragged chunks and the voice was silent.

Now she knew things were going to change . This was no hallucination brought on by weed and absinthe. This was connected to the events of last year.

There was no other logical explanation. A full twelve months after Jason Franklin had been caught and sectioned for what he had tried to do, it seemed that he had been right all along. And that meant that all hell was going to break loose.

She grabbed her fleece and slid into it. She didn't bother looking in the mirror: she didn't care what sort of state she was in and, for the first time since she was five, she left without cleaning her teeth.

She took her keys from the dresser, picked up her swipe card and pocketed them both.

Those whispers – exactly the same ones Jason Franklin had heard. The ones that had driven him to destruction.

And weren't they all *oh-so-pleased* that he had been stopped just in time? She remembered the smiles of relief on the parents' faces at the start of the new term in January as they dropped their loved ones off at All Souls. Thankful that there was no maniac around their children determined to burn the college to the ground, regardless of who was in it.

Good God, she had been just as relieved as well – at the time when the fires started she had only just left for home. If she'd stayed another night as originally planned she'd have been caught up in it.

Thanked my lucky stars that night, didn't I? She shook her aching head in disgust. *And all this time we should've been thanking him.*

Or helping him. She stopped suddenly and glanced at the calendar. December 20th. Almost a year to the day…

The hallway was deserted. The door to Dan Bailey's room was not just unlocked but open. Not like him. Even if he'd gone for a run as he did every morning he would have locked the door.

She poked her head around the door. His rucksack and suitcase lay on the bed. Open to reveal clothes, books and toiletries, ready for his trip home to his parents.

Something was wrong. His mobile phone was there as well, and she knew he always took that with him for his runs. An icy chill prodded her stomach.

She approached the communal bathroom. Empty. The pristine porcelain of the toilet and sink basin gleamed in the golden light slicing through the frost coated window. No more vomit from Rob Benson – as if that was possible, after what he'd ejected over her laptop – but she also noticed that there was no condensation on the mirrors. No water on the shower curtain. With Dan's fastidious, almost anal fixation with personal hygiene – a shower before a run, then one afterwards - that spelled trouble.

Wherever he's gone, he hasn't gone willingly.

She ran down the stairs, nimbly avoiding the fire extinguishers that lay on the floor of the first landing. Knocked from the wall mountings by Rob's drunken exit, she assumed.

She pushed open the door. Onto the gravelled path that bisected the court, she headed for the archway by the porter's lodge leading to Trinity Street and away from All Souls College. Her trainers kicked up small flurries of snow but almost slipped on the harder, frozen layer beneath. She grunted, forcing herself to slow down. The sunlight was stronger now, the reflected glare from the snow of the Court making her eyes hurt. She stared at the ornamental fountain and the gaping hole in the lawns next to it. Chunks of earth were covered by tarpaulin that in turn was covered by fresh snow. Barriers marked out with hazard warning tape surrounded the grave that awaited the culmination of the Founder's Feast tomorrow night, which was unnecessary seeing as no-one but Fellows were allowed to walk on the lawns.

And who'd want to get close to an open grave, anyway? she thought with a shudder.

The cold air was agony to her aching head, but it was at least clearing the alcohol fog.

She folded her arms over her breasts and trudged cautiously to the lodge. She heard the gentle hum of early morning traffic and bicycles clattering down Trinity Street filtering through the archway.

Old Court itself was completely silent. And there were no signs of life from the lodge, either. She tried the door, frowning when she found it locked.

She was alone. That wasn't too worrying – at least she wouldn't have to face John Franklin. She shuddered again, and this time it wasn't down to the cold. God, that man gave her the creeps. If Jason Franklin really was insane it was no surprise when you considered who he had for a father. She would never forget the sight of the head porter repeatedly slamming the head of Jason into the low wall of the fountain – his own *son*, for God's sake! –an expression on his face that could not be mistaken for anything other than pure enjoyment.

That hadn't 'reasonable force' used to overpower an arsonist. It was nothing less than pure hatred. And like everyone else associated with the college of All Souls, she had wondered why it was so intense. But no answers were forthcoming. She'd heard rumours, but that was all they were. Rumours. It was something Rob had asked about last night when he brought the first round of drinks. And she could only –

She blinked. She'd seen something out of the corner of her eye, a brief movement outside the tiny chapel. Something red…and green.

The doors opened. A woman's head peered out…and then sharply withdrew as her eyes met Emma's.

Stacey!

She let out a strangled cry. There was no mistake. The red hair – as wild and unkempt as her own - was a sodden mass that flicked droplets of sea water on the dark oak doors before disappearing into the stone confines of the chapel.

Emma could smell the salt tang of the ocean waves that had killed her sister. The aroma of putrefying flesh and intestinal gases as the body was dragged from the harbour two years ago now filled the cold, silent court.

Her head swam with the memory and she felt the frozen ground beneath her feet tilt violently. She sank to her knees and vomited.

She stared at the vomit steaming on the fresh snow for a long time. Anything rather than look to the chapel entrance.

I have to know.

She climbed to her feet and looked around her. The court was still devoid of human life.

But what about the chapel? Human life in there? It couldn't be. Stacey Robertson was dead. Whatever had disappeared into the chapel, it was not her sister. Someone was playing a sick joke.

Just like the voices I heard earlier? The voice of Stacey on my mobile? That's no joke, Em.

She had to know. She had to find out. Stepping over the rapidly cooling vomit and onto the grass of the lawns, she made her way to the chapel.

The doors weren't closed, but they had been pulled to. She put a shaking hand on the knob and pulled it towards her. The droplets of sea water had run down the timber, forming small shining crystals of salt.

The doors swung open on rusty hinges. She stepped in and her glasses steamed up. She took them off and wiped the lenses on her jeans. The musty smell of old, damp stone filled her nostrils. She couldn't detect any aroma of seawater now.

Sunlight coming through the open door provided the only illumination, not enough to completely banish the darkness. She replaced her glasses but could only just make out the pews and the altar. The carved image of Christ loomed over the silver eagle on the lectern, His agonised expression hidden by the shadows. She shivered. That sculpture gave her the creeps.

The building was tiny, an apology for a chapel. It had none of the grandeur or ornate decoration that other Cambridge College chapels boasted – the Fellowship didn't even have a chaplain amongst its numbers - but it had something unique. A wooden carved representation of the Passion that was unlike any other she had seen..

Christ's legs were folded at the waist, the knees pointed to the left. A wickedly blunt nail entered the right ankle and came out of the left behind it, pinning both to the wood. Two more nails shattered the wrists, not the palms, the fingers clenched inwards like claws, the fingernails penetrating the palms and drawing fresh blood. His head was slumped on His right shoulder, the crown of thorns penetrating the skin.

She walked slowly towards the altar, her mouth dry. The snow on her trainers melted, soaking into the faded, threadbare carpet that led between the cracked and chipped pews. The winter sun rose higher, and Christ's face was reclaimed from the darkness.

The expression wasn't one of beatific sacrifice – it was an all too human representation of physical agony. The flesh coloured paint was unnervingly close to the real hue of tortured human skin, right down to the mottled blue and purple patches of the bruising meted out during the buffeting. His piercing blue eyes were wide and staring, the shining pupils dilated. The mouth was open in a silent scream, the thin lips curled and the yellowed teeth broken. The fresh blood trickling from the nail and flagellation wounds were a vivid scarlet in the glare of the December sun.

She heard the sound of dripping water. She frowned, and cocked her head.

There it was again. A steady drip-drip-drip, of liquid falling on stone. She thought of the seawater falling from Stacey's red hair and put her hand to her mouth.

This wasn't seawater. The coppery aroma was unmistakeably that of blood. Blood dripping from physical wounds and falling to the stone flags.

Emma let out a strangled cry as she saw the source. Around the nails pinning Christ's wrists to the cross something glistened and squirmed. Fresh blood, running from the gaping wounds to the ends of the trembling fingers before falling to the floor.

The head of Christ then raised itself from the shoulder. Thorns from His crown were pulled free from the taut muscles in the arm with a wet sucking sound. The emaciated chest rose and fell, shuddering breaths taken and exhaled. Breath that misted in the cold air of the chapel.

The head turned to face the intruder. Emma was frozen solid, immobile, under the gaze of the figure that was no longer made of painted, carved wood. The terrifying expression fixed her to the floor as surely as the nails held the flesh of Christ to the cross.

His eyes had changed. The piercing blue irises were now scarlet: blood-red irises that encircled the rapidly shrinking pupils, constricting them, as though squeezing them out of existence. The lips moved slightly. More mist rose into the air to accompany the barely audible words.

"Confess your faith…"

There was no trace of agony or fear in Christ's expression now. The lips were twisted into a mocking smile as Emma opened her mouth to scream.

"Confess your faith unto him who said All Souls are mine…"

The words were louder now, clearly audible. Calm, confident and commanding, accompanied with mocking laughter.

"All Souls are mine…and ALL SOULS IS MINE!"

The laughter at the thing's own joke increased in volume, echoing around the stone walls of the small chapel and drowning the scream that tore from Emma Robertson's lips.

It wasn't just the blasphemous words, nor the animated carving of a leader sent to free mankind from death and evil. It was because the words were delivered in a woman's voice. A young woman's voice that was painfully familiar.

Stacey's voice.

Emma's scream finally drowned the laughter of the abomination on the cross. Blotted out everything. She was oblivious to the closing of the chapel doors behind her.

She was oblivious to the slow, measured footsteps of the man who walked towards her with outstretched arms.

FOUR

As Rob drove down Cherry Hinton Road Andy regretted his sharp words; Rob hadn't meant to rub his nose in it, but it was something that wasn't going to be forgotten and would have to be discussed in length at some stage. And there was no doubt about it – Rob Benson would have to be fully informed of his mission in Cambridge. It was only fair. Besides, he had a feeling he might need some assistance, no matter what shape it came in.

He stifled a yawn. He had managed to get some sleep on the train journey, but not enough. The lack of sleep and the stress of the previous night's events were catching up with him. Hopefully he could have a good sleep at Rob's house before phoning Pearce and getting his instructions. At least he hadn't dreamed about the horses again.

He ran a finger along the cold pane of glass, noting the dried dog saliva with disgust. The windscreen was smeared and grimy with stale cigarette smoke, enhanced by the bright sun glaring through it. Andy saw crushed Coke cans and McDonalds cartons scattered along the floor of the cab. Rob hadn't changed much, still a slob. And he was aging. A small but noticeable beer gut poked through the webbing of the seatbelt: his three-day-old stubble was grey around the mouth, his shock of light brown hair was greying around the temples, and his eyes were yellowed and bloodshot. The Eternal Student was showing his age.

He reeked of booze, so had obviously been on some bender last night. Probably another college bar, crashing the end of term parties. Just as they had both done, so long ago during his own, all too brief, student days.

Seeing the familiar landmarks – the train station, the War Memorial, the shops and pubs along Hills Road– it seemed to Andy that he'd never been away. It was hard to believe that it had been fifteen years.

"Things changed much?"

Rob glanced at him, noted that Andy was trying to lighten the mood.

"Cambridge? Not really. Media attention disappeared after the All Souls event last year…uh, Anglia Poly is now Anglia Ruskin, but you probably know that –

"Phil Lotson." Andy said suddenly. "He still lecture there?"

"As far as I know." Rob's nose wrinkled. "Jesus, that stinks. You just shit?"

"Blame your dog. I might need to see Phil at some point. Can you arrange a meeting?"

Rob looked at him. "You serious? You're the last bloke he'd want to see."

Andy smiled. "Don't think I don't know that. He's doing some work on All Souls, isn't he?"

Rob indicated left and changed gear, ready to pull into The Paddocks. "He hasn't updated his website for a while. That guidebook he was working on…knowing him it'll be either finished or binned. Haven't seen it in the shops so I'm guessing the latter. Fuck me, that reeks! You sure you ain't dropped your guts? Either of you?"

Jasper barked. Andy sniffed the air. There was something now.

"Christ," Rob muttered as he brought the vehicle alongside his work place. "Smells like something died in here."

"That collision you had yesterday. Any blood might've seeped through to the engine block. Hot metal, cooking blood…"

"Wouldn't smell that bad, surely?"

Andy raised his eyebrows and gave Rob a hard look. "Depends what you hit."

Rob shuddered.

Granta Office Supplies was a medium sized warehouse in the centre of the Paddocks Industrial Estate. Most of the warehouse was given over to the storage of stationery and assorted office products, placed on display cases and shelving for retail and trade customers to browse through. A small trade counter faced the machine sales showroom just past the main entrance and as they drove past Andy and Rob could see a large queue of people forming a queue behind the small Christmas tree on the trade counter. In the distance Andy could see shining lights and the glow of computer monitors emanating from the main sales office at the back of the warehouse. Fake snow was sprayed in the corners of the windows. Unnecessary now, Andy thought.

Rob saw that the double doors of the goods-in entrance were open. He swung the Transit around and slowly reversed in. He cried out as he put his foot to the brake. The wheels spun on what must have been ice.

"Shit! That was close…"

"Something wrong?"

Rob frowned and leaned over the wheel. "Apart from that stink? Yeah, this van's been handling like a pig this morning. Brakes are for shit as well. Thought it was just the state I was in, but…"

"You still loaded? I noticed that there isn't much give in the suspension."

Rob shook his head as he pulled the key out of the ignition. He shivered as he opened his door and stepped out onto the snow. "No, all unloaded yesterday. My van was empty when I went to…"

Andy narrowed his eyes. *When you went to All Souls.*

Rob turned his eyes away. "When I parked up. I walked to Emma's, I'm sure of it…" he patted his thigh, a gesture for Jasper to follow. The dog bounded out hurriedly, skidding on the snow as if he couldn't wait to get out of the Transit. Rob looked at Andy.

"You coming in, or d'you want to wait while I load up?"

Andy regarded Rob steadily. "I think I'd better come in."

Following Rob and his dog into the despatch area Andy saw a small, wrinkled man in black overalls, a fleece and a woollen beanie cap with the Granta Office Supplies logo. He was knelt in the loading bay, hunched over various sealed packages scattered on the concrete floor which he half-heartedly attempted to sort into some form of a delivery route.

Andy looked around him. This area of the warehouse was small and crowded. Pallets of photocopier paper, shrink-wrapped filing cabinets and boxed segments of office furniture were pushed against the walls. At the far end Andy could see metal racking, each bay containing various items of stationery and office supplies waiting to be wrapped and despatched. In front was a pair of empty two-sided cages, each bearing a laminated label stating RETURNS, next to a yellow Hyster counterbalance forklift truck connected to the battery charger. It hummed contentedly to itself, a strange accompaniment to the Christmas songs playing on the battered radio Andy turned his attention back to the gnome-like figure on the floor,

A scowl that looked like it was a permanent fixture, maybe even a trademark, creased up his face and made him look older than his forty-four years. Despite the non-smoking signs scattered throughout the despatch area, a thin black roll-up smouldered between his lips, the scent of Drum Gold mixed with liquorice paper filling the air. Flecks of ash fell on the warehouse floor like snow from a nuclear winter.

"Andy, meet Jim Maskell, Granta's Chief Elf."

Jim looked up from the packages and straightened his back, groaning. His scowl deepened when he saw Rob.

"Less of yer bloody lip, boy," he spoke in a broad Fenland accent. "I ain't in the fuckin' mood."

"You never are, you miserable old fucker. What's up? Santa knocked you off the good boy list?"

Jim spat out the dog end and crushed it under foot. His eyes narrowed as he caught sight of Andy.

"More bloody passengers, Robbie? You might as well start up a taxi service. And since you ask, I ain't in the mood 'cause of what young Harrison promised his new client."

Rob wandered over to the despatch desk and flicked through the delivery notes. He grinned at the mention of Terry Harrison .

"Oh yeah? What's Kiss-arse been up to now?"

"He's arranged us to – *get that fuckin' dog away from them chairs!*"

Andy followed Jim's wrathful glare to see Jasper's leg cocked against one of the more expensive high backed executive leather chairs.

Jasper froze, a thin stream of piss halting in mid flow. He looked warily at the warehouse manager. Then he sniffed at the small puddle, wagged his tail in self-approval, and scampered off to Rob.

Rob sat down and helped himself to Jim's pouch of tobacco as Jim scuttled off to the executive chairs, growling and muttering obscenities. Andy turned to Rob.

"How long have you had that dog, anyway? Never took you for a pet fan."

Rob lit his roll-up and shook his head. "Not mine. He's Geoff's dog." Smoke clouded above him as he leant over and fondled the dog's ears. "Of course, now it looks like he isn't coming back, I guess I'm a full time caretaker, eh boy?"

"Did you say Geoff?"

Rob looked up, visibly surprised at Andy's terse reaction.

"Yeah. Geoff Michaels." His eyes narrowed. "Name familiar to you?"

Andy walked forwards. His hand reached into his jeans pocket. Jasper's ears flattened and his lips drew back.

"Steady, Jas," Rob laid a hand on the collie's head. "He might have a sweetie for you. Andy, if that came from an advent calendar I hope it ain't been in your pocket for too long."

Andy didn't smile. He took out the photo, unfolded it and handed it stiffly to Rob. "Geoff Michaels. Is that him?"

Rob almost swallowed the roll up. "Fuck, yeah! That's him – and that's a more recent photo than the police released." He turned the photo over, frowning when he saw the address written on the back.

"His last known address. Yeah, my house. He was lodging there." He handed the photo back. "Care to tell me what your involvement with him is?"

Andy didn't answer. He glanced at the scrawled address on the back of the photo, folded it up and returned it to his back pocket.

Fucking Pearce, holding out on me already. He must have known Michaels' last address was Rob's house. He must therefore have known that Rob was the old college friend Andy had spoken about.

He knew and said nothing. So why was that? Was Rob involved in this in some way?

"Rob. I'm going to come clean with you. I'm look – "

A door slammed shut. All heads in the warehouse turned to face the newcomers.

"Ah, shit. Kiss-arse and The Fat Controller." Rob stood up and crushed his roll up underfoot. "Tell me later, Andy."

Andy could see why he was called The Fat Controller. Mark Higgins was wheezing with the effort of walking from the main sales office into the warehouse. His hair was greying but his features were youthful. His chubby face was red, as though someone had given both cheeks a good slap. Or perhaps he'd seen the state of the van.

At the sight of Rob he scowled and waddled over to the despatch desk, the open jacket of his cheap grey suit flapping as much as the piece of paper he brandished in his hand.

"I want a word with you, old sport!" His voice was high pitched, almost a squeak. He halted at the sight of Andy. His watery grey eyes flicked over the cold, unsmiling visage of the nightclub bouncer, a brief appraisal. He gave Andy a look that said *I'll worry about you later* and then held the paper in front of Rob's face.

"A letter of complaint, Robert! The second one this week. Your dog seems to have bladder control issues."

"Oh Christ, not again. Where was it this time? " Rob took the letter gingerly. "Bloody hell. Thought we'd been discreet…naughty boy."

Andy saw that Rob was trying to keep his face away from his boss. It was down turned, facing the dog with a glare. He was trying to stop Higgins from smelling the booze on his breath.

"Discreet?" The cheeks were getting redder. Andy could have sworn that there was more heat coming off them than the fan heater beside him at Jim's desk. "A leak behind the skips of the college kitchens! You call that *discreet*? We were lucky not to lose that account. If it happens again, old buddy, the dog goes! Why do – what's that smell?"

Andy saw the relief in Rob's eyes when Higgins turned his attention to the floor. With a sigh, Higgins bent down and picked up the dog end. "How many times do I have to tell you, old sport…"

"The bloody dog should go *regardless*. You know the company's policy on animals in the workplace. And this waste of space should go as well."

All three men were silent at these words. They turned their heads to watch Higgins' companion, who had been inspecting the front of the Transit, walk towards them.

So this is Terry Harrison, the man Rob calls Kiss-arse, Andy thought. He was young, early twenties at the latest. Good looking, and he obviously knew it. Visibly self-assured to the point of arrogance. A frown and a sneer that looked like it came on automatically whenever he was talking to those he considered underlings. Fashionably scrunched and gelled blonde hair, stubble on the designer side, a kid who believed that image was everything. The three-piece suit was an expensive and classy wool mix, the shoes were neatly polished and buffed, Italian leather by the looks of them, and the silk tie alone would have cost Andy two nights' wages.

"Talking of animals…who's your new friend, Benson? Still collecting the waifs and strays of Cambridge, are we?" He looked Andy up and down, his lips drawing back in distaste. "Where did you get this one? Looks like he should be in prison, raping blokes in the showers."

"Keep your sordid little fantasies to yourself." Andy smiled mirthlessly. "And for your information…yes, I have been in prison, and no, I had no fun and games in the showers. Don't judge me too harshly, sunshine. After all, we can't all be *Apprentice* rejects, can we?"

Harrison's eyes flashed in anger.

"That was a long time ago," he hissed. "Even Lord Sugar admitted he'd made a mistake in sacking me."

"All right, all right," Higgins flapped his hand irritably. "Robert, I believe there's been a change of plan with the new account. Terry wants you to take the furniture today."

"I know it was arranged for January," Harrison stared at Rob with greater disdain than he had given Andy. *No love lost between these two*, he thought, watching Rob grudgingly take the delivery note.

"But I thought it would make a good impression if we got this done today. Hopefully they won't see the impression *you* made on the firm's van." He glanced at Higgins, a sly smile on his face at this new dig at Rob. "Have you seen the dent on it?"

"Van?" Higgins scowled at Rob. *"Explain yourself, old buddy."*

"Coupla pissheads had a pop at it last night when it was parked up." Even Andy was impressed by the speed and ease with which the lie slid from Rob's lips.

"Nothing major, just a crease in the bonnet. I'll fill out an incident form before I shoot off."

"A couple of drunks, eh?" Harrison sneered. He sniffed theatrically, the implication clear. Then he frowned. He could smell something far worse than stale alcohol.

It was a stronger, more powerful version of the stench Andy and Rob had smelled earlier. Andy's eyes followed Harrison's, turning to Rob's Transit. Whatever it was, it was not coming from the radiator. It was coming from the rear of the vehicle.

With a hard look thrown at Rob, Harrison walked to the back of the Transit. Higgins and Rob watched intently and Jasper was suddenly motionless. Andy knew then something was wrong.

Jasper's ears were flat on the top of his head, his whole body stiff. Hackles were raised and his lips were drawn back from his teeth. A growl.

Fear. The dog was all too aware of the source of the smell. And he was terrified of it.

Terry Harrison had the rear doors of the van open and stared in horror at what lay within. He turned away as the stench hit him, doubling up and retching.

Andy moved slowly towards the vehicle. He shook his head in disbelief at what his eyes were telling him. *Well, that explains the smell. The next question is: how the fuck did it get there?*

The wooden floor of the cargo hold was coated in dried blood. Sticky pools had congealed around the huge, black-furred mass that lay on its side. Its shattered abdomen continued to seep dark, rank blood that coated the stinking mass of entrails coiled alongside it. Its mouth was open, blackened lips parted in either a silent scream or cry of rage. Its eight inch tusks were yellowed but wickedly sharp. The glazed, dead eyes of the boar were open, and seemed to be staring directly into Rob's eyes in silent accusation.

It was an hour later, van emptied and then loaded again, that Andy Hughes, Rob Benson and the dog Jasper left the warehouse of Granta Office Supplies and set off into the snow covered streets of Cambridge. This time, Andy was driving.

They had switched seats just before leaving the industrial estate. At Andy's insistence, and Rob was happy to oblige. A pounding headache and nausea from his hangover and the feeling that something terrible had happened last night – all these were hard enough to handle. But this was something else. He'd hidden his reaction well enough in the warehouse, managed to stop himself from passing out as the concrete slab of the floor swayed under his feet and bile rose in his mouth. The others were too busy holding onto their breakfasts to notice.

But no way was he fit to drive. For the first time since he'd arrived, he was glad of Andy's presence. He glanced down at Jasper, curled up on the middle passenger seat, still trembling. Then he looked in the side mirror as the warehouse disappeared from view. The dead boar had been safely dragged into the loading bay, away from curious eyes, while the management figured out what to do with it.

It was nice to have seen The Fat Controller and Kiss-arse sweat, to do some real work for a change. The boar must have weighed over four hundred pounds, and they'd all had a merry time trying to roll the thing off the van and onto a pallet. It was Andy who had suggested they use the forklift.

He had leapt into the seat of the Hyster, effortlessly manoeuvred it around the tight confines of the warehouse. Even Jim Maskell, who had spent a few years working at the Pet Crematorium, had looked sick as Andy slid the tines into the gaping belly of the dead beast. A quick adjustment of the forks with the side shift, and then he raised it, pulling the carcass out of the van and onto the pallet.

Most of it, anyway. A few small pieces of putrefying flesh were stuck to the wood panelling, and a length of intestine remained attached to the left tine as Andy reversed the vehicle. The other end remained embedded in the boar's innards, the length of intestine stretched taut and then snapped, spraying Harrison with its semi-liquid contents.

It had taken Rob half an hour to hose out all the blood and stomach contents. Even then the cargo hold still reeked. It would take weeks for the smell to fade completely. God knew what the customers would think when they received their orders today. Yet another thing Higgins hadn't been happy about.

Higgins, Maskell and Harrison hadn't believed his protestations of innocence. *No, of course I can't explain how that thing got there. And why the bloody hell would I have put it in the van anyway? Wild boars do not roam freely through the streets of Cambridge.*

"Some sick joke played on me. After all, what was my last drop yesterday? The Catering Office of All Souls College. Hey, go easy on the speed, will ya?

"I had a run in with the Head Chef there, some horrible fat cunt called Cassell. Won't go into the details…"

Andy smiled as he pelted down Hills Road. "Something to do with a dog's full bladder, I'd imagine."

"Round of applause. I'd left the van – open and unlocked - for about five minutes. Plenty of time for him and one of his lackeys to shove a dead boar in…."

"You're joking. After the effort it took us to get the thing *out* of the van?"

Rob sighed as he lit a Mayfair. He didn't notice Andy grimace at the smoke blown in his direction.

"I know, sounds bloody ridiculous. But I wouldn't put it past All Souls to phone up and complain that I've nicked the meat for their feast tonight. Who'd be silly enough to eat that monstrosity, though? Jesus! Watch where y'going!"

The driver of the black Honda Andy had almost driven into shook his fist furiously and mouthed silent obscenities until Andy glared coldly at him.

Rob snorted and turned away. Boar…

He remembered that the boar used for the Founder's Feast of All Souls was hung for several days beforehand. That would explain the God-awful stench – a creature already decomposing, a further night spent rotting away in his van. Even the subzero temperatures of a bitingly cold winter night had no slowing effect on its putrefaction.

But if that was the case, the fur and bristles would have been peeled away. The carcass would have been gutted and bled. No, this boar didn't come from the kitchens of All Souls. And he *had* driven home last night. Parked up in the kitchen area while he went to see Dan and Emma, so he'd returned and driven back the way he had came in.

Through the woods of All Souls…perhaps it was there he'd hit it. Nah, that was ridiculous. Surely?

Shit, back to square one. Still none the wiser as to what happened last night. He tried to ignore the dream. The familiar surroundings of a dark, snow-bound wood…

Rob leaned over Jasper and flicked the blower onto full blast. There were still some damp patches on his jeans. On closer inspection he realised that they weren't all caused by water spraying from the hose. Some of the patches were dark red.

He shuddered, took a deeper drag on his cigarette and turned back to Andy. After the incident with the boar he had forgotten about the picture Andy had shown him.

"Andy, we don't have a lot of calls today. I'm guessing that as All Souls is one my last calls you're going to be good enough to stay with me all day, yeah? Good. That's plenty of time for you to tell me what your involvement with my missing lodger is."

"Hello, Cambridge Pet Crematorium. How can I help you?"

"Oh, good morning. I wonder if you could help me…" Mark Higgins' throat was dry. This was ridiculous. But, Jim Maskell had recommended his previous employers – as long as his name wasn't mentioned – as being the most sensible option.

"I have a large animal that needs removing from my premises. I believe you can transport large creatures, dispose of them?"

"Yes sir, we can. What type of animal is this? And will you be requiring individual or group cremation?" The young woman on the phone was courteous, efficient and professional. This made the whole episode even more surreal. *I wonder what's the strangest request they've ever received?*

"I don't care how you dispose of it, I just want it gone!"

A suspicious pause. "Where *exactly* is this creature, sir?"

He replaced the receiver without answering. He sat back in his swivel chair, gut straining against the buttons on his shirt. He massaged his smooth cheeks with his forefingers. Two circles clockwise, and then two circles anticlockwise, repeated until cramp or jaw ache sets in...

It was a habit he had developed recently when stressed. He'd tried to stop it, realising it made his cheeks even more flushed than usual, and was a sure sign to his staff that he was feeling under pressure.

But damn it, who wouldn't be under pressure after what he'd had to deal with this morning? He stared at the replaced handset. He'd panicked, gone off on the wrong track. More concerned with getting rid of the animal as quickly as possible rather than thinking the situation through, considering its full implications.

A knock on the door.

"Come in," he said wearily. He forced himself to sit up, removing his fingers from his cheeks.

"Did you have any luck with the Pet Crem, sir?" Terry Harrison looked behind him before he closed the door. The walls were thin here, so he was making sure he was out of earshot before he raised the issue.

"No Terry, I didn't. Did you seal the warehouse door?"

"Yes, sir. It's off limits to all the staff, now. No-one gets in."

"Very well. Terry, stop calling me sir. It won't get you any brownie points. And they're not 'the staff' - they're your colleagues."

"Even Benson?" Harrison's face went slightly pink with the admonishment. "Did you smell the booze on his breath? And he smokes in the van. He can't be here for much longer, surely?"

"No, I think Mr Benson's days are numbered." He didn't like to admit it, especially not to this backstabbing, careerist little shit. Rob Benson had his flaws but the customers liked him, his workmates liked him, he got all the work done and that was all Higgins had asked for.

Things were different now, though. The drinking was becoming a regular problem since his friend and lodger had disappeared. He was going off the rails, there was no doubt. And that little stunt at the kitchen of All Souls could have severe repercussions for the firm. The Colleges had their rivalries, but they all talked to each other in one way or another. Word would get around about the customer-facing representation of Granta Office Supplies. *A borderline alcoholic, chain-smoking in the company van, accompanied by a ragged mongrel that pisses on client premises.* No, the office supplies business was tough enough without losing clients due to the actions of a delivery driver.

But as for the dead boar in the van...Higgins knew that Rob was innocent of this. The look on his face had been as shocked and bewildered as those of his colleagues. So had someone put it in the van deliberately? A slight aimed at the company? If so, why, and by whom?

He noticed Harrison's smirk.

"Damn it, what is it with you and Rob? It's over this Emma girl, isn't it?"

The smirk vanished. As suspected. *How bloody childish can –*

A short, strident tone from the phone on his desk. An internal call, the display telling him line 6 – warehouse. He picked up the receiver.

"Hello, Jim. Look, don't worry, old sport. I've phoned Spicers, today's delivery has been called off. We won't get it until after Christmas." *Plenty of time to get rid of that bloody boar.*

"I don't think we need to sort anything out, Mark," Jim Maskell's voice sounded rather distant on the phone. As if he was calling from miles away rather than the other side of the building.

"How do you mean, old buddy?"

"I – I dunno how to describe it, boss. I think you'd better come and have a look-see fer yerself."

"On my way." Higgins put the handset down gently, almost gingerly, realising his hands were shaking. *God, what now?*

Terry Harrison followed him without being asked. Higgins stood back to allow him to peel away the hazard warning tape that had sealed the access door to the warehouse.

When they entered, Higgins could see why Jim had sounded so strange on the phone. He was kneeling on the floor next to the boar's pallet, shaking his head slowly.

"Just when you thought this shit couldn't get any weirder…" Jim spoke to the two arrivals without looking up. Mark Higgins silently agreed as he watched Jim releasing handfuls of scooped-up dust and – *what is that? Ash?* – from the concrete slab floor.

The pallet was empty and the boar was gone. The black, four hundred pound mass of rotting, stinking fur and flesh had been replaced by a huge pile of finely ground particles and brittle, grey-white sticks. A closer look told Higgins that they were…

My God, it can't be. They're bones.

Even the stains of black blood and reddish slime on the floor had gone, along with the putrefying stench. The warehouse of Granta Office Supplies no longer looked or smelled like a slaughterhouse.

Now it looked like someone had emptied out the contents of a crematorium incinerator. Higgins shivered at the thought, telling himself that it was down to the chill breeze creeping in through the gap in the exterior doors.

That breeze played over the arched collection of bones in the centre of the pile of gnarled and curled sticks that must have been the beast's ribcage. The ash fell gently from the bones. Jim tentatively touched one of the ribs. It disintegrated, transformed by a single touch into yet more ash.

The breeze grew stronger. The ashes became swirling patterns writhing across the warehouse floor as the wind sighed through the gap in the doors, a mournful lament for the beast that had passed on in more ways than one.

FIVE

In the depths of a freezing Cambridge winter, Philip Lotson's dreams turned to the gloriously hot summer they had all enjoyed six months previously.

He smiled in the warm, enveloping pleasure of the memory and kicked his legs under the duvet. Kelly murmured sleepily, a frown creasing her sleeping features, and rolled over.

And in the dream his wife turned to him and kissed him gently on the cheek, smiling as his beard scratched her pert lips. She leaned over and Phil felt the punt sway threateningly.

"Steady on, Kelly!" He laughed, clutching the wet side of the punt. She laughed with him and threw her arms around his neck. The punt rocked again. In the seat opposite them Nick rolled his eyes and clucked his tongue, embarrassed by the unrestrained display of affection his parents were showing to the world. He looked knowingly at the punt chauffeur and shook his head.

Phil tilted his head and looked back, seeing the amusement on the inverted face of the chauffeur. The pole shifted from one hand to another, raised to a near horizontal angle as he steadied the vessel in the water.

"Not embarrassing you are we, Nicky?"

Their son just rolled his eyes again, further embarrassed by being called Nicky. He reached for another Alpen bar from the cool-box.

"Not too many of those, son," Phil warned. "You'll make yourself sick."

Nick laughed as he peeled the wrapper from the cereal bar. "Only one thing's making me sick at the moment." He puckered up his lips and made wet kissing noises, laughing at the face his father made.

"You wait till you're older and you get married. Then you'll know what real sickness is." That earned him a playful slap.

Phil wiped a bead of sweat from his brow. It was going to be a scorching hot afternoon. He was pleased his schedule had allowed him this rare opportunity to spend a day out with his family. Kelly had gently pushed him, reminding him that the holidays his academic calendar provided shouldn't all be spent locked in his study at home or the aisles of the university libraries, working tirelessly on his books.

Take some time out for once, she'd told him as she entered his study that morning. *You delivered the last book well ahead of schedule, they're not going to push you this time.* It was rare enough that Kelly managed to get any time off from the payroll company what with the staff shortages, and Nick was spending too much time glued to his Xbox 360 and the satellite sports channels when he should have been out in the fresh air – especially on rare, glorious days like this one. Phil had tried to put her off, claiming he was on a roll with the book.

She shook her head, pushed his swivel chair back from the desk and climbed on top of him. Her hands had snaked around his shoulders and pulled him closer, burying his face in her cleavage. One hand strayed lower, unbuckling his belt. He had groaned in pleasure as her fingers went to work, buried his face deeper in her breasts.

It had been two hours before they were ready to leave.

In front of them the river flowed lazily, winding its way along the backs of the college buildings. Sunlight glinted on the rippling waters and the dampened gunwales of the passing punts. One vessel came too close to theirs, dangerously overfilled with Italian language-school students clutching bottles of Stella and Apple Sourz.

"Bloody idiots," Phil heard the young Scudamore's punt chauffeur remark. "That's going to tip over at any moment..."

Should've taken the guy's advice and gone Grantchester Meadows way, he thought ruefully. *Every bugger goes down the Backs on a day like this. Thank God Kelly insisted on a chauffeur.*

Their own punt turned gracefully into the bend of the river, the vessel tilted to create a keel and plying a straighter course than Phil could ever have managed.

The Bridge of Sighs rose above them. Sunlight caressed the panes of glass lovingly, turning them into dazzling panels of pure silver. They darted forth in straight lines, a contrast to the shimmering shadows of the waters that rippled along the ancient masonry of the bridge and college buildings.

He blinked his eyes against the brightness, wishing he'd brought his sunglasses. The sunlight was getting brighter. He opened his eyes and blinked again, trying to shift the red blotches that stained his vision.

"Phil, are you okay?"

"I'm fine. Just a bit dazzled, that's all." He rubbed his eyes. Hell, the redness was getting worse now. Everything seemed to be tinged with red. The walls of the colleges, the grassy banks, the waters of the Cam...

He sat bolt upright as he realised why everything was hued in that colour. The punt rocked violently and the chauffeur cursed as he tried to steady the vessel once more.

The redness wasn't caused by sun-damaged retinas. He knew that now. The crimson hue lapping at the Bridge of Sighs was cast by the waters themselves. Water that clung to the hulls of the punts like scarlet treacle, clinging possessively to the upraised spruce poles as they were lifted from the water with each forward stroke. The sun continued to shine from a cloudless July sky, making the river of blood they were floating on gleam and glisten sickeningly. He cried out, a strangled sound that refused to leave his throat. Kelly and Nick looked at each other nervously.

She put a worried hand on his shoulder. "What's wrong, hon?"

"The river! Can't you see…" his voice trailed off as he stared into her bewildered eyes.

"What about the river?"

He couldn't speak. *Why can't they see it? It can't be just me, surely?* He twisted around and looked up at the punt chauffeur. The young man stared down at him warily.

"Try and keep still, sir. Carry on moving like that and you'll have us all overboard."

Phil swallowed nervously at the thought of plunging into *that.* He forced himself to keep still, closing his eyes tightly. The sun beat down on his closed lids, as if trying to force them open.

"Just try and relax, okay sir? Enjoy the ride…"

Phil kept his eyes shut, teeth clenched in fear. The sunlight ceased its assault on his eyes for a brief moment as they passed underneath the kitchen bridge of St John's, and then it began again.

The river bent to the right sluggishly and Phil could feel the punt slowing as its navigator fought against the viscous fluid. He opened his eyes and looked up. To his left, Trinity Hall and Clare College. To his right, the Garret Hostel. *Keep looking up, don't look down, don't look down…*

Kelly and Nick were ignoring him. With strange, faraway expressions on their faces they were fumbling inside the cool-box, pulling out cling film-wrapped pieces of pastry. They unwrapped them hurriedly, cramming the pies into their mouths with ravenous haste. Chewing noisily, swallowing each mouthful with none of the delicacy they normally used when eating.

Pies? he wondered, trying to concentrate on what his wife and son were eating and not the river of blood that carried them. They didn't eat pies or pastries; Kelly wouldn't allow them in the house, or indeed anything with cholesterol and saturated fat. He was lucky enough that she allowed him the hot cross buns he devoured daily.

A piece of pie filling slipped out of Nick's mouth. He frowned in annoyance before picking it up from his lap and thrusting it back into his already full mouth. Phil could see that it was meat of some kind. The smell hit him. Sharp, gamey meat that didn't look – or smell – cooked properly. As Kelly chewed her portion a few drops of blood emerged and dribbled down her chin. She continued eating, oblivious. Phil's stomach heaved. He was thankful they didn't offer him any.

He became aware of a sound behind him, like curtains moving in the breeze of a newly opened window. He turned around - slowly this time, remembering the chauffeur's admonishment.

The punt chauffeur's clothes had changed. Gone was the regulation uniform of waistcoat and straw boater. Now he was clad head to toe in robes of dark material that rippled in the still, oppressive afternoon air. No breeze.

The robes were topped with a heavy hood that covered the young man's face completely. It was only when he lowered his head and stared at his passenger that Phil could see the face had changed.

Most of it was cast in shadow. Shadow that dulled the white glare of fleshless cheekbone and grinning, lipless mouth. Shadow that could not match the blackness of empty eye sockets staring directly at Phil. The mouth opened slightly, words emitted like a breeze rustling autumn leaves in a graveyard.

Relax, sir. Enjoy the ride.

Skeletal fingers gripped the pole, thrusting into the water and moving the punt faster along the river. The chauffeur was in a hurry to get to their destination.

Phil tore his eyes away from the thing behind him, saw that the punt was approaching the wooded banks of All Souls College. It was then that he saw what was happening to Nick. He tried to scream but nothing came out.

Nick's mouth opened and half-chewed pie meat fell out just as his neck opened. Starting at a point below his left earlobe, the cut moved quickly, a perfect curve joining up with a matching point below his right earlobe. A cut that came from nowhere, as if sliced by an invisible knife. Phil could see severed pieces of the windpipe and the base of Nick's tongue through the clinical slash just before it was hidden by a descending curtain of blood.

And then his wife. Her scream was muffled by something unseen as her stomach opened beneath her white vest top. More cuts slammed into her chest, stabs this time rather than the elegant slash that had killed his son. Miniature explosions that made her judder and shake violently in her seat. Her arms thrashed wildly at her unseen assailant, striking nothing but thin air. More punts passed serenely, their occupants completely unaware of the carnage happening in front of them.

The waters around the pole gurgled as it was lifted and bent round to propel the punt towards the tree-lined banks of All Souls. It came alongside the earthen walls, the wood kissed the earth and the punt was still, the sunlight blotted out by the dense canopy of the ancient oaks.

Nick's lifeless body slumped backwards, his head thrown back so that the hole in his neck opened wider, an obscene smile. Kelly's silent head dropped onto Phil's shoulder.

And then Phil felt something prodding him in the stomach. A sharp, pointed object, probing inquisitively at his slack belly before sliding in effortlessly, agonisingly.

A figure emerged from the shelter of the oaks, advancing cautiously towards the punt. Horror and bewilderment on his features.

Through his blood-streaked vision and the physical waves of agony crashing into him with each knife thrust, Phil Lotson slowly recognised the man climbing into the punt. A man he hadn't seen in over fifteen years. In a voice that no longer sounded his own, he said *"Andy?"*

Andy Hughes looked down at the blood on his clothes. Stared, uncomprehending, at the bloodstained knife in his hands.

Phil climbed shakily out of bed. The cold sweat on his body chilled him further as he left the warmth of the duvet and Kelly. He stood on trembling legs, looking down on her. In the dawn light peeking through the gap in the curtains she looked calm, serene, a small smile playing on her lips at whatever dream she was having.

He took a deep breath that misted when he exhaled. He shivered and rubbed his clammy forehead. *Why?* He'd never had nightmares, not even as a child. So why now? That hot July day had ended with a ploughman's lunch at the Anchor and then a film at the multiplex. So why had this...*obscenity* happened?

He knew the answer. He dressed quickly, squinting at the digital clock on the bedside cabinet. Seven thirty. Three hours before his appointment. He'd shower later and change into some fresh clothes then.

During that punt journey along the Backs they had not stopped at All Souls College, they'd just passed it as they had passed the banks of the other riverside colleges. For it to appear in a dream like this – and *now* – meant his research was getting to him. He was spending too much time looking into its enigmatic past.

But that wouldn't be enough to cause a nightmare of such intensity, surely? To see his loved ones die so horribly, so graphically. And to die *himself*....he rubbed his eyes and swallowed noisily.

This wasn't just a nightmare. This was a warning.

But warning me against what? To stop work on the All Souls story? Or to stay away from Andy Hughes?

Phil shivered at the memory. Andy Hughes was history, probably still in prison for all he knew. A shame, a real tragedy. Such a gifted student, but a troubled one as well. It was perhaps inevitable that it had ended the way it did. A relief for them all. Especially Kelly.

He looked back to her sleeping form. He could see her smile grow wider as she rolled over, pulling Phil's share of the duvet around her. Her head moved back and forth, snuggling into the pillows. She purred contentedly and pulled the duvet over her head. The dim glow of the clock's display cast a red veil over her like blood on a shroud.

He had an impulse to wake her, to hold her to him. He fought the temptation.

No, let her sleep. Don't bother her with this ridiculous nightmare, she'll only tell you to abandon the book.

Perhaps that wouldn't be such a bad idea he thought, as he closed the door quietly and made his way to the small landing. Blood on a shroud? Jesus, it was definitely getting to him.

He walked past Nick's room. The door was ajar and a cold breeze was coming into the hallway. God, he'd slept with the bloody window open again. Amazing how that kid never felt the cold.

He peered through the gap in the door anyway, just to check. He shivered in the cold and saw the window wide open, the curtains drawn right back. Nick was asleep at an odd angle, the duvet wrapped and twisted around his small body. He was snoring gently but his head was tilted backwards…

…as if waiting for the knife. Phil shuddered at the thought. He crept over to the window, footing his way through the minefield of Xbox 360 game cases and CDs scattered on the floor.

Through the windows he could see the snow capped steeple of St Andrew's Church and its surrounding gravestones. He shivered and pulled the window closed.

Nick didn't stir. His face looked flushed; perhaps he was coming down with something. Not surprising when you go to sleep with the window wide open and the radiator switched off. He thought about waking him, but then dismissed the idea.

Just because I've had my sleep disturbed, why should I disturb his? He closed the door and made his way downstairs. The central heating kicked into life and warmth began to filter through the house.

Disturbed. He shook his head sadly as he entered the kitchen and filled the kettle. Ridiculous, really. It wasn't even as though he'd uncovered anything overly disturbing in his research. But it was consuming him; there was no doubt about that.

It was a far cry from his first book. *Besieged* – an in-depth retelling of the siege of Colchester during the second Civil War - had been received with rapturous reviews and pleasantly surprising sales. The Times Literary Supplement had praised his lucid style, the clear prose complimenting the solid background of scholarly research and factual reasoning. The book's success had no doubt helped him to become Senior History Lecturer at Anglia Ruskin University. The youngest the university had ever seen, given the position a mere three years after taking his first post as lecturer. And this without a PhD or even an MA – just a postgraduate certificate in higher education.

That had caused a few ruffled feathers. But he had been a success in the role: that could not be denied. In those three years he had raised the overall grade average by forty percent. The History department of the former polytechnic was now one of the most respected in the country, even making number nine in the Sunday Times' University List. When interviewed about his success he'd been asked what the secret was and he had shaken his head, saying he wasn't sure there was a special formula, it was merely a question of raising the right level of enthusiasm and commitment in his students. His lectures and seminars were almost legendary. His next book was eagerly awaited and he was financially better off, now able to afford the three-bedroom semi in Chesterton and to marry Kelly.

That had ruffled a few more feathers, he thought as he took the milk out of the fridge. Relationships between tutors and students were not encouraged, but they happened. She was a mature student, twenty-five years old when she started her course in the early 1990s, only four years younger than him. The warning from his colleagues had fallen on deaf ears. But it hadn't been Kelly's fault that his work had faltered, that his reputation was crumbling. It was his fault alone.

His next book had been eagerly anticipated. But he had gone off in a different direction. A small independent publisher had asked him to write a short book on the possibility that Matthew Hopkins had not died but had journeyed to the New World and had a hand in the Salem witch trials. This theory was held in such derision by leading academics that many eyebrows were raised when the rising star of Anglia's history department actually took the time to write a reasoned argument that supported the hypothesis. If *Witchfounder General* had flopped then it wouldn't have been a problem, but the sales were phenomenal and it spent six weeks on the bestseller lists. Poor reward for the knock his professional reputation took. The reviews were not as kind as the royalty cheques.

The small independent publisher was not so small anymore. And they wanted to capitalise on the success of the book.

He poured milk into the mug, squeezed the tea bag dry and placed it on the drainer. After a few sips he felt warmth restored and the effects of his nightmare subsiding. He even felt hungry. He eyed the opened pack of hot cross buns next to the breadbin and remembered the same supermarket brand had been toasted, buttered and placed in front of him when he signed the next contract.

He could have told them to bugger off. The time spent researching *Witchfounder General* had been at the expense of his students. He was standing at a crossroads and he knew it. Another book like this would finish his academic career.

But the commissioning editor had been very persuasive. The next book they wanted would not involve any controversial historical theories. It would not damage his reputation as a scholar. And the advance would be three times the amount they had paid for the Hopkins book.

What we're after, Phil, is a book on the dark side of Cambridge. Go on, have another bun. Extra cinnamon in these ones, you'll love 'em. Legends and folklore, yes books like these have been done to death. But this is the first time that this subject will have been written by a serious and respected historian.

Phil had almost choked on his buttered bun. *Respected? Did you hear wha*t History Today *said of* Witchfounder General? *I can't afford another book like that.*

The editor had smiled expansively, waving a dismissive hand. *This will be different. The first time a book with such a localized theme will be available in bookshops all over the country. A guaranteed bestseller. Interest – non-academic interest – in this city is growing. People want to know more, especially after the incident at All Souls last year.*

Phil smiled grimly to himself as he turned on the grill. That editor was no dummy. He was trying to capitalise on an incident that had put Cambridge in the headlines of every major tabloid and broadsheet almost one year ago. Amazing to think that some people *still* believed there was a supernatural element to the incident, and of course the events there had raised interest in the seemingly archaic practices of other university colleges.

He knew what the publisher wanted. Sensationalist tales of madness and murder, ghosts and Satanism that could be flogged to a gullible public. The fact that the author of *Cloisters, Courts and Corpses – the Dark Side of Cambridge* was a respected historian would increase the plausibility of the contents.

Phil placed the cut halves of three buns on the grill pan and slid them under the glowing red element. He sliced off thin wedges of butter, put them on a side plate and put them in the microwave.

And what if I can't give you what your book needs to succeed? he'd demanded. *All I can write about is the usual legends. The ghosts of dead Masters haunting Corpus Christi. The connection of Selwyn College with the work of the Psychic Institute. The sightings of Oliver Cromwell haunting his old college of Sidney Sussex, a bit peeved because he's lost his head. It's tired old tosh that's been done a thousand times before. What can I do to make this different, saleable – but more importantly, of serious literary and historic merit?*

The reply had been swift. *Start with All Souls. That's never been done before. Give the readership a sense that something is hidden, something dark and sinister. That'll sell the book.*

Literary and scholarly merit wasn't important, he thought sadly as he turned the buns over and replaced the grill pan. Just an optional extra. And *Cloisters, Courts and Corpses – the Dark Side of Cambridge* would put the final nail in the coffin that held Philip Lotson's academic reputation.

"So why did I do it?" he thought out loud as he set the microwave timer for five seconds, just enough to soften the butter. "Is it money, does that matter more than my career at Anglia?"

No, of course it wasn't. He couldn't put into words the reason he had accepted the commission, signed the contract with buttery fingers. Perhaps it would be a bit of light relief. Perhaps he could really succeed in making Cambridge folklore worthy of historical merit…

No, that wasn't it either.

Stop kidding yourself, Lotson, he told himself as he spread the softened butter onto the buns. *You're writing it because of All Souls. Because you know that there's a real mystery there. Not any crap about ghosts or dead Masters but the simple mystery of why no one has ever written about the college before.*

Yes, that was it. A college of that age and heritage had to have some interesting episodes in its history. It had been the first college built in Cambridge. Technically, Peterhouse was the oldest of the University's establishments, founded in 1264. All Souls had its first statutes fifty years afterwards, but it had been established as a place of learning in the Fenland landscape long before a group of refugee scholars made the arduous journey up from Oxford in the thirteenth century to escape persecution.

There were countless volumes of college histories available to the general public, either online from the colleges' digital archives or from city bookshops and the Cambridge Collection in the Lion Yard library, each describing the individual college's contribution towards the development of the University, the region and its association with many key periods in British history.

And yet no such volume was available – or even in existence – for All Souls. The only known story was the connection with Elizabeth Woodcock and the 1799 meteor strike and, of course, the events of last year.

Phil took the plate of buns and his mug of tea back upstairs to his study. He powered up the PC and sat back in the chair, chewing appreciatively. Hot Cross buns, an Easter treat, five days before Christmas.

Well, why not? It was his only vice, and hardly a dangerous one. Still, his belly was getting quite rounded these days, in spite of the fact that in best Cambridge academic tradition he cycled everywhere rather than drove.

Sorry, Kelly, can't munch on rabbit food all the time. Certainly not as harmful as the pasties and meat pies that he had devoured in his younger days…

Meat pies. He shuddered at the memory. He put the remnants of the bun down and logged onto his email account. He took a sip of tea.

One email. One that almost had him choking on the hot, sweet liquid.

Subject: All Souls Research.

Sender: david.searles@allsouls.cam.ac

It couldn't be. He opened the email, read through the first few lines. He shook his head in wonder.

An invitation to All Souls College to discuss his book. An offer to assist with any research materials, any interviews, a full, guided tour if he so desired. Helpful, friendly. A complete contrast to the defensive, suspicious and less-than-helpful attitude he had received from other members of All Souls when he had requested assistance.

This was from David Searles - the Master of All Souls himself. But Philip Lotson was uneasy. Two things disturbed him.

The first was that the email had been sent this morning, at exactly the same time he had woken from his dream. Coincidence, surely. Nothing to be worried about, he tried to tell himself.

What was more worrying was the postscript on the email.

Please come at midday. Do not announce your visit. This meeting has not been approved by the College Council, but I feel it imperative that we talk.

Not approved by the College Council…only Searles wished to speak to him. Phil thought carefully before typing his response. He would meet him, of course. But he had a feeling that something else was wrong. There was a strange tone to this email. Phil could just imagine the haste with which it had been composed.

Sent just after he had woken. Had Searles had a similar dream? And why summon him today? Why not after Christmas – or at least, after the Founder's Feast tomorrow?

*Imperative that we talk…*Phil frowned as he sent his reply. The Master of All Souls was not just a worried man.

He was a frightened one.

SIX

Even by midday Andy could see Rob Benson's hangover showed no signs of abating. Andy's less-than-experienced driving around the narrow streets of central Cambridge didn't help. As he mounted the kerb on Bridge Street he heard Rob's resting head bang on the passenger window before emitting another self-pitying moan.

"Sorry, Rob. Been a while since I've done this." He pulled on the handbrake and grinned at the dog. Jasper grinned back. He had enjoyed the drive as much as Rob had suffered it.

"So you keep saying…" Rob blinked at the bright sunshine gleaming off the Cam. A bus blared its horn as it swerved past the Transit and he winced at the sound. Andy turned and saw angry smears of human faces behind the condensation on their windows, mouthing silent curses.

"Okay, one HP toner for Parsons, 3 Quayside. I'll do this one." Rob paused.

"Andy?"

"Yes?"

"When you turn the van round, watch out for cyclists. You almost twatted two down East Road. Don't make it third time lucky."

Andy smiled thinly. Being away from Cambridge for so long he'd forgotten the mobile minefields that were city cyclists. He could swear that the ones that had emerged from the Zion Baptist Church on East Road had dropped from the sky.

"And…if Emma calls, keep her on the line." Rob looked worried. "I mean it, man. That girl's never off her phone. And after what you told me…well…" He folded the delivery note, put it in his fleece pocket and slammed the door shut.

Andy heard the side door open, Rob rummaging amongst the cargo of paper boxes and wrapped parcels for the toner cartridge. The side door slammed shut and Rob slowly walked to his destination. Head bowed, shoulders slumped, as if he was going to his own execution.

Poor Rob, Andy thought. It had been a hell of a morning for him. The nightmare, the dead boar, and his own sudden – and far from welcome – visitation.

That hadn't helped matters. After telling him that Pearce had commissioned him to go to All Souls to track down Geoff Michaels, Rob had changed colour from white to green. It had made him fret over this Emma girl all morning, and so Andy Hughes did not have much of a navigator to help him with the delivery route..

Andy looked out of his window, watching pedestrians hurry past, eager to get back to work or back to the Christmas shops, anything to get out of the biting winter cold. Further ahead he saw bollards lower to allow the bus access to St John's Street, snow shaking from the roof as the driver pulled into the narrow cobbled road.

He didn't have any answers about this Emma girl. If she was travelling home today as planned she might be stuck in an area with weak signal, her phone's battery might have run dry, anything. Or she might have been so disgusted at Rob's behaviour that she was blanking him. That hadn't put his mind to rest, either.

"What do you think, dog?" he said to Jasper. The collie cocked his head, the left ear folding inside out and falling flat again as he faced Andy. "Roberto worrying about nothing? Or is this connected to your master?" He gently unfolded the ear and scratched it. "Don't miss your real daddy much, do you? Or are you hiding it?"

The dog licked his hand. Slowly, almost sadly. None of the manic restlessness Andy had witnessed earlier was here now.

"Yeah, you miss him. As do two other people. Three, if you count your caretaker. Guess he's never been the same since Michaels' moody either. But why is the general consensus that All Souls has the answer? Just because he was last seen there doesn't mean he *stayed* there."

Well, he'd find out soon enough. The delivery was expected at All Souls at noon. While Rob met up with Kiss-arse and assembled the furniture, Andy would 'disappear' into the buildings of the college and begin his investigation.

Not that he was looking forward to going there. It was the incident in All Souls that had destroyed him fifteen years ago, and he had no urgent hurry to visit the scene of his crime. He shivered at the thought, but waiting for it was worse. Hanging around, anticipating. At least when he got there he could get on with the task he'd been sent to do.

Unless Pearce has hidden a few other surprises for me. He scowled at the thought.

Well, won't know until we get there, will we? He decided to turn the van around, just to give him something to do until Rob came back.

He glanced in the side mirror and saw no vehicles were approaching. He popped the handbrake, spun the wheel and collided with something that made a heavy, metallic clattering sound as it crashed onto the road.

Like the passers-by on their way to the city centre, he froze, a horrified stare at the sight in front of the van. Rob's words came back too late. *Don't make it third time lucky.*

The mountain bike was emerald green, with an oversized tube frame and rusting bull bars on the handles. The rear wheel spun in the air. The rider, thrown a clear six feet from his bike, was a male in his late forties. His helmet had taken the full brunt of the impact with the pavement, Andy could see that by the deep scratches on the yellow plastic, and it looked like his thick rucksack had helped cushion his fall. But the body had taken some punishment as well. The rider sat up slowly, gingerly touching his knees and wincing.

Andy opened the door and jumped onto the ground. The rider leaned forwards, clutching his right elbow. Andy could see a hole in the green tweed of the jacket's elbow, a white shirt speckled with blood spots.

"Are you okay, pal?"

"Do I fucking *look* okay, you bloody idiot?" Fury replaced pain in the man's eyes. "And if you say 'sorry mate, I didn't see you' I won't be – "

Pain. Fury. Then recognition.

"Andy Hughes." A hollow laugh. *"Andy bloody Hughes!* You always said that you'd kill me. Come back to make good on your promise, eh?"

Andy was uncomfortably aware of the scrutiny from the crowd of shoppers and lunch-breaking workers. They had formed a semi circle around the injured man and were in that awkward stage between going to help the injured man and waiting to see what would happen. But having his name called out and tied in with the word *kill* was not how he wanted to be remembered by them.

"Sorry, chap, I... *Phil?* That you?"

Philip Lotson got to his feet, still clutching his elbow. He staggered, almost slipping in the slush that was even now freezing again. This time the bystanders were even more reluctant to advance. They were keeping a more than healthy distance. Philip Lotson became aware of the audience. He flexed his right forearm, rolled his elbow.

"Thank you ladies and gentlemen, I'll be fine now." He turned to Andy. "Won't I, Andrew?"

"How can he drive in a vehicle like this? You can't even see through the damn windows…disgusting. God knows what his house is like."

"I'll be finding out later," Andy replied. "I'll take a picture for you."

Phil was wiping the smeared grime on the passenger side of the windscreen with the sleeve of his jacket – and his good elbow. He stopped and stared hard at Andy.

"I'd appreciate that." He had to shout to make himself heard over the roar of the fan heater. "I'd also appreciate you telling me why you're in Cambridge."

"I'm not here to kill you, Philip. I can assure you." Even over the roar of the blower his softly spoken words were distinct, perfectly audible.

"So that attempt was just a bonus, was it?" He sighed. "Okay, I take that back. You're not here to see me… or Kelly, I hope?" A harsh, protective glare.

Jasper looked uncomfortable. Andy reached down and switched the engine off. Pointless having it running: they wouldn't be going anywhere until Rob got back. And with both of them talking and exhaling in such a confined space the cab was warm enough for now.

Andy leant his right elbow on the steering wheel and faced Phil. His face was impassive.

"Phil. I am not here to cause Kelly any grief. Or you, for that matter. I don't expect either of you to forgive me for what happened, but please try and remember that it was a long time ago. I haven't come to Cambridge for…for *that.*

"But I need your help. I'd asked Rob to put us in touch or arrange a meeting." A thin, humourless smile. "No need for that now, as you can see."

Phil snorted and stared at the Quayside.

"Funny how meetings with you always end up in someone getting hurt."

Andy took a deep, self-calming breath. *Let that one pass, he's right after all.*

"Phil. I need to know everything you can tell me about All Souls College."

Phil turned back and stared at him.

"Why the interest? I'd have thought you'd want to forget All Souls, especially after what happened there."

"I've had a long time to forget it," Andy said with a slow nod. "But someone wants me to do a little digging." *Should I tell him about Pearce? No, best not.* "Geoff Michaels is Rob's lodger. Or rather was."

Phil nodded, a suspicious look in his eye.

"That I know," he said warily. "He disappeared last year. Stress of exams, family expectations…"

"Breaking up with his girlfriend, money worries, and so forth. Yes, I know the official story. But his parents aren't happy with that. And…they want me to help find him."

Phil was silent. Andy had thought he'd say something dismissive, to voice the same thoughts he'd had when Pearce gave him the job. *Why ask you? What makes them think their son will still be there?*

Instead Philip Lotson silently watched the passing human traffic on Bridge Street. His brows were furrowed.

"Andy. I met up with Rob Benson a few months ago. First time I've seen him in years. He's of the same opinion. He doesn't believe Geoff went…willingly. He thinks the answer lies in the college as well. I told him that was rubbish. Part of me still thinks it is. But…"

He turned and faced Andy directly. His face was grim, pale and his eyes were red rimmed. Andy knew this was not the after effect of his collision with the van. This was something else.

"Your book." Andy said grimly. "Rob told me you've started it off with All Souls. Something's not right, is it? What have you found, Phil?"

Andy almost turned the engine back on to get the heater moving, but he knew it wasn't the cold seeping into the van that made Phil Lotson shiver.

"That's the problem, Andy. I've found nothing about that college. Apart from the basic details in the college prospectus and their brochures for the corporate catering market, the events of last year…nothing."

"What about the college's own archives, surely they have something?"

Phil snorted. "I'm sure they do. But you try getting to see them. Most of the colleges have been very forthcoming and helpful, many of the Fellows love talking about their college's legends. The President of Queens spent a good two hours with me, just to make sure I knew everything there was to be known about their phantom punter.

"But All Souls…that's a different matter. I tell you: everyone I spoke to, from the Head Porter to the Senior Tutor – even the bloody *gardener* – were abrupt to the point of rudeness. The Bursar virtually accused me of cashing in on one of their darkest moments, and the others made me feel that I was accusing them of hiding some secret."

"Defensive." Andy checked his watch. *Come on Benson, what's keeping you?* "Guess they don't like to be reminded of last year's events. Media must have been pestering for weeks on end after last year…"

"And just when they think it's all blown over, some nosy book-writing git wants to dig it all up again. That's what I thought to begin with. Until this morning." He told Andy about his email from the Master. "Hence my trip out today."

"Very helpful all of a sudden. Perhaps he just wants to make sure you're not going to put anything unauthorised in, or to play down the events of last year."

Phil didn't answer. He was chewing his fingernail and rubbing the sore elbow. He looked like he hadn't had much sleep.

"Have you been having any nightmares recently, Phil?"

Phil turned his head, too quickly.

"Nightmares? No coincidence, Andy. He sent an email at exactly the same time I woke up from one. *Exactly* the same time. As if he knew about it…"

"Or had one himself?" Andy suggested.

"If he did, I hope to God it was nothing like mine. I wouldn't wish it on anyone. It felt…too real for a nightmare. Kelly and Nick…" he swallowed noisily. Then a deep breath, his eyes squeezed shut, before continuing. "Last summer, when I took Kelly and Nick punting for the first time. The dream was an exact recreation of that day, a perfect memory - apart from the ending. They were killed, Andy. Sliced to pieces before my very eyes…"

Now Andy had the explanation for the drawn expression and the bloodshot eyes of his former tutor.

Andy bit his lip. It was obvious Phil really loved Kelly. And his kid…Andy would bet that Phil Lotson was a great father. A perfect family man. It made his own behaviour fifteen years ago that bit more shameful.

Phil's eyes opened again, glanced briefly in Andy's direction. They narrowed as they fell on him. *Something else was going on here.*

"What is it, Phil?"

When Phil told him his hands clenched on the steering wheel. *Christ, no wonder he's scared of me.*

"You've…you've never dreamed of me doing anything like this before?"

Phil shook his head. "No. Not even…not even back then."

Andy exhaled and relaxed his grip on the wheel. "Well. Guess that's something." *Why a knife, for Christ's sake? And why now?*

It all seemed even more sinister when taking into account the other events of the last twenty four hours. His calling to Cambridge. Rob's little 'adventure' last night. The carcass in the back of the van, which seemed to have a connection with the kitchens of All Souls. And this Emma girl? The way Rob was acting it sounded like her silence had been enforced, because her disappearance was out of character. Andy's shaven scalp prickled. Absence. Out of character…

Jen.

Everything was swirling around the college of All Souls like the clouds of a building hurricane. A storm was coming.

Another shaken, pallid face appeared next to Phil's, distorted by the filthy smears on the glass. It made Phil jump. He groaned in pain as Jasper leapt over him and planted his front paws on the door handle, his rear claws digging into Phil's belly. The dog barked a welcome at Rob, more saliva spraying onto the glass that Phil had just cleaned. The tail beat against Phil's face, hairs sticking in his beard. He coughed, wincing, and tried to push the animal away from him.

Andy couldn't help but smile at the sight. That changed when Rob opened the door and stared dully at the occupants of his van.

Jasper jumped onto the ground, sniffing around the bag of warm doughnuts he'd purchased on the way back to the van.

Rob's face was pale and drawn. He looked like he was having difficulty standing. In his other hand was the company's mobile phone, which threatened to slip from his shaking fingers.

"Rob?" Phil's voice was filled with concern as well. Even Jasper had calmed down. He sat on the freezing pavement without protest, tail no longer thrashing. His warm brown eyes stared with loyal concern for his master, the tempting aroma of the doughnuts forgotten.

Rob acknowledged Phil with a nod. He stared at Andy and raised the phone.

"You won't believe this. Jim's phoned me, gave me an update on the pig. It's gone."

"That's quick work," Andy replied. "How did they get rid of it?"

Rob shivered as he replaced the phone. "You don't understand, mate. They didn't get rid of it. It's gone. As in disappeared. Vanished."

"Vanished?" Andy's fingernails dug into the vinyl covering of the steering wheel. "How could it just…vanish?"

"No idea. Jim went outside to put some grit down on the path, came back and the pig had…well, he said it looked like it had been cremated. Higgins and Kiss-arse came over and then the ashes…blew away. He said nothing remains of it. *Nothing.* Not even the smell."

Phil Lotson turned to Andy. "Vanished…cremated pig? What's all this about?"

"Not a pig," Andy replied. "A boar. A wild boar. Turned up in his van this morning. He doesn't know how it got there." He stared meaningfully at Rob.

"Wait a minute." Phil said quickly. "A boar. Cremated?"

"Think so." Rob nodded shakily. "Jim said it was all ash and charred bone – until it blew away."

Phil stroked his chin thoughtfully. He stared hard at Rob.

"A cremated boar…and no trace remains?"

"Might be a couple of bloodstains I missed when hosing out the van."

"No. It's all clear in there," Andy said.

Strange, when he had placed Phil's bike and his own heavy rucksack in the cargo hold to clear space in the cab for three men and a dog he had noticed that the putrid stench had gone. As though it had never been there to begin with…

"Curiouser and curiouser," he whispered.

"More than that." Phil's voice was hoarse. "You are aware that the cremation of a boar is the culmination of the Founder's Feast of All Souls?"

Andy and Rob stared at him.

"Guess we'll find the answers when we get to All Souls. See if your friend Cassell is around, wondering who's stolen his carcass."

Rob grinned at Andy's comment. "More likely got his knob shoved up a Christmas turkey." He took out a doughnut, offered it to Jasper who took it gently, almost daintily. Then to Phil. "Want one? I almost got us some bacon rolls. But after Jim's call, the last thing I wanted was burned pig."

Phil shook his head.

"Not like you, Phil. Well, you need to lose some weight anyway. Why aren't you on your pushbike, anyway?"

"Ask your chauffeur."

Andy grinned at Rob's questioning glare.

"Third time lucky, as you said."

"Oh for God's sake…"

"His bike's in the back of the van. Not much damage that I can see but I suggested we drive him to his appointment."

"Appointment?" Rob stared at Phil suspiciously as he fed Jasper a second doughnut. "Where?"

"Same place you're going." Phil put a restraining hand on Jasper's thrashing tail. "I have an invitation to meet the Master of All Souls."

Andy Hughes drove the van back up Bridge Street with no further bike-related incidents. The red brickwork of Magdalene College glowed festively as they passed.

Andy was silent, concentrating on the drive, remembering instantly the best way to get to All Souls. *Funny, only been back a few hours and it feels like I never left…*

Castle Hill. Northampton Street, then down Queen's Road. The Backs.

Andy felt himself relaxing, physically and mentally, as his eyes drank in the scene that symbolised all that was best about Cambridge. He marvelled at the icy beauty this harsh winter had bestowed to the expanse of trees, lawns, pasture and gardens of the riverside colleges. The silvery brown waters of the Cam flowed lazily, as if on the verge of freezing, as they carried away academic memories on their way to the fens. The Courts and gardens of most of the older colleges were visible, each linked by a bridge to the border of parkland on the west side. The sycamores and horse chestnuts, jealously guarding the vision of historic splendour from traffic-bound passers-by, had now been forced to relent. Their leaves had long since fallen in lazy showers of gold and russet, allowing brief glimpses of the hallowed architecture to those stuck in the slow moving queue of traffic on Queen's Road.

The serene beauty of the Bridge of Sighs, Venetian-inspired splendour sitting uneasily with the red brick of St John's College. The elegant neo-Classicism of Clare College's western façade, its seventeenth century bridge spanning the freezing waters of the Cam, effortlessly linking New Court with the river. This enhanced the illusion of Clare being more a palace than a place of learning; an ice palace, snow and hoar frost glinting seductively on its gables. Then, the gothic Perpendicular majesty of King's College Chapel, enrobed in snow and ice.

The past was alive, and never more beautiful than on a morning like this. Winter brought out the visual beauty of Cambridge's architecture unlike any other season. Andy shook his head. Amazing, just a glimpse and he was back in scholar mode. Noting everything about his surroundings, the dates they'd been created, and the history behind them. Phil would be proud of him –

He noticed that Phil was quiet, rigid in his seat. His eyes were fixed firmly on the road ahead of them, avoiding the splendour of the historic backdrop.

Of course, Andy realised. *His nightmare was in summer rather than winter, but it was on the Backs that he dreamed his wife and boy were hacked to pieces. By me.*

At the black metal screen that composed the West Gate of King's, a Marshal in distinct purple livery blew into his hands and stamped his feet. A reminder of ancient times, a guardian on duty at the college's most vulnerable point of entry.

There was no Marshall at the entrance to All Souls, Andy noticed as he pulled the Transit onto the access road. There was something else.

"Why are we stopping?" Phil asked.

Rob pointed. "That's why. Looks like we ain't going any further."

The West Gate to All Souls College was an intricately arranged series of wrought iron railings in black and gold. Six feet high, each railing terminating in an arrow-shaped point. A metal plaque with the name of the college and an engraved image of a boar's head in gold was affixed to the right hand section. When open, it was wide enough to allow entrance for delivery vehicles, but this morning not only were the gates closed but the gravel path leading up to them was blocked by a metal bollard supporting a No Entry sign.

Rob leaned over and peered at the words underneath the red circle. "Well, that's new."

ALL DELIVERIES AND VISITORS – REPORT TO EAST ENTRANCE, KING'S PARADE.

"Awkward," Rob muttered around a fresh cigarette. "Bollards have been put up on the East Entrance as well. Have to park up and walk the furniture. Still, no problem."

Andy stared at him. *You don't want to go through the woods, do you? Frightened of what you might remember? Well, tough shit Roberto.*

Rob's thumb froze on the lighter's wheel as Andy Hughes jumped out of the cab.

The bollard was one of the pull-up, fold-down variety, with a padlock securing the top ring and preventing anyone but key-holders laying the obstacle flat. Well, that was the theory anyway. The top loop was too long. With one impatient upward pull and a disdainful shove, the bollard crashed down onto the gravelled pathway. He pushed the gates aside and returned to the van.

Two stony faces glared at him.

"That might cause problems, Andrew. I'm meeting the Master, don't forget. I'm sure they closed this off for a reason."

"Probably because of Rob's little adventure here last night." Andy said. He closed the door and put the van into first. "Anyway, I'm doing you guys a favour. I don't think either of you are up to walking much."

He released the handbrake and put his foot down.

"Welcome to All Souls, gents."

At the top of the right gatepost, a security camera swung round from what Andy had thought was a fixed position, overseeing the access via Queen's Road. It circled a full hundred and eighty degrees, then rose, following the van's progress as the vehicle ignored the twenty mile per hour speed limit and sped up the gravel path to the rear buildings of All Souls College.

In the porter's lodge, Head Porter John Franklin stared at the West Gate monitor with cold, mounting fury.

"That the van that was here last night, Street?"

A gruff Yorkshire accent answered from behind the door. "That's the one, Mr Franklin. The guy in the passenger seat was here last night."

The same that hit one of Her children, Franklin thought. He toggled the joystick, bringing the van into focus. Then a frown creased his craggy features. His steel grey moustache twitched as another thought struck him.

He pressed the rewind button, back to the point where the bollard had been pulled down. The driver of the van was in the bottom left hand corner of the monitor, only just there.

But the digital image was unmistakeable. He recognised the shaven head, the cold, deep-set eyes with their unnatural shade of green, and the fixed frown. After fifteen years, he was back.

Franklin went cold. He leaned forward, ran his index fingernail down the frozen image of Andy Hughes' face. Just over the eyes.

Perhaps it was anger at the prospect of the danger Hughes' return represented that made him press too firmly on the CRT screen.

Or perhaps the physical energy he had expended on the woman had made him forget his own strength.

The screen cracked. His finger remained, immobile, fixed on the emerald eyes of the driver long after the image vanished and the blood ran to the white cuffs of Franklin's shirtsleeves.

"*Hughes.*"

SEVEN

Gravel and snow were scattered by the Transit's wheels as the van sped up the path leading to the bridge. The stone chips bounced up and rattled in the wheel arches, sounding like machine gun fire.

Jasper had both paws up on the dash, nose pressed firmly to the cold glass of the windscreen. Excited at the speed and rocking motion of the van, his tail whipped back and forth again.

"Christ, Andy! Slow down!"

Comes to something when Mr White Van Man is scared of a little speed! Andy said nothing as he drove over the bridge, but reduced speed. Gravel hit the stone balustrades of the bridge, fell through the pillars and sprinkled the icy Cam below.

He was tense. His fingernails dug deeply into the vinyl of the steering wheel. He felt his heart hammering and adrenaline coursing through his body

For the first time in fifteen years, he was back in the place that had destroyed him. In the side mirror he saw the camera turn and follow the vehicle's progress. He frowned. *You know we're here, don't you?*

They left the bridge and the gravel path ran ahead in a straight line for about thirty yards, before it disappeared into a line of oak trees.

A heavy shroud of snow covered the skeletal branches. Leaf litter and rotting acorns formed untidy heaps that peeked through the snow, and he wondered why the gardeners hadn't been sent to clear them away when they fell in the autumn.

A breeze sprung up, forcing the topmost branches to shed their snow, and it was at that moment that Andy could see there were four or five rows of similar trees behind.

Remnants of the original, ancient wood that was cleared to make room for the college. He smiled grimly. A local history module from one of Phil Lotson's classes. Some of his teachings he would never forget.

Andy noticed that Rob had become silent. He had shrunk back in his seat, his eyes half closed as though trying to sleep – or trying not to remember what happened last night.

As they drove through the wood the gravel driveway shrank, narrowing on both sides so that the lower branches scraped noisily on the van's bodywork. The screeching forced Rob's eyes open, and put Andy's teeth on edge.

The path became narrower, nothing more than a frozen dirt track, the gravel disappearing altogether.

"I guess this is why they don't want delivery vehicles down here," Andy murmured as the rear wheels of the Transit spun noisily on the freezing mud.

They made slow progress through the wood. These trees were ancient. Judging from the huge girth of the trunks and the increasing number of boles jutting like open sores, these oaks had been here for hundreds of years. Above the ancient canopy the sky seemed darker, the trees taller and more closely grouped as they progressed, casting deep shadows. The college buildings disappeared from view. And all the while, the teeth-grating shriek of wood on metal accompanied them, branches smacking against the windscreen so loudly that even Jasper jumped back with a startled whine. As though the trees were following a command to halt the unauthorised passage of this metal intruder. As he forced the van deeper onwards, Andy had a strange sensation, a feeling that they were being watched. And not by camera lenses or human eyes

He told himself he was imagining it. There was no sign of life – not even any birds fluttered from the trees as they advanced. But the feeling remained. And he could tell by the silence of the others that they felt it too.

Finally, the exit materialised. The track widened and the traction improved. The skeletal fingers of the ancient oaks retreated, leaving the bodywork in peace. The light improved and the winter oaks became no more than shrinking reflections in the side mirrors.

A quick glance at Rob and Phil confirmed Andy's suspicions, that they had been just as unnerved by this strange passage as he was. Jasper's ears were back and nothing more than a low whine escaping his closed lips. Quiet and subdued.

Andy turned his attention to the buildings in front. The stone façade was about ten yards away, a carved archway in the wall allowing access.

"Cloister Court," Phil remarked. It was impressive, but unsettling. The medieval range of cloisters and covered walkways were made of the same blackened clunch stone that made up Old Court. The buildings were too tall and close together to allow much sunlight to fall on the whitened lawn. The midday sun made little impact on the gloom.

The cold, stone cloisters were empty, the lancet windows dark and inscrutable. No lights were on in the rooms beyond. The atmosphere was still, timeless. *An ecclesiastical structure abandoned by man and God alike... shit, where did that thought come from? That wasn't from Phil's class.*

A gateway in the centre of the facing range ushered them from the claustrophobic court and into New Court. Larger than Cloister Court, the lawn twice the size, less enclosed, less oppressing thanks to the presence of newer architecture.

To the right was a jumble of late nineteenth century buildings of crumbling red brick and unknown purposes. Smoke billowed from narrow chimneystacks that Andy remembered belonged to the college kitchens. Rob's nervous face confirmed it. He shrank in his seat as they passed the loading bay and the open service doors. A fat, white-overalled figure stood by the rubbish skips and glowered at the vehicle.

"Say hello to your friend, Rob." Andy turned the wheel, grinning at the dirty look Rob gave him, and entered the last gateway. The one leading to Old Court.

The gateway was too narrow, the stone walls curving inward to form a tunnelled roof that would do serious damage to the van's bodywork. Or so it seemed.

"Go on, Andy. It may not look like it but you can get a bus through there." Rob smiled thinly.

"You been this way before?" Phil asked nervously, involuntarily cowering in the seat as the stone tunnel came closer.

"Yep. This is the way I came last night, when I saw Emma." A pained expression crossed his face. Andy gave him a knowing look.

And the same way you left, isn't it Roberto?

He had to hand it to Rob, though. The tunnel was a tight fit, so Rob had done well to get the van through without scratching it, the state he was in last night.

A loud, plastic-sounding smack reverberated around the cab. Andy cursed when he saw the nearside mirror suddenly snap back on its hinges into the window pane.

"Amateur," Rob grinned. As soon as the van exited the archway he wound the window down and folded the mirror back. He grimaced and shook his fingers theatrically at the cold contact.

The enclosure of Old Court was not as claustrophobic as its fellows. The sun had managed to climb over the turrets and ramparts of the front range and was in the process of adding some light – if not warmth – to the chilly enclosure. Andy shut the engine down and climbed out.

On the pathway frozen snow – still frozen despite the midday sun – crunched under their feet. The only sound they could hear. It was hard to believe they were in the centre of a bustling university city.

He scanned the arrangement of buildings in front of him. Similar to the range they had seen in Cloister Court, but the huge Gothic façade and medieval fortress-style double doors of the Great Hall were the obvious difference. As they walked past Andy saw the doors were firmly bolted shut. Ice coated the extra long, elaborately wrought hinges. *Another barrier, another layer of defence,* he thought. *No entry.* He turned and stared at the octagonal stone fountain in the centre of the Court – and the snow covered mound of earth next to it.

"That's where they bury the boar after the Feast," Phil said quietly. The black and yellow striped ribbons rustled softly in the breeze. Andy glanced at the hole the hazard-warning tape barricaded and shook his head.

Phil pulled his jacket closer around his body in an attempt to keep out the chill breeze.

"Andy. Don't you ever feel the cold?"

"Of course."

"So why don't you wrap up? At least wear a hat. The amount of heat you must lose through your head…"

Andy didn't reply. Through the gateway he could see Jasper standing on the dash, peering mournfully through the windscreen.

"Hold on a bit, boy," Rob called. "Back soon. I'll let you have a scamper over the lawn."

"No, you bloody won't!" Phil snapped. He pointed to the *KEEP OFF THE GRASS* sign on the edge of the court. A rule Phil was determined to respect, Andy realised as he watched him stick to the flagstones that surrounded the grass. He smiled. Of course, walking on the lawns in college is a privilege for Fellows only. *Academic courtesy, eh? Well, when in Rome…*

His smile faded when he saw the footprints that led to the chapel. *Two sets.* One quite small and obviously formed by a woman's shoes, trainers probably; the others larger, heavier. A trail made by a man's heavy boots.

There was something else that wasn't right. The larger footprints went to the chapel and back out again. The woman's footsteps only went one way. Into the chapel. And yet…

He squinted his eyes against the harsh glare of the winter sun. There was no mistake. The small wooden doors were closed and padlocked shut. No-one was going in.

Not now, anyway. But those footprints are fresh, they were made less than two hours ago.

"How long will this meeting take, Phil?" he heard Rob ask.

"Not sure. An hour, maybe two."

"That's probably how long it'll take us to set the furniture up." Andy turned and examined the delivery note in Rob's hand. "I'd be very surprised if your mate Kiss-arse actually bothers to help us out."

"Oh, he'll piss off the minute the ticket's signed." Rob snorted. "Phil, we'll be in the van when you're finished. Give us a call when you're ready."

Phil nodded absentmindedly, not even aware of the bit of paper with a scribbled mobile phone number pushed into his jacket pocket. Andy could see that his mind was on his surroundings and his imminent meeting with the Master.

They entered the porch of the Main Gate. Ahead Andy could see through the open gateway to Trinity Street, the entrance they were supposed to have used. Now he could hear sounds of normality – pneumatic drills and diesel generators, road works, and the ringing of bicycle bells.

The door to the porter's lodge was wedged open, as though the inhabitants were unaware of the cold. Or relished it. He took a deep breath and fought to control his shaking.

Keep calm, Andy. It was a long time ago.

The lodge was just as he remembered it. Heavy oak panelling, a bare stone floor. Dingy lighting. Pigeonholes took up one side of the lodge. Normally stuffed with internal mail and memos to students and Fellows, they were mostly empty for the Christmas vacation, apart from one or two that had some unclaimed Christmas cards. Cork notice-boards took up the opposing side, covered with notes ranging from rowing fixtures and adverts for recitals to stern notices from the University administration regarding disciplinary procedures for various acts of misconduct. Two tiny Christmas cards were pinned to the nearest board to Andy. He flicked one open, noting the scrawled seasonal greeting *To Franklin and Co.: Have a good 'un! First VIII*

A few strings of thin tinsel were draped over the top of the corkboards, along with a one-foot high, sparsely decorated Christmas tree on the counter, a half-hearted attempt to bring some seasonal cheer to the gloomy, Dickensian office. *Scrooge would've loved this*, he thought. *Fifteen years on and nothing's changed.*

Even the old cash register, used for the sale of postcards and pens, feeble souvenirs of the college, was the same one from the 1960s.

The only nod to modernity was the flat panel PC monitor and the bank of CCTV monitors to the left of the counter. Six monitors, each one given continuous feed by the dedicated cameras mounted at strategic points around the college. Andy noticed that the one covering the Queen's Road access point – the access point they had used without authorisation – had a large crack running down the centre.

Behind the counter the lodge stretched back to reveal three men. Two porters, thickset men in their late thirties, sat in reclining chairs, drinking coffee and reading newspapers. Their heavy black coats were buttoned up against the cold, but they were obviously not going to ask the head porter to put the heating on or close the door.

The head porter himself looked far older than Andy Hughes remembered. The neatly trimmed moustache and swept back hair were steel grey now, and the lines in his forehead and around his eyes were deeper, more pronounced. But those cold blue eyes hadn't changed. They were still bright and sharp; watchful, appraising. They blazed: lighting up with icy malevolence when they met the cold, clear gaze of Andy Hughes; a blaze of recognition and hatred.

Go on Franklin, say it. Just bloody say it.

John Franklin said nothing as he pushed himself away from the counter. He folded his arms, the biceps bulging through the sleeves of his thin white shirt as he did so.

He was tall, equal to Andy's six foot two, but he carried himself differently. An upright posture and disciplined movements that only those of previous military experience seem to possess.

Hasn't let himself go, then, Andy thought. *And here he is in rolled up shirtsleeves with the door wide open. What's he been up to?*

Unlike his underlings shivering in their overcoats Franklin seemed unaware of the cold. His face was flushed, as though he'd just returned from some arduous physical activity – after all, there was some blood seeping from a plaster on his right index finger. Or perhaps it was anger and hate keeping him warm.

"Hughes." Low, barely restrained tones in a familiar Edinburgh brogue. An anger that was kept in check, disciplined enough not to allow it in his voice. "I take it that was your van that came through the Queen's Road access. Working for Granta Office Supplies now, are we?"

"More of a consultant." Andy stood firm, meeting Franklin's baleful sneer with a disdainful look. He was aware of Rob and Phil behind him, silent. Shrinking back warily from the tension between the two men, aware that it could explode into conflict at any moment. All of them knew what had happened in the bar of All Souls College one summer's night fifteen years ago. And Andy's sudden appearance at the college was a grim reminder to Franklin. *No wonder he hates me.* Andy permitted himself a smile.

"Performing a risk assessment on delivery routes taken by our drivers. Researching new ways to enter old college buildings, that sort of thing."

Franklin's face went scarlet. The two porters behind him lowered their newspapers, picked up their distinctive bowler hats, and headed for the door.

"Now, Franklin. We have a delivery to the Master's Lodge. Your *boss*. He's expecting the furniture any moment now – as well as a meeting with my good friend Mr Philip Lotson. Do you really want to keep the Master waiting?"

Franklin's eyes flicked from Andy, to Rob and then Phil before settling back on Andy. The porter turned away abruptly. He reaching for the phone, lifted the handset to his ear, and pressed a direct dial button.

"Franklin here, sir," he spoke quietly, almost respectful, while keeping a hate-filled glare fixed on the man in front of him. "I have …Philip Lotson and two delivery men from Granta to see you. You may wish to…oh. Very well, sir." He replaced the handset, a look of surprise on his flushed features. "You can go."

"Pass me one of those maps." Andy pointed to a pile of photocopied plans of the college grounds. "It's been a long time since I've been here. I don't want to take a wrong turning. Who knows what trouble I'd cause this time?"

Franklin took a deep breath. Exhaled. Then snatched the top copy and slammed it onto the counter, rattling the PC monitor and the change within the cash register. Rob winced.

Neither he nor Phil said anything about the exchange until they were out of the lodge. Then Rob exploded.

"What the fuck was all that about? You winding him up on purpose?"

"Relax, Rob. He won't say anything." Andy examined the map with distaste. A poor photocopy, and badly drawn, the lettering on the individual buildings was barely legible. The Master's Lodge was just to the left of Cloister Court. Strange. The woods on the map were represented by a thin line, as if it was just a screen of single line trees rather than a full wood.

"Just wanted to see if he still remembered me." He lowered the map and nodded through the smeared window of the lodge. Franklin stood rigid, arms folded.

Yes. Still a fan, I see.

Back through New Court and its smoking kitchen buildings. Through the gateway into Cloister Court with its silent, oppressive galleries. Through the last court and facing the oaks again. Even Andy shivered this time. He looked at the map on his lap. Had to turn right here…

The Master's Lodge was a handsome two-storey structure adjoining the north side of Cloister Court. As Andy brought the van round to face the main frontage he was reminded of the late sixteenth century Long Gallery of the President's Lodge at Queens. Like the Queen's building, it had Tudor half timbering and white plastering. Frozen ivy clung to the timber, stretching greedily around the walls. In the centre of the Lodge was what looked to be a tower – or rather, a half-tower, bulging from the gallery almost organically, as though the structure had grown naturally rather than been built by human hands . Transoms of black timber provided dramatic frames for the mullioned windows that gaped darkly from the Lodge, overshadowed by stark gables that cast them into shadow, further darkness. There didn't appear to be any lights on.

Andy parked the van and stepped out. Phil and Rob followed warily. Jasper needed no encouragement to stay in the van. No sound from the wood they had passed through, no sign of life from anywhere else in the grounds. The noise from the city centre was once again missing. Andy turned from the woods and faced the door.

The door was set in the back of a wooden porch in the centre of the half-tower. Heavy oak, the top curving gracefully and rising to form a half-arch. The doorknocker was blackened iron, carved in the shape of a boar's head. Andy noticed Rob shudder as he put his hand to it. Another reminder of the beast in his van.

The striking of the knocker was deep and full, three sonorous thuds echoing through the porch way as Andy slammed the boar's head onto the wood with more force than was necessary.

The broken silence resumed, more evident and pronounced as the echoes faded. Andy, Phil and Rob waited quietly, none of them speaking.

Rob took a last drag of his cigarette, realised it was burning to the filter and stubbed it out on the door knocker, in between the beast's eyes.

Phil knocked his hand away with a disgusted cry. The stub fell to the ground just as the door opened.

Professor David Searles was a tall man – not quite as tall as Franklin or Andy, but not far off. He was dressed in a perfectly tailored grey suit and a sober dark tie that gave a certain dignity to the man wearing it. Not that he needed it, Andy thought. Searles was a man whose pose and stature showed an effortless dignity and grace. And yet…

There was a certain downbeat aspect to this man. The straight back looked forced, as though he was fighting a temptation to slump those rigid shoulders and bow his head, to give in to the worries and pressures of his role.

It was his face that betrayed the posture of his body. The face was long, the chin prominent without being pointed. The smoothly shaven features and thinning fair brown hair with streaks of grey in the temples belonged to a man in his late fifties, but the dull, tired look in his hazel eyes made him look older. As those eyes took in the sight of Andy Hughes they flickered, almost imperceptibly, but Andy noticed it. A look of apprehension – or was it recognition? Couldn't be. Searles was invested at All Souls just after Andy had left Cambridge; he wouldn't have known Andy at all.

The smile that followed was forced. "You must be the gentlemen from Granta. And you must be Philip Lotson." The eyes turned to Phil who smiled in greeting. "I've heard a lot about you. It's a pleasure to meet you at last. Please, come in."

They followed the Master of All Souls into the lobby. The interior reflected the exterior in terms of age and the sense of antiquity. Deep mahogany wainscoting, richly varnished. The rug which ran along the parquet floor was a rich umber adding to the sense of gloom in the passageway. It would've helped if there were some lights on, Andy reflected. The whole place smelled musty, a museum odour of old stone and wood.

Searles led them into a room that ran off the left side of the lobby. Like the lobby, the lower halves of the walls were encased in dark mahogany and the soft pile carpet was a rich scarlet. Bevelled windows magnified and distorted the wintry scene from the Fellows' Garden, grossly swelling the snow-capped oaks into monstrous, unnatural formations.

A large, ancient desk stood forlornly in the centre, the oak chipped and cracked, with jagged splits in the legs. In front were two wing-backed chairs in saggy green leather upholstery, again carved of oak but in slightly better condition than the one behind the desk that Searles now took. He reclined, steepled his fingers and smiled at Rob.

"As you can see, the working furniture of my study has seen better days. Your company's very generous offer couldn't have come at a better time."

"Yeah, we're all Santa's little helpers," Rob muttered. "Has Kiss-ar - has Terry Harrison got here yet? I didn't see his motor outside."

"Not yet." The Master gave Rob a sympathetic smile. "Don't worry about putting the desk together. If you'd care to leave it in the lobby I'll give him a hand to assemble it when he arrives."

Still stood in the doorway, behind Rob and Phil, Andy frowned as he saw Searles' eyes flick in his direction.

"Although I might even make him do it all himself. That young man seems a little too cocky for my liking. I think a little honest toil – to which I am certain he is unaccustomed – will do him some good."

Rob laughed at that, but Andy didn't. He saw the Master's eyes turn to him once again. A knowing look. *You don't want me or Rob hanging around, do you?*

"Besides, I'm sure you two have a lot more deliveries to be doing this afternoon. That would explain your apparent haste in arriving here."

"Guess Franklin had some words, did he?" Rob shuffled his feet.

Searles smiled. "I must apologise for my head porter's abruptness. Ex-military man, so not the world's greatest diplomat. However, he has a point. I decided to close off the Queen's Road access because we are having difficulties with delivery vehicles. The courts are too narrow to accommodate anything larger than a car, and the trees outside Cloister Court are becoming damaged. They are very old trees, as Mr Lotson knows. Living history." Searles sighed. "The events of last year - and the attempted sabotage - have made us very protective of our college. I explained all this to young Terry when he took the order. Perhaps he neglected to pass the details on?"

"Wouldn't be the first time. If - "

"As I said, I'm sure you have more work this afternoon." The interruption was smooth and well mannered, not brusque, but a dismissal nonetheless. Andy's eyes narrowed as Rob failed to take the hint.

"No rush, boss. All Souls is our last drop. We're giving Phil a lift back, so - "

"In that case, please feel free to wander through the college grounds. Explore the courts, the gardens if you wish. Or have a meal in the Buttery. I think you'll find that our kitchens do some very warming festive lunches, ideal for keeping out the winter chill.

"I shall telephone Mr Franklin and inform him that you have free access to the parts of the college that do not require a security pass." Again, he looked at Andy while speaking to Rob. The message was clear: *leave us alone. But explore the college. We have nothing to hide.*

Andy nodded in acknowledgement of the offer, but said nothing. It was too much of a coincidence. A free reign around the college on the same day that Phil Lotson was invited to discuss the history of the college. And the remark about the kitchens… it made Andy remember the complaint Rob's boss had made about Jasper intruding in the kitchens. And it was the kitchens that would be preparing the boar for the Founders' Feast tomorrow.

No, this is no coincidence. Searles is giving us some clues. Time to play Kojak.

"Come on, Rob. I could do with something to eat. Let's drop the desk off and go. Phil, we'll catch you later."

Rob walked to the doorway, a bewildered expression on his face, his eyes never leaving the Masters'. Andy moved aside to allow him to pass. He smiled at Searles knowingly before leaving. Searles nodded his head once but didn't smile. As Andy closed the door he heard the Master's voice.

"Well, Mr Lotson. I believe we have much to discuss." Andy paused before leaving, taking in the tone and delivery of the words. The Master's voice was tremulous, the voice slightly high pitched. He'd done well to cover it so far but now it was obvious.

Phil was right. The Master of All Souls was a frightened man.

EIGHT

Phil gratefully accepted the large measure of whisky the Master offered. The lead crystal tumbler was heavy in his hands, the vessel of high quality. As was the liquid that burned a welcoming path down his throat, warmed his body and alleviated the pain in his elbows. Single malt, matured over fifteen years. He sighed with pleasure.

The Master sipped his whisky delicately, thoughtfully. His chair was turned to the bevelled windows that offered a distorted, almost surreal view of the Fellows' Garden. Phil followed his gaze, watching the sun shine on the spires of King's College Chapel, temporarily banishing the dark winter shadows from the painstakingly trimmed lawns. The borders were empty, yet well maintained and free from any visible sign of weeds. Only the snow and ice held them prisoner.

"A bitterly cold winter," the Master remarked as he cradled the tumbler in his delicately formed hands. "Just like last year."

For a tall man, Phil noticed that his hands were rather small. The fingers constantly moved, caressing the tumbler, tapping on it, circling the rim. He wondered if the Master had recently given up smoking, and was trying to find something for his hands to do.

No, it's another tell-tale sign of his fear and anxiety, he realised. And at the mention of the words last year, he knew Searles' anxiety was kindling. He was preparing himself to discuss not just the history of his college, but the attempted destruction of it. Last year.

"Do you, mind, Master?" He had opened his jacket pocked and retrieved the digital Dictaphone. Searles shook his head.

Phil placed it on the desk and rested his index finger on the record button.

"I hope you don't mind me asking, but…why exactly did you ask to meet me? Everyone else I spoke to was reluctant to discuss last year's events, especially when they knew I was putting it into my book. The general response was that the past should be forgotten, left to rest."

Searles sighed heavily as he turned from the window. The sun was sinking rapidly behind the ecclesiastical horizon. The shadows in the Fellows' Garden were lengthening.

"The past can never be forgotten, Mr Lotson. And it never rests. It lives on in the present alongside us, whether we are aware or accepting of it - or not. As men of history I think we are both aware of this."

Phil was reminded of the introductory seminar he gave to all his first year students at Anglia Ruskin. *History is not a dead subject. The past lives on.* He shivered and took another sip of the whisky.

Searles wasn't just voicing the same sentiment he held. His tone of voice suggested that his view of what constituted the past and how it lived on was markedly different to Phil's. The Master continued.

"I asked you to come today because I wanted to make sure you have the full facts before proceeding with your…book." There was a look of distaste. "Quite a come-down, is it not? I'm certain your energies and talents could be better spent on more academic pursuits than this…this tourist pamphlet."

Phil was silent. *Not you as well, Searles? Or is this just for the benefit of the tape?*

"Still, each to their own. But be warned. The last thing I want is last year's episode to be sensationalised and distorted as it had been by the tabloids…and some of the so called 'qualities', for that matter. I am aware of the reputation and reviews of your last work, so you can understand my apprehension. Hopefully by giving you the full, detailed facts you will be certain to provide a more rational account of that night's tragedy and will avoid the ridiculous, supernatural labels that were attached to us. I need hardly remind you that one of our own members, Professor James Freeland, sadly succumbed to the same madness. Our academic reputation suffered considerably. Only now are we beginning to regain credibility in the eyes of the academic world."

Phil took another sip of the whisky. A larger one.

"I understand that that itself had been a problem even before last year. If you don't mind me saying, Master, All Souls has been a perceived as a bit of a joke – some would say even an embarrassment to the University. The Council of the Senate has never had a Fellow of All Souls in its membership. No member of the college has ever had an opportunity to vote on the Graces put before the Senate.

"It is even rumoured that if it were possible for a college to be removed from the University the Council of the Senate would have voted for your exclusion a long time ago."

Searles smiled thinly.

"I've heard this also. Because of the college's…chequered past, and it's far from illustrious present. The archives compiled over the years would have blown away all the myths and rumours that enshroud our college like the festering cobwebs that they are. We have a fully competent IT department, our own web design team. It is a tragedy that we were unable to transfer our archives into the digital realm because of the fire that destroyed the papers. All those records, the correspondence of previous Fellows and alumni of All Souls…lost forever.

"Which is why a complete history of the college will never be written. Anything before 1799 will never be known because of the fire in the library. What you may have uncovered in previous histories of the University, any fragments of local newspaper reports relating to the college, are all that remains. You know as much as anyone else does of the college."

The Master looked directly at Phil. He stopped playing with the glass tumbler. His fingers were now relaxed, the crystal leisurely resting in them as he reclined in his chair. He cocked his head to the sound of banging and scraping in the lobby beyond; muffled cursing that could only have come from Rob Benson. He winced at the sound of wood and plastic wrapping being scraped before continuing.

"What you really want to know about is the custom of the Founder's Feast."

"Indeed, Master." *And why you've summoned me here. But that can wait.* "There seems to be no record of the Feast's origin, or why it is necessary to continue it to this day. A Founder's Feast…but there is no name of the Founder.

"A mystery. Your college is nothing like the All Souls of Oxford, or indeed any other Cambridge College where the history of the founder and the role of the college can be traced back to religious reasons.

Searles merely smiled. Phil continued.

"And the Founder's Feast…the choice of meat for the main dish…well, taking into account the college's medieval origins, that's understandable. But why is the carcass of the consumed boar ceremoniously marched through the grounds of the college? Why are the remains buried in the centre of Old Court?"

"Tradition, Mr Lotson. Purely and simply a matter of tradition. As the boars are no longer available in the woods that grew on the site of the college, an organic smallholding in Thetford provides our meat yearly. Boar flesh is no longer the delicacy it once was, but this supplier has succeeded in raising animals that come extremely close to the original beasts that were once prevalent in primeval European forests. Its taste is quite distinct from most people's experience of wild boar flesh."

Phil asked for the address and website of the smallholder and made a mental note to ask some questions. Perhaps see some footage of these unique creatures growing up, see what resemblance they had to this thing that Rob claimed was in his van this morning. *Jim said it was all ash and charred bone – until it blew away...*

The Master handed over a piece of paper with the details of the smallholding. "Are you quite all right, Mr Lotson? You seem a little pale."

"Yes...fine. Ate too much for breakfast, that's all. Please, continue."

"Very well. It seems an eccentric tradition, bestowing upon a dead, half-eaten animal a funeral with honours that only a human being would enjoy. But participating in this ceremony is a...singular experience. A sense of purpose overcomes you. When you help carry the beast to its final resting place you feel that you are honouring it, thanking it for its sacrifice. It dies so that its flesh may give you life. It's the way the original enactors of the ritual must have felt.

"No other academic institution in the world venerates such a tradition. We believe it adds a unique charm to All Souls, distinguishes us from the other Cambridge Colleges. As such, a ritual that we feel duty and honour bound to respect, and continue."

Phil stroked his beard. 'Charm' was not the word he would have used for such a bizarre ceremony. *Respect and continue?*

"And so, it keeps the past alive?"

Searles nodded. "Most definitely. You need to understand the origins of the foundation and the boar's association with the annual Feast to appreciate the ritual.

"The college has a wild boar's head as its crest, as does Queen's – but that particular college, one of our illustrious neighbours, earned it through its association with Richard III, one of its major benefactors. We have it for far older reasons." The Master was watching him intently now. There was no trace of the fear and anxiety that plagued him earlier. It had drained from him, as easily as Phil drained his Scotch.

The Master poured him another without asking.

"All Souls stands on old ground, Mr Lotson. Very old ground. It was a college of learning even before the refugees from 'the Other Place' set up home here.

"No trace of the original building has survived. Very little is known of the college's purpose, the scholars who studied there. Or even what those studies consisted of. It is understood that the site of the college was situated in a small oak wood, the remnants of which survive to this day. Some of the older records referred to the existence of an institution known as Drunemeton."

"Or Nemeton," Phil was conscious that he said the word too quickly, too eagerly. "Nemeton being the Latin term for sacred grove."

"Yes," the Master sighed scornfully. "Druidism. Of course, the Celtic priesthood died out long before religious colleges were introduced, but because ours was built on a site that had some connection to a druidic centre of learning, All Souls has long suffered an association with a barbaric priesthood. Ridiculous, really. Whatever was studied in the college before All Souls was founded: it certainly was not druidic lore."

"You must admit, though, the evidence of a direct link is there." Phil told himself to calm down. He was starting to babble, over-excited. "Your own, living tradition of the Feast."

"In what way, Mr Lotson?" Searles smiled condescendingly.

"Burial of the boar…it shows a remarkable similarity to one of the fertility rituals practised by the Celts. Mixing the flesh of the boar with seed corn and then burying it in the fields to promote fertility.

"The boar was certainly a sacred animal to them," Phil continued. "It was treated with reverence, awe, because of supposed magical properties."

"A beast that linked this world to the Otherworld. I know my mythology, Mr Lotson. But I'm afraid I'm going to have to disappoint you if that is the approach you wish to use for the inclusion of All Souls in your book." Searles shook his head.

"Really, Mr Lotson, you should know better. The tradition was there before All Souls was founded because wild boars were scarce at this time. The development of a riverside port into a thriving medieval city meant the woodland in which the boar thrived was no longer available. And on the day the foundation stone of All Souls was laid - the twenty-first of December, 1299 - a single boar was seen running through the woods. The first seen for decades. It was hunted, killed and eaten at the feast to mark the founding, and its remains buried in a patch of ground that was to become Old Court."

"But some were uneasy with this. A pagan act committed on the day a Christian college was founded, dedicated to God."

"Indeed. The new college's reputation suffered. All Souls had difficulty attracting new scholars. Those who did put the superstition behind them naturally enough found nothing untoward in the college, and pursued their studies with religious devotion. But they were few and far between. Which explains why we remain one of the smallest colleges in Cambridge. Of course, the Tripos diversified: there were more subjects to study. The college grew, but never thrived." There was sadness in his voice.

It wasn't surprising. Phil knew that there was suspicion from the other colleges, who could never accept that a college performing a pagan ceremony was granted statutes to establish it as an official and legally recognised centre of Christian teaching. But most of the suspicion, which turned into outright hostility, came from the townsfolk.

"The 'Black School.'" Searles was reading his mind. "A label invented by superstitious townsfolk that stuck for centuries. Stories of devil worship, necromancy, all sorts of superstitious claptrap; that was what All Souls was known for in spite of its eminent academic reputation. Throughout its history, there has always been a section of the community that wished to see All Souls burn." He sighed. "1381 - the Peasants' Revolt – if it hadn't been for the quick actions of the militia, it would not have been just the University records in Great St. Mary's Church that burned. Then 1799…the 'Divine Judgement', as the Master of Christ's college called it."

Phil nodded slowly. 1799. The year All Souls was almost destroyed completely, without human hands.

There was anger in Searles' voice as he continued. "It is incredible, some would say scientifically impossible, that a stone of that size didn't create a larger explosion. This, for many, is proof that it was a warning: a judgement from God rather than a desire for total oblivion.

"The meteorite hit the library in Cloister Court. Many were killed in the terrible conflagration that ensued, including the Master, Charles Harvey. A tragedy: in both human terms as well as financial and material. It took many years for All Souls to recover, to rebuild. But the college endured. It could never shake off its tragedy, but all involved were certain that it would never happen again. Meteorites, like lightning, rarely strike in the same place twice. However…"

"One man, seriously disturbed. Taking the place of a…heavenly missile. Thank God he was stopped before he caused any damage."

The Master rubbed his eyes wearily.

"It wasn't God we owed our thanks to. It was the quick thinking of our head porter that prevented his son causing a disaster."

"But God was the *reason* this young man gave for his attempt to destroy All Souls. He saw himself as the second Divine Judgement, a human incarnation and punishment for the past 'sins' of this institution. And the supposed continuance of them." Phil saw that Searles' eyes were red and swollen when he replied.

"Jason Franklin is an extremely unbalanced individual. His father will vouch for that. If you can get him to talk about it."

Phil's eyes gleamed. *This was it.* A direct link with the head porter, John Franklin. Now he was getting somewhere. He noticed the annoyance in Searles' eyes.

"Please do not think for one moment that John Franklin will ever discuss this matter with you, an outsider. He feels very bitter and angry about that night, even blames himself for it."

Ah. Better tread carefully here.

"How long has John Franklin been head porter at All Souls?"

Searles stroked his chin thoughtfully. "It feels like he has been here forever. It is hard to imagine All Souls without John Franklin. My understanding is that he took the role of duty porter in 1985 soon after he was discharged from the Army. He took to the job straight away, and became head porter in 1990 when the previous holder of that title, Dennis Vaughan, died in his sleep at the age of eighty six."

"Franklin has a military background, then?" That was news to Phil.

"Yes, 3rd Parachute Regiment. An…honourable discharge after the Falklands campaign." Searles' eyes glanced downwards. Phil picked up on the lie straight away and made a note to pursuer that further. *Franklin left under a cloud. Curious…*

"And he came here? Why's that?"

"He'd been a student of All Souls in the 1960s. A degree in economics and politics, and then Sandhurst for officer training. He always said he'd return. All Souls was in his blood, he once said…"

"His son, Jason Franklin, must be in his early twenties now. What can you tell me about him?"

Searles took a deep breath. "Very little, Mr Lotson. Suffice to say that he was the physical result of a whirlwind romance with a barmaid from the Radegund Arms that ended badly. The child was taken into foster care at the age of six due to domestic problems, amid signs of increasing mental instability. His mother wanted nothing to do with him. It seems that walking through the college, when his father allowed Jason to shadow him and learn his duties, had an adverse affect on him. He read too much, soaked up too many lies. He claimed to see and hear things. Voices, whispers, faces crawling out of the wall…as I said, it was the first signs of his paranoid schizophrenia, and it exacerbated the domestic strife at home."

Domestic problems? That was news as well. The mother never came forward after Jason Franklin's committal last year.

Domestic strife…wonder if that means Franklin beat his son, taking out his anger at the embarrassing behaviour with physical violence? He looks the sort of man who would turn to that as the first resort.

And an ex-Para, a Falklands veteran…a dishonourable discharge? Phil opened his mouth to speak but the Master raised a hand.

"Please, no more on this subject. Franklin has confided in me alone about his son, but he doesn't wish others to know. I'm sure you will respect his right to privacy when you write this section of your book." Searles regarded Phil steadily. "I really hope you will resist the temptation to sensationalise this sad affair. The damage attempted on All Souls was the result of a mentally disturbed young man acting out his tortured fantasies. A tragic affair, one we are all deeply affected by. The media treated everyone concerned abominably. I trust you will have more discretion and respect."

A reasonable request, spoken by a man saddened and distressed. He looked tired, as if the effort of retelling the All Souls story had drained him. Searles raised his glass to the window, examining the whisky. The red sun dying through the windows turned it a brilliant colour, gold and scarlet. He drained it, closed his eyes and took a deep breath. It felt like an age before he opened them.

"Perhaps I can give you a tour, Mr Lotson."

The air was colder than it had been when they stepped out of the porch way. The day was dying and the temperature dropping further as a result. Rob's dog had his nose pressed against the windscreen of the Transit, whining. Phil patted the dented bonnet of the van as he passed.

They walked along the gravelled driveway towards Cloister Court, the only sound in the silent clearing the crunching underfoot of frosted gravel chips and snowflakes.

Phil looked at the frozen oak trees, finding it hard to believe that just a few hundred yards beyond them there was a bustling road, thick with cyclists and cars. Life. It felt that the wall of trees had not just blocked them from view but had swallowed all sound as well. An ancient barrier: cutting the members and visitors of All Souls off from the twenty first century.

"How old are those trees exactly? When we drove through them earlier it seemed they were positively ancient."

"Those oaks? Older than the college," the Master replied, buttoning his overcoat. "The trees in the centre of the copse were fully mature even before All Souls was founded."

Phil pondered this. "They present difficulties for vehicular access, don't they?"

The Master halted. He turned and stared thoughtfully at the oaks. "Indeed. We tried to tarmac the path to make it easier for cars and commercial vehicles to access, but low lying roots and stumps still provide obstacles. One of our Fellows ruptured his fuel tank as he wandered from the track last week on a stump that we thought had been cut away. It seems that all efforts we make to provide access through the wood are thwarted by the very trees themselves. So, following a revised risk assessment, the College Council determined that all vehicular access is to be made via Trinity Street.

"Of course, with the present road works and the restricted access times, it makes life awkward for those with cars. And vans." Searles looked back to the parked Transit. He paid close attention to the dented bonnet.

"Tell me, Mr Lotson. How long have you known those delivery men from Granta?"

The question took Phil by surprise. "Rob and Andy? Since they started their history degrees at Anglia Ruskin in the 1990s."

"They're graduates?" The Master frowned.

"Rob is…just. Andy was forced to abandon his degree in the first year. A real shame. He was one of the best students I've come across, would've had a fine academic career if he hadn't been forced out."

"Forced out." Searles looked thoughtful. "Yes, I recall Franklin telling me about this…individual. Fifteen years ago. And now he's back. Why?"

Phil thought carefully before answering.

"Spending Christmas with Rob, I believe. They were good friends many years ago, I believe they got in touch with each other on Facebook…" he rambled on, wondering why he was lying on Andy's behalf.

"I see," Searles nodded before walking ahead. They continued along the gravelled driveway through Cloister Court.

The Master knew he was lying – if anything, David Searles would have a better understanding for Andy Hughes' presence in Cambridge than Phil. But he didn't press the issue. Perhaps that's another test, Phil thought as they approached Old Court. They turned into a gateway on the left hand side of the Court, a wide spaced alley that cut a swathe through the frowning structures. The doors were open and the Great Hall of All Souls swallowed them.

Phil's breath exploded from his lungs. Now he knew what breathtaking *really* meant.

The cold clunch stone exterior gave no clues as to what to expect. He'd seen pictures of the Great Hall before, in the college's prospectus and various university architecture text books. Impressive even then, but no picture could do full justice to the effect the Hall had on a first time visitor seeing with his own eyes.

The interior was astonishing. Not just because of its cavernous size – one hundred metres long, forty metres wide, thirty metres tall – but because of the richness of decoration. They stood on brightly varnished floorboards which gleamed with reflected electric candlelight. Phil looked up at the chandeliers. *Yes, fake candles, but pretty convincing.*

In the centre of the Hall were five trestle tables, backed by heavy oak dining chairs. The floor consisted of marble tablets that portrayed the arms of the University, golden lions rearing from a red background quartered by a white cross. To the left was a huge Tudor fireplace underneath marbled mantle tiles. The grate was clean and gleamed blackly. The walls were covered in rich, exotic wallpaper with flowing patterns of red, cream and gold to give the impression of medieval tapestries. Arched, transom windows with tracery that wouldn't be out of place in the finest Gothic cathedrals reluctantly allowed the dying sunlight to seep through the blue and red stained glass.

At the far end of the Hall was a screen, carved in oak in a Neoclassical style: wooden columns with gilt flourishes supporting an impressive, yet oppressive triangular portico. In the centre was a gilded carving of a boar's head, the eyes blazing scarlet.

My God! Rubies for eyes! Phil's jaw dropped lower. The precious stones glared down at the two men, a guardian angered by this unwarranted intrusion into its domain.

The screen surmounted a raised plinth which stretched from one end of the Hall to the other, providing a dais for the long table below. This was High Table, where the Master and Senior Fellows would sit, facing the five lower tables as they consumed their meals in superior isolation. *Academic equivalent of being above the salt, and just as medieval,* he thought.

The tables were already set and laid with silver cutlery that gleamed in the electric light and nestled on red leather placemats. Normally for Formal Hall, Phil thought, the weekly occasion when all members of the college, Fellows and undergraduates, would sit and dine together. All Souls was one of the few colleges to make this compulsory.

Not that it would be a trial to eat here, he thought with a trace of envy. But not this time. Term was over, the students gone home for Christmas. This was set in readiness for the Founder's Feast.

He looked again at the screen. Yes, that was oak. Strange how the wood had darkened and mellowed with age. It looked ancient, but not wearied or distressed with the passing of the years. Scrupulously maintained, he thought as he walked along the marbled centre. He was aware of the mess his shoes were making with mud and melted snow, but something caught his attention that banished guilt from his mind.

In the centre of High Table was a spherical object. Not resting or mounted on it, because only the top two thirds of the object were visible. Mounted *in* the table, in a specially carved hollow to hold the rock. He gingerly placed a finger on it.

It was approximately twelve inches in diameter. Smooth and highly polished. Black, with thin traces of red and green. Phil raised a hand to touch it.

"No. Please don't do that."

He turned and stared quizzically at Searles, who had now walked over to join him.

"The Divine Judgement," Searles said in hushed tones that echoed around the cavernous Hall. "The meteorite that struck the Great Hall in 1799. A permanent reminder of the chequered history of All Souls."

Phil felt a sense of awe. In this city of ancient architecture and timeless tradition, a body far older than the human race - maybe even older than the Earth itself - had travelled distances incomprehensible to human minds to land on the oldest college in Cambridge.

It humbled him, realising that human conception of time was nothing, mere seconds in the clock of the cosmos. It was easy to understand why mystical connotations were made with this object. Especially as it had travelled of all places in the universe, here to Cambridge.

To destroy. Phil shivered.

"Just a lump of rock, refuse from outer space," the Master whispered. Whispers that became echoes. "And yet so much more. If you were a religious man you could easily convince yourself that it was a gift, or a message from God."

"Or a curse." *Divine Judgement's got a chilling ring.*

"Quite." The Master stroked the air above the polished spheroid with his delicate fingers. They appeared to tremble. "Are you aware of the Black Stone that is so precious to the Muslim faith? Pilgrims to Mecca make their way to the Kaaba, to raise their hands to the black stone embedded in the south-eastern corner. To receive energy they believe radiates from it. Muslims believe Gabriel gave the stone to Abraham, a symbol of the covenant between God and Man. It is a meteorite just like this."

"And so much more," Phil replied. He jerked away from the stone, shocked by how powerful his own whispered words were in the Hall. He looked back at the stone, forced himself to keep his next words as quiet as possible. Something about this stone demanded humility and respect. "For Muslims it's proof of God's existence and love for His creation. For anyone associated with All Souls, it looks like proof of God's anger."

"For disturbed minds, yes. Proof that human evil receives the justice it deserves from higher powers. As young Jason believes."

"Why's the rock kept here? Surely it should be in a museum."

Searles shook his head. "It must never leave. We have had requests…well, *demands*, from the Senate that the rock be donated to the Fitzwilliam Museum. We have resisted. We are not superstitious or overtly religious men, Mr Lotson, but we do respect our college's traditions. Just as the boar is consumed and eaten every year without fail, the stone *never* leaves All Souls. The tradition has it that as long as the meteorite remains, evil will never return to All Souls. God's wrath in physical form, the most powerful means to prevent the Dark One regaining a foothold. Read into that what you will…*but tradition must be respected.*"

Phil stared at Searles in bewilderment. One of a group of highly intelligent and learned men, clinging onto a past that meant nothing. Continuing an outdated feast ritual for which the purpose had been forgotten and jealously guarding a meteorite that should be now sitting in pride of place in the geological section of a good museum. Even to the extent of not allowing outsiders to touch it.

Just what the hell motivates these people? No other college in Cambridge was like this one. No wonder rumours flew. Phil stood away from the meteorite and stared hard at the Master.

Searles is lying. No way is this adherence to ritual borne out of respect for tradition. There's something else. Something Searles wants to tell me, but can't.

"I hope you don't mind me asking this," he said, the words still booming. Damn it, how could you have a quiet conversation here? "When you emailed me this morning you said the meeting hadn't been approved by the College Council. You said it was 'imperative that we speak'. As if...well, like you have something else you want to tell me."

Searles raised his eyebrows. "Nothing underhand about the meeting, Mr Lotson. The Council didn't approve it because they don't take you seriously. I wanted to meet you to satisfy myself you were a professional scholar, that you wouldn't sensationalise or twist our story." His eyes flickered over Phil's head, his words spoken too quickly. And there was fear in the man's eyes.

What are you afraid of, Searles? You're the Master of All Souls. What've you to fear in your own college?

He turned back, looking to where Searles' nervous gaze had landed. He saw a red light glinting, and wondered why he hadn't noticed it before.

Perhaps it wasn't so surprising. He'd been so overwhelmed by the beauty of the Great Hall and the conversation with the Master about the Divine Judgement that only now was he aware of the CCTV camera. A faint hissing sound accompanied the red light above the black lens, as though the operator was zooming in on their faces.

Searles turned and walked rigidly towards the doors. At last Phil had his answer. *Constant surveillance. The meeting's being watched. Monitored, recorded. Hidden microphones.*

Phil felt anxious to be away. He followed Searles, and both men left the Great Hall.

The red light of the camera and the ruby eyes of the boar followed their exit.

NINE

"Any memory yet?" Andy asked.

Rob dropped another cube of sugar into his coffee and stirred it with shaking hands. He raised it to his lips and saw Andy staring intently at him.

"Yeah. I just remembered that Emma has this amazing tattoo of a scorpion on her tit. I asked her if she was going to get a pair, but -"

"You know what I mean."

"I don't know, Andy." He sipped the coffee. "That drive through the woods earlier…it triggered something. Something scary. But I still can't remember."

"Nothing at all?" Andy sat back in the plastic seat and stared hard at Rob. Around them the Buttery was almost deserted. Hardly surprising with less than five days to go to Christmas. Two surly catering workers, their overalls spotlessly clean with the lack of custom glared at them behind the serving counter. The smell of stale chips and lasagne filled the air.

Unlike the rest of the college buildings, the Buttery was just like any other normal, modern cafeteria. Formica tables half-heartedly covered with paper Christmas-themed tablecloths. Small tubs of ketchup and vinegar sachets. A spotlessly clean wooden floor. A festive menu by the serving hatch offered basic roast turkey and all the trimmings for less than £3.00.

Not today, though. Vegetable lasagne and chips was the only main course available.

Apart from the wild boar and red onion baps. Rob had turned green when he saw them on the hot plate. A Buttery Special, a tie-in with the Founder's Feast tomorrow.

Sure you don't want one? Only £3.50, two for six quid.

Just coffee, thanks.

"Tell you this, though. If I was that pissed it's amazing I got the van through the wood at all. Lucky not to get a ruptured fuel tank with all those stumps and roots hiding in the dark." He shivered – or perhaps shuddered, Andy thought.

Hiding in the dark…he remembered how dark and oppressive the woods had been, and that was in broad daylight. He didn't like the thought of going through them at night. But that's what he'd have to do later when he returned to All Souls. No way could he go anywhere near the porter's lodge.

Andy sipped his black coffee thoughtfully, gazing at the threadbare plastic Christmas tree in the corner by the Fire Exit. The fairy-lights seemed brighter now – or was it because it was getting darker outside?

Yes, definitely darker. The overhead strip lights flickered and hummed into life, an attempt by the catering staff to banish the midwinter darkness. Andy had started to feel more relaxed with each moment that passed in the college. But the darkness changed that.

"We'll check on Emma's room while we're here. Can you at least remember where *that* is?"

"No need for satire, Andy. 'Course I bloody remember." Rob looked at his watch. "Fuck me, half three and she *still* ain't called! She ain't going to be there now."

"No harm in looking, is there? Might see one of her hall mates, they could have some idea."

"Nah. Dan Bailey was the only one left, and he fucked off somewhere last night." Rob scowled. "I'm gonna have words with that tosser in the New Year. Sold me some well dodgy gear - "

"So she was alone last night?" Andy lowered his mug . "Apart from you, of course."

"Yeah. Usually nothing to worry about because security's pretty tight. CCTV in all areas, swipe card access for the main buildings… since last year security's really tightened up."

CCTV…and I wonder who was watching the monitors? Perhaps John Franklin had been monitoring the college grounds on the night Geoff Michaels sneaked in and disappeared. Andy drained his coffee.

"Still got it?"

"Got what?"

Andy sighed. "The guest pass Emma got you. Do you still have it?"

Rob raised his eyebrows. "Think so. Be at home, though. Why?"

"Let's hope that Franklin hasn't cancelled it. If they use the system I think they do, that swipe card will be active for 48 hours." He smiled coldly. "You and Emma might have made my job a bit easier. Come on. I think young Jasper needs a walk."

Jasper needed more than a walk. Andy was reluctant to have the nervous and full-bladdered dog coming with them for longer than necessary, but he saw there was no way the dog was going back into the van without human company. He retrieved the toner cartridge from the van, checked the label matched what was on the delivery note, and slammed shut the sliding door.

"Is he normally this jumpy?" Andy asked. Rob attached the lead to Jasper's collar.

"He's manic, you've seen that. But..." Rob scratched the dog's flattened ears. "I guess he's spooked by this place as well."

Andy looked at the unlit windows of the Master's Lodge. There were two sets of footsteps in the snow that lead from the locked door. Phil and Searles had gone for a wander, and Andy wondered where the Master had taken him.

The Bursar's office would have been hard to find using the poor map from the porter's lodge, but Andy had noticed one of the CCTV monitors was fixed on a small set of buildings in Old Court. He'd also noticed a rather large man squeezing his way into the narrow doorway of the centre building, clearly labelled J stairway. That was where they headed.

Andy noted the entrance to the Bursar's office was via one of the traditional Cambridge narrow spiral staircases. No wonder the fat man struggled.

"Rob. I'll take the delivery." *I want do a little digging.*

Jasper and Rob waited outside. It would have been pushing their luck to bring an animal into the offices. Especially after Jasper's little 'visit' to the kitchens.

J stairway wasn't just narrow, it was dark. A bulb had gone and no one had bothered to fix it. For the second time that day, Andy made a journey that was darker than it should've been. The stairs were slippery, melting snow from his boots making the passageway treacherous. When he got to the top of the staircase, still in darkness, he could barely read the brass plate on the doorway. SIMON DAVIES – BURSAR. The badly fitting, almost warped door was outlined in pale yellow by the lights in the Bursar's office behind. He could hear a man's voice, raised in anger, shouting in what sounded like a one-way conversation.

He rattled the doorknob then pushed the door open.

It was a small office, cramped and unsuitable for the work expected to be performed within. In the right corner five-foot high bookcases full of overflowing lever arch files formed a small cage for the petite, middle-aged woman burying herself deeper into her cardigan, shrinking into her seat and edging her head closer to the keyboard as though she was about to be physically attacked.

The room was made smaller by the huge bulk of Simon Davies in the other corner. He stood in front of his desk with a corded telephone handset clenched to his reddened face and spittle flying from his thick lips. He had a ginger beard in a Tudor style and muddy brown eyes that bulged in their sockets and threatened to burst from a face scarlet with anger. His jowls strained for freedom over his shirt collar, despite the top button being undone and the grey striped tie loosened.

"I don't bloody care what your excuses are! You promised me three workers for tomorrow night. *Three!*" He glowered at Andy. "I know it's the Christmas party season, I know you're swamped with requests...but All Souls' Founder's Feast is a renowned event. It should take priority over office parties for a bunch of chavs – *just what the hell d'you think you're doing?*"

Andy had dropped the toner cartridge on the Bursar's desk, spilling some of the untidily stacked sheaves of paper. Realising Davies was speaking to him, he raised his eyebrows questioningly.

"Drop off from Santa. You've been a good boy this year." He held out the delivery note. "Sign and print."

If Davies' face had been red before, it was purple now. Spittle on his fat lips turned into flecks of foam. The plastic of the handset threatened to break.

"Calm down, pal. Your head looks like it's going to come off."

The tense silence was broken by a nervous titter from the woman in the corner. Aware of the Bursar's eyes blazing in her direction, her smile vanished and she buried herself back into her work.

"Ms Cox will sign the delivery note," Davies' voice was strangled. "And you would be advised to improve your customer service skills. Granta Office Supplies, isn't it? I'll be having words with Mr Harrison when he arrives."

Andy's back was towards him. He grinned and winked at the lady in the corner. She smiled nervously at him as she signed the paperwork.

"*Your boss*," Davies added meaningfully. He was about to say more when he realised there were noises coming from the phone. "Yes? Oh. Well, if that's the best that you can do...very well. Email me the young lady's details, CC it to Ms Cox as usual. A copy of her CV...I take it she has silver service? Very well. Tell her to report to the kitchens tomorrow morning, eleven a.m." He slammed the handset down and glared at Andy's amused expression.

"Can't get the staff these days..." Andy's words brought another nervous laugh from Ms Cox and another glare from the Bursar.

The glare softened and became a look of recognition. Davies turned and grabbed his coat from the top of a filing cabinet.

"Judith, I have to leave. An appointment with Mr Cassell. Be sure to get that invoice from Ocean Wave Direct cancelled. And we're overdue a credit note on the last cancellation, chase them up. Then you can go." He pushed past Andy on his way to the door.

"And the compliments of the season to you." Andy's words were addressed to a slammed door. He shook his head and turned to Judith.

"He always like this?"

She looked visibly relieved to have her boss out of the room. She took off her glasses and wiped them with the corner of her cardigan. Davies' spittle had travelled a long way.

"Recently, yes. He was a perfect gentleman when I first started, but…he's becoming unbearable recently. Under a lot of stress, snapping at the slightest little thing..."

"Seemed in a real hurry to be gone just now." *But that was because he recognised me. Wonder who he's really gone to see?*

Judith Cox frowned. "Yes, I thought that was strange. But then, he's a strange man. And this is a very strange place. Not a popular place to work. That phone call he had now was with from an employment agency that sends catering workers to us. Since last year, no one wants to work here, especially not on the night of the Founder's Feast."

"I can imagine," Andy said with a nod. "Lightning never strikes twice, but…"

Judith examined her glasses in the overhead light and put them back on. "But best not to take chances. Is there anything else I can help you with?"

Andy paused. She hadn't been here long, she wouldn't know about Geoff Michaels. And he couldn't very well rifle through the records of the Bursar's office while the secretary was still there. But…

"There is one thing. A friend of mine went missing some time ago, I don't know if you have any information on him?" He pulled out the creased photo and passed it to her.

She examined it carefully. "He looks familiar. I can't say I've seen him around the college, though. But I only started two months ago." She handed the photo back to Andy.

"Sorry. I think I recognise the face from the *Cambridge Evening News* last year. Missing student, isn't he?"

Andy nodded solemnly. "Geoff Michaels."

"Hmm, yes. It's familiar now. Of course, he disappeared just before the incident with the college, so his story was forgotten. The police believe he had reasons for disappearing, they don't suspect 'foul play'…but you do?" Her eyes narrowed behind the half moon lenses, becoming more suspicious and appraising.

"Let's just say it was out of character. And he was last seen at this college. The police have ruled out any connection, but I've a feeling they couldn't be bothered to investigate properly." *Or had been told by a higher power not to push the college.*

"Well, I'd like to help you, young man, but I don't see what I can do." She glanced at her monitor. "Ah, the young lady's details have just come through. I'd better print these out for Mr Davies…" She looked back at Andy. "I tell you what. If I hear anything, find out anything that might help you I'll let you know. How's that?"

"That would be great," Andy smiled warmly.

"What's your email address?"

He paused. "A phone call or a text might be better. Here's my number…"

As he wrote it down he thought *this is bloody ridiculous. What's Pearce thinking, sending me off to be Mike Hammer?*

He must've known Andy would stick out like a sore thumb. Physically he was instantly recognisable. His history meant that he would not be forgotten by certain people in Cambridge no matter how many years passed.

And it was obvious that no one was going to remember Michaels, or have any trace of him within the college. For Christ's sake, most of the college had gone home for the Christmas break. What was he going to learn from people who weren't here?

Pearce must have had some other reason for sending him up here. But what?

Perhaps a call tonight will shed some light, he thought as he handed the piece of paper over to Judith. *Not much else I can do until then.*

"Thank you…Judith."

She smiled warmly. Almost motherly, he thought, before adding, "And have a Merry Christmas."

As he headed for the staircase he wondered why her smile had frozen.

Rob shook his head as he flicked his Mayfair stub into the hole. The darkness swallowed the orange light, extinguishing it more effectively than stubbing or crushing underfoot could do. He stepped back from the barrier with its ribbons of hazard warning tape and wondered again at the bizarre ritual the college of All Souls saw fit to enact year after year.

The hole was near the ornamental fountain on the lawns of Old Court. A good six feet away, to ensure that the excavation didn't interfere with any of the pipe-work of the fountain which was still active. Rob wondered at the cold water jetting into the fast approaching twilight. *Why bother? Must have no end of problems with freezing pipes. And why no shoring on the hole? Christ, it's six foot deep…*

The hole was a grave. This was where the cremated carcass of the boar would be laid to rest.

"Nutty bastards," he growled as he lit another cigarette. "What d'you reckon, shitbag?"

Jasper didn't answer. He was too busy inspecting the fountain. Cold water sprayed up his nose and he snorted wetly. His back legs got a little too close to the hole, so Rob pulled the lead gently.

"Ease back, boy. Don't want *you* vanishing as well..."

He stared at the crumbling façade of the single Hall of Residence opposite him. Like the rest of the buildings that surrounded Old Court the rooms were in darkness. No lights shone through the drawn curtain blinds. There was no way Emma would be there now. He sighed and checked his mobile again. No new messages, no calls. The hangover had gone now, and although he wasn't completely alert he was more convinced now that Emma's disappearance was not down to her disgust at his behaviour last night.

So where the hell is she? He wished he'd known her parents, perhaps he could've called them and found out...no, if she had disappeared that would upset them even more.

He forced himself to accept an uncomfortable fact. The last place Emma was seen was All Souls College. The last place Geoff Michaels had been seen. Vanished, just before the 21st of December.

No coincidence. And neither was Andy Hughes' presence in Cambridge. Rob wondered if Andy knew more than he was letting on – or if he was in the dark as much as he was.

Jasper cocked his leg against the octagonal base of the fountain, and a golden sprinkle provided a colourful contrast to the clear jet of water shooting upwards from the stone basin.

Steam rose and the snow turned yellow before melting and dripping into the black hole of the boar's pit. It seemed an age before Jasper finished. He lowered his leg and sniffed the darkened stone base of the fountain with a sense of pride.

Rob saw movement in the corner of his eye. He turned quickly and saw a bulky figure in black exiting J stairway.

Simon Davies froze. His fleshy jowls dropped in disbelief at what he saw. He shouted something that Rob could barely hear. Rob grinned and shrugged.

The Bursar turned in disgust and reached for his mobile. Rob heard him bellowing into the handset. He sighed.

"Well done, Jasper. Dropped me in the shit again. I bet he's grassing me up to Franklin as we speak..."

Jasper grinned at him. He was squatting, his tail raised high in the air. He licked his lips, eyes half-closed, and then...

"Shit." Rob closed his eyes. *Here we go again. Twice in two days.* "What's wrong with you, boy? First the kitchens, now the lawn." He pulled out a small black bin bag from his jacket pocket. After yesterday's episode, he wasn't taking any chances.

"Shouldn't be on the lawns, anyway. The Cambridge Grass Police shoot you on sight for even walking on the lawns, let alone dumping on them." Behind him, in the distance, he could hear the sound of a door opening and slamming shut. Heavy footsteps crunching through the snow.

Jasper growled. His ears went flat, lips drawn back in a snarl of fear. Rob turned to see what was spooking him. A cold lump of bile rose from his stomach at the sight of the head porter advancing purposefully towards him.

Not now, please. I really don't need this. He raised a placating hand, swallowing nervously.

"Look, I'm sorry about this, chap. I'm just about to clean it up…"

Franklin paid no attention as he stepped over the low chain link fence and onto the grass. He didn't reply, didn't even look at Rob. His attention was fixed solely on the dog.

Franklin grabbed Jasper's collar with a swift movement of his left hand and dragged the helpless and now terrified Jasper off the ground. Holding him at arm's length with no effort, watching the collie's paws scrabbling in the air as the collar began to cut into his windpipe.

Franklin lifted him higher, the dog's hind legs a clear two feet above the snow covered lawn. His struggles increased: his pain and terror voiced by his muted, strangulated whines.

Rob was frozen with horror and disbelief at what the head porter was doing. Franklin just stood there without a single visible trace of exertion. No sweat, no reddening of the features.

Not even anger. Instead, the eyes glinted and the corners of the mouth creased upwards.

"No control of your bowels, laddie? Perhaps you need a lesson in housebreaking."

Rob moved quickly, his frozen stature shattered and galvanised into action by the sight of Franklin's right hand clenching into a fist, huge hairy knuckles bulging and whitening. Fresh blood began to seep from his bandaged finger. Rob saw the arm moving backward, saw where the fist was going to land. Had to get there before it –

He was inches away from Franklin when the fist shot forward with lightning speed into the dog's soft belly. Jasper tried to howl, a terrible, strangulated cry of suffering. He twisted and jerked in the head porter's relentless grip like a gallows victim.

Jasper was dropped to the floor, left to convulse in agony in the snow. Franklin had seen Rob coming, and wanted both hands free to deal with him.

Rob ran into the head porter with a speed and momentum that knocked both of them to the floor. Rob felt the solid, muscular bulk of the man give way before his charge, heard a satisfying grunt of surprise. He raised his knee and powered it into Franklin's groin as he reached for the neck with both hands.

He felt the steel-like muscles in his hands, tried to dig his nails into the flesh.

But Franklin wasn't about to give in so easily. His arms, splayed outwards on the ground, folded in sharply, his hands transformed into devastating pile drivers that crashed into Rob's ribs.

Rob felt his lungs explode, his whole body struck numb and powerless by the double blow. He slipped from the porter's body to join the still-convulsing Jasper. His vision clouded, black fog threaded with fine lines of red and blue, and through it he could make out a huge, blurred bulk rise from the ground, towering over him. He twisted on the snow, the frozen, close-cropped blades of grass beneath like needles in his skin. He fought the urge to vomit.

He saw a booted foot come into focus. Black, leather-coated steel toecaps, aimed at his mouth. Pulled back, ready to launch.

Rob felt Jasper twitching behind him, a warm canine body growing colder. He could see Franklin's grinning face leer down at him in gleeful anticipation of the pain about to be inflicted.

"Franklin!" The shouted name echoed around the frozen medieval confines of the Court. It had the desired effect. Franklin's foot remained where it was. The grin remained though. More mocking: contemptuous even, as it turned to face the man who had interrupted his work.

Rob raised himself off the grass, tears of pain streaming down his cheeks. It was a while before he could feel relief at the vision of David Searles and Phil Lotson hurrying to his rescue.

"So what did you learn, Phil? Anything juicy?" Rob winced as he climbed into the driver's seat and slammed the door shut.

Phil's eyes blazed as he held Jasper in his arms and slammed the passenger door shut. "All Souls College? Arseholes College, more like."

Rob lit a cigarette. The tobacco drew racking coughs from his pulverised chest. Jasper whimpered softly.

He'd stopped convulsing after Searles had pulled Franklin away but was still in a lot of pain. When his coughing faded Rob put a concerned hand on the collie's speckled head. The dog licked it slowly, the tongue trailed rather than attacked with its usual ferocity. Rob felt rage building in him, a rage that was far colder and darker than the winter night now drawing in.

"I can't believe they let a man like Franklin work in such a position of authority," Phil fumed. "The man's a psycho! No wonder his poor son flipped out if that's the only male role model he had."

Rob looked in the side mirror, back to the Master's Lodge. Andy came out, slamming the door behind him in disgust.

Shame you were too late to witness it, Andy, Rob thought. *You'd have made that bastard suffer…*

But Andy had heard about it. Coming from J staircase, seeing Rob and Jasper in obvious agony. Seeing Phil scream in fury at the smirking Franklin. Seeing Searles stand motionless, a curiously distant look on his face.

Andy wrenched open the passenger door. He was breathing heavily, deeply, his eyes narrowed.

"Nothing's going to be done, Roberto. He's not doing anything."

"Of course he isn't," Phil said. "Searles is terrified of Franklin."

"Why?" Andy snapped.

"Jump in, Andrew. Let me explain. Robert, are you sure you're fit to drive?"

Rob nodded.

"Who's the Master, who's the servant? Who runs the college, Searles or Franklin?"

Phil smiled grimly at Andy's question. "It's always been said that it's the porters who run Cambridge colleges. When Searles contacted me I was under the impression he was scared of something – or someone. I think now I know who that someone is…"

Rob and Andy listened intently as Phil told them about the meeting with the Master. Rob twisted the key and engaged first gear, anxious to be away. In his side mirror the cloistered college buildings shrank and vanished into winter darkness.

The headlights didn't seem to make much impact on the last barrier to their exit from All Souls. The trees seemed thicker somehow, the branches longer. They trailed down to the ground and across the driveway, the last of the snow falling to the floor.

A vague memory of something black and monstrous looming from the shelter of the trees stirred in his mind. A memory of last night.

His hands shook on the steering wheel. The memory was vague, but he knew now this was where he'd collided with the boar.

He flicked the lights onto full beam to battle the enshrouding gloom of the wood. At the other side of the cab Andy was silent. Still breathing deeply, eyes narrowed in anger – and thought.

He's planning something…or is he scared? Does he feel out of his depth for once? 'Cos I know I fucking do!

It felt like a long time before the trees thinned out sufficiently for him to see the rush hour traffic building up on Queen's Road.

TEN

The darkness outside the window told Judith Cox it was time to call it a day. She glanced at her watch. Six thirty. Yes, definitely home time. Not that there was much of a home to go to, but at least it was away from here.

She took off her half moon glasses and rubbed her eyes wearily. The throbbing in her temples had increased and she felt utterly exhausted. Low blood sugar hadn't helped. She eyed the untouched tuna salad sandwich with its curled corners of wholegrain bread. A lunch forgotten and ignored thanks to her workload and the deadlines set by Davies.

Davies. God, at times she felt like she was in a Dickens novel. The office was small and cramped, the inevitable result of modifying a section of the older part of the college for business use. Sometimes it felt like the roof was conspiring with the walls to close in on her and crush her. And if they failed, Davies could do the job just as effectively.

Hard to believe that he'd been such a gentleman at her interview for the post of Bursar's Secretary. She glanced at the calendar, noting the date. Good grief, was it really only two months ago? It felt like years. Davies had smiled apologetically as he took her to the top of J stairway, the autumn leaves following them in on the chill October breeze. *Not an ideal working environment, I'm afraid. But your duties will be much lighter than those employed in the main College Office.* That should have been a blessing. With no Praelector or Dean in the Fellowship, the traditional duties of Senior College members were spread unevenly – and it was the admin staff who shouldered most of the burden. She herself was employed to provide secretarial support to the Bursar, handle incoming calls and the filing.

That soon changed. Over the following weeks it became clear to her just how much work she was expected to do. The Bursar was hardly ever in the office, but each morning an email would be waiting for her, listing her duties for the day. And they weren't just the usual secretarial chores. Invoices were to be queried, spreadsheets updated, cashbooks reconciled. All Souls queried every single invoice it received, holding off payment for as long as possible, finding any excuse to demand a credit note or a full refund. This morning was a classic example, Judith being ordered to withhold payment to a catering supplies firm because of the wrong type of flour delivered to the kitchens – even though it had been the Catering Office who had messed up the order.

It hadn't taken long for Simon Davies to show his true colours. The smiling, friendly gentleman at her interview, the one who had sympathetically listened to her harrowing life story and assured her that she would receive nothing but full support and co-operation from the Fellows and the admin team, was a brutal taskmaster. The workload increased, the deadlines were tighter – and she was expected to stay behind to cope. Last week she'd refused to stay behind to complete a mailshot for the college alumni, the annual invitation to the Founder's Feast. It had brought Davies out in a rage. He'd slammed his coffee mug down on her desk, leant over and shouted in her face.

Why d'you think you're being paid so well? Did you really think you'd just be doing the odd bit of filing and answering the telephone? For Heaven's sake, woman, if you can't cope you can bloody well leave and let me find someone more capable!

She shuddered at the memory as she shut the PC down and turned off the monitor. She felt a hard ball rise in her throat, obstructing her breathing. The tears would follow soon. The psychiatrist had told her that she had to give in to them, never suppress them. They were healing tears.

But it was hard. When the tears began she was instantly transported back to the school reception. The same shuddering, wracking cries: the sensation of the world spinning out of control. She was convinced it would happen again, despite the advice the bereavement counsellor and God knew how many support groups had given her.

She glanced out of the narrow window: saw the cold full moon rising in the sky. *I could've told him what to do with his bloody job. Why didn't I?*

She took her coat from the hook on the door and pulled it on. The face in the moon sneered at her, as contemptuous and knowing as Davies' had been when he'd laughed in her face.

Go on, then! Walk out! See if you can find anything better. How long has it been since you've had a full time job, Ms Cox? How many of your job applications and CVs have been binned because of your admittance of mental health problems? Just be grateful this college has given you a chance that no other company would...or ever will!

The tears rolled freely down her cheeks now. She had come along so well, had made such progress. No one who was unaware of her past illness would ever have suspected that the strong, forthright personality emanating from the diminutive middle-aged frame was a painfully built construction. Even she had sometimes forgotten. The clinical psychiatrist who regularly assessed her had been impressed by the strength of character. No longer weak and self-effacing, now more confident and prepared to stand her ground, fight her corner…and with a few harsh sentences that strength had evaporated, dissolving in the acid of the Bursar's words.

She sniffed, wiped her tears away with the cuff of her coat. That attack wasn't just uncalled for, it was callous, cruel. Davies had listened with such sympathy and understanding at her interview, shaking his head sadly as she relayed the details of her descent into clinical depression and mental illness after her marriage collapsed. He'd clucked his tongue at the history of Steve Cox and his womanising, angered by the man's lack of love and respect for the woman who had supported him during his frequent bouts of unemployment with her pittance of a school secretary's wages. The Bursar had been as kind and concerned as the psychiatrist who had charted her inevitable decline towards nervous breakdown.

She had blamed herself in so many ways. And not just for the miscarriage. She had sought solace in food, all too aware of Steve's dwindling regard and physical interest. Cakes, crisps and chocolate created a vicious circle, the weight she put on turning him away from her even more. Her bouts of weeping, her lack of interest in the things she used to enjoy, the increasing self-loathing. Her psychiatrist had pointed out the fact that Steve was the only man she had ever had a serious relationship with, her shyness making her nervous around men ever since her school days. It was only to be expected that she would feel despair as the only man she had ever loved grew distant. And not just distant. Contemptuous…even hateful. As though he blamed her for the loss of their child.

And then that hateful evening. Parents' evening. Collapsing on the front desk in the school as the hallway filled up with proud and anxious parents. Mothers *and* fathers, husbands *and* wives. Working together for their children. Concerned or optimistic about the future. Anxious or hopeful of their offspring's talents and potential. Families. Mutually respectful. Mutually loving.

The despair had exploded in her like a bursting dam wall. The tears and racking sobs at what she would never have with Steve had broken her: the pain she had bottled up for all those years coming through with a vengeance, a malevolent genie free at last and hell bent on destroying the hated vessel that had imprisoned it for so long. She didn't remember the ambulance arriving, the sedatives, the first night in Fulbourn hospital.

But she remembered the treatment, the confidence building therapy. Painful, slow, but it changed her life. It made her see how she had been her own worst enemy, how she had punished herself for things beyond her control. That had taken time. The support groups had enabled her to come to terms with, if not get over, the miscarriage and in the meantime Steve left, seemingly pleased that her illness had given him an opportunity to leave guilt-free.

All for the best, she told herself again. But always hard at a time when families should be together. Her first Christmas alone.

Thank you…Judith. And have a Merry Christmas. That strange, skin-headed delivery man was the only one in the college to wish her Merry Christmas. The tears had almost come then. But why burden him with her problems? He seemed to have enough on his own plate without worrying about her. He had looked concerned, though. Sympathetic.

Not a man to get on the wrong side of, though. She smiled at the memory of the stand-off between the deliveryman and her boss. The only time she had seen Simon Davies at a loss for words and actually scared. Perhaps it might make the Bursar treat her a little better in the future.

I should coco, she thought sadly. She glanced at the printed CV on her desk, the one sent by the recruitment agency, and remembered she had to pass that to Cassell in the kitchens on her way out. Employing the St Neots girl would be his decision. She shuddered. As bad as Davies was, at least she didn't have to work with Cassell. That man gave her the creeps. She hoped that this Jennifer Callaby was made of stronger stuff than she was.

She picked it up, shouldered her bag and switched off the lights. Darkness reclaimed the Bursar's office. Even the moon had disappeared, moving to shine on another dark section of the college.

She made her way down the narrow staircase, her shoes throwing sharp echoes around the silent stone walls. She gripped the banister tightly, her fingernails gouging into the wood. *Damn it, when are they going to replace the lighting in here? This is an accident waiting to happen…*

She froze suddenly, aware that she was no longer alone. Around the darkened corner of the lower flight of stairs she could hear footsteps steadily approaching. A man's footsteps.

The bulk of the figure was huge and imposing in the darkened stairway, the porch light from the open door leading to Old Court casting shadows that loomed upwards, a dark forewarning of the man approaching.

The Bursar looked upwards towards her. It might have been down to the gloom in the dimly lit stairwell, but the strange expression on his face made Judith Cox feel threatened. Simon Davies had something clutched in his right hand, something that made sharp, rustling noises.

She took a sudden step backwards as he advanced and raised the thing towards her. Her mouth opened. The CV dropped from her hand, landing in a flurry of paper on the stone steps as the scream left her lips.

Judith Cox stared dully at the cellophane wrapped package the Bursar was holding up to her. She almost laughed. The forthright thrust, the stabbing motion Davies had made had almost made her scream and the Bursar looked just as startled as she felt. Only now could she see that the bouquet of flowers wasn't a weapon.

He lowered his eyes and swallowed. And she could see then that it wasn't just her reaction that had made him so ill at ease. This was a man who was not used to giving flowers to a woman, or perhaps any demonstration of affection. She couldn't recall him ever saying he was married. Neither had she ever noticed a ring on his finger.

"I'm sorry Ms Cox…Judith. I didn't mean to frighten you like that. But I won't be here tomorrow, so I knew this was the only time I would be able to speak to you before…" His words trailed off. His eyes met hers and she saw genuine concern in them. And something else, something she had never seen from Steve.

Guilt and shame.

"I've thought a lot about the things I said to you today. They were terrible things, words that should never have been said." He gestured again with the flowers, the cellophane crinkling as he offered them to her. More slowly this time. "Not much of an apology, but…"

She took the gift with still shaking hands and inspected them. She still felt on edge, her heart racing. One eye on the flowers, one on the Bursar.

Roses and chrysanthemums. A festive, winter collection. Nothing extravagant but that didn't matter. The gesture was something.

Davies straightened himself and let out a deep breath.

"I feel awkward talking to you in the dark like this." A weak smile. "Shall we go into the office?"

She nodded, then turned to go back up the stairs.

Once inside the office Davies sat down in his swivel chair and gestured for her to take the seat opposite. She placed the bouquet on her own desk, next to Callaby's CV.

He sat hunched over the desk, hands cradled, eyes still reluctant to meet hers fully. Finally he looked up, fiddling with the knot of his tie.

"Flowers don't say enough, Judith. And I'm not sure words will be enough either. I can only start with a full and sincere apology. I'm really, really sorry Judith."

She said nothing.

Davies rubbed his eyes. She saw now how red they were, how pale he looked. He was not sleeping well – if at all.

"I've been under a lot of strain the past few weeks." He attempted a smile, and now she saw his Tudor beard had flecks of grey that she hadn't noticed previously. "I know you feel that I've left you to take care of all my duties, but believe me I'm doing more work than you think. And it's taking its toll on me.

"I'm not excusing myself. I just hope you'll accept that my behaviour and my treatment of you has been...out of character. You're an excellent worker, Judith. I hope you don't feel the urge to move on, find alternative employment."

"How could I?" she replied dryly. "What with all my CVs and applications being binned by other companies reluctant to give me the generous chance that the college has. Your words, Bursar."

He winced at her response. "I'm dreadfully sorry. I cannot apologise enough. We have sincerely undervalued you, Judith. That will change, I assure you. As soon as my immediate tasks are finished I will ensure that the College Council completely reviews your contract. A substantial salary increase, a lessening of the workload...I'm not making false promises, nor am I stringing you along. I'm asking you to bear with us through a very difficult time."

Judith narrowed her eyes. She'd never imagined that the day would end like this. He seemed sincere and genuinely apologetic. And yet...

Why the sudden turnaround? Why's he so anxious for me to stay?

"Is there something else you want to tell me, Mr Davies?"

He sighed and glanced at the bouquet resting on her desk. "This is a difficult time for All Souls, Judith. The first anniversary of that terrible night...it has cast a pall over the Feast. Nerves are frayed, particularly those of us who were there that night. And it made us realise the common misconceptions society has about madn – mental illness."

She sat back in the chair, arms folding. *Yes, this is the real reason.* No longer afraid of her boss: the self-built strength, the forthright personality she had constructed for herself after the breakdown, was returning. She glowered at him and he lowered his gaze, staring at the toner cartridge on his desk. He fiddled with the Granta Office Supplies label as he spoke.

"We have to show an example. All Souls has been the centre of one...unbalanced individual's actions, and the media has been quick to condemn, to label unthinkingly. But I've been thinking..." he looked up. "Since you've been with us, Judith, have you seen or heard anything unusual?"

Oh, for God's sake. "Let me guess," she said, tight lipped. "Are you asking if I have seen the visions that Franklin's son said he'd seen? Heard the whispers that told him to burn the Great Hall? Are you implying that just because I spent some time inside a mental hospital that I'm as insane as he is – as he *still* is?"

Davies shook his head frantically, eyes bulging. "No Judith, that's not – "

"Let's get one thing clear." She stood up suddenly, her diminutive frame for once filling the room, making the Bursar's hefty frame seem small and insignificant as he cowered from her. "I suffered from clinical depression which led to a nervous breakdown. It is *totally* different to what Jason Franklin is afflicted with. I never had ghostly visions, heard strange voices telling me to destroy things. What I went through could happen to anyone. No-one thinks it'll happen to them until it does." Fluorescent light reflected off her half moon glasses as she moved her head closer to his. She could see now just how tired and drawn his eyes were. "I'm glad you feel guilty about your earlier comments, but I still find it sad that you think all mental illness are one and the same. But that's your problem - "

A thought struck her, cutting her off in mid sentence. Tired, drawn eyes – but also fearful. And not just fear of her anger. She knew now why Simon Davies had been losing sleep.

"My God. You've seen something, haven't you?"

The Bursar gave a weary nod. "Two nights ago, when I left the Master's Lodge. Passing the walls of the chapel, I heard…whisperings."

"Whisperings."

"Judith, there was no one around. I was on my own, and yet I heard voices. Horrible voices, saying terrible, evil things. I was scared, terrified. And…" he closed his eyes, rubbed the stubble above the bearded jawline in a despairing fashion. "They were voices I knew. People I – I had known."

"*Had* known," she repeated hollowly, all anger evaporating from her as what he was implying hit home. Voices of the dead. "What were they saying?"

He gave a muffled sob. His lips parted, his index fingernail poking a gap in his teeth to stifle any more cries. Finally he took his hand away and replied.

"Things I can't possibly repeat. Just thinking about them now makes me want to scream. These…voices were describing horrific acts of violence, told of people screaming in agony." He looked up at her with haunted eyes. "Screaming in agony long after they had left their bodies…screaming about the thing that was destroying them."

The walls and ceiling of the Bursar's office were no longer conspiring to close in and crush Judith Cox. They were moving far away. Instead the floor was threatening to take her. She grabbed the armrest of the chair, pulling it towards her. She sank into it gratefully.

"And you…have you told anyone?"

Davies shook his head. "I haven't told a soul. Except you."

Judith took a deep breath. "Worried they'll think you're mad, Bursar? Far better to ask if someone with a proven track record of loopiness has experienced it." She regretted the harsh words instantly. The man was clearly frightened, disturbed and doubting his own sanity. He needed a friend.

Judith knew all too well how he felt.

"Mr Davies, I've seen nothing out of the ordinary. Don't forget, I only see the porter's lodge, this room and the car park. My diet keeps me from the Buttery." She patted her slowly slimming stomach. "I wish it didn't, the food there smells wonderful. But I think it's a worthy sacrifice…" Self-esteem was a lot easier to regain when you had your weight under control, she felt. "You said you were working too hard, Mr Davies. And with the anniversary, the Feast approaching…is it possible that the events have been playing on an overtired mind? It must be easy to think you're hearing voices, especially after what happened to young Franklin and the attention it received."

"Autosuggestion. Perhaps. But it felt so real, so concrete…"

She didn't know what to say. She turned to her desk and picked up the bouquet. She pulled it towards her, hugging it.

Davies saw the gesture and smiled sadly. "I think you'll need to put those in water pretty soon." He saw the CV, revealed now the flowers had been lifted.

"That's from the St Neots girl, yes?" he stood up slowly, visibly forcing himself to be professional, in control once more. "I have some more work to be doing here, so I'll take that to Mr Cassell. I know you don't like going near him."

Judith smiled appreciatively. "Thank you, Mr Davies…Simon."

Davies flicked through the two stapled sheets of A4 paper. "Truth to tell, Judith, I don't like going near him either. None of us do. Not a pleasant man at all. But…a master of his craft. Like Franklin, a necessary evil." He frowned at his words, as if a new thought had struck him.

"Pay no attention to me, Judith. Please, think about what we've discussed. I won't be seeing you until the New Year, I believe? Have a Merry Christmas, Judith."

She smiled in appreciation, wished him the same, and stood up. She closed the door behind her and left with the flowers under her arm.

The moon painted the frost bound lawns of the Old Court with cold silver, but as she stared up at it she felt it was no longer mocking her. Now the night was filled with promise and new potential. Two Merry Christmases, and her boss confiding in her. Perhaps things could improve for her at last.

She hitched her bag over her shoulder and strode purposefully down the cobbled path towards the porter's lodge, walking quickly to keep warm. The cold was biting, tearing right through her heavy overcoat. She shivered, her body shaking and causing the wrapping of the bouquet to rustle.

A flash of white at the corner of her eye made her stop. She turned, stared at the centre of the Court. Next to the barricaded burial pit for tomorrow's boar, the fountain's jet of icy water stopped. She glanced at her watch. Eight o'clock. Strange, the fountain was shut down at nine every night. The white vapour of shimmering droplets hung in the air like a fading spectre before vanishing completely.

There was something else, just behind the fountain. And now the water pump of the fountain had shut down she could see more clearly what was there.

There were four of them. Two in front, two behind: four points of a perfect square. Moving slowly and purposefully, the tall slender frames hidden by the billowing white robes that fluttered and rippled impossibly in the still, breezeless air.

Their faces were hidden by heavy hoods of the same material, but by the shape and formation of the fabric she could see that the heads were down turned. Concentrating on the lawn and each measured step they took, mindful of the great weight they carried on their cradled shoulders.

A heavy structure made of thick, dark wood. Some kind of stretcher – it had to be, she told herself, to carry that shrouded figure that lay on top, peaceful and serene in death.

The bag slipped from her shoulder. It wasn't a stretcher. It was a bier.

A funeral procession.

A procession headed right for her: a white clad quartet that seemed unaware of the stone fountain that lay between them and hers. A quartet that passed through the obstacle as though it wasn't there.

Onwards they came, passing over the lawns and heading for the cobbled pathway on which she stood, immobile, rooted to the spot with astonishment. Five yards separated them. Then four. Three.

Now she could see movement in the shrouded figure they bore to her. The folds of the silken material twitched and ruffled, the object they carried awakening. Or returning to life.

The bearers of the bier halted abruptly, aware of the movement of their cargo. The bodies straightened, towering over her. The heads raised.

As one, they turned inward; the free arms of the two on the left moving upwards and across, pulling the sheet away from the body on the bier. The hoods fell from their faces.

The faces turned back to stare at her, the fleshless mouths each bearing a hideous grin. White, skeletal grins that were luminescent in the cold moonlight. Empty eye sockets the bright moon couldn't illuminate, pits of utter darkness that stared impossibly into her own eyes.

It wasn't the skulls that made her scream with horror. It was the figure they were carrying to God knew what final, unhallowed resting place.

The skin of the diminutive, naked figure was pale and waxy in the moonlight. She writhed soundlessly in agony as she clutched the swelling in her belly. Long, sweaty tangles of mousy brown hair snaked obscenely over the edge of the bier as the head thrashed from side to side, uttering screams that could not be heard, only remembered. Judith remembered well.

The swelling in the woman's belly shifted, moving downwards. She arched her body upwards, as if offering herself to the heavens and the thing within slipped smoothly from the lips of her bared vagina in a glistening mass of black fluid and grey tissue. A soft, shapeless lump of ravaged flesh that the woman picked up and held to her, crushing it to her breasts. And now came weeping that was just as soundless as the screaming, but far more terrible.

The mental and emotional anguish of a life lost before it could be fully created and given to the world, far outweighing the physical agony of an aborted childbirth.

Judith stared at herself on the bier, felt herself going back in time to that terrible day when she had lost her baby and began the slide towards breakdown. The skeletal pallbearers stared sightlessly at her, mocking her with their burden. *Her* burden.

A voice. A gentle but firm grip on her shoulder. She turned slowly, unable to tear her eyes from the grief stricken woman on the bier who was staring back at her with pain an accusation, as if she was blaming Judith for the loss of her child.

Blaming herself…

"It wasn't my fault!" she screamed. "I didn't want it to happen!"

"What's wrong? Wanted what to happen?" The face Judith was screaming into looked at her with concern.

John Franklin tightened his grip on both of her shoulders. She blinked, took in huge gulping breaths of cold night air that ravaged her lungs. She heard a hissing sound, a watery gushing noise that could have been blood pouring from the ravaged foetus. She turned, looked back to where the funeral procession was standing.

The ornamental fountain had come back on. Its cold jet of water was the only moving thing on the lawns.

"Ms Cox, whatever's wrong?"

Judith stared, uncomprehending, into Franklin's eyes. Looked back again at the fountain. Turned and buried her head into the porter's chest.

She felt his muscular arms fold around her, a strong hand stroking her head. "Easy now. Easy, now…"

She stood like that for a long time as the tears wrenched themselves from her, another fountain on the cold and lifeless lawns of the Old Court.

Franklin looked up to the solitary light in the window of the Bursar's office. Davies stared back at him, his face blank and expressionless.

ELEVEN

Phil was quite happy to be let out at Elizabeth Way and cycle the rest of the way home. He told Rob that he needed some fresh air in his lungs after the smells of the van – and Jasper.

Andy Hughes wasn't fooled. He saw the nervous glance Phil threw in his direction as Rob pulled his mountain bike out of the Transit. *Just don't want me anywhere near Kelly, do you? Just in case your dream was a premonition…*

Phil and Rob were speaking quietly, the conversation inaudible over the roar of the heater and the idling of the engine. Finally the rear doors were slammed shut, Rob climbed back into the cab and put on his seatbelt. Andy didn't acknowledge him, just kept his eyes on the side mirror. He watched Phil pedal away, expertly weaving his way through the lanes of traffic on the roundabout, the rear light flashing and the bulk of the rucksack swinging on his shoulders.

"How old's his son, Rob?"

"Ten or eleven, I think. Why?"

Andy closed his eyes. *Ten years old. Good God.* And to think, it could have been him being the father rather than Lotson…

No, don't think like that. Put it out of your mind. You've got more important things to worry about…

"No reason." He was surprised by these conflicting feelings. His love for Jen was rock solid, he'd never even considered cheating on her – and God knew he'd had plenty of offers from some of the younger women at The Porterhouse.

But now, being amongst the ghosts of his past reminded him of his first love. *True what they say, you never forget your first.* That love had never really died, in spite of the way the relationship had ended. Perhaps it was just as well he didn't see Kelly.

He patted the dog's head. Jasper had recovered remarkably well after Franklin's assault, but was still somewhat subdued. They'd both keep a careful eye on him, especially for signs of blood in the urine or stools.

"What next, Andy?" Rob indicated, pulled away and joined the traffic on the bridge. "You ain't eaten all day. Fancy something?"

Andy shook his head. "I need sleep more than anything else, Rob. Just a couple of hours, and then I'm going to phone Pearce, see what he's got to say for himself." He wasn't ready to phone Jen yet. And he hoped that the sleep would be dreamless.

Rob scratched the stubble on his chin. "Why's he holding out on you? What's he got to gain by keeping you in the dark like this?"

Andy couldn't answer.

Rob didn't say much on the journey back to Thoday Street, but Andy knew he himself wasn't great company at the best of times. And with less than two hours sleep in the last twenty-four, with a job that was turning into a real mystery and the ghosts of his past crowding around him, he was even less inclined to polite conversation. The radio was turned on, the usual Christmas songs playing. That made the silence between them even more awkward. Andy's plans for Christmas with Jen were well and truly shot, and Rob…

He glanced at Rob. Both parents dead. He was on his own as well.

Thoday Street was deserted. Apart from the usual kerb-mounted parked cars, their windscreens already turning an opaque white with the falling temperature, the Transit was the only thing that moved.

Rob mounted the kerb outside his house, shut the lights and the engine down and turned to his passengers. In a mock upper class tone, he grandly announced:

"Welcome to the Cambridge Hilton. I'm ha-fraid there is no portering service today…he is too busy beating up defenceless ha-nimals what have been shitting on his lawns."

Andy smiled as he took his bag out of the Transit. Throwing it over his shoulder, he slammed the side door shut and turned to the house.

Jasper trotted past him, squeezed past the railings of the small garden gate and sat by the door.

"Recovered very well, haven't we, shitbag?" Rob smiled, pointing the key at the van. The hazard warning lights flashed once with a single beep and a solid click of central locking. He put the Transit key in his pocket and took out the house keys. He frowned as he saw the lump sticking out of Andy's holdall.

"Your missus didn't do the packing then?"

Andy glared at him.

"Guess not."

The house bore the marks of a semi-student dwelling occupied by one single male: dirty plates and cutlery in the sink, carpets that had never felt the suction of a vacuum cleaner and a sculpture in the living room that could only have come from the mind of someone who was still a student at heart.

On the far wall, on a wide shelf besides the television, beer cans were stacked against the wall, tapered to a point where a single silver can of Becks Vier touched the ceiling. And true to the spirit of the season, Rob had thrown some tinsel around the base of his beer pyramid. Andy shook his head and lowered his holdall next to a paper-strewn mess that probably had a coffee table underneath. Jasper sniffed it, eyes bulging with happy curiosity.

"Nothing in there for you, boy. And I see your caretaker didn't bother getting a Christmas tree for you to piss on…"

"Cutbacks, my friend," Rob called from the kitchen. He lowered the coffee jar and turned to Andy. "Not much point having a tree for one…well, two, but you know what I mean."

Andy nodded stiffly.

"Come away from there, shitbag. Santa's sack it ain't…"

You got that right, Roberto, he thought. He looked at the plastic swipe card lying on a copy of the Christmas *Radio Times*.

"This the guest pass that Emma gave you? Mind if I…?"

Rob waved a hand. "Help yourself."

Andy picked it up, pocketed it and headed for the staircase.

Geoff Michaels' room came as a surprise. It was dusty but tidy, everything neatly stacked away in cardboard boxes and plastic packing crates. Andy blinked at the smell of dust burning on the light bulb when he flicked the switch – obviously the room had not been entered for some time.

"Parents didn't take anything away then?" he asked Rob, coming up the stairs.

"The plod took a few items. His old dear took some photos, clothes – sentimental things – but left the rest here. Waiting for his return."

They stared at each other knowingly.

"Hope springs eternal," Andy muttered as he took the lid off the nearest packing crate. Inside were lever arch files and ring binders, stuffed with what looked like marked essays and coursework. Andy flipped one of the files open, scanned the title page. A 1500 word essay on the presentation of the sacred and the secular in the plays of Euripides – marked down for typos, spelling mistakes and incorrect references. Andy felt his eyelids drooping just looking at it. But then, that was probably the tiredness catching up with him.

"Not much to explain why he went AWOL, Andy. Believe me, the filth went over everything." He frowned, a thought striking him. "Unless…"

"Pearce thinks the police were, at best, rather lackadaisical with their investigation. At worst..." he smiled humourlessly.

"Collusion? But why would cops be helping a University college to keep this under wraps?" Rob had a cigarette in his mouth, but stood in the doorway to light it. Andy guessed Geoff had been a non-smoker. Even with him gone, and unlikely to ever again occupy the room, Rob Benson was unconsciously respecting his wishes.

"Perhaps the college is more powerful than people give it credit for. Something's going on there, without a doubt. Phil's interpretation of the Master's meeting is proof of that."

Rob blew smoke behind him. "Question is...what?"

Andy sat on the bed and rubbed his eyes. "I can't think at the moment. Some shut-eye, a call to Pearce, and then I'll have some answers." *Or more questions*, he thought with a grimace. His shoulders slumped, his head titled forward. He began to unlace his boots.

"Rob, I'm going to crash out for a bit. Can you give me a call in a couple of hours?"

Rob took a deep drag of his cigarette, eyeing him strangely. He nodded.

The light was switched off and the door closed. Andy swung his body onto the bed and lay back. The mattress welcomed him all too easily. Sleep claimed him, and took him to a world of blood, snow and fire.

He was still searching, he knew that. But not for Geoff Michaels. And not at the college of All Souls.

He was no longer even in the city of Cambridge. He was trudging through thick snow in a flat, featureless landscape, heading for the only distinguishable feature. His feet were numb with the cold, his gloved hands thrust deep into his jacket pockets in a vain attempt to keep warm.

He didn't know how long he had been battling through the snow, how many miles he had travelled. It didn't matter. He'd finally found what he'd been looking for.

A mound of snow, approximately eight feet long, sloped upwards to form a mound that stood four feet high. When he saw it he knew he was too late. The woman he was searching for was dead.

No, there's still hope, he told himself desperately.

He knew he was fooling himself. There was no hope, not now. The temperature had dropped to eleven degrees below freezing on the night she had vanished, three nights ago. Three nights of heavy snow, falling on a prone body in an isolated field, layer after layer building up and freezing solid. A cavern of ice and snow, her final resting place.

A frozen tomb.

He knelt down by the drift, ignoring the dull ache of cold ice that penetrated his denim clad knees. He touched the side of the tomb and wondered why tears formed in his eyes, why he was mourning a woman he had never known.

He tilted his head back, eyes to the heavens. The clouds were steel grey, no attempt made by the midwinter sun to break through the leaden covering and give warmth to the land below. He could feel his tears freeze on his cheeks.

"Elizabeth," he whispered. The solitary word broke the silence of the dead, snow-bound field.

And with the utterance of that name, something else was broken. Another sound filled the air as his voice faded and died. A dull, rhythmic pounding, like a dying heart beat. It took his cold-numbed mind some time to work out where it was coming from, to register what was happening.

The snowdrift was breaking up. Soft, fluffy layers of virgin snow that had fallen earlier today, another cold shroud for the woman lying dead in the field, fell soundlessly to the ground. Tiny, barely distinguishable lines appeared on the ice walls, zig-zagging from bottom to the top, branching like the dead limbs of a tree. Cracks that widened, opening into fissures as heavy, muffled pounding broke the walls of the tomb from within. Chunks of ice fell to the ground, forcing Andy to back away.

The pounding ceased, as if the occupant was aware that its prison had been broken. It was free to leave.

The hand came first, slim delicate fingers that were unmistakeably female. The blue tinged fingers were clenched into a fist, knuckles bruised and scraped raw by repeatedly banging on the walls of the tomb. Blood that had flowed from the knuckles was frozen, but the fluid oozing from the torn and broken fingernails was fresh. The fist unclenched, sensing the fresh, colder air that greeted it, the palm opening as though in supplication.

Or a plea for help. He moved forwards slowly, wary. He reached out his hand, stretching over the broken wall. A soft, barely audible moan greeted him as he clasped the frozen, ravaged hand.

"Elizabeth!"

He reached into the ice shelter – it was surely no tomb now, she was alive, thank God, she was *alive* – to take her other hand, to look into her eyes, to reassure her, to thank God that…

There was something clutched in her other hand, something heavy and warm. Something that fell into his hand, a thing he knew was stone – and yet was alive. Elizabeth's arm dropped, sank back into her ice shelter, her gift given.

It was a carving made from a heavy black rock, with traced patterns of some green and red coloured minerals on the flat, obverse side. A rock that was warm to the touch. A rock that was alive.

The carving turned itself in his hand and he saw the face smile in welcome. A human face; peering through a carved framework of twisted oak, holly and mistletoe leaves. The white mistletoe berries gleamed like pearls, the holly berries glistening like blood droplets. The face itself bore an old man's features. Aristocratic, commanding. But so *old.*

Heavily lined, cheeks wrinkled and creased with an age that no human being could survive. But it was the eyes that held Andy's rapt gaze.

Eyes full of weariness, as though they had seen more than their fair share of suffering and tragedy. And also strangely knowing: possessed of a knowledge that was too great, too powerful – too dangerous – to be shared with others.

Eyes that were exactly the same shade of gold-flecked emerald as Andy's own. They flashed in recognition, expectation. The lips widened in a smile of gratitude and relief.

Relief. He almost dropped it in horror. Because he suddenly knew what it wanted from him. He tore his gaze from the hypnotic glowing orbs of the carved face and looked at the woman lying in the ice shelter.

He had called her Elizabeth, but he didn't know why. The face that smiled up at him with blackened, cracked lips and dull grey eyes: the voice that called out to him in a hoarse whisper, they belonged to Jennifer Callaby.

"Charles," she murmured. *"You came for me. I knew you would…"*

He tried to call her name, her real name, but it wouldn't leave his lips. All he could utter was the name he had spoken previously. The words tumbled from his lips, words he had no control over, words that made no sense to him, delivered in a voice that was not his.

"Elizabeth… *I am not here.* I am still in All Souls. This is Impington Common… the meteorite broke in two. Your horse was startled, it threw you. You know what has come to pass…"

Her eyes widened. She opened her mouth to scream.

Andy looked at the carved piece of rock in his hands. The piece that broke away from the heavenly messenger headed for the college of All Souls.

"…this is the Divine Judgement. But it is not complete."

He held the rock closer and examined the carved human features. *Carved by whom?* It had broken from a rock that had travelled millions of miles through the cold depths of space. It had never been on Earth before.

Around the vegetation that disgorged from the open mouth, all through the crown of thorns and leaves, the traces of red glowed and pulsated like molten lava. It was getting hotter.

You know what must be done. Say your farewells…and prepare yourself.

"I love you, Elizabeth. Please, forgive me. This is the will of God…"

The tracery pulsed scarlet, then orange, then bright, searing yellow. Flames erupted from the open mouth and the eyes, tearing up his arms. The intense heat melted his fingers, skin crackling and burning, fat melting like candle wax, bone turned to charcoal.

His arms collapsed inwards, bringing the carving to his chest where the hungry, unearthly fire continued its devastating work.

The roaring of the fire blotted out his screams of agony. But nothing could deafen the anguished howls of grief that came from the woman in the ice shelter. It was a sound he took with him.

The sound accompanied him back to consciousness, back to the bed of the missing student, back to the darkness of a Victorian terraced house in Cambridge on a winter night - the cry of a woman he had called Elizabeth, but knew to be Jennifer Callaby.

He brought his knees up to his chin, grasping his legs with shaking hands. He could have sworn his trouser legs were sodden and cold with the melted snow of the field he had trudged through. He squeezed his thighs and knew his legs were dry. No snow.

But heat. Still the unearthly heat burned his shaven scalp. He gingerly touched his forehead, wincing at the pain that felt like fresh sunburn.

The source of the heat was still here. He could feel waves of it coming from underneath the wooden framed window, just by the pillow. Relief was a tangible, soothing sensation that seemed to cool his burning body.

The radiator. Rob had obviously cranked up the central heating and the radiator had become a furnace that burned his forehead when he rolled his head from the pillow in the clutches of his wild dream.

Wild dream…bit of an understatement, he thought as he swung his still-trembling legs over the side of the bed. . *Even worse than the wild horses….*

He opened his eyes and waited for them to adjust to the darkness. Geoff's boxes and plastic crates were strange and unwelcoming silhouettes, ghosts of an academic life in frozen transit.

It made Andy wonder what had happened to all his own text books and study materials when his own academic career had been violently ended.

Reaching in his left pocket, he pulled out his mobile. The time on the mobile's display screen read 19:33. He'd been asleep for less than two hours.

Straight to voicemail. He took a deep breath and tried to remember if he'd keyed in her parents' number. Yes, he'd put it in this morning, just before phoning Rob. Scrolling down the alphabetical list, it should have been under S…no, nothing there. He scrolled backwards, found it under J – Jen's Parents.

It felt like an age passed before the phone was answered. The light from the handset's display cast a sickly green pallor around the room.

"Hello?" A female voice, but not Jen's. Her mother, Sandra.

He took a deep breath before replying.

"Mrs Callaby. It's Andy – Andrew."

The silence that followed was almost as cold as the night outside. He'd expected it, but he didn't have time for it. Not now. That dream had too many parallels to Phil Lotson's dream.

"Mrs Callaby, I'm sorry to disturb you. But it's important. Is Jen – "

"Jennifer wants nothing to do with you, *Andrew*. I can't believe what you've done." The voice faded, Andy guessing she was waggling the handset angrily in front of her husband.

"Neil, listen to this! That Hughes man has phoned!" The voice returned to the mouthpiece. "Do you realise she was in tears when she got here?"

Andy fought to control his anger. *Shut up, you sanctimonious old boot! Tears are the least of our problems…*

He stood up and reached for the door. Movement would at least help calm him. He blinked in the bright light of the hallway as he walked slowly down the stairs, annoyed that his legs were still trembling. Anger, or fear for Jen?

Probably both, he admitted to himself.

"…she should have left you ages ago, I never felt she was safe with you…"

"Well, that's what I'm calling you about, Mrs Callaby. Her safety." He nodded to Rob, who was sat on the sofa rolling a spliff. Jasper lifted his head from Rob's lap and stared at Andy, Rob instantly moving both elbows upwards to prevent the dog's jaws knocking the joint from his hands.

Andy felt all attention was on him. Two pairs of eyes in this room and two pairs of ears in St Neots. With any luck, *three pairs of ears.* "Is she there?"

A pause. "Yes."

"Good. That's all I wanted to know." He sighed. "I suppose it would be too much to ask to speak to her?"

No answer.

"Okay, I don't want to ruin your Christmas. Just tell her I've got every intention of respecting her wishes, but…I want to know that she's safe."

The pause was longer this time. Andy could hear the sound of a paper rustling, an elderly male voice coughing ineffectually. A door closing, soft shoeless feet padding across the carpeted floor in the rapid way that Jen always did when the post had arrived or there was something exciting she wanted to share with Andy.

Then barely audible whispering between two females…he sighed with relief. She was there. She was safe.

"Thank you, Mrs Callaby. Have a Merry Christmas. Jen, I love you." Pressing the end button before the mother could reply or deny, he sat down on the sofa heavily. He frowned at the cracking sound that greeted him.

He looked underneath him and pulled out a crumpled polystyrene container. Pieces of lettuce and red cabbage stained orange with chilli sauce peeked from the side. He tossed it onto the coffee table with disgust. It flipped open, and the remains of a kebab glared at him. Jasper cocked one ear at it then looked away. Even he had standards.

"Jesus."

Rob shrugged as he lit his spliff. "I know, the place is a tip. The maid's gone skiing."

Andy pondered the display on his mobile. Rob followed his gaze.

"Thought you were going to phone Pearce, not the mum in law?"

Andy stared at him, his eyes watering against the thick cloud of skunk Rob breathed his way.

"What's up, chap? What makes you think your missus is in danger?" Rob hiccupped on the strong smoke and blinked.

"Just a dream. Well, I say *just* a dream, but I'm not sure Mr Lotson would agree."

"Ah. Something on the same lines as his, yeah? What happened?"

Andy told him, describing the dream with as much detail as he could bear to remember – the burning, the agony, the awareness of death. The stone with the carved face. And the woman called Elizabeth, who was Jennifer.

Rob noted how much Andy shook with the retelling. Andy was aware of Rob's scrutiny. He eyed Rob's spliff.

"Wanna puff?"

Andy glared at him, and Rob visibly flinched. Reminded that Andy Hughes' hatred of any form of drugs was still as unshakeable as it had been when they first met. And following recent events, it was more fierce than ever.

"Sorry, forgot," Rob mumbled and took another puff. "She called you Charles, then. And this Elizabeth – it was definitely Jen?"

Andy nodded.

"Impington. Now why's that ringing bells? Charles, Elizabeth, frozen field at Impington…no surnames? Shit."

"You disappoint me, Roberto." Andy smiled. "With a 2:2 in history and all your time in Cambridge, I'd have thought you'd be an expert in local history by now."

Rob shrugged languidly, the skunk taking rapid effect. "White Van Man syndrome has knocked it all out of me. Sorry, but this is one for Phil. He'll know. I'll give him a bell later, see if he can shed some light." His eyes glazed. He slumped in the sofa, reaching under Jasper's belly for the TV remote. He pointed it at the TV and pressed the power button.

"Don't leave it too late," Andy warned. He stood up and reached for his holdall. He knew only too well what Rob could be like after a couple of spliffs, and it looked like very little had changed over the fifteen years.

Back up the stairs, into Geoff's room. He placed the holdall on the crumpled duvet, noting the dampness of sweat on the pillowcases. He shivered at the memory of the dream.

Forget it. Back to work. He unzipped the holdall and pulled out the black fleece-lined jumper and black jogging bottoms. Beanie hat and trainers – black as well. He'd be unseen going through the wood at the rear entrance of the college grounds, but he needed to be as discreet as possible on the way there. An evening run, burning off some calories in preparation for the annual festive blow out – perfect, and the beanie would disguise his baldness.

He changed quickly, deciding not to shower until his return. He rearranged the remaining contents of the holdall, ensuring the weapon was fully covered, and zipped it closed. Then he picked up the phone and dialled Graham Pearce's number.

Rob was drifting, struggling to follow the plot line of an episode of *The Simpsons*. Otto the bus driver was staying at the Simpsons' home, but Rob couldn't figure out why. He gave up, and contented himself to giggle at the hyper-coloured images instead. Jasper was unusually calm, but was easily explained as a combination of the assault on him at the college earlier and the effects of the second hand smoke from Rob's joint.

"That's what I think, anyway," he muttered, caressing Jasper's flopping ear. Jasper closed his eyes and settled down to sleep, resting his head on his paws.

For the first time in twenty four hours, Rob Benson finally felt at peace. The incident with the boar, Emma's disappearance, Andy's arrival – all faded. Because he was not in a position to get answers, there was no point in searching for them. Not at the moment, anyway.

And that bloody dream of Andy's…Christ, Andy Hughes was not the sort to suffer nightmares. Inflict them, yes. Wake up in a cold sweat, trembling, and in an immediate hurry to call his missus – no, that wasn't him.

"Or is it?" he muttered to the sleeping Jasper. "P'raps we've misunderstood Mr Hughes. Been fifteen years, after all. Everyone mellows given the chance."

A loud slamming sound made Jasper jerk awake. Rob followed the dog's gaze, realising that Andy had left the house without saying goodbye or where he was going.

"Goodnight, Andy. Enjoy yourself." He made sure Andy Hughes had really gone before adding "Twat."

Jasper raised a quizzical ear.

"Don't look at me like that, shitbag. Don't tell me you're getting used to him?" He pointed the glowing red end of the joint at the image of Homer on the TV.

"As the yellow Poet says, this is not *Happy Days*, and he is not The Fonz."

He reached over Jasper's wagging tail, searching for his mobile. With the spliff back in his mouth he tried calling Emma again. Still no response.

"Shit." He pressed the end call button and stared thoughtfully at the dial. *Don't leave it too late*, Andy had told him.

"Who the fuck does he think he is, anyway? Bollocks to him." And yet…even in his befuddled state, the description of Andy's dream had made an impact. It was too much of a coincidence that he, Rob and Phil had had nasty dreams in the last twenty-four hours – nightmares that felt too real to be dreams, which felt like warnings.

"Well, just this once…" He took a final drag of the joint, breathed out happily and dropped the butt into the overflowing ashtray. Pressing the mute button on the remote, he selected Phil Lotson's home number and called. Jasper closed his eyes again and began to doze.

"Hello, Kelly. It's Rob. Yeah, not bad thanks. All set for Christmas? Good stuff. Look, is the old man there? I need a word."

Rob frowned. Kelly didn't sound her usual cheery, bossy self. *Something wrong there. Still, what's Christmas without a few bust-ups?*

Phil's voice sounded strained. "Are you alone, Robert?"

The cloud of skunk lifted slowly from Rob's brain. "Yeah, Andy's gone to – well, he's popped out. You okay?"

"Popped out. I see." A heavy sigh. "Would he be popping into All Souls be any chance?"

"I'd imagine so. He didn't exactly give details…"

"Robert. If you can, get hold of him. *On no account is he to set foot in that college.* Do you understand?"

"Andy Hughes is not the sort of bloke you tell what and what not to do. What's the problem?"

"It's for his own safety, Robert. Make that very clear to him. I've just received a call from Sam Dawson. He works at the Phoenix Unit in Fulbourn."

"Go on." Rob's fingernails were white with the pressure he put on the handset. He knew all too well who was held at the Phoenix Unit.

"Jason Franklin has asked to speak to me, tonight. About the dream he had last night. About the dream I had this morning…and a dream Andy Hughes had less than an hour ago."

"Fucking *what*?"

"He's read our minds, Robert. Or invaded them. He says there's a connection to the college…and that we're all in danger."

Rob's jaw dropped. He had difficulty replying, and it wasn't all due to the weed.

"I'll explain more later on. I'm going to see Franklin in an hour's time. The visit isn't authorised by the hospital so Sam's going to help me get in."

"Stay there, Phil. I'll come and pick you up."

"No. Kelly's taking me. You just try and get hold of Andy, stop him going anywhere near the college."

Easier said than done, Rob thought as he hung up.

"What now, shitbag?"

Jasper raised his head and stared at Rob warily, as if to say *You sure you're safe to drive? Remember what happened last night – but you can't can you, you were too pissed up and stoned to remember. Want to take that risk again?*

"Well, let's see if he's left any clues. Pearce isn't the only one holding out, I'm sure Andy isn't giving me the full SP either. Let's see what's in Santa's sack." He moved to the door, feeling surprisingly clear headed as he walked up the stairs.

The door was open. Andy's jeans and sweatshirt were on the bed, neatly folded. Odd, that. Why did he change without having a shower?

The holdall was on the floor, next to the packing crates containing the remnants of Geoff Michaels' academic career. The bulge was still there. Rob knelt down and unzipped it.

Underneath the clothes were two items. One was wrapped in tissue paper. It was heavy and cold, and felt like stone. He put it to one side.

It was the second item, covered in bubble wrap and brown parcel tape that took his interest. And made him recoil in horror when he realised what it was.

TWELVE

Phil leaned forward in the passenger seat and held his hands above the air vent, trying to warm them. He was amazed the car had started at all. It had taken him ages to scrape the ice from the windscreen, but the battered Rover 216 had rattled into life with surprising speed, as though it knew its passenger had an important appointment.

Kelly negotiated the treacherous roads expertly, and he looked at her with undisguised admiration. She'd only been driving for three years, had seen it as an essential task after Phil failed his test for the sixth and final time. She'd passed first time and even now he felt a twinge of envy. She was a natural, a born driver who performed behind the wheel better than most men of her age.

"I'm sorry about this, Kelly. I'll – "

She changed gear and waved a dismissive hand. "Don't apologise, hon. I'll invoice you for the petrol on Christmas morning, how's that?"

He smiled, tried to feel relieved at her attempts to lighten the mood.

"You tried to get in touch with this Franklin boy before, didn't you? What happened?"

"They wouldn't allow me anywhere near him. Family only." And that had been before he'd started work on the new book. Official access to Jason Franklin had been denied to the press who'd been all too eager to add colour to the All Souls tragedy: it surely would not be granted to a writer whose intention was the same.

Official access, anyway. What Sam Dawson had offered Phil was anything but official. It was the only way he was going to get to see Franklin, so he wasn't too worried about Sam's flouting of the regulations. He was more concerned with the fear in Sam's voice. Not the fear of someone being physically threatened – psychiatric nurses were probably so well trained and had sufficient back-up that fear shouldn't be an issue – but another kind of fear altogether. Coupled with Franklin's desire – or need – to see him more than Phil needed to see him. And that was worrying.

The Rover's headlights picked up the sign that pointed to Fulbourn Hospital. Half an inch of snow framed it, and more was falling from the sky to join it. "Left here. It's not the main building; it's one of the villas."

She frowned, changed down two gears and pulled into the access road. The gatehouse loomed on their left, a Victorian red brick building which looked like a gingerbread house underneath its icing sugar coating of snow.

The villas were originally built for the long stay patients, and the sad incurables who would remain under the protection of the Trust until they died. A series of unconnected, single storey buildings, based on an attractive villa design to make them appear the opposite of what they really were. Holiday homes, rather than long stay mental institutions.

Kelly slowed the vehicle to the 5 mph limit. The road that carried the Rover was well lit. Streetlamps housed in clear globes shone benevolently through the frosted chestnut and sycamore trees, onto the empty and derelict buildings.

"Odd. I thought these were all emptied out, everyone moved into James House or the new ward at Addenbrookes?" The grounds behind the villas had been given over to a new business park.

Phil nodded. "Most of them are, but some acute facilities remain." *Phoenix Unit being one of them*, he thought with a shudder.

"Past George Mackenzie House, just before Springbank, that's where it - "

They came to it before he finished his words. The Phoenix Unit was a villa identical to the others, except that the colour and condition of the beige masonry meant it had been built very recently. Purpose built.

A basketball hoop loomed behind the building like a futuristic gibbet. Kelly swung the Rover into one of the few parking spaces in front. The only other vehicle was a blue Renault, which Phil supposed was Sam's. Odd that there were no other vehicles, he thought. Surely Sam couldn't be here on his own?

Phil pressed the release catch on his seatbelt and turned to Kelly. She looked worried.

"I'm not sure how long I'll be. Perhaps it'd be better if you went home, catch up on some sleep."

She looked doubtful. She glanced nervously at the sign proclaiming PHOENIX UNIT.

"Not house, not ward…unit. How clinical can you get?" she muttered. "I'm not going anywhere, Lotson. Nick's okay, it's just you that needs babysitting. I'm staying."

She folded her arms and looked at him defiantly. Her elfin features were illuminated a sickly orange by the dashboard light.

He smiled guiltily. "I don't deserve you, you know that?"

"I know," she smiled back. "Good to hear you admit it at last."

Phil leaned over and kissed her full on the lips. "I love you, you bossy cow."

"Love you too, Lotson," she said and kissed him again. She drew back, casting an apprehensive eye on the glass doorway of Phoenix. "Take care in there, okay? If *he's* dangerous, what are the rest of them like?"

He hadn't thought about that. He hadn't considered what Franklin's fellow inmates were like. Or how many of them there were. He looked at the lone Megane. His words were an effort to reassure himself as much as Kelly.

"I'm sure everything'll be fine. Places like this don't take any chances. And he's not as dangerous as the media make him out to be." *Crap liar.*

She stared out of the windscreen. "You didn't tell me what happened in your dream this morning."

"Just a nightmare, love. Nothing serious."

"You never have nightmares, Phil. Why start now? And why won't you tell me what happened?"

Like I'm going to tell you.

"It's connected with this Franklin guy, isn't it? Or is it Andy Hughes?"

Andy Hughes. Yes, I dreamed you and Nick were sliced to pieces and Andy was holding the knife. Feel better now?

"I'll tell you later, Kelly. I promise, okay?"

It wasn't okay, but she didn't comment. He kissed her cold cheek and stepped out of the car. He raised a hand in farewell, smiling with a confidence he didn't possess.

An icy wetness stung the back of his neck. He looked at the night sky warily, noting that snow flurries were returning. Now it was colder. Another treacherous night.

The sound of keys turning in a lock made him turn suddenly. The glass door opened and Phil Lotson was face to face with Sam Dawson.

Sam had always been a big man. Even in his first year at Anglia, he towered over Phil. Six feet four, even taller than Andy Hughes, with a stocky muscular build that had increased over the years. Muscles rippled down his bare forearms, and his pectorals bulged menacingly through his thin black T shirt as he closed the door behind Phil.

Another one who doesn't feel the cold, Phil thought. His hair had grown as well. A thick mane of dirty blonde hair that straggled around his shoulders. His small grey eyes fixed Phil in an appraising stare. Then a broad smile broke out on his wide face. He shook Phil's hand vigorously, pointed to Phil's belly.

"Well, well, well. Who ate all the pies, then?"

Phil laughed back. "Leave it, Sam. I get enough grief from my current students, don't need it from my former ones."

Sam nodded, still smiling. "Things okay with you? Kelly all right?"

"She's great, Sam. We've got a little boy – well, not so little. Nick's eleven next April."

"Eleven! Christ, it's been a long time. My Suzie's expecting our second any day now. Don't think Tim's going to enjoy having a baby sister, but…" his gaze fell and Phil could see the uneasiness in his eyes. This was no time or place for a reunion. "I didn't want to disturb you like this, but…well. Come this way."

Phil followed him down the hallway to the kitchen. Everything was shiny and new, from the glistening lemon paintwork on the walls to the bright blue carpet tiles. Bold, vivid colours. The kitchen was large and immaculate, the cookers and fridges as clean and gleaming as the kettle that Sam now filled. Phil looked around and saw the open serving hatch that was a portal to the sitting room. The same décor as the hallway, with luxurious easy chairs in green upholstery scattered around the room. Framed pictures of modern art reproductions hung on each wall. He noticed that there were no panes of glass covering them, and the TV was firmly fixed to the far wall. He looked at the locked drawers on the kitchen units and knew that only Sam – or whoever else was on duty – would have the keys to the sharp steel utensils within.

The kettle clicked off. Sam poured boiling water into two clean mugs as he spoke. "The Phoenix Unit was open for six months before they put Franklin here. They moved me from the High Dependency unit to here, said I was the best man for the job…the same month Franklin was admitted, funnily enough. Said I was the right man for the job, but that was bollocks. It was more down to my size."

"What is this place, exactly?" Phil took the steaming mug, shaking his head at Sam's offer of milk.

"This is a private unit. It has nothing to do with the Fulbourn Trust. The folk here have relatives who pay to keep them here."

"Don't like the sound of that."

"Nothing sinister in it, Phil. They still follow the legal process." Sam took a sip of his own coffee. "When you're sectioned it's initially for six months - an approved social worker, a GP and a community psychiatric nurse sign the papers and the patient's reviewed after that period. Some are sent home after that, or into the care of the community…we get the ones who can't be sent back, the ones who no-one admits officially can't be cured."

"Like Jason Franklin," Phil whispered, and wondered why he'd lowered his voice. "Where is he?"

"He's in his room at the moment, getting something for you."

"Sounds ominous." He tried to make the remark sound casual. "What is it, a petrol can?"

"Artwork. Stuff he gets up to in Occupational Therapy." The way Sam said that implied the artwork was more dangerous, more threatening than a full petrol canister.

"You're not on your own here, are you?"

Sam smiled grimly. "The joys of working for a private firm. Cutbacks mean Phoenix only has three auxiliaries each on eight hours shift."

"Only one? With someone like Franklin here? My God, that's – "

"Asking for trouble," Sam finished. He shrugged. "Let's just say the other two – and the relief – are as physically imposing as myself. It has its advantages. How else could you get to see Franklin?"

And now I'm here I'm not sure I want to meet him…

"Something you need to consider, Phil. I report to the clinical psychologist, a bloke called Longhurst at the end of each shift. They're not meant to discuss individual cases, but he does with me. Wants to know what he gets up to at night, if he sleeps, if he doesn't why not, how many times he goes for a shit…"

"Which sounds as though he's a special case."

"Very special," Sam said quietly. "Not because of the celebrity status. He's got the board very worried."

"Is he a problem patient, then?"

"Oh, he's a problem, all right. But not just in terms of violence. He was raging when he came here last year, but the right treatment has…well, suppressed it." He shuddered and lowered his mug. "Phil, I never saw rage like it. I've dealt with some cases in my time, but this rage...it was barely human. He shows no signs of it now, but it's there. Waiting to spring like…like a genie from a bottle. "

Phil swallowed nervously. *Genie from a bottle*…and he thought back to Andy Hughes and his former student's own rage.

"As I said, that's not the only cause for concern. When you meet him, you'll see for yourself. When you see his artwork, you'll understand. Problem patient doesn't even start to cover it."

"I would prefer the term service user to patient…" a well-spoken but irritated voice spoke from the serving hatch. "Problem or otherwise."

Phil whirled round, almost dropping his coffee mug in shock. Jason Franklin was leaning over the counter, arms folded and propped on the Formica. In the frame of the serving hatch his slim build looked sinister and foreboding, a trapped wild animal.

And a silent, stealthy one, Phil thought. He hadn't heard Franklin approach. *How long's he been standing there?*

"We are clients, not patients. I keep having to remind Mr Dawson here of that fact."

Sam was silent, staring at Franklin through narrowed eyes. His fists were clenched. Franklin turned away and smiled at Phil. He unfolded his arms and extended a hand.

"Mr Lotson, thank you for coming at such short notice." Franklin frowned at Phil's slowness in accepting that handshake. Phil took it cautiously, half expecting his arm to be wrenched through the hatch and his whole body dragged, bruised and bleeding, into the sitting room where Franklin could work on him.

"Relax, Mr Lotson. Don't believe the hype." He released Phil's hand after a brief but firm handshake. "I'm not fond of fava beans and nice Chianti, either. Now, Sam, I can't hold a conversation like this. Come in, the pair of you."

Sam moved to the kitchen door, into the lobby and opened the door that led to the sitting room. Phil followed warily, and couldn't help but notice how quickly Sam had reacted to Franklin's request.

No, not request. That was an order, and Sam obeyed instantly. For a moment Phil was back in the Great Hall of All Souls, wondering who the master was here and who the servant. In that respect, Jason Franklin was just like the head porter.

Franklin leant back against the counter. Relaxed, confident, and not as imposing as he had seemed in the kitchen. There was little physical resemblance to his father. He didn't have the head porter's narrow, hard features or his bulk. He was of average height, not much taller than Phil, with a slender, lithe build clad in a navy Reebok sweater and faded grey combat trousers. There was a two day growth of pale stubble on his chin and his light brown hair was tousled and unwashed. He ran a hand through it and Phil saw how small and delicate the fingers were, just like David Searles'.

Jason Franklin gestured to two chairs with a relaxed sweep of his arm. "Sit down. Relax, for God's sake."

Phil found himself sitting down cautiously. Sam had taken his seat instantly, another order obeyed without question – but with resentment. Phil looked at him, wondering at the mixture of fear and hatred in his eyes. Sam's fingers dug into the green fabric upholstery.

Franklin inclined his head, staring at his Vans trainers for a moment before looking up again. "Well, Mr Lotson. Why do you think I summoned you here?" Arrogance, a self-satisfied smirk.

The eyes bothered Phil. The irises were an unusual shade of green, a bright emerald speckled with flecks of gold.

Exactly the same colour as Andy Hughes' eyes.

Jason Franklin's eyes had a different quality, though. They didn't contain Andy's hard, resentful glare. They had a singular look.

A look that everyone interviewed in the wake of last December's events remembered clearly and had described in the only word that could be used.

Madness. Seeing it now, Phil knew what they meant. The way Franklin stared at them both was a manner in which he had never been scrutinised before. It wasn't bright and gleaming, it wasn't wide eyed and staring. It wasn't the glazed stare of heavy medication, either – he'd either found a way of avoiding his meds or was unaffected by it.

The look was one that spoke of living in a different reality to others, though much more so. A gaze that spoke of some hidden knowledge, a terrible and ancient secret that set him apart from others more than his madness could ever do.

Or maybe the madness is a result of that knowledge, Phil thought with a shiver. Franklin's eyes narrowed. Then he smiled.

"Do I make you nervous, Mr Lotson? Knowing what you dreamed this morning? Knowing what your friend dreamed earlier today as well? Does that scare you?"

"Should it?" A challenge had been thrown down, a gauntlet cast. Phil wasn't going to be intimidated.

"I think it should. A real nightmare, wasn't it? Your wife and son – and then you. Gutted like pigs in your punt, your blood flowing to join the scarlet waters of the Cam."

Phil started. He rose from the seat.

"How could you possibly know - "

"And it's almost as bad as the dream Andy Hughes had less than an hour ago. Rob Benson's dream was a picnic in comparison. How do I know, Mr Lotson? It's quite simple. I know because I was there. I shared your dream. I stood by you...I *died* with you.

"Heavy stuff, yes? I know more than you can possibly imagine. And I know that you, and your family, are going to die if you don't listen to me." Those eyes bored into Phil's, the self-satisfied smirk gone. The terrible knowledge burned like a flare. Phil wilted under the glare and felt the seat rushing up to take him.

"That's it, Mr Lotson. Sit back, sir. Enjoy the ride..."

"Franklin..." Sam warned.

"*Shut it, Dawson.* You don't want me to tell Mr Lotson the things I know you got up to in the past, do you?" Franklin turned back to Phil, his snarl replaced with a sad smile.

"You'd think it would be a great gift, the ability to see into people's minds, wouldn't you? All the hopes and dreams of your fellow man laid out in front of you. No. Instead you see the filth that lurks in people's minds, the immoral shit that sloshes around their souls." He flicked his gaze back in Dawson's direction briefly. "It's a curse, Mr Lotson. Simple as that. Because I no longer have any control of whose mind I can read. And it can drive people mad. Weaker, less resilient people have collapsed under the strain."

"But not you?" Sarcasm dripped from Phil's words. Franklin was highly intelligent and extremely articulate, that was obvious and already well-documented. He had the arrogance and conceit that went with the self-awareness of his intelligence. But was he really unaware of his condition?

"If you're not mad, why are you here?"

Franklin laughed. He seemed genuinely amused by Phil's remark but it wasn't a pleasant laugh. "'To speak truth, the world is but a great Bedlam, where those that are more mad, lock up those who are less.' I'll let you work out who said that."

Phil wasn't impressed. "It's only the truly insane who have no doubts about their sanity."

Franklin shook his head, irritated. "No, Mr Lotson. It's only the truly insane who ignore the warnings all around them. Who punish and incarcerate those who have the awareness and the guts to heed those warnings and do something positive."

"Positive? Like trying to burn down a building with people in it?" Phil sneered. The newspaper reports were accurate, then. Jason Franklin still believed he was right to do the things he'd done, regardless of the cost to human life. *You arrogant, self-righteous bastard.*

The moment that thought ran through his mind Franklin's breathing quickened. Twin spots of red appeared in his stubbled cheeks and the slack muscles in his arms tightened. Phil was aware of a discomforted shuffling in Sam's seat but he kept his eyes locked firmly on Franklin's impossibly emerald eyes. It was time to take a gamble.

"Sam, would you mind if you left Jason and myself alone for a moment?"

Even Franklin looked surprised by that. Sam coughed.

"No can do, Phil. Sorry."

Phil turned in his chair. "Please, Sam. Jason is not going to attack me or give you any cause for grief. Remember, he wanted me here."

Sam glared at Franklin. "I'm not happy about this, Phil. He's not to be trusted, he plays games with you."

Franklin rocked gently back and forth on the edge of the Formica counter.

"I think Mr Lotson's suggestion is a good one. As he says, I'll give you no cause for grief." He grinned. "Twenty five quid or seventy five. Leave now and I'll say no more."

Sam's sharp intake of breath sounded like the hiss of a venomous snake ready to strike. Phil stood up and put a hand on his shoulder.

"It's okay, Phil, I'm going." He stood up abruptly and unclipped a small rectangular object from his belt and handed it to Phil. "This is a Man Down alarm. At the first sign of trouble squeeze the two buttons together. That'll have the Old Bill down here faster than it'll take for me to finish kicking the shit out of him."

"That won't be necessary Sam. Trust me." Phil took the alarm without breaking his stare with Franklin.

"Trust," murmured Franklin after Sam left, closing the door to the hallway without locking it. "Interesting choice of words."

Phil walked over to Franklin and placed the Man Down alarm on the counter. He stepped backwards and asked "What do you mean?"

"That only confirmed it." Franklin pointed to the black plastic unit lying within easy reach. He didn't pick it up. "You send the security out to show that you have no fear of me. So that I'll feel more relaxed and comfortable in your company: more willing to confide in you. Bloody stupid. The consultants tried that on me when I first came here."

"No need. He seems more scared of you than you are of him."

"Because I know what he is."

"And that is?"

"Cheap. Very, very cheap." Franklin cocked an ear to listen for approaching footsteps, or the shuffling of an eavesdropper trying to keep silent. "Well, he's not earwigging. He trusts your judgement."

"Why did you call him cheap?" Phil kept his voice low. He hadn't intended the discussion to start like this but he was intrigued. Whatever Franklin knew about Sam Dawson, it was something Sam was disturbed by, something he wanted to keep secret.

"Twenty five pounds for a blow job. Seventy five for full anal." Franklin laughed at Phil's dropping jaw. "Have to pay your way through college somehow, and I get the impression he enjoyed it far more than he would flipping burgers for McDonalds."

Phil's eyes narrowed. "And you knew this by…looking into his mind? Or just listening to rumours from other staff? I know which is more likely." It was still news to him though: he'd always remembered Sam surrounded by good looking girls. And he was married, with a second child on the way…

"You believe what you like, I know the truth. I knew the minute I was admitted here. But I only told him I knew tonight. To make him get you in here."

Phil nodded slowly. Blackmail – and it worked, it had got him in. Sam was taking one hell of a risk but he obviously felt he had no choice. "Well, I'm here. Now you can tell me why."

Franklin walked away from the counter, slowly and purposefully towards him. Phil's back stiffened, his grip on the rapidly cooling coffee mug tightening.

Franklin stood over him. Then he took Sam's seat and sank into it.

"I shared your dream, remember? Can you remember what the punt chauffeur looked like?"

Phil stared at Jason Franklin and his jaw dropped. Now he imagined the young man's features hidden under a black cowl. Remembered the face smiling down at him in the punt. "Oh my God…"

Franklin shook his head. "I know, it's amazing, isn't it? That's never happened to me before." He leant back languidly in the chair, his thin hands clasped behind his neck, staring at the ceiling. "The psychiatrists would have a field day with this one. The symbolism: the blood in the water. You and your family punted down the Cam by a mythical representation of death. And you paid the ferryman – in blood."

"So who wielded the knife? Was that you?"

"Not me." A frown. "There was someone on the bank who had the knife after you died. Someone you know. Someone who had their own dream: who's bringing their own share of blood and death with them. Andy Hughes."

"So what's this all about? Why the dreams?"

Franklin shrugged. "To be honest with you, I'm not entirely sure. But it proves that I was right all along. Events are in place, Mr Lotson: events that will bring an end to the evil in All Souls. Why you've been dragged into it is a mystery."

"Perhaps it's a premonition. A warning not to get involved."

"That would be the best answer, wouldn't it? No, there's something else…tell me, what have you found out about the college so far? What did the Master tell you today?"

"Nothing much. Just that the only dark events in the college have your name stamped all over them."

Franklin grinned. "Well, he would say that, wouldn't he? And you believe him?"

Phil didn't answer.

"No, of course you don't. You know he's hiding something. And he's scared, isn't he? Why do you think that is?" Jason Franklin sighed. "I bet he said no-one else has heard the whispers. Let me tell you this: I'm not the only one who has heard them. And this year, more people are going to hear them."

Phil scratched his beard. "You really believe this? You refuse to consider that these voices are nothing more than the whisperings of your own disturbed mind?"

Franklin cocked his head and grinned smugly. "Come off it, Mr Lotson. I don't hear the voices anymore. Not because of effective drug therapy but purely because I'm not on college grounds anymore. They keep giving me the shiny little pills though: they think I still suffer delusions. 'The voices in his head are gone, that's a start. But oh dear, he still believes he's some sort of chosen one. Still has visions of pseudo-religious figures telling him to destroy.' They tried to say it's my way of rationalising my crime, my madness. But not anymore. Now they don't know what to say.

"They're scared, Mr Lotson. None of their drug combos stop the visions I have, and they're not going to accept my explanations, are they?"

"It's hard to believe that what you heard were really the souls of the dead, Jason."

Franklin shook his head firmly. "Not when I mentioned names. Gave physical descriptions of how they died, how old they were, who their family members were… you'd think that would be enough for someone to request an investigation into the college. Instead I'm reviled and hated by the relatives of those who've disappeared. They think I've used their life stories to weave in some 'elaborate web of fantasy' as one of the tabloids called it."

"Okay, go back to these…visions. What form do they take?"

"Here." Franklin pointed to the coffee table. On top of the stack of old newspapers and dated magazines were several sheets of neatly folded A3 paper.

"This is what I see in my visions. Of course they won't let me near the art materials in the Occupational Therapy room now, not after they saw these. And don't ask me how I got hold of the pens. Crayons and felt tip pens wouldn't have the same effect." He winked.

Phil unfolded the first picture. A pen and ink sketch of a clearing in a densely wooded area. No, wait, it was…he squinted and pulled it closer.

A woodland glade. An oak wood. Jason Franklin had used fine point pens to draw in meticulous detail the leaves on the trees, the boles in the ancient trunks. There was no snow in this picture, the oaks were in full summer splendour but there was no mistaking what this was an illustration of. The path that led away from the clearing and into the middle distance was the same one he, Andy and Rob had driven through this afternoon.

But through the gaps in the trees Phil could see no trace of the medieval stonework of the college buildings. Above the tree line, the sky was darkening. Heavy clouds vanished before night's relentless onslaught, the sun retreating as though afraid to linger and illuminate the scene below.

A massacre. A horde of men in ancient armour: breastplates and shields glistening black with blood that spurted from their hopelessly outnumbered victims. Men and women, children also, clad in rough tunics and animal skins. Screaming soundlessly as short swords and spears were thrust into their exposed bodies with cold, calculated precision.

Their agonised expressions were a contrast to the cold, impassive stares of the soldiers who despatched them with clinical efficiency. Neither enjoyment nor horror at what they were doing but professional indifference. It was a job, nothing more.

It was their attitude to the grim task that made the whole scene so terrifying. If there had been even a trace of triumph or satisfaction on the killers' faces it would have been a bit easier to accept, because at least they would have been expressing some form of humanity.

Perhaps Jason Franklin had intended that, to draw attention to the all too human faces on the helpless victims. The agony, the terror, the bewilderment. And then Phil noticed other members of the group. Four men, older than the rest and dressed in white robes. They too were being slaughtered, they too were in pain. But there was no trace of fear or despair on their faces. Instead there was cold fury, a rage that burned from their ink-drawn eyes and transcended the page.

Rage and knowing. Knowledge that one day this terrible slaughter would be avenged.

Phil lowered the picture with shaking fingers. "Very impressive, Jason. Very... graphic."

"And very real. What I've drawn actually happened in places all over the country as the Roman war machine sought to destroy the strongholds of the old religion. The isle of Anglesey is best known for the slaughter of the druids, but it wasn't the only site. You recognise the woods, don't you?"

Phil nodded. "The glade isn't there anymore, but yes, those are the woods at the west entrance of All Souls. Was this from a book you read?"

"From a dream. Two months ago."

"And were you a...participant in this dream, like you were in mine?"

Franklin's eyes bored into his. "Oh, yes. I was there. And how I wished I could wake up from it. But no matter how many times they stabbed me, speared me, I remained. My arms were cut away, my stomach run through again and again...and still I lived."

Phil looked closely at one of the white robed figures, the expression of hate. "And judging by this...prayed for vengeance."

"You're catching on, Mr Lotson. Look at the next picture."

Another drawing of the glade. This time, the butchers and their victims had gone. No blood stained the ground. This time the sun shone on a cold winter's morning. Snow weighed down the limbs of the oaks. And in the middle, a huge fire burned voraciously, surrounded by a circle of twelve figures dressed in robes identical to those worn by the four in the last picture. Within the leaping flames a figure stood. Arms held aloft, head raised to the skies: an expression of agony on his face as the flames consumed his flesh. And something else.

Rapture. Phil looked up. "And this? A sacrifice?"

Franklin shook his head. "An offering. A voluntary one. I was in the circle, I watched the thirteenth member walk, of his own free will, into the fire."

"But why?"

"I don't know. I was in the body but not their minds. I could see, smell, hear – certainly feel. The agony was real. The cold morning air and the heat of the flames plucking at my robes: the smouldering as I got too close – all real. But I was an observer, nothing more. This time I couldn't share their thoughts."

"Does it make any sense to you now?"

"The next dream did." He gestured to the third picture.

All Souls College, last December. This time Franklin had used coloured inks to show the destruction he had hoped to recreate in the Great Hall. Bright red and gold with more muted yellows gave the inferno a presence that felt so real Phil had the impression that if he put his fingers to it they'd come back scorched. And within there were writhing, tortured figures. Their expressions showed none of the rapture on the offering in the previous picture. Just pure agony.

"This was no dream, was it? This is what you came so close to achieving."

"With one difference. I've been working on this for some time, but I only drew this section an hour ago. When your…*friend* Andy Hughes woke from his dream, I knew what I had to put down. Look to the left, by the chapel. Above the flames. See?"

Phil followed Franklin's pointed finger to the object that was hurtling from the heavens. "The meteor," Phil mumbled. "The Divine Judgement."

"Look closely. See the face beneath it, in the flames."

A human face, peering through a framework of twisting oak leaves and mistletoe branches. The face was that of an old man. Aristocratic and commanding. Heavily lined, cheeks wrinkled and creased with an age that no human being could survive. The eyes were a piercing, unearthly emerald colour, filled with despair and knowledge – knowledge of some ancient secret, something too powerful – or disastrous – to be shared with others.

The eyes… Phil looked from the drawing to Franklin's eyes. And then back to the picture again.

The faces were different. But the eyes were the same, and not just the unusual emerald colour of the irises. The knowledge, the sharing of an ancient secret. Jason Franklin had it.

"The dead are screaming for release. The meteorite, the Divine Judgement - it will flare again, Mr Lotson. All Souls is going to burn. And when you know just what has happened there, you'll beg to help me start the fire."

THIRTEEN

Andy Hughes kept a steady pace on his way down Mill Road, a gentle, easy jog rather than the full pelt he wanted to break into. His Maglite bounced in the rear pocket of his jogging bottoms alongside Emma Robertson's swipe card. His breath misted in the night air, clouds forming in front of him and breaking apart as he ran through them. His nostrils twitched in disgust at the smell of kebabs and cheap burgers that permeated the empty street. The conversation with Pearce played through his mind like a looped tape recording.

I'm not holding anything back, Andy, I promise you. I'm receiving very little in the way of information myself.

"Liar," Andy breathed as he crossed over to Parker's Piece. In the harsh glare of the streetlamps he could see the snow on the grass was cut savagely by meandering bicycle tracks and the footsteps of Christmas shoppers.

"You knew Michaels and Rob Benson were housemates."

I was asked not to relay that information. The people searching for Michaels have set rules. Terms and conditions of the job, you might say.

"Rules? What bloody rules?"

And then Andy had heard something in Graham Pearce's voice that he'd never believed possible. Fear.

"So you're frightened, eh, Pearce?" He paused by the central lamppost in the park known to generations of undergraduates as Reality Checkpoint, marking the boundary between the central university area and the 'real world' of non-academic Cambridge.

He stared at the dancing metal figure of the carp at the base of the pole and he smiled with nostalgia. It was rumoured that the name 'Reality Checkpoint' had been painted on it in the mid seventies by students from his own university, when it was the Cambridgeshire College of Arts and Technology.

A good place to pause, he considered. The eyes of the carp glared at him, as if recognising him as an Anglia Ruskin alumni and blaming him for the vandalism committed on its home. He stared back, frowning at the memory of another pair of eyes that burned into him…

An elderly woman approached, clutching a Galloway and Porter carrier bag full of books. She scowled at him and walked by. Andy froze as he watched her head off in the direction of the police station on Parkside, then relaxed when he saw her join the queue for the National Express coach opposite the station..

"Get a grip, Hughes," he muttered, more quietly this time. After regaining his breath he broke into a slower jog, passing the University Arms Hotel and into St Andrew's Street.

"They're not his parents, are they? Who the fuck are they?"

Andy, I can't tell you…too much is at stake. The party who commissioned me insisted on complete anonymity.

"I fucking bet they did." Downing Street, Pembroke Street, running against the one-way traffic filtering into the multi-storey car park. He passed Pembroke College, St Botolph's Church, heading for Mill Lane.

So why was I chosen? Be honest, Pearce, I couldn't have been your first choice for this Mike Hammer bullshit.

Pearce had sighed on the other end of the phone before continuing. *I think you know the answer to that yourself, Andy. You were requested by the aforementioned party.*

Gave me a good reference, did you? Andy had laughed. *Sounds like I'm being set up for something. Why don't I just walk away from it?*

He was on King's Parade now. King's College Chapel and the university church of Great St Mary's reared above him, their snow-dusted pinnacles reaching for the stars in the night sky above. He ran past a young couple taking pictures of each other against the railings with their camera phones, into the road and overtook a slow moving cyclist.

Nothing to stop you, Andy. But the other party will not be happy. They mentioned Jennifer. Didn't go into details, didn't say what would happen to her…but advised me to mention her name if you were thinking of walking away.

What could he do? Jen was incommunicado at the moment, her bloody mother wouldn't believe him if he tried to warn her. So even though he knew he was walking into a trap, he had no choice.

There was one upside. For once, he knew Graham Pearce was telling the truth. During that telephone call he had realised Pearce was too terrified to lie. And for someone to be able to put the frighteners on Pearce…this was obviously someone not to be messed with.

Not yet, anyway, he snorted as he jogged through the claustrophobic surroundings of All Soul's Lane. Clare College to his right, All Souls to his left, hidden by the blackened clunch stone. *But as soon as I found out who they are, heads will roll. No one threatens Jen, no one.*

Onto the Backs, the Cam glinting blackly in the winter starlight. The West Gate of All Souls College was still closed, the sign ordering deliveries to be made to the Trinity Street gate, frozen with the fresh dusting of snow that had fallen this afternoon.

Andy came to a halt, breathing deeply, the sweat rising from his body like mist. He eyed the line of traffic on Queen's Road, satisfied that no passers-by were taking a nocturnal visit to the Backs. He was alone.

He stood in front of the West Gate, watching the CCTV camera complete its sweep. He waited, watching it sweep back in his direction, during which time he retreated into the shadows of the gateway. Satisfied that it no longer had him in its range he made his move. He ran to the gates, took hold of one of the railings and hauled himself up the six-foot distance to the top. He balanced precariously on the spaces between the wickedly sharp points of the railings, took a deep breath, and leapt over. He hit the gravelled pathway and rolled. Looked up at the camera, sweeping his way, he pulled himself into the shadows of the brick gateposts.

He was in. Now he needed to get to the point Pearce – or rather, the other party – had insisted on.

But before he could get to the chapel he had to get through the wood first. In the daytime, with companions and a vehicle, it had been unsettling. *God knows what it's going to be like now,* he thought, heading down the path in a rapid sprint, anxious to be over the bridge and into the trees before the camera faced him again.

The oaks welcomed him with bowed, heavy limbs and darkness. Fresh snow began to fall and he disappeared from the outside world.

Far from Reality Checkpoint, he thought grimly

Jason Franklin watched the Rover drive off into the night. He waved a sarcastic farewell and turned to Sam Dawson who was securing the entrance door.

"Given him a fair bit to think about, haven't I? What do you think he'll do next?"

Sam gave him a disgusted look as he clipped the Man Down alarm back on his belt. "Probably won't be getting much sleep, that's for sure. You sick bastard."

Franklin grinned as Sam turned on him. "Just telling the truth, Sammy boy."

"*Your* truth, maybe. Go on, fuck off back to bed."

"With the nut-jobs? Don't think so, not sleepy anymore. Think I'll do some more drawing."

Sam snorted and pocketed the keys. "Do what you bloody want, but stay the fuck out of my way. You mention my past again – to *anyone* – and I'll rip your fucking head off. You don't scare me." He pushed past Franklin and headed back to the kitchen.

Yes I do, Sam. Jason Franklin smiled as he wandered back to the ward. He wasn't going to do any more artwork. He had an appointment with the man in the mirror.

He looked in the open door; saw the three beds with their sleeping occupants as faint silhouettes. Jack Bailey, Mick Appleton and Steve Langley. Poor fuckers, he thought. Society's waste: chucked into the human equivalent of a rubbish bin.

He was under no illusions. He and the other three patients - service users…no, scrub that, *inmates*, were classed as beyond hope. Their disorders were beyond the reach of drugs and psychotherapy, but no one was going to admit it officially, that some patients were doomed to their disorders for the rest of their lives. No one was leaving the Phoenix Unit alive.

He'd heard rumours, mainly from the catering staff that dropped off the cook-chill meals every day, that the Phoenix Unit was going to be closed down and the four inmates transferred to a private complex on the South Coast – Fairlight House, where the Private Finance Initiative that ran the unit were based. Another cost-cutting exercise, although it was more likely that the companies based on the business park had something to do with it. Not a good selling point to clients and prospective customers that you share your office grounds with a loony bin.

A rumour that was confirmed when he read Longhurst's mind. The prick. The chief clinical psychiatrist hadn't even bothered to let the ground staff know, obviously under orders from his superiors. *Can't have unrest in the camp before the big move, can we Longhurst?*

Jason Franklin had debated whether to tell them or not, but then decided against it. It would spoil the surprise. Besides, he had more important things to be getting on with. And he knew he wouldn't be in the Phoenix Unit when the move came. The Elder had plans for him.

He hoped that the plans would come to fruition quickly. He was beginning to feel his own grasp on reality – his truth – slipping away. The dreams and visions were physically draining, and emotionally harrowing. They always had been, but now he was reaching the end of his endurance. It was twelve months of being locked up in the cuckoo farm that was killing him. He didn't belong here.

Every day he looked at his fellow inmates and wanted to break out. The worst times were evenings, just before bedtime, because they all had the same vacant, slack jawed expressions, their eyes gazing lifelessly. The heavy sedatives blurred the boundaries between their individual disorders, they were all the same. Zombies created by the medical staff, because they were easier to deal with. The physical strength was weakened, the threat of violence reduced to acceptable levels of risk. All brain-dead: shuffling into the lounge to gape at the TV until it was time for individual treatment or Occupational Therapy.

That was the most depressing time, he thought as he walked into the bathroom: the patronising tone of the OT leader as she passed out the crayons and chalks and 'invited' them to draw what they liked. No pencils, and none of the fine liner pens he'd so cherished for his art, nothing with a point that could be used as a weapon.

In spite of that, he had to admit he was quite pleased with the results. He'd managed to impart a vigour and emotional depth to the pictures that transcended the limitations of the kiddie materials he was given. He'd like to have claimed all the credit, to think that the fear flashing in the OT bitch's eyes as she saw his work was down to his artistic talent. She didn't know about the pens he'd managed to steal from Longhurst and hide, ready to use in the night hours. Not as weapons, though – but to draw the true images he'd witnessed, to do them full justice on paper

All great artists were misunderstood by society, the majority of people lacking the emotional responses required to interpret the work correctly. Instead, they were so quick to persecute them, to jump on their artistic endeavours and force them to admit that what they produced was *wrong*, was *sick*. That they needed therapy, curing.

What do they bloody know anyway? With a snarl he switched on the lights. How could they possibly understand, to truly realise that his work was not the sick product of a twisted mind or, in Longhurst's view, the product of a mind unable to distinguish between reality and fantasy, a mind enslaved by delusions, personal demons that could only be controlled by chemicals?

That was Longhurst's crucial mistake. In the last session with the clinical psychiatrist he'd emphasised the word control over cure. He'd admitted that Franklin would never be free of his disorder. He'd lost it then.

It's no disorder. How many times do I have to tell you? It's a gift. It's proof that there's a greater being that cares about the human race, wants its survival.

Longhurst had smiled condescendingly, but glanced at Dawson behind him. Jason had forced himself to calm down. He'd taken a deep breath and tried to calmly explain, once again, what The Elder was doing.

My talent has been developed, my art is better than it's ever been – not because I've been inspired, but because a greater power is working through me, using me to get the message across.

Yes, Longhurst, you can smirk. Think it's funny that this power has chosen me to be its representative, to impart its message? Fuck you!

Longhurst had asked, quite calmly, what that message was.

That society holds its values too dear. Human life is sacred? Wrong, wrong, WRONG! Human lives are sources of power, great power. And some have to be used as such, to safeguard the majority.

His artwork proved that. The Elder told him often enough – often in a tone of despair as it realised that Jason Franklin's message had been ignored.

He told Jason not to let Longhurst know that drastic measures would soon be taken. Others would be called upon, summoned to Cambridge. They would be compelled to assist, to die if necessary. Too much was at stake now.

Jason Franklin stared at the plastic mirror above the washbasin. Shatterproof, unbreakable: and therefore useless as a weapon. It had other uses though.

He wiped the condensation away, grimacing at the slimy dampness that clung to his palm. Stubborn trails of smeary mist remained on the mirror, distorting the reflection that stared angrily back at him, a twisted gargoyle that simmered with impotence and rage, frustrated by its imprisonment.

Now, what would Longhurst make of that? Another inner demon? He smiled at the thought and the gargoyle's face lightened.

He breathed gently on the plastic surface. The Elder would speak to him now, surely. At least now he confined his appearances to one location, and a time agreed at the last meeting.

In the past it had been awkward, to say the least. The Elder would appear unannounced, when Jason was unprepared. A face in the wall, a voice on the radio. A figure on the TV screen. And sometimes, more frustratingly, The Elder would appear on the face of someone Jason was talking to. That was unsettling, watching their features contort and remould into the wizened and timeless visage of the one who trusted him, Jason Franklin, to destroy the evil hiding in the grounds of All Souls College.

He could understand why people were scared of him when that happened. Hearing The Elder's voice, seeing his face when no one else could. It was unfortunate that the label of schizophrenia could be applied so easily to this: another symptom, another piece of proof for the doubters. It happened once in the Phoenix Unit, during his second interview with Longhurst, and he had to make certain it never happened again.

The Elder had listened to him at this point, and agreed to his request not to visit him in this manner again. He promised to appear at a more discreet location and time.

The mirror in the bathroom would be their agreed rendezvous. The features had unlined, became youthful again, and the piercing green eyes that were weighed with ancient and terrible knowledge had diluted to the pale blue of Longhurst's supercilious gaze.

Looking at the mirror now, Jason Franklin couldn't help but laugh. That must have been an absolute gift to Longhurst – his patient's personal and most vivid delusion, the semi-religious deity, taking over the doctor's face, speaking through him! Jason knew he'd had to tread carefully with him, didn't want him knowing that he could see the darkness within his soul. Far better for him to believe, as Lotson had done, that the things he could see were gleaned from idle gossip. The Elder had warned him about this, that the misuse of this additional gift would cause others to fear and hate him, far more than his 'condition' ever would.

And now a new gift. To share dreams. Even The Elder had been surprised by that, and for the first time Jason Franklin had detected a trace of fear in those timeless eyes when he'd been woken this morning and spoke to him in the mirror.

Why? Surely this had been a gift from The Elder, an ability to bring those who could destroy the Fellowship of All Souls closer together? Philip Lotson wouldn't have believed him if he hadn't been told in every crucial detail the dream Jason Franklin had witnessed, had appeared in.

Staring at the mirror, he breathed out and asked: "What now? What do I have to do now?"

The mirror dripped condensation into the washbasin. He stared around him, anxious that the others might hear. No stirring from the beds. The bathroom was empty and silent.

Now he was concerned. The Elder had ordered him to meet him here, after Lotson had visited and been informed of his role. So where was he?

A terrible thought. Had he angered him in some way? Was it too late to stop the evil in All Souls breaking through?

Has The Elder abandoned me?

He cried out in despair. But the mirror was still. Even the droplets of condensation were indifferent to his anguish. He slammed his fist against the plastic, feeling the material quiver with the force of his blow. He slammed into it again. It quivered once more, but more strongly, more pronounced, like he was hitting a giant piece of rubber. His reflection wavered and the surface rippled like the waters of a dark Scottish loch, hiding ancient monsters.

Then the transformation. His reflected face, blending into that of the other who stared at him from beyond the mirror. His eyes took on a more luminescent, unearthly shade of green with pupils that were black pinpricks. The vegetation disgorged from the mouth, ivy and holly and oak branches waving like tentacles, the mistletoe and holly berries gleaming brightly. The condensation disappeared, evaporating instantly.

The vegetation crawled around the edges of the mirror as it always did at these meetings. A framework formed around the portal, and then the vegetation was still. Now The Elder could speak.

The eyes settled on him, the pupils dilating, twin pools of darkness that held him transfixed.

Jason. The voice was a sibilant whisper, like waves from a prehistoric sea washing over shingle, an autumn breeze in distant, primeval woodlands. The voice of the Earth, the spirit of the planet.

But with a new, and disturbingly human tone. One of urgency, anxiety. Fear. Jason swallowed nervously. His hands clenched the plastic side of the washbasin, his legs shaking. *Something's wrong, The Elder never speaks like this.*

"Elder. What's wrong? Lotson's been told: he won't admit it, but he believes. His next step is to meet Freeland, see the physical evidence with his own eyes."

It is not enough, Jason. The messengers have already been prepared. They are singing to Andraste as we speak.

Jason nodded. It was the night before the Feast that the offerings were prepared. So why was The Elder so concerned about it?

The Fellowship knows it will not be enough. They will complete the ritual, and then Andraste will tell them to offer one more. One who has yet to be taken.

One to make up for the failed propitiation last year.

Jason Franklin felt as though he'd been punched in the stomach. The walls spun, the tiled flooring reared up to take him. He forced himself to stand upright, to continue facing the mirror.

Of course, it made sense. He'd interrupted the offering. The soul had been despatched, but the Communion hadn't taken place. Geoff Michaels' spirit had been allowed to escape.

"They must have known," he said. "Andraste would have ordered them to prepare three this year."

The Elder shook his head. The vegetation rustled softly, as though caught in a gentle breeze.

She lulled them into a sense of security. Once again, she lied. She will force them to be reckless, to take a victim without careful planning. It is this that may work in our favour.

"How come?" Jason frowned.

They will take one who is precious to the man in the blood-dream. The man who wielded the knife...the man who burned with the Divine Judgement.

"He's the one whose dream I shared earlier. Elizabeth Woodcock and the Divine Judgement. Andy Hughes. Why is he so special?"

I do not know for certain. But he has a power…a darkness in him that even Andraste fears. If his beloved is taken he will tear down the gates of hell to rescue her. Andraste knows this; she is sending her children to stop him.

Jason shuddered at this. He knew all too well what form the children of Andraste could assume.

Those in the woods are being formed at this very moment. And if he prevails, another awaits him in his friend's warehouse. You must help him. He must be persuaded to assist. You must persuade him.

Jason laughed, the echoes swallowed up by the face in the mirror rather than echoing around the bathroom.

"Easier said than done, Elder. Remember where I am. How do I get out, and how do I get him to help?"

The eyes glowed. *A way will present itself. Be prepared, be ready at dawn.*

"Dawn? That soon?" Jason raised his eyebrows. The escape was going to be sooner than expected. "Then what?"

Make your way to the Nemeton. You will meet him there, and he will be bringing the icon. Then he will know. The rest will be up to him. There is no more we can do. If the final offering is made, Andraste's return is assured. But if he can stop it in time…there may be hope. The eyes looked away.

I must leave you now, Jason. This is the last time we will speak here. I can do no more for you.

"No!" He couldn't stop the cry escaping his lips. "You can't leave me, I need you!"

The Elder smiled sadly. Those impossible orbs softened, something that looked like sympathy and regret within them.

You no longer need me. You need to look within yourself. Face your past, the night you've buried for so long. In that respect at least, Longhurst is correct. It will free you…but not in the manner he expects.

"What night?" he screamed. "Why can't you stay?"

There are rules, Jason. Rules even I do not understand, but must follow nevertheless. You have done well…but now we part.

The framework of winter foliage shrivelled and died. Chunks of dead brown leaves fell to the floor. The face of The Elder shifted, the eyes losing that penetrating green, the features softening into those of a man in his early twenties that stared back at him, despair, bewilderment and loss in his eyes. His hands slipped from the plastic washbasin and he fell to the cold, damp tiles of the bathroom floor and its carpet of dead leaves.

Leaves that stiffened, became sharper and more solid. Turned to silver.

He lay on the floor, surrounded by fragments of the unbreakable mirror and began to weep.

FOURTEEN

Simon Davies stood outside the college chapel and steeled himself to enter. The door was open, and he knew the Senior Tutor was already in there. He swallowed, knowing that Nicholas Nasen would have no difficulty in preparing himself for the offering tonight. He would not be feeling the dread, the sickening anticipation of performing an inhuman act of suffering, the fear that went with it.

One thing he'd never associated with Nasen was fear. To see him cycling on the towpath on cold winter mornings, a megaphone bellowing orders and criticisms to the First VIII in a quest to ensure that All Souls remained Head of the River, he looked every inch the formidable figure he was. Not overly tall, five foot nine, but stockily built, with grey hair cropped to a military standard. Exactly the same length he had during his army days. A permanent scowl was etched on his wide face and the eyes were piercing blue orbs beneath the heavy lids which saw right through you: assessing your strengths and weaknesses with just one brief stare, knowing exactly what sort of man you were. What you tried to hide. No wonder he and Franklin got on so well – and had done so ever since they first met, fighting in the Falklands.

Even though he was in his sixties, the Senior Tutor was mentally the strongest one of all the Fellowship, Davies admitted to himself, and he should've been invested as the Master of All Souls. He would never shirk from his duty, nor expect others to fail in their task.

It was for that same reason Davies was thankful David Searles had been selected. At least he had weaknesses. At least he was *human.*

Nasen, the Senior Tutor…along with Franklin and that monster Cassell, they made an unholy trinity. They were the power behind All Souls, there was no doubt.

I'm just a bean counter, a glorified accountant. Searles is just a figurehead, nothing more.

Davies glanced behind him at the empty Court. Judith Cox had long since gone home.

Poor woman. He shuddered to think what she had witnessed here but he could guess. Her miscarriage was the catalyst for her mental breakdown; it could only be assumed that was what had been visited upon her. Andraste always used your past against you. It was her way of ensuring your compliance or your self-destruction, to make you aware you were your own worst enemy. He'd watched Franklin escort her to her car: had wanted to tear down the stairs and run to her, hold her in his arms, tell her everything would be all right…

He sighed. Nothing would be all right. Had he himself not heard the whisperings? Had Andraste sensed his weakness, and was testing him, punishing him? He wondered if Cassell, Franklin and Nasen had heard them. If so, what did they do? Ignore them? Or listen to them, recognise that Andraste was angry with them all, and would require more appeasement this year? But it was pointless getting them to admit to it. They'd see that as weakness, the path to self-destruction as witnessed in Jason Franklin.

He eased open the chapel door another couple of inches. He could hear whisperings within –human ones, thankfully. He went in.

The interior of the chapel was smaller than the exterior suggested. Or perhaps it was the thick shadows that made it look smaller than it actually was. The candles on the altar had been lit, the scent of melting wax and burning wick combining with the aroma of cold stone and damp oak; the smell of a church that was not used often. The Bursar shook his head sadly. They would be using the candles in the basement shortly, why not use the electric lights in here? He knew the answer, though. Nasen liked it this way. It was imposing, creepy, putting you at a disadvantage. It made you fear.

He walked down the aisle between the rows of dark oak pews, the shadows leaping from the wooden seats with each flicker of the candles. Above the altar, the carving of Christ loomed. The flesh-coloured paintwork looked sickly yellow in the flickering candlelight, the blood trickling from the nail wounds a vivid scarlet.

The Bursar stared at the face of Christ and saw again why the carving was unique. The expression wasn't one of beatific sacrifice; it was an all too human representation of physical agony. The eyes seemed even wider than usual, the dilated pupils even blacker than the shadows. He noticed that the lectern with its eagle had gone. He knew where it was now.

Beneath the carving, at the end of the front pew, sat Nicholas Nasen. Aware of Davies' approach, he turned and inclined his head curtly. The nearest he gave to a greeting.

"Are you prepared, Bursar?" Gruff, blunt tones. Like Franklin and Cassell, the Senior Tutor never used the names of the Fellowship, only their titles. Formal and distanced, another hangover from his military service.

"As much as I ever can be, Senior Tutor." Davies took the pew opposite. "Are the others here?"

"They're waiting below." Nasen stared back at the carving. "It will begin shortly."

As it always does, the Bursar thought. His shoulders slumped. With a resigned sigh he said, "Then we'd best join them."

"Not yet, Bursar." Nasen's hand was raised, but he never took his eyes away from the carving of Christ. "We need to talk. Franklin told me about your secretary."

Davies swallowed nervously. "Another trick of Andraste. I'm sure it's nothing to be concerned about –"

"I'm not referring to her…visitation, Bursar." The hand was still raised. But now it folded in on itself, fingers curling, nails into palm. A fist.

A fist clenched in fury that came crashing down onto the pew. The crack of splintered oak reverberated around the small chapel like a gunshot. Davies almost jumped, and Nasen turned on him.

"I'm referring to the person she was last seen visiting. Franklin followed her after she drove away. *She's about to contact Freeland!*"

Davies' mouth gaped. "Freeland! But…why would she…"

Nasen stared at his scraped knuckles. Blood began to seep from them. "Ms Cox is a very strong character. She is not stupid. As Franklin led her back to her car she said: 'Jason was right after all. Freeland has the answers.' And she said she was going to see him. Tonight. We believe that this Hughes character sowed some seeds, and when Andraste tormented her…well, she obviously saw that as proof."

"Proof," the Bursar muttered. They both knew what that meant. If Freeland had the evidence still…

"You need not concern yourself with her. Franklin has informed me that she's at home in Swavesey. She's packing a few items for her trip to see Freeland. I have instructed him to take care of the matter."

Davies' head swam. He let out a strangled cry and stared at the eyes of Christ.

"Pull yourself together, man." Nasen snapped, with visible contempt for the Bursar on his harsh features. "Franklin has his own ideas of discretion. The police will suspect nothing. A simple mechanical tinkering – the brakes on that Focus of hers needed looking at anyway. The A14 will be treacherous tonight with the severe ice, and there's fresh snow on the way..."

Davies rubbed his knuckles against his mouth, his eyes squeezed shut.

"You would do well to take a leaf out of Franklin's book, Bursar. It is bad enough that the Master weakens…but to have two of the Fellowship falter could destroy everything. Remember why we do this, Bursar. We owe it to mankind. We do this for the love of humanity."

"Humanity." Davies let out a high-pitched laugh. "We do this in the name of humanity, do we? It's so easy to forget!"

"Never forget, Bursar. *Never.* We have other problems to deal with; Ms Cox is the least of them. Phillip Lotson and Andrew Hughes both visited today. Lotson saw the Master, gave an interview without consent from the College Council." His lips drew back. "And Hughes came to see you and Ms Cox. Didn't you think it was odd? Didn't you spot his resemblance to Charles Harvey?"

Davies frowned. "There was a slight resemblance, I'll admit, but…"

"No coincidence. If he and Jason Franklin meet, the outcome could be catastrophic." Now Nasen looked nervous, but Davies told himself it was a trick of the light, a false impression brought about by the flickering candlelight. "Steps will have to be taken. Hughes will have to be dealt with at some stage, but our immediate concern is Lotson."

"Why Lotson?"

Nasen licked the blood from his knuckles. "Simple, Bursar. I have it on good authority that Lotson was summoned to the Phoenix Unit tonight. There's only one reason he could be there. Only one person he'd be visiting."

"Which means he'll be visiting Freeland at some stage."

"Precisely, Bursar. Franklin's talents will have to be called upon again."

Nasen glanced at his watch, holding it at an angle to the candles to read the display.

"They'll be conscious now. It's time." Davies followed the Senior Tutor to the sacristy. Inside, the carpet had been rolled back to reveal the hinged wooden door that the members of the College Council knew all too well – and where it led to.

The door was propped open by the missing wooden lectern. The eagle's carved head looked upwards as if screaming against the weight on its shoulders. Simon Davies knew the feeling.

With slumped shoulders and shaking footsteps, he followed Nicholas Nasen down the flight of cold, damp steps to where the rest of the Council waited.

Andy Hughes knew it was impossible. It was just a small wood in the middle of a modern British city, for God's sake.

He closed his eyes, held them shut for a full ten seconds, breathed in deeply. Then he exhaled and opened them. But his eyes weren't lying.

The trees had closed in on him. Flashing his small Maglite behind him, he could see his footprints implanted on the frozen snow, leading to him. From their point of origin was nothing. The path had vanished.

The lights of the college that had beckoned through the gaps in the trees had vanished as well. He turned slowly, holding the torch outwards, carving a circle of light in the sylvan darkness. The snow on the branches was illuminated in a strange shade of blue. The crunching of his Nikes on the frozen snow was the only sound. That and his deep, heavy breathing. Nothing. No pathway leading in...and nothing leading out.

"Bollocks," he hissed. "There's always a way..."

He walked in the opposite direction of the footprints and stared at the trees barring his way. He could squeeze through the gap between the trunks but after that there were more obstacles, more trees to get round. Not a problem in itself but without a straight path to follow he'd be lost. He shook his head in wonder. Lost in a tiny wood like this...holding the torch up he could see no end to the wood in sight.

Well, can't go backwards...

He pushed through the lower branches of the first pair of oaks, wincing at the lumps of snow thrown down from their limbs and landing on his neck. He shrugged them off and pushed forwards. On foot he had a better impression of just how ancient these trees were. The boles stared hungrily at him, gaping holes of blackness that seemed to stretch to the centre of the earth itself. The trunks were wider, thicker than he remembered.

A noise. A twig cracking? He looked downwards, surprised that there was little in the way of leaf litter. Just frozen earth beneath frozen snow.

The noise again. Behind him. He turned and stared. And dropped the Maglite in disbelief at what he saw.

The torch fell to the ground with a soft plop, but remained pointed in the direction of the thing that was breaking through the hole in the ground, illuminating the thing in all its horror.

It was identical to the boar they'd pulled out of Rob Benson's Transit earlier, but the tusks were smaller - and sharper. The black bristles on its hide and dorsal crest gleamed in the torchlight as it heaved itself from the hole in the ground. Andy blinked, his mouth open in horror. The hole was rectangular, cut by human hands.

How the hell did I miss that? Identical to that in the lawns of Old Court, where the boar would be consigned to at the end of each Feast...a dead boar. A half-consumed boar.

Identical to what came his way now. The eyes were dull and opaque, all spark of life extinguished. Except for a tiny pinprick of scarlet within each centre.

The legs propelled the impossible thing forwards: the front trotters and the hindquarters powerfully gouging huge chunks out of the frozen earth. Clumps of mud that bounced up into the gaping hole where its belly and innards had been.

Andy picked up the torch and backed away slowly. He felt frozen wooden fingers prodding his back. The boar opened its mouth and hissed like a snake. No steam from condensing breath. No warmth. No life…*and yet not dead.*

It leaped at him, its powerful hindquarters easily launching three hundred kilograms of beast into the air. Andy twisted, fell to the ground and rolled in the opposite direction. He watched the dead boar crash into the trunk of the nearest oak, its trotters scrabbling wildly on the wood, snow shaken from the tree by its impact. It turned, fixed him in its sights and launched itself again.

This time Andy wasn't so fortunate. Its forelegs crashed into his chest, knocked him to the ground and punched the breath from his body. His head hit the frozen ground and he cried out in pain. The beast's snout forced itself into his belly, the wickedly sharp points of its yellowed tusks tearing through the material of the sweatshirt, piercing the skin.

Pushing upwards, they would have passed through into his diaphragm if he hadn't brought both hands crashing down on the top of its head, twin pile-driver blows that gave no pain to the creature but certainly prevented the tusks going any deeper. He forced downwards with flattened palms, a vain attempt to push the beast away.

It responded with impossible strength and power, its trotters scrabbling on the ground, finding purchase on his thighs. He grunted in pain, felt the tusks gain power once more, knew it was only a matter of time before he was speared…

His palms felt like they'd been pressing down on thistles. God knew what that creature's hide was made of, but he knew they couldn't be the bristles found on any normal boar. He forced his palms outwards, moving downwards; each hand finding an ear. Horrible coarse material, like old bone wrapped in ancient parchment.

He twisted and pulled. A loud rending and popping sound filled the tiny clearing as the boar's ears came away in his hands. Without pausing, without planning, without thinking – just reacting – he reached for the eyes next, those cold, dead, sightless orbs. They popped like cold overripe plums beneath his gouging thumbs.

Then the elongated snout, tearing and twisting. This didn't come away, but the soft fleshy parts of the tip were crushed to a pulp between his hands. No blood came forth, no warmth released by this piece of flesh.

No pain registered in the boar, either, it continued to battle as though unaware of the destruction being wrought upon it.

Andy fought with a blind rage and unconscious fury, the genie released from its bottle as it had been less than twenty-four hours ago. He gained the upper hand, twisting his body over, mounting the boar. He had its tusks in his hands now, his knees crushing the beast to the ground. He bent the head back, saw its lower jaw open… and then with a speed and expertise that surprised even himself, he took his right hand from the tusk, reached into the mouth and wrenched the animal's tongue from its roots.

It flapped noisily as he tossed it into the snow. Then the legs, twisting them violently in his hands, hearing the rapid popping and cracking of sinews being broken, of joints twisted from their sockets.

It still moved as he got to his feet and examined his handiwork. It dragged itself forwards on broken limbs, its slack jaw and mangled snout trailing on the snow. Its eye sockets still seemed to see him, fixing him in a glare that was doubly impossible – neither eyes to see nor life to power it – but was there nevertheless.

Andy felt the sweat cool and freeze on his body, steam wafting into the night air to meet the fresh flurries of snow that started to fall. He was aware of the cold, liquid sensation of trickling blood – or its equivalent - on his thighs and stomach. But he was alive.

The beast sagged into the snow, its movements becoming more sluggish with each second that passed. Andy didn't wait to see if it stopped altogether; he turned and despite the pain in his gored abdomen he ran.

He could see a lightening of shadows in front, and realised that he was on the right track at last. Each step was agony, but the faint glow of lights from ancient buildings fired him onwards - as did the sound of snorting and snuffling behind him. More than one creature made those noises – he knew the boar that had attacked him was not alone.

Through the cloisters and archways, his breath misting and his vision blurring into a haze of dark red, he powered his body onwards. Only when the sounds of the boar faded into the night did he allow himself the luxury of slowing his pace.

It was an eternity before he reached Old Court and laid tear-filled eyes on his destination: the chapel, where Pearce had told him to go.

He moved slowly towards it, hugging the cold clunch walls to share their shadows.

His hand on the door handle, he put his ear to the gap between the double doors and listened. No sound, perhaps it was empty. Take a chance, he thought. He took a deep breath and pulled the door open.

Simon Davies had always wondered why the robes were white. It was stupid and impractical – it showed the blood too clearly.

But it was part of the ritual, a tradition that could not be broken, nor even questioned. Everything had to be followed as the previous generations had followed. Nothing could be left to chance; one slight error, one tiny deviation from the propitiation could have dire consequences for all. Andraste would not forgive a second time.

Through the narrow eyeholes of his wooden mask he looked around the cellar, taking in the white robed and masked figures of the other members of the Council. There should have been no way of knowing who was who. But they knew. They all knew. The eyes gave everything away.

Cassell and Nasen's were the only ones that weren't filled with fear and self-loathing. They roamed the crypt, eyes fixing on the others and glaring, forcing them to be strong.

Remember your duty. We do this for the love of humanity.

Their eyes rested on those of the Master for considerably longer. It was he and his hesitation, his weakness, which had almost brought disaster upon them all. His anguished eyes, red from weeping, were the most noticeable. Davies sympathised, shuddering at the thought of the responsibility on Searles' shoulders.

The two figures in the centre of the circle they formed were barely recognisable as human. When they still had their limbs: still had eyes, lips, nose and ears – Davies knew that even Nasen had felt pity then. Knowing that this man and woman had friends and loved ones. Fathers worried sick about their disappearances. Mothers who would surely have killed themselves if they knew the suffering their children were undergoing.

That was all gone, now. The skin removal had reduced the offerings to something less than human. It should have made the penultimate stage of the ritual easier: knowing the offering no longer had a tongue with which to scream, eyes to weep and plead, ears to hear the sound of their own flesh being torn apart. The removal of all five senses, total sensory deprivation as demanded by Andraste.

But it wasn't. This was the hardest part of all. This was when the Council were confronted with the final result of their work. A human being reduced to nothing but a quivering lump of raw meat that begged for death and an end to its suffering. Each member of the Council knew that death that would soon be granted. And that the indescribable suffering in the crypt was a mere prelude to what would follow when the offering left this plane to join Andraste.

The dismembered torso of the student Dan Bailey still quivered, even when the head was finally cut away. Davies had to turn away and force himself not to vomit, but that made him see the ravaged remains of what had once been Emma Robertson.

He saw Nasen remove his mask, a signal that this stage of the propitiation to Andraste was complete.

Davies took off his own mask, found himself staring at the bloodshot eyes of the Master. Searles blinked, and red fluid seeped from beneath his eyelids.

Blood had spurted into the eyes holes of the mask when the Master made the final cut on the woman. He was ashen-faced, the blood from his victim the only colour on his face. He was sobbing.

The Council placed the masks on top of their folded robes. They left the scattered joints of meat to be collected by Cassell, and the others filed up the steps leading back to the chapel.

Their steps were heavy, but Davies sensed a tangible feeling of relief in the cold air of the chapel. The hardest part was done. At least he would not have to be involved in any more killings this year. He thought about Judith Cox and Phillip Lotson but forced it out of his mind. *Franklin's task, his responsibility. Not mine.*

That relief evaporated when he came face to face with the carving of Christ. The eyes were open, staring at the Council accusingly.

Remember your duty. We do this for the love of humanity. Davies swallowed thickly and lowered his eyes.

Then raised them. The face of Christ…

The mouth was open, but not in a soundless scream, and no longer silent. The sound of mocking laughter filled the small chapel. Female laughter.

Not enough…one more…I DEMAND ONE MORE!

Davies froze. Even Nasen looked alarmed, as his horrified gaze met the Bursar's. His fingers loosened and his knife fell to the floor, the sharp clattering of metal on stone almost deafening in the confined space.

SEARLES…you know of whom I speak. She comes tomorrow…take her and prepare her…

"How many more?" Searles cried in anguish. "Dear God, how many more?" He sank to the floor, kneeling at Christ's feet. The carved face stared downwards at him with undisguised contempt.

She will suffice…for now. But then you must –

The voice of Andraste stopped as the door of the chapel swung outwards. The candles fluttered, the shadows even more animated.

Illuminated in the glow of the lampposts of Old Court, the bleeding, black clad figure stared in shock at the animated carving of Christ that writhed and squirmed on its wooden prison.

The Council turned as one and stared at him. Silence filled the small chapel, tension mounting between the members of the Council and one who had dared to enter the chapel during the ritual.

Davies recognised him as the delivery driver who had entered his office earlier. He stared at the blood seeping from the man's black sweatshirt, saw the torn patches and knew that this man had entered the college via the woods. He had confronted the children of Andraste and had *survived.*

For a brief moment, hope fluttered in Davies' heart. Perhaps this was a sign. Perhaps this man was the one who would –

The silence was broken by the roar of female fury that emanated from the lips of Christ.

Charles Harvey has returned…kill him. KILL HIM!

Davies was pushed roughly aside by Nasen, who reached for the fallen knife and advanced towards the intruder.

Andy limped out of the chapel and into Old Court. He turned to see the black clad figure of one of the porters running to him from the lodge, his hand raised with something that gleamed metallically in the glow of the lamp lights. A gun, aimed at Andy.

Nasen was almost on him. A knife behind him, an automatic pistol in front of him...and the screaming, unholy voice coming from an image of one who promised to deliver Mankind from death and evil. For the love of humanity.

KILL HIM…he will destroy you all…KILL HIM!

Andy Hughes ran.

FIFTEEN

Phil Lotson was still shaking as he drained the third vodka. Kerry took back the empty tumbler and was about to pour another.

"No. No more." He hiccupped and ran his fingers along his jawline, his nails rasping against the greying beard. "I need to keep a clear head if I'm going to meet Freeland."

She almost threw the bottle on the floor. Instead she slammed it down on the dining room table hard enough to knock over the Christmas table centre decoration. Small, red-painted plastic berries fell from the fake holly sprigs and rolled across the white cloth. Phil's eyes widened as he took in Kelly's furious expression.

"You're having a laugh, surely?"

Phil raised a weary hand. "Kelly, listen – "

"No, *you* bloody listen! Two hours I was sat in that car, wondering if you were going to come out in one piece. Wondering what that nutter was telling you, what shit he was filling your head with!"

Phil sat back in the dining room chair. His shaking subsided as the alcohol took effect, but seeing the enraged look on his wife's face almost made him reach for the bottle and pour another measure. *A really bloody big one.*

"Shit? You have the bloody nerve to tell me that what I'm uncovering is *shit*?"

"You're being taken in, Lotson! First this Searles bloke: now the nut-job arsonist – for Christ's sake, get a grip. There's nothing sinister about all this. Freeland left under a cloud, didn't he? Because he's just as loopy as that porter's son!"

He sighed and looked past her, into the open doorway that led through to the lounge. The Christmas tree lights were off; Nick had been as good as his word and remained in his room after they drove to Fulbourn.

"Nothing sinister? Then you explain to me how Franklin's kid managed to describe my dream in every detail. You explain why Searles *lied* to me about the smallholding that supplies the boar for their feast."

"What?"

Phil sighed, reaching in his jacket pocket for a piece of folded paper. "These are the contact details Searles supplied. Address, phone number, website. Guess what? None of it exists. Searles knew I'd find out, but he lied anyway. Question is - *why*?"

Her features softened as she pulled out the opposing chair and sat down. Her shoulders slumped and he could see genuine weariness in her eyes now.

Shit, I should have realised how much this is taking out of me – and my family's suffering as a result. But then, she hadn't been as wound up as this when he wrote *Witchfounder General*. This was more than a snappy – albeit justified – reaction to his selfish neglect of them.

This was fear. She could scoff at Jason Franklin's testimony, laugh in disbelief at the information he shared with her on the drive back to Chesterton – but deep down she knew there was more to it.

This is why she doesn't want me contacting Freeland – she's terrified of where it's going to lead. He didn't know where it was heading – Freeland might be just as insane as Franklin, in which case no problem.

But insanity had its causes.

"Kelly, I promise you." He leant over the table and took her hands. "Nothing I'm researching is going to put you or Nick in danger."

Her voice was subdued. "I wish I could believe you, Phil. But you won't tell me about that dream you had this morning, so I *know* it involved me and Nick."

He looked at the plastic holly berries in the space between them. He released her hand, reset the table centrepiece and scooped up the red globes. He held them in the palm of his hand, staring at them intently, too guilty to meet her eyes as she continued.

"You know why Searles lied about the smallholding – he wants you to dig deeper. He wants you to get to the bottom of this – but he's too scared to do it himself. What's that, if not a warning?"

She's right, he admitted to himself glumly. *Even Jason Franklin implied as much.*

He looked up and smiled weakly. She took the berries from his open hand and flicked them onto the carpet, smiling back.

"Take that as a hint, Lotson. The carpet needed a Hoovering, anyway. Get to work!" She playfully punched him on the shoulder, choked back a sob, and took the bottle back to the drinks cabinet.

Phil Lotson stared at the paper in his hands. The details of the smallholding, lies, make believe…and on the other side, in Jason Franklin's unusually elegant handwriting, the phone number of James Freeland.

A warning. And yet…he had to know. One phone call wouldn't hurt, surely? Besides, Jason was convinced Freeland would be in, even recommended the time to call him. *Eight-thirty, phone him then. You'll be pleasantly surprised…*

He heard rustling from the kitchen, the sound of the pizza they were about to have earlier being unwrapped and placed in the microwave. The smell of pepperoni and cheese filled the air and he realised he hadn't eaten anything since the hot cross buns at breakfast – apart from that doughnut Rob had offered him in the van.

Strange, even in the most foreboding of circumstances his appetite was never affected. But not this time. For the first time in his married life, the thought of food did not appeal.

Now I know something's wrong, he told himself. He had to know. He stood up from the dining room table, the paper clutched in his hands. He went through to the front room and picked up the telephone.

Kelly threw the kitchen foil in the swing bin and rubbed her eyes wearily. God, four days till Christmas and she was worn out already. At least she'd saved enough annual leave to take off over the Christmas period. The building society could get by fine without her.

She took the salad bowl out of the fridge and began mixing it. Bloody stupid really, neither of them felt like eating now but she hated the thought of waste. She began layering the salad onto three plates – she assumed Nick would still want something, if he hadn't helped himself to any of the Christmas goodies in the fridge.

This had all been prepared and ready for the sit-down at six pm – and then that bloody call from Phil's former student had changed all that.

Had to drop everything again, didn't you Lotson? She stabbed the cherry tomatoes angrily. *Everything on hold for your bloody book.*

"Books," she muttered. Not that this was the first time. The amount of times Phil had forgotten appointments and arranged days out, because he had his head filled with ideas and research materials for his books.

Phil had always had a slightly distracted air about him, one of the things she had found so appealing when they first met. He was a breath of fresh air amongst all the pretentious and self-important tossers she'd met in Freshers' Week.

But I thought the same about Andy Hughes, didn't I?

Passionate and dedicated to the study of history, but never taking things too seriously. Always ready to have a laugh and a pint – one of the things that endeared Phil to his students, and one of the reasons she and Phil had developed such a close relationship. Meeting in the Bakers Arms every Friday had become a tradition: initially a chance to chat about her work, bands they enjoyed, books they read. It was only a matter of time before it developed into something more.

No regrets, she loved him as much today as she ever had. And he had helped her get over Andy Hughes, there was no doubt about that.

He still had that boyish enthusiasm and charm, a blasé attitude to everything that complimented her desire to get things done quickly, rather than clashed with it.

But when he was seriously involved in a side project – be it a book or his thesis – it was like watching someone slipping into dementia. He forgot the most important things, times - even dates - for his seminars, dental appointments, and family matters. Focussed intently on the project at hand.

But it was worse this time. She had an uneasy feeling when he announced that he'd signed the contract for the follow up to *Witchfounder General.* She knew the subject matter of the book would focus on All Souls eventually.

And that'll be the death of us, she'd almost told him. She had kept quiet, knowing how melodramatic that sounded, but his dream this morning was proof. She opened the microwave door and pressed a knuckle onto the pizza. Still cold. She slammed the door shut and pressed the two-minute button.

She'd been woken by his cries. She had turned, saw the sweat pouring from his face, but shrank back in terror rather than waking him. Because the words he were uttering confirmed her fears.

The pleading, the cries…

*…please don't cut them. No…oh, my darling, what have they done to you…Kelly, what have they done to you…*And he was reaching to the ceiling, his hands clutching, grasping something he believed was close to him.

Holding it to his chest, burying his face in it.

…Nicky! Oh, my poor, poor boy…

When his eyes flickered, she had shut hers, feigning sleep. It was something she was good at. She had no choice. Hearing him mutter the name *Andy…*

Andy Hughes. She took the pizza out of the microwave with trembling hands. That was worse than All Souls. His name hadn't been mentioned for over ten years. Until now.

And he turned up today, for Christ's sake! She dropped the steaming pizza on to the chopping board and reached for the knife block. Her fingers tightened a little more than necessary around the bread knife.

Ten years. What a difference a decade makes…I'm not the same person anymore, I wouldn't make that mistake again.

"Lotson! I don't hear a Dyson in there! You want some dinner or what?"

A muffled sound of assent came from the front room.

"Okay. Give Nick a call, will you?" She began cutting the pizza, the serrated edge effortlessly parting the stuffed crust. Melted mozzarella flecked with green herbs oozed onto the chopping board and she thought back to Andy Hughes, to the night ten years ago when she had watched him kill.

In the name of love, eh? She remembered spitting at him as the police dragged him from the college bar. The confusion, the mixture of emotions…if Andy hadn't stepped in, she'd be dead by now, she knew it. Phil had stood by and done nothing. Andy had had the balls to do what Phil should have been man enough to do…but he'd gone too far.

She'd hated them both that night. Almost as much as she hated the two students who had tried to rape her.

They were dead. They'd paid for their crimes – or their attempted crimes – with the ultimate cost. But Phil and Andy…

What sealed it for her was the blazing look of hatred Andy had thrown at Phil as he was dragged into the police van. Words spat out with hatred.

Bastard! I'll fucking kill you for this, Lotson! That wasn't Phil's fault. How could Andy blame *him* for it? He was the one who'd lost control, not Phil.

She lowered the knife. *All have to take a side at some stage, don't we?* She took Phil's side…and then his hand. Married, while Andy Hughes burned in fury and hatred in a prison cell.

It should never have happened. None of them should have been there. That was the first time she had been in the grounds of All Souls and she had vowed never to go back.

The sound of the gate in the back garden opening brought her back to the present. She raised the kitchen blind and looked out.

The trip light was triggered, illuminating the snowbound garden – and the man entering.

She dropped the blind but kept hold of the knife. And for the first time since she gave birth to Nick she screamed.

Rob Benson popped the handbrake of the Transit and swung out without indicating. Jasper barked, tipping over in the seat. Rob ignored him.

He didn't feel befuddled with skunk now. Seeing the things Andy Hughes had brought with him had had a very sobering effect.

The van lurched off the kerb, hitting the icy road and threatening to go into a spin. The lever arch file containing Geoff Michaels' work fell to the floor, on top of the wrapped gift.

"Unbelievable, isn't it, shitbag?" Rob was angry. Angry at Andy Hughes, for bringing this shit to his doorstep: angry with Geoff Michaels, who'd walked needlessly and unwittingly into the lion's den: angry at Jason Franklin, who seemed to know everything but was feeding information selectively; but most of all, angry with himself.

All this time, the reason why Geoff disappeared – staring me in the fucking face!

He drove quickly, anxious to get to Phil Lotson's house as quickly as possible, to show him what Geoff had written.

Jasper was subdued, not his usual manic self. For once, Rob Benson would not need to clean the inside of the passenger window.

More than subdued, Jasper was frightened. His lips had drawn back and his ears were flat on his head. Snarling at the thing in the footwell.

"Relax, shitbag. It's just a Crimbo pressie." He glanced at the thing on the floor. Some of the gift-wrapping had come away and he could see bubble wrap coating something that looked like stone.

The streetlights of Mill Road reflected off the pregnant bellies of low cloud giving birth to yet more snow. He flicked the wipers on. At the end of Newmarket Road, he waited impatiently for the lights to change. Only the pedestrians had the green light.

Rob looked back to the lights. Still red. Behind him, the driver of a silver Mini Cooper blared his horn. Jasper sat bolt upright.

Rob forced himself to be calm. There was no hurry: he'd called Phil, told him to expect them both.

Phil had sounded oddly distant, though. He'd wanted Rob off the phone as quickly as possible, said – or rather whispered – that he was about to make a call. Something he wanted to keep quiet from Kelly, obviously. And Rob had the nagging feeling it was something to do with All Souls – or Andy Hughes.

Perhaps both.

Jasper's growling was low and muted. He lay on the seat, nose on paws, eyes fixed on Andy's gift.

Still the red light. Traffic building behind, more horns blaring.

"Calm down, for Christ's sake." He pressed the stereo button, turned the radio to one of the local Advert FMs. He was in time to hear a traffic report.

The A14 was at a complete standstill, due to a Ford Focus crossing both lanes and slamming into the cab of an articulated truck. Rob closed his eyes: hearing these sorts of reports on a daily basis never desensitised him to the tragedy of someone dying on the road. He offered up a silent prayer to whoever was listening that the driver had survived.

At least this explained the traffic hold up. All points north of Cambridge were well fucked.

Jasper's growl turned to a piteous whine.

"For God's sake," Rob sighed. He reached over, grunting at the restrictive webbing of the seatbelt, and picked the present up.

It felt warm to the touch, which was strange. Perhaps it was just the insulation from the packaging.

"'Merry XXXmas!' God, how cheesy is that?"

Brown parcel tape sealed the bubble wrap. He tore it open and made a closer examination of the strange carving.

It was about nine inches in diameter, roughly circular, and hewn from black stone. It was smooth and polished, with a fine tracery of red and green running through. It smelled old; similar to the scent of musty churches on damp days, but far older. He flicked it over, and met the gaze of the face carved in the stone.

It was an old man's face that stared at him through a frame of twisted oak and holly leaves and mistletoe branches. Painted berries in red and white glistened wetly, as though snow had recently melted from them.

But it was the face itself that held his attention. The forehead was heavily lined, the cheeks wrinkled and creased with an age that no human being could survive. And the eyes…

They could not have been the work of a master craftsman or production line mould. It might have been a particularly vivid pigment in the emerald paintwork used for the orbs…but they seemed *too* vivid, too *alive*. Filled with the pain of carrying the burden of some terrible, ancient knowledge.

Jasper growled nervously, but Rob paid no attention. Those eyes held him, refusing to let him go, and drawing him in.

Emma.

He sat bolt upright, wondering where the word had come from. The radio? He stared at the factory-fitted unit.

It is too late for her. She sings for Andraste.

He looked back to the carved face. Now he knew where the words came from.

The green eyes bored into him, the pain and ancient knowledge all too real, a tangible presence that the face in the leaves seemed to be trying to impart to him. The mouth opened, the encircling vegetation that formed its halo twisting and writhing. He could feel it moving in his hand, the ivy and acanthus leaves fluttering like moths trapped in his hand.

He cried out, tried to drop the stone, but his fingers were firmly fixed around the stone halo, as though coated in Superglue or Araldite. Jasper barked furiously, his hackles raised and his claws digging into the upholstery of the seat. Spittle flew onto the topmost part of the carving's face with a sizzling sound as it evaporated.

Rob Benson could feel heat coming through the stone. His fingers twitched where they made contact with the carving, smoke from burning skin rising into the cold air of the cab. He opened his mouth to scream, and the green eyes widened, the black pinpricks of its pupils dilating, widening.

Take me to All Souls. Take me to the Nemeton…

The pain was unbearable. His fingertips were blackened, scorched stumps that wept clear fluid and melted fat, dripping down the burning stone like candle wax. The stench of burning meat filled his nostrils and had his bile rising.

The Divine Judgement must be revisited…for the love of humanity, there must be no failure. PROMISE ME!

Rob cried out in agony, his scream drowning out Jasper's frantic barking.

PROMISE ME!

"Yes! Christ, yes, I promise…just stop the *pain*…"

The pain didn't relent. Black smoke obscured the glowing carving. Rob Benson cried out one more time, clenched his teeth, his eyes firmly closed against the cloying, acrid smoke. He thrust the thing away from him, smashing it into the bulkhead. He heard cracking and splintering, the sound of the plastic barrier breaking, and then a hissing, bubbling sound. The sound of plastic melting: reforming around the red-hot thing that assaulted it.

His hand came free. He opened his eyes, weeping at the sight of his ravaged palm, ragged skeletal tips peeking through the melted stumps of his fingers.

The pain and self pity was forgotten when he looked at what he had done to the Transit's bulkhead.

The stone carving was firmly centred. The plastic had moulded around the stone halo, and where it met the vegetation even the plastic had turned green. The eyes were closed, the lids squeezed shut as if in agony. The mouth remained open, the thin branches of ivy and oak leaves frozen in the act of disgorgement. The stone berries were dull, no longer gleaming. Everything about the face was still. Frozen.

Or trapped, Rob thought with bewilderment. The pain was gone. He stared at his unblemished hand, extended the undamaged fingers. He looked at the now silent Jasper, sitting on the floor.

From under the glovebox, Jasper stared back at him, ears flat against his skull. He licked his lips and wagged his tail once.

Rob jumped at the sound of horns blaring. He stared at the empty stretch of road beyond the lights of the roundabout. Elizabeth Way was clear.

With shaking hands he released the handbrake and put the van in gear. He drove slowly, his eyes firmly fixed on the road that spanned the frozen Cam. He tried to ignore the things he saw on his peripheral vision. The whining dog cowering in the passenger footwell and the face of his newest passenger.

"She sings for Andraste? What the fuck does that mean?" He turned the radio volume up to blot out the memories of that voice. The traffic had eased, but Chesterton still seemed to take ages to get to.

It was the flaring of brake lights in front of him that made him think the eyes were reflecting red in the windscreen, surely.

"Okay, Kelly. Calm down." Phil took the knife from her trembling hands and placed it on the chopping board by the rapidly cooling pizza. His hands trembled just as much as hers, and the calming words he uttered were forced.

The knife was exactly the same one he had seen in his dream, wielded by Andy Hughes. And he was here, in the kitchen of their home.

Kelly retreated, her eyes still fixed on Andy. Phil couldn't believe what he saw.

Andy Hughes had been attacked by something. His black jogging bottoms and sweatshirt were torn and ragged in several places and soaked in blood. He was breathing heavily, deep and barely controlled exhalations, and sweat drenched his face.

Andy followed Phil's eyes and lifted the torn flaps of his sweatshirt. Kelly gasped at the fresh blood seeping from the twin incisions on his washboard stomach.

"What the hell happened to you?" Phil said hoarsely.

Andy didn't answer. His face was flushed from his exertion and covered in scratches that looked like they'd come from tree branches. Phil thought back to the drive through the woods on All Souls this morning and realised where Andy had been.

"Didn't waste any time, did you?" Phil sighed.

Kelly clutched his shoulder.

"Who have you attacked this time? See you came off badly for a change." Her words were hissed, and Phil was surprised to see Andy rock back on his feet, visibly pained by Kelly's question. And there was something else on Andy's face, something Phil had never seen. Something that explained why he had run at a break-neck pace from the centre of Cambridge to the house in Chesterton.

Fear. Andy Hughes had seen – and fought – something that scared him. *And for someone who knows no fear, this can only be bad news*, Phil thought with a shudder.

Kelly noticed his shudder and stared searchingly into his eyes. He smiled, tried to be reassuring, but Andy spoke first.

"Phil…Kelly."

Her eyes flashed.

"I'm sorry to come here like this…but I had no choice." His breathing was slowly returning to normal. In spite of the run and the battle he'd gone through, he was recovering quickly. Phil could see Andy had kept himself in prime physical condition over the years. Remembering Kelly's relationship with him, he felt a brief flicker of envy.

"I need to talk to you about All Souls. I was there tonight." He leant back against the closed door and closed his eyes. No matter how fit and healthy he was, he was only human. Now he'd reached his destination, he was visibly flagging.

"You won't believe what I saw, what I fought against..."

Phil said nothing. He took Kelly's arm from his shoulder and walked over to the sink. He took a glass from the drainer and filled it with cold water from the tap, passing it to Andy.

Andy nodded his thanks and drained the glass. His face was losing its flushed colour. Now he was looking pale, and not just from the loss of blood.

"Into the front room, Andy. You're going to pass out." Phil took his shoulder and motioned him towards the door. He took a tea towel from the drawer and handed it to Andy.

Kelly gave him an angry look, but relented when she saw the change in Andy's colouring, saw him staggering to the hallway door with the tea towel held to his bleeding stomach. She nodded and pressed herself back into the wall to allow them to pass by.

Andy frowned at the lights glinting on the Christmas tree. He swayed on his feet, and Phil led him to the sofa before he could collapse onto the tree.

Andy sank into it gratefully.

Phil stared at him, waiting for him to speak first. Outside he could hear the sound of a vehicle approaching. Headlights swung through the gap in the curtains. Andy stiffened.

"That'll be Rob," Phil said evenly. "He called me earlier, said he had something he wanted to show me. About Geoff Michaels. And about *you*."

Andy smiled ruefully. He released the pressure on the towel and peered thoughtfully at the twin puncture marks on his abdomen.

"About me? Sounds like he's been rummaging in Santa's sack. Naughty boy, couldn't wait for Christmas..."

Kelly had opened the front door. Phil could hear an excited barking from Jasper. Rob's dog could smell the pizza.

No, not Rob's dog. Geoff Michael's dog, Phil reminded himself.

"And Geoff Michaels?" Andy shook his head. "I don't know what Roberto's found out, but I'm guessing this much. Geoff Michaels is dead. He was killed last year...where his body is now, God only knows. But he was murdered."

Phil stared at him. A cold fist rubbed its knuckles down his spine.

"You're sure about this?"

Andy looked up as the door opened. He nodded to a white faced Rob and turned back to Phil.

"He wasn't the last. Someone else was murdered tonight. I saw the blood on their hands, on the knife." He pressed the towel back to his abdominal wound and grimaced. "And splattered across the face of the Master."

Phil sank back in the sofa. "The Master's involved? Then – "

"They're *all* involved."

Kelly was in the doorway, her hand held to stop Nick coming any further down the stairs. Rob Benson stood with an overflowing lever arch file in one hand.

Jasper cautiously moved to Andy and sniffed the blood dripping onto the white rug. His hackles rose and he backed away, snarling.

Andy raised his head and stared at the Christmas tree. In a voice that trembled with barely suppressed rage, he said:

"The Master and the Fellows of All Souls College. They're killing people."

SIXTEEN

Jasper stared quizzically at Andy from the centre seat. Even though he'd showered and changed into some of Phil's spare clothes there was a scent that remained on him, something that unsettled the dog. That was nothing compared to how unsettled Andy was. He stared in horror at the Green Man on the van's bulkhead.

"What the *fuck* …"

It was the carved face from his dream. Right down to the disgorged vegetation and the eyes.

…this is the Divine Judgement. But it is not complete...

Rob glanced at the carving with a worried expression. "Yeah, sorry man. It was your pressie from Jen."

For a moment the carved face was forgotten. Andy turned and glared at Rob.

"What? You've been in my bag?"

"Cool it, man!" Rob glared back. "Of course I've been in your bag. No, I didn't put that thing up there. You wouldn't believe me if I told you."

Andy felt his eyes drawn to the carving firmly fixed on the plastic bulkhead. He shook his head in disbelief. His fingers brushed the remoulded plastic gingerly, tracing the join between the stone carving and the bulkhead. There was none. It was as though the two materials had become one, had fused, melded. Impossible.

"Try me."

Rob's version of events chilled him. The fire that had burned Rob sounded just like that of his dream. *The Divine Judgement must be revisited…for the love of humanity, there must be no failure.*

"And what the hell is Andraste?"

"Let's hope this old boy Phil talked about has got the answers to that thing. As for the other thing you brought with you, Andy…"

While Andy had showered and changed into some of Phil's old clothes, Phil had made the call. After laying eyes on the thing in Rob's van, after reading the notes in Geoff's dissertation, he had known what to do. Even he was surprised by the response.

Come round tonight. As soon as you can.

Perhaps he'd had bad dreams as well.

"Just as well I did bring it. I don't like the sound of it, Roberto. Phil going all the way to London, tonight…on Jason Franklin's recommendation? It's not right."

"We've been through this, Andy," Rob sighed as he headed back down Chesterton Road. "It's worth the risk. If Freeland has real, hard physical evidence of…of what you've discovered, then it makes sense to get it. Go to the Old Bill, let them handle it."

"That's bollocks," Andy snorted. "Look at what Michaels wrote in his dissertation. All those things pointed to All Souls, and they missed it? I'm telling you, they're keeping out of it. They've had their orders."

"Sounds a little paranoid to me."

"I've dealt with the police. You haven't."

"And others," Rob spat. "You going to tell me about the combat shotgun you brought with you? When the fuck were you going to tell me?"

"When I had to. You shouldn't have gone rummaging through my bag. I couldn't leave that in the house, and I had a feeling that Pearce was holding out on me. I thought it would be good insurance if things got nasty."

Rob shook his head as he turned onto Newmarket Road. "This Pearce bloke knows some nice people. Not an ordinary pump action or a revolver – no, it has to be a Franchi SPAS 12 combat shotgun. You don't use those to turn over post offices - you use them in war zones!"

Andy narrowed his eyes. "You seem to know your guns pretty well."

Rob shakily lit a cigarette. "Few years back I went to Bratislava for a mate's stag weekend. We went wild with handguns, machine guns – the SPAS 12 was an added bonus."

Andy was silent. Smoke drifted towards him.

"You're fucking lucky I didn't tell Phil or Kelly about this. Why the hell did you agree to take it?"

"It was a favour. And Pearce is not the sort of bloke you say no to."

Favours and promises made in prison were cast iron deals – *I get you the SIA ticket, you look after this piece for me* - especially if the bloke whose mate on the outside had pulled the job for Pearce. It wasn't as though he'd had any choice. But he'd been stupid leaving it in the attic, he accepted that. And stupid to think that Rob wouldn't go rummaging.

Still, this could work out well. Rob's used this gun before, so he might come in handy…

Andy closed his eyes. After the hot shower, the bandaging and the liberal shots of whiskey, fatigue was catching up with him. But he couldn't sleep. He didn't want to sleep.

But he didn't want to talk, either. He looked at Rob smoking his cigarette and felt a twinge of contempt.

Or is it resentment? He asked himself. *Rob had the chance to finish his degree, and what's he done with it? Fuck all. Acting like the Eternal Student with a dead end job while my chances of a shot at academia went up in smoke. What would I have been by now if that night hadn't happened?*

He told himself to calm down. *Over-tired and stressed out. Cool it, Hughes. Rob's your only friend right now. Besides, there are more important things to be angry about…*

The A14 and A303 passed in a blur of oncoming headlights that glared so brightly he had to close his eyes.

When he opened them he was surprised to find the van coming to a stop outside a modern, modest two-up, two-down in cream coloured brickwork that shone brightly in the glare of the Transit's headlights. To the left of the door with an artificially frosted glass panel was a small brass plaque that read *New Rectory*.

"Was I out?" Andy asked groggily.

"Long enough to get to Swaffham Prior."

Andy nodded slowly, massaging his stiffening neck muscles. He looked at the clock on the dash. God, he'd been out cold for forty minutes.

Without dreaming. Small mercies.

Andy stepped out of the van and saw why Rob had put the van in gear. He almost slipped on the icy sloping pavement that led down to the Rectory. He hung on to the van door that threatened to swing out of control, and looked behind him.

The two rounded towers of the churches that shared the same churchyard – a result of lordly piety and rivalry in medieval times - soared into the night sky. The paved pathway sloped upwards for about twenty metres before turning to the left and disappearing behind the yew trees that marked the perimeter of the graveyard.

Rob rang the doorbell. Andy turned back and saw a distorted black shape moving through the frosted glass panel. The door stuck in the jamb as the occupant pulled it. Andy could make out a frown on the bearded face as its owner pulled the door inwards again.

"Touch of damp, mate?" Rob smiled in greeting.

Reverend Ian Wilkins smiled ruefully. "Yes, I should have had the door planed before the cold weather came, but…the ferocity of this winter took me by surprise."

A frown crossed the vicar's broad face as he looked in Andy's direction, his bushy eyebrows bristling. The vicar was in his late fifties, Andy guessed. The short black hair was darker than it should have been, obviously dyed, and there were heavy lines in the pale, broad face. His blue eyes had a distinct glazing in them that spoke of developing cataracts. His face revealed his true age, belying the sprightly and youthful movements his body made.

"Took us all by surprise, vicar. Did Philip Lotson tell you we'd be coming?"

The vicar continued staring at Andy, a frown that was one of recognition, as if to say *I've seen you before but I can't remember where.* The same look the Bursar had given him earlier.

The frown was replaced by a look of horror when the vicar's eyes moved to the thing in the van.

He strode out of the doorway in slipper-less feet, unheeding of the snow that soaked his socks. He pushed past Rob, put both hands on the dent of the still-warm bonnet and stared, enraptured at the carved face.

"Where did you get this?" His voice was high-pitched, tremulous with excitement.

And fear, Andy noted. "My girlfriend got it for me. Christmas present." He followed the vicar's rapt gaze. "You know what this…this thing is then?"

"I think so. You'd better come inside. Both of you. You might be able to help me."

Rob and Andy exchanged glances. *Help you? It's us that need helping…*

Rob opened the driver's door, whistling for Jasper to come out. The clergyman stuck his head into the cab, seemingly oblivious to the black and white torpedo of fur and flesh that jumped out, sniffed his ankles and whipped a tail against his thin trousers.

"Can you bring this carving inside, young man?"

Rob laughed. "We tried, pal. It won't come off. It's stuck fast."

Andy watched silently as the vicar tested Rob's statement. After a moment Wilkins came out of the cab, shaking his head in wonder and inspecting his fingernails. There was a small drop of blood on the knuckles of his left hand.

"And before you ask, we haven't used Superglue, Araldite or Sticks-Like-Shit." Andy said, reaching into the cab to pick up the lever arch file that contained Geoff's dissertation. "Neither of us have a clue what's holding that thing up there. Any ideas?"

Wilkins stared at him, his eyes shining through the glazed cataracts.

"I think so, young man. Come with me."

Wilkins led the way, stooping to stroke Jasper's head on the way. Rob followed then Andy, who paused to wipe his feet on the WELCOME mat on the porch.

Rob and Andy stopped dead at the foot of the stairwell. Rob froze, and Andy felt the blood draining from his face. He stared in horror at the heads mounted on the wall above the banister rail. Even Jasper, perhaps sensing the similarity between these heads and the one mounted on the van's bulkhead, paused in mid-step.

"Jesus Christ," Andy whispered, ignoring the disapproving look Wilkins threw his way.

Six carvings of foliate heads grinned down at him. Wooden faces, painted in various hues of green, their wild staring eyes finished in a brilliant emerald gloss. Black pinpricks of pupils gleamed. Vegetation disgorged from their mouths, spreading around the framework of their faces like a halo.

Now he knew why Philip Lotson had arranged this meeting at such short notice. And now he knew why Geoff Michaels had spent so much time with the Reverend Ian Wilkins while working on his dissertation.

"A little hobby of mine," the vicar sighed as he closed the door. "At least, that's how it started. I'm afraid to say it's become more of an obsession now."

"Not to worry," Andy said tightly. "Phil gets quite obsessed with his work as well."

Wilkins looked at him shrewdly. "Mr Lotson. Yes, we've spoken a great deal. It was Phil who came to me for help on the Elizabeth Woodcock chapter of his current book. Has he not spoken to you about it?"

Andy frowned. "No. Should he have?"

"I see," Wilkins sighed. "Well, all in good time. Come this way, gentlemen." He led the way up stairs.

Andy followed, his eyes firmly fixed on the vicar's back and away from the dead gaze of the carvings.

"I've only recently put them up. My wife never allowed my collection to go beyond the realms of my study." He paused on the final step. He spoke to the newel post. "She died last year. Lung cancer. And she never smoked a cigarette in her life...

"Since then I've devoted all my spare time to the study of these remarkable images. Church business isn't exactly demanding these days, so this...keeps me busy." At the top of the stairs, the landing led to three rooms. Above the lintel of each door, another carved face stared downwards.

"Veronica hated these things, said their eyes followed her across the room. Now I feel a sense of peace with them around the house. They comfort me...I don't feel alone."

Andy said nothing.

"What you see are cheap replicas that I've collected over the years, from various cathedrals and museum gift shops. I've managed to obtain original carvings from churches that have…succumbed to the ravages of time. I keep these in a safe place."

"What's the appeal these carvings have to you, vicar?" Andy asked. Wilkins smiled, pointed to the lever arch file Andy carried.

"The same appeal they had to Mr Michaels. Yes, I recognised the handwriting on the spine." He took the file and leafed through it. "They represent a real mystery. Pagan fertility symbol? Gargoyle? No one knows the real purpose of the Green Man, or has a definitive explanation of his origins. But everyone who sees one understands – instinctively, you might say – that the face in the leaves represents something very deep and very important to mankind. Perhaps our origins or our relationship with the natural world. He is an archetypal image. An icon, if you will."

Andy stared hard at the large display case mounted on the far wall facing him. The stone faces here were not replicas. The musty and unmistakeable smell of ancient stonework refused to be imprisoned behind the glass. It was pungent, yet strangely soothing and reassuring, like the welcoming smell of a cooling, empty church on a hot summer's day.

Some of the carvings were faded, their features almost erased by centuries of English weather. Some, carved in wood and clearly taken from ends of pews and misericords, had been carefully restored and lovingly polished. The smell of varnish accompanied the musty aroma of stone.

They all had something in common, though. They were disgorging vegetation, and they all looked to be in pain.

"The Green Man in anguish," Wilkins said in a low voice. Whispered, respectful, as though he was at a funeral. "The most…disconcerting aspect of these carvings."

Rob backed into the study, a finger raised aloft, and clearly associated with Jasper. The collie was sat on his haunches, grinning happily in the doorway. Rob turned back to Andy and the vicar.

"Okay, I think he'll be cool now." He nodded to the folder Wilkins had open. "Geoff was quite taken with these things as well. I didn't realise how much work he'd put in until I read that."

Wilkins nodded. "Geoff has done his research very well. I see he quoted extensively from Kathleen Basford's book, *The Green Man* – the first, serious scholarly exploration of the theme. She was obsessed with it – and she was a botanist at Manchester University, a scientist, no less. Obsessed…" his voice trailed off as he stared at the picture in Geoff's folder.

It was an eight by ten inch glossy of a carved foliate head, with a Post-It note attached. On the yellow paper, Geoff had written: *Keystone from window – Chapel of Nine Altars, Fountains Abbey, York.*

Andy peered at the picture. The foliate head was cold blue stone: the eyes open wide, blank, lacking pupils. The foliage emerging from its mouth took the form of thick branches that entwined around its chin and spread upwards to form a crown.

"I thought the Green Man was a pagan image? How come you see so many of them in churches…Christian centres of belief?"

"The Christian church never fully vanquished the old religion. The still-holy world of forests and sacred groves, rivers and springs was impervious to the new religion. So…the church took over these old bastions and rites from the past and assimilated them. However, the old gods were seen as very real threats by the pre-medieval church…to their faith or to their power, I'll let you decide which." He smiled sadly.

"Some see the Green Man as a demonic figure, old gods rendered impotent by being trapped in holy stone – hence the anguish. There are three types of Green Man. The foliate head, completely covered in leaves; the charmingly titled 'bloodsucker' head, where vegetation sprouts from all facial orifices, and the one that always fascinates me: the disgorging head, where vegetation emanates from the mouth of the Green Man. This is what you see here. And, of course, in your van."

Andy felt cold as they walked over to the window next to the display cabinet. Wilkins pulled the curtains apart and they looked down onto the van parked on the path. The porch light was still on and they could just see the carving on the bulkhead. *Disgorging vegetation*, Andy mused.

"Why is it called a Green Man?"

"It was Lady Raglan who coined the name 'Green Man', back in the nineteen-thirties with *The Green Man in Church Architecture* in *The Folklore Journal*. She was convinced its origins lay in the figure known as Jack-In-The-Green, or Robin Hood – the central figure in the May Day celebrations throughout Northern and Central Europe – convinced that it was associated with vegetation myths and the notion of sacrifice."

"Sacrifice?" Andy's face hardened. Wilkins was staring at him again – in that cool, appraising way he had done earlier.

"Offered to the gods…to ensure the land prospers, and mankind survives."

Rob and Andy looked at each other. *The Divine Judgement…for the love of humanity.*

Wilkins flipped a few more pages of the dissertation.

"It's a theory that is still in doubt, of course. I did tell young Geoff not to read too much into it…" He sighed as he looked through the dissertation. "Oh dear. I see he's rather run away with himself here. Hmm."

"Sorry chaps, I really need a smoke." Rob had a Mayfair in his mouth, the unlit tip shaking visibly.

Nicotine withdrawal, or fear at what he was being told? Andy wondered.

"I'll see you outside."

They waited until the front door was closed and they could hear sounds of footsteps and dog claws on the frosted path outside. A flare of orange, then grey smoke rose into the night air.

Wilkins turned from the window and gazed at his collection behind their glass prison.

"It's been suggested that the Green Man is in anguish to express the death of nature. 'All greenness comes to withering' as the medieval poem says. What we are looking at are the faces of the dead, in despair and agony."

Andy thought about that for a moment. His eyes never left the carving on the van's bulkhead. He noticed Rob had his back towards it, hunched over Jasper and petting him, shivering in the cold as he sucked hard on his Mayfair.

"But the greenery springing from the mouth…surely that's a sign of new life?" Andy asked. "Rebirth in the face of death, hope of life eternal. That may explain why the Church kept them in their buildings – life eternal is the same message you share with the old religions."

Wilkins raised his eyebrows in surprise. "Yes, you could be right. But look at the Green Man in your van. Tell me what makes it different to the ones you see here."

Andy frowned. "The vegetation. Something different…"

"Yes. There are three types of foliage to be found in the mouth of the Green man. Vine leaves, the symbol of Bacchus, or Dionysus. Acanthus, sacred to classical and Northern European traditions as a symbol of rebirth. And oak, sacred to the druids." Wilkins flipped through the folder, searching for something. "Yours has the latter... and something else. The greenery you have on there is not symbolic of spring. You have holly, ivy, mistletoe…all winter plants.

"It's unique. Kathleen Basford knew about this one….ah, and I see Geoff Michaels did as well." He showed Andy the picture.

A photocopy, a line drawing of a foliate head.

"This didn't warrant an entry in her book because she wasn't certain it existed. She went to the place it was seen last, to try to find clues as to its whereabouts…and to find out who carved it. She was unsuccessful."

There was no mistake. The illustration was that of the Green Man carving in Rob's van.

"The last place it was seen was in the chapel of All Souls College."

Andy felt the floor lurch beneath his feet.

"And Geoff Michaels was determined to follow the trail, was he not?" Wilkins stared hard at Andy. "I wonder what he discovered."

He flicked back through the pages.

"Seems he read some of Ms Basford's notebooks. What's interesting is that the last time this carving was seen was in February 1799 – just before the meteorite hit the college. It was never seen again. Until now."

He closed the folder and placed it on top of the glass cabinet. He folded his arms and gave Andy a hard look.

"So tell me, young man. How did your lady get hold of it?"

"I think she got it at a stall at a folk festival. Each year they sell all sorts of pagan and gothic knick-knacks – like this." Andy pointed to the collection. "I had the feeling it was no replica, but…it's not usual stone, either. Black stone."

"Black stone?" Wilkins frowned. His eyes took on a faraway look. "Black stone… like that in the Great Hall. How is it affixed to the van?

"You won't believe this, but…" and he told Wilkins Rob's description of the event.

"Fire…" Wilkins eyes glazed, and Andy thought for a moment that the cataracts were returning. He blinked, and the vicar continued

"Fire, black stone…incredible." He looked away from the window. "Does this mean nothing to you?"

Andy frowned. "I'm looking to you for the answers, pal."

"The name Elizabeth Woodcock? Is it not familiar?" There was earnestness in the vicar now, as though he was in the presence of someone powerful – or holy.

"Should it be?" And then it hit him. Perhaps it was Rob's description of the fire that burned when holding the carving.

A fire from the Heavens…'forgive me, Elizabeth. This is the will of God.'

"Anything to do with the Divine Judgement?"

"Everything." Wilkins opened a drawer in the base of the display cabinet and pulled out a cardboard folder. He opened it and took out what looked to Andy like a facsimile copy of an ancient newspaper.

"The Cambridge Independent Press and Chronicle. Dated ninth of February 1799, a week after the meteorite hit All Souls. This is a report of the consequences of the particularly vicious winter that gripped our region in that year – rather like the one we're suffering now.

"Three deaths were reported. Rebecca Freeman, a sixty year old woman who froze to death on the Ickleton-Chesterford Road. John Limner, a shepherd from Woodditton, who died on Newmarket Heath. But it's the third death that has relevance to us." He held the paper up to the light and read aloud.

"'An Impington woman named Woodcock has been missing since Saturday and is supposed to have perished in the snow. She left Cambridge at about six o'clock in the evening and not withstanding a diligent search her body has not been found. The mail coaches have in many places been entirely stopped by snow and the mail forwarded on horseback…' It goes on about the state of the region for a while. Elizabeth Woodcock was the wife of Impington farmer Daniel Woodcock. She rode to Cambridge each Saturday to sell surplus goods on the market. She was quite a drinker by all accounts, and met up with friends at the Three Tuns on Castle Hill for a good old booze up before heading back home.

"Well, this particular Saturday was the second of February. The storm she rode out in had worsened on her way back to Impington. Drifts built up along the dykes and the trackway was barely visible.

"Half a mile away from home it was reported that a meteor flashed through the sky." He paused, and Andy nodded for him to continue.

"It seems that a piece broke from the Divine Judgement after it hit the college and flew along Woodcock's path. Her horse reared and threw her.

"Now, she was quite the worse for wear at this stage. She'd drunk extra to 'keep out the cold' and it probably did keep her warm, but it sealed her fate. She tried to get up but was too drunk to stay upright. She fell unconscious and the snow, whipped up by the wind, formed a drift around her while her horse found its own way home. Her friends, family and distraught husband searched for several days before reluctantly giving up. No one could survive temperatures of that severity. They waited for the thaw.

"But Elizabeth Woodcock was not dead. The drift froze around her, imprisoning her…"

Andy felt chills running down his spine. *A cavern of ice and snow, her final resting place. A frozen tomb…*

"She kept warm with controlled sips of whiskey from her flask and liberal intakes of snuff. She forced a hole in the top of the drift – igloo, I suppose, tied a piece of her torn petticoat to a branch and thrust it through. Of course, being on the part of the common so far from the path, no one saw it, until a week later." Wilkins turned to another page.

"Sixteenth of February. 'Her voice and pulse were as strong as in full health. Her legs appeared like those of a drowned person and mortification had taken place in consequence of their being buried in the snow.' Frostbite, in other words. She lost most of the fingers on both hands."

Andy remembered the bloodstained, torn nails of blackened fingertips, feebly scratching at the roof of the ice tomb. He shivered.

"This is a piece from the Impington church parish register. 'On the eleventh day of February 1799, Elizabeth Woodcock, wife of Daniel Woodcock, died aged 43 years of a lingering Disease in consequence of a confinement under the snow of nearly eight days and nights, that is to say from Saturday the second until Sunday ye tenth day of February 1799.'"

"Hell of a story," Andy said. "To survive for that amount of time…"

"In sub zero temperatures, with nothing but snow and snuff." Wilkins smiled. "She became something of a celebrity. People would travel from miles around to visit her – and bring a bottle for her! Sadly, it was the drink that killed her. The doctor's report of her death noted that her passing had been 'accelerated by spirituous liquors afterwards taken – procured by the donations of numerous visitors.' A plaque in Impington Church shows her as a beautiful woman sleeping peacefully in an ice cavern, looking for all the world like Snow White in her glass coffin…are you all right, young man?"

"Yeah. Reminds me of a dream I had this morning."

Wilkins's eyes narrowed. His fingers tightened on the paper. "Go on."

"I dreamed I was looking for her: didn't know why I was looking, or who she was. But when I found her…she didn't look like a forty-year old farmer's wife. She was a beautiful young woman…spitting image of my girlfriend. And she was holding onto something. A black rock, carved into a face…"

The colour drained from the vicar's face.

"My God," he whispered. "Did she…did she say anything?"

"She couldn't speak much, but she called me…called me Charles."

"Charles Harvey," Wilkins said in a hollow voice. "It's true, then."

"What's true?"

Wilkins rubbed his eyes and sank down into the office chair next to his desk. "Some of Elizabeth's visitors were distressed at the sight of her, so much so that her husband forbade anyone to see her until three weeks after her ordeal. After the fear had subsided and her ravings ceased. She'd screamed about being burned alive, by a fire from Heaven."

My God, Andy thought. He stiffened.

"Holy fire, come to punish us all…and her in particular. It was Elizabeth Woodcock who first used the words Divine Judgement to describe the meteor strike.

"Not just that. She'd had no previous contact with people, no one told her of what had happened to All Souls College on the night of her disappearance. And yet she *knew*. She knew the college had been the target. When she came out of her fever, she told Daniel that it was the fire that had kept her alive. All Souls is five miles from where she fell. She wept uncontrollably, refused to tell her husband more.

"Daniel Woodcock went to the Three Tuns on the night of his wife's disappearance, knowing that was her last port of call before her fall. The landlord told him that Elizabeth had come in looking extremely upset, and he'd listened in on her conversation with the other farmer's wives. He was reluctant to tell Daniel what he'd heard. He eventually confessed."

"What was it?"

The vicar stared deeply into Andy's eyes. "She was pregnant. Pregnant with the child of Charles Harvey."

Charles…forgive me. "And who was Charles Harvey?"

"Charles Harvey was the then Master of All Souls College. The Master who was the first to die when the meteorite, 'God's Divine Judgement', struck the Master's Lodge and set the whole College afire."

Andy took a deep, steadying breath. "I don't believe this."

Wilkins shrugged. "I don't blame you. There's no proof that Elizabeth Woodcock was having an affair with the Master, and it sounds highly unlikely. What would a distinguished academic of such standing be doing risking his position for carnal affairs with a farmer's wife? Daniel never believed either. Until the baby was born."

There was a strange look in the vicar's eyes as he continued.

"Again, there is no proof. No entry in the birth register for a child named Woodcock in 1799, and the doctor made no mention of pregnancy when he made his report."

"But you believe?"

"Yes I do. Because the surviving Fellows of All Souls took great interest in Daniel Woodcock following his wife's death. Some visited him, asked him – with deepest sympathy and respect, of course – if Elizabeth had been with child. This is noted in a conversation with the priest at Impington, a conversation that the priest in question recorded. The Fellows of All Souls suspected something between Elizabeth and their leader."

"But why were they so interested in this child?"

"It was a rule at this time that Fellows of the College remain unmarried – and they were forbidden to have children. Children have been born out of wedlock for thousands of years, but I don't believe it was the prospect of a scandal hitting their already beleaguered college that so worried the Fellowship. It was noted by the Impington priest that when Daniel answered in the affirmative…they all looked positively terrified. 'As though the end of the world was upon them.'"

"What then? What did Daniel do?"

"Daniel Woodcock sold his farm and moved out of the area. His name does not turn up in any other parish register in these isles – Phil Lotson has tried finding him, but to no avail. He either moved abroad or changed his identity. The sale of the farm is the last written record we have of Daniel Woodcock."

Andy caught the emphasis. "Something was *heard*, then?"

Wilkins nodded. "In 1817 a man named Peter Hughes was tried and executed for the murder of Joseph Burling. Burling was the Bursar of All Souls, and the last surviving Fellow who witnessed the fire of 1799. Hughes claimed it was self defence, that Burling had tried to kill him and his son...the court was unconvinced. No one believed a drunken, penniless, itinerant labourer would be threatened by an esteemed and wealthy academic. The son was acquitted, but his father went to the gallows.

"I mention this because the physical description given of Peter Hughes matches that of Daniel Woodcock. I firmly believe they were one and the same person. And that the last Fellow of All Souls College who witnessed the Divine Judgement almost succeeded in his goal – of killing the son of Charles Harvey."

"Where was this, exactly?" Andy's mouth was dry.

"Quite a way from Cambridge." That strange, appraising look was back in the vicar's eyes.

"A small market town in Oxfordshire called Wallingford. I believe they have a yearly folk festival...some interesting carvings for sale..."

Jennifer Callaby slammed the door shut. She heard disapproving words from downstairs and closed her eyes.

She resisted the temptation to throw herself on the small single bed and bury her head in the pillows. For God's sake, she felt like she was a teenager back at home again rather than a thirty year old woman! Nothing had changed.

How did it come to this? How can the clock be turned back so quickly? She knew the answer, but didn't want to admit it to herself.

I have to: she told the shaking reflection in the dresser mirror. She didn't recognise herself. Her eyes were red-rimmed and sunken, her cheeks hollow and her skin flushed. She ran a shaking hand through her cropped red hair and wrinkled her nose. Needs a wash, she thought absently. *When did I clean it last?*

She had caught sight of the phone number on the caller display, just before mum put the phone down. It had been a Cambridge number. Andy had come after her.

She didn't know how to feel at first. She had told him not to come, to leave her for a while. But on the drive up to St Neots, as the parent's home got closer, she'd had time to think about the events.

She knew she hadn't overreacted. She'd gone up to the attic to bring down her suitcases and that's when she found it. The shotgun. At least, she thought it was a shotgun. It looked like some monstrous, futuristic cannon.

After the initial shock her first thought had been *Pearce*. The SIA licence Andy held would never be renewed by legal means, not with his record. Only someone like Graham Pearce could pull strings like that.

And he'd wanted a favour in return. A temporary home for the weapon. It was the final straw. She had climbed down the stepladder with shaking legs, eyes brimming with tears to their room where she hurriedly packed and then to the sitting room, where she wrote out her letter to him.

How could you, Andy?

Of course he couldn't tell her. She couldn't blame him for trying to keep his past under wraps. For trying to protect her from the dangerous parts of his life that would not let him go. Perhaps if she'd hidden his present on top of the wardrobe, and she'd never seen the gun it might have been different.

What he'd done last night was no different to what he'd done fifteen years ago. He'd gone too far again. Could she live with that?

She'd asked herself that as she came into St Neots. She still didn't have the answer. She remembered her mother's words, her warning when she told them she was moving in with him.

That's not just suppressed anger in him, that's rage. It isn't normal. Mark my words, Jenny, he's a walking time bomb. And you'll be caught in the fallout.

God knew, the relationship had been hard recently. Something had been bothering him: he was even more edgy than normal but he wouldn't open up to her. The strong, silent type taken to the extreme. And it wasn't just the favour he had done for Pearce.

Only at night did he reveal his demons. When he was asleep he tossed and turned in their bed, punching the walls as he dreamt.

That was terrifying. There was a rage in him that was trying to escape its prison. His beautiful green eyes with flecks of gold in the irises gave no hint of the turmoil beneath. It was a rage he had hidden well, but couldn't suppress indefinitely. It had to break free sometime. And it had done last night.

She knew she still loved him, had done ever since she served him a veggie burger at the Wallingford Bunkfest three years ago. She couldn't deny that it was a physical attraction at first: the hard muscled body and shaven head of the man running the security had woken something in her, something she thought had died after the divorce with Mike. His support was strong and silent, few words spoken, just the comforting presence of him and knowing he was there. That was priceless, especially after her burger van business went to the wall.

Money had been tight the last few months, but they'd managed. Andy had been angry that he didn't get the head doorman position at The Porterhouse, but extra shifts brought the pennies in when the agency couldn't find her any catering work.

She wondered if he'd opened his present yet. No, he always insisted they open their gifts together – after the Christmas roll about on the carpet, of course…she smiled sadly.

Perhaps there is a chance. But I need time first. And going to her parents was a bad idea. The minute she'd dropped her suitcase in the hall her mother had looked at her with a supercilious smirk, an 'I told you so' look in her eyes.

That look soon disappeared. After an hour's sleep and then hearing her mother launch into a lengthy diatribe against Andy, while her father buried himself in the Radio Times, she picked up the telephone and began phoning the local employment agencies, looking for work. She plugged her laptop in and emailed her CV to one firm that was looking for workers to help out at some college celebration tomorrow night.

Can't sit on my arse watching DVDs and stuffing myself with sausage rolls, mum. I've always been a worker, you know that.

At least wait until after Christmas!

Christmas is five days away, mother. I'm not going to sit here and listen to you slag off my boyfriend.

Ex-boyfriend, Jenny. You're not going back to him.

Mum! Just piss off!

There was a knocking at the door. She wasn't given time to answer before it opened and her mum stuck her head in. The smell of baked mince pies came in with her.

"Jenny?" There was no hint of concern on her hard, pinched features. Just tight-lipped annoyance at her daughter's petulance.

"Go away, mother." *Mum! Just piss off!*

"No, I will not go away. You'll listen to me when you're under my roof. There's something you need to know – "

"I know you had no right to put the phone down on Andy." She folded her arms tightly across her breasts.

"Jenny. It's for your own good. I'm proud of you for leaving that animal – "

"He's no fucking animal!"

Her mother managed to tighten her lips further. She took a step forward.

"You know he killed two people."

"Yes, mother. And I know why. Anyone would have done the same." *Would they?*

"History's repeating itself, Jenny. That young man he put in hospital last night? I've just heard on the news. He's dead. The police went to your home to arrest him. It won't be long before they come here, asking questions."

Jennifer Callaby didn't need to look in the mirror to know that her cheeks were no longer flushed. She could feel the blood draining from her face, felt a chill running through her entire body.

Now everything had changed.

SEVENTEEN

Philip Lotson tightened his scarf and stared at the tower block he was expecting to meet Freeland in. He tried not to listen to the fading sound of the Rover's engine, Nick staring bleary eyed from the sleep he'd had on the journey down to Peckham. Kelly wasn't going far, just to drive around until she found somewhere civilised to park.

She promised him she wouldn't be too far away. *The first sign of trouble, call me – I'll be there in a shot!* He'd laughed at that, trying to suppress his own fear. Of what Andy Hughes was bringing on them…and what was waiting for him here in Fellows Court.

Phil shook his head in wonder. Crazy, it sounded like a complex of luxury flats for the wealthy retired. It was the complete opposite. The courtyard was empty, not a soul around. Too cold even for the junkies and pushers, and for that he was grateful. The roller shutter doors on the garages were scrawled in obscene graffiti, some totally illegible, others written in such strange handwriting that it was a different language. A solitary football, half deflated, lay on the walkway leading to the courtyard. He kicked it half-heartedly, watched it limp into a pair of broken Grolsch bottles.

The lobby was as empty as the courtyard, only here the graffiti was more noticeable, in something approaching English. The smell was stronger as well, stale urine and old excrement mingling with the scent of damp, rotting plasterwork. The lift doors were battered and dented, the visible signs of three decades of drunken abuse, poverty-fuelled fury and alienation vented via booted feet on metal. He didn't even bother to see if it was working. He took the stairs.

He made his way slowly up the concrete steps, thankful that at least the lights were working. By the time he had reached the twelfth floor he had worked up a sweat that chilled rapidly in the cold air. A piss-stained mattress greeted him, the brown smears on the fabric looking like a skeletal grin. He thought back to this morning's dream with the ferryman and shuddered.

The flimsy doorways to the flats drifted past him. He looked at the left hand wall for the odd numbers. Eighty-seven, eighty-nine, ninety-one…

Ninety-three. This was it. No doorbell, no knockers like the boar head on the Master's Lodge. *My God, from All Souls to this. Two different worlds…two different nightmares.* He wondered if the naming of the block was an irony Freeland appreciated.

He rapped his knuckles three times on the thin, cheaply varnished door. There was a stirring sound from within, the sigh of an old armchair releasing its occupant, soft treads of worn slippers shuffling over carpet to the door.

Phil heard the sound of a security chain disengaging then a deadbolt being released. Useless security methods to safeguard a door that could be kicked down faster than picking the lock, put there to give some peace of mind. Something better than nothing.

The door swung open invitingly. No hesitation. Freeland knew it was him.

The face at the door was pale and gaunt. Thick black rings circled watery, bloodshot eyes that hadn't seen a single night's undisturbed sleep for a long time. The drooping face was supported – if that was the word – on slumped shoulders that were once broad and powerful, a rower's shoulders. His grimy blue shirt spilled out of his frayed brown corduroy trousers. A hand was extended in greeting. The voice was rich and cultured, but there was an underlying accent, a hint of Estuary that he made no attempt to hide or emphasise. Proud of his roots but not wallowing in them.

"You're earlier than I expected, Mr Lotson," Freeland said with a weak smile. "But you're very welcome."

The tiny flat reflected the dilapidation of its occupant. Once, the rooms would have been bright and new, the epitome of sixties modernity and a triumph of urban planning. Now, like the rest of the flats in the rotting tower block, it was a grim affair of peeling wallpaper: damp, cold and reeking of decay.

A threadbare Satsuma coloured carpet cowered from the skirting boards. The man sat in the brown leather armchair in the centre seemed to be doing the same.

Around him were chipped pine bookcases stuffed with various academic works that sat incongruously with the creased and bent spines of Catherine Cookson paperbacks. In the far corner stood a s black ash computer desk, stained with coffee mug rings, with an old CRT monitor. There was a humming sound from the PC.

Phil stared at the small photo Blu-tacked on the side of the monitor. A smiling woman in her fifties hugged a handsome young man in ceremonial academic robes. His hair was long and unkempt, threatening to dislodge his mortar board. One hand proudly brandished a scroll of paper, the other lovingly draped around the old woman's shoulders.

Phil recognised the setting straight away. The grounds of the Senate House in Cambridge. The date printed on the base of the frame gave the year 1969. James Freeland must have been eighteen or so then, a confident, talented young man just starting on his academic career. A world away from the broken, ancient looking man sat opposite him. Professor James Freeland sighed as he saw the object of Phil's attention.

"She told me that was the proudest moment of her life. Her only son graduating from Cambridge…and how proud Dad would've been as well."

Phil looked away from the photo and stared at his feet, remembering the pride his own parents had felt and shown when he graduated. Freeland smiled wistfully.

"He died when I was three. Accident on the docks. I hardly knew him, but I remember how long it took Mum to get over the loss…and how she struggled to bring me up. Working all hours in the laundry, a few extra notes earned here and there working the bar in the working men's club. Not enough to pay the mortgage though. Hence this flat being her last home…and it broke her heart."

He'd moved to a small drinks cabinet to the left of the PC. He lowered the drawer and took out a small bottle of cheap dry sherry.

"She grew old before her time, Mr Lotson. It was only when I got my undergraduate place in Cambridge that she…grew young again. Every time I came home for the holidays she beamed so much I thought her cheeks would crack. Especially Christmas. She loved this time of year. " He took out two tiny glasses and filled them to the brim. He passed one to Phil. "She was so proud of me – but was more pleased that I was happy in what I was doing. That I'd found my calling. Not many dockers' sons went to Oxbridge at that time, Mr Lotson. Certainly none from the inner city pit they had a cheek to call my school. And when I graduated, told her I'd won a scholarship to work for a doctorate…she was over the moon. 'Make your mark on the world, Jimmy!'

"The only thing that would have made her happier was to see me married. She often asked me why I hadn't found the 'right one' yet." He smiled ruefully. "And then she said 'I don't care if you're one of them homosexualists, Jimmy. Just as long as yer '*happy*.' The smile vanished, and Freeland stared into the sherry glass.

"It was only when I came back here last year, when I told her what my duties as a Fellow of All Souls consisted of…why none of the Fellows are married. She knew then." Freeland indicated the leather armchair. Phil sat in it, or rather fell. The springs had gone long ago. Freeland pulled up the swivel chair from the PC desk.

"I would say Merry Christmas, but…well, I don't see much point in keeping it any longer. This will be the first one without her, so…"

"Jason Franklin told me she'd…passed away. I'm sorry, Professor. How did she die?"

Freeland smiled thinly. "He didn't tell you?"

Phil shook his head.

"Little shit." He drained the sherry, swallowed and winced. "On her way back from church in September she was attacked and killed. After learning what I've done during my time at All Souls she got religion pretty damn quick. Felt my soul needed as much prayer as she could give it. Maybe she's right…but prayer won't wash away my sins."

He reached for the bottle and poured another measure. "It didn't stay in the headlines for long – killings around here are so commonplace that no one bats an eyelid over the murder of a defenceless old woman anymore. But…"

He choked back a sob. His voice cracked.

"…on the steps of the church itself. Mr Lotson, it was like a butcher's shop. And…and oh, so familiar…"

Phil frowned, but remained silent.

"They haven't caught the murderer, and they never will. I am responsible for my mother's death, Mr Lotson. No one else but me. I ran away from All Souls, to forget what I've seen, *what I've done.* And she died because of it.

"They killed her to show they can reach me, with impunity, any time they want. They could've killed me, left her out of the equation. But this is how they operate. To punish me for abandoning the Fellowship, killing me isn't enough. They prefer to destroy your spirit, your reason for living, to leave you in the pits of despair and self-hatred. They learned too much from *Her*." His voice was a snarl, and Phil almost physically recoiled from the hatred now unleashed.

"I want to die, Mr Lotson. Seeking a kind of redemption? Absolution for my sins? Maybe I am. These are evil people, Mr Lotson. And to think I believed them, trusted them…" Tears ran down his cheeks, tears of anger as well as self-pity. He sniffed loudly. "On the third day after it happened, it came home to me. I knew then. Not just how wrong I'd been, but how wrong they were – because this was an act of desperation as well as evil. They think it will shut me up, that if I talk I'll be branded as loopy as Jason Franklin. 'Poor fucker, lost his mum to a junkie's blade…now look at the paranoid shit he's coming out with.'" He wiped his nose on the sleeve of his shirt. "They can pull strings, Mr Lotson. Get me sectioned…put me in the same unit as young Jason. And then they can take their time over me."

Phil remained silent, waiting for Freeland's outburst to finish, waiting for the room to stop spinning, waiting for the similarity to his interview with Jason Franklin to fade.

"One thing before I tell you what is happening at All Souls, Mr Lotson. That everything Jason Franklin told you is true. Are you ready to die?"

Phil was on his feet, the sherry spilling down his trouser leg. *"What?"*

Freeland wiped the tears from his eyes. "A new development. The minute I saw this, I almost hoped you wouldn't come." He turned to the PC and moved the mouse. The screensaver disappeared, to be replaced by a webpage.

"BBC news website," Freeland said quietly. "Did you wonder why the traffic on the A14 was so bad tonight? There's your answer."

The picture was a twisted nightmare. What looked like a Ford Focus enveloped within the gaping maw of an articulated truck's engine housing. The heat from the fire had been intense. The metal on both vehicles was twisted, black and smouldering, the barrier the Focus had crashed through curling and enveloping them both like some mechanical python. Thankfully, he couldn't make out any human remains.

"The driver of the Ford was a woman called Judith Cox," Freeland said with a tremor. "She was on her way to see me…and she was killed before she had a chance to see what's brought you here now."

"An accident," Phil said in a low voice. He was aware of the sherry soaking through his trouser leg now, and considered asking Freeland for a top up. "A terrible tragedy, but with the road conditions, these things happen – "

"No," Freeland said emphatically. "No accident. Murder. But no way to prove it. The Accident Investigators will reveal that the vehicle was in a poor state of repair – faulty brakes, leaking steering fluid – and the driver had a history of mental health problems, was coming off her medication too rapidly…"

"You know all this? How?"

"I just know." Freeland stared unblinkingly into Phil's eyes. And for a moment, when he looked beyond the moistness of tears shed from the reddened eyes, Phil Lotson had the unsettling sensation that he was back in the Phoenix Unit under the mocking scrutiny of Jason Franklin. He blinked, shook his head, and the sensation passed – but only when Freeland looked away.

"This is why I know they're getting desperate. Innocent people died on that road, purely to prevent one woman getting here and discovering the truth."

"And yet I made it here. Alive." *God, but for how long?*

"Yes." Freeland nodded stiffly. "Alive. That's why there's hope. But I have to tell you now: once you have this information, this proof, you are going to be in terrible danger. You can walk away if you wish, I wouldn't blame you. I know you're a family man," he added wistfully.

"Why me? Why can't you deliver this…this evidence? Why are you relying on an outsider? *And more importantly, why the hell did you sit on it for so long?*"

"I've been silent for too long, I accept that. A part of me still believed that what they are doing is right, is just…is *necessary*. And…God forgive me, Mr Lotson, I was wallowing in self-pity, self-hatred. Thinking of my loss and how it paled into nothingness compared to those families whose bereavements and suffering I helped to cause. I'm an Eastender, someone who's proud of their roots…but, no macho bollocks, no illusions. I'm a weak man and I know it. And I hate myself for it. Fuckin' mummy's boy…"

Phil looked away, back to the webpage. The tarmac had melted in certain places, reformed around pieces of metal into twisted, horrifying shapes that resembled outstretched human arms, clawing the road in agony.

"And that changed tonight, when she phoned me." The Estuary accent retreated. Self control was resumed. "In one phone call I learned about the strength and courage of one woman, and it put me to shame. What she saw tonight was a very personal thing, an event she'd tried to keep hidden – even from herself. She saw a vision of herself, undergoing a shattering and agonising miscarriage, years ago."

Phil turned back to Freeland. "A flashback?"

"No, not a flashback. She saw herself, her *younger* self, carried through the grounds of All Souls College – in the third person, you might say. She saw her younger self go through the miscarriage all over again."

Phil didn't say anything.

"She thought she was going mad, she didn't suspect that an outside force was responsible for showing her this. I had to talk to her, to tell her what was going on. But then, as you spoke to Jason Franklin earlier, you know why this happened."

"I know why he *thinks* it happened."

Freeland narrowed his eyes. He closed them, took a deep breath and then opened them again.

"Okay. Let's back track a little. What exactly did he tell you inside Phoenix?"

"He told me about the whispers, the voices he heard at night. The dreams of going back in time…and his relationship with someone he calls The Elder."

"The Elder. Yes. And he told you why he tried to burn the college buildings down?"

"To free the trapped souls he was convinced had been imprisoned…that fire could not only cleanse and purge the evil, it could force it to release the ones it had… enthralled, was the rather melodramatic word he used."

Freeland smiled grimly. "Enthralled souls…All Souls. Melodramatic, but also ironic."

"He's convinced that his 'task' must be completed before December the twenty first ends…before the final stage of the Founder's Feast. And he said I'd beg to help him." That still made him shudder, the gleeful way Jason Franklin had said it. As though he knew Phil was going to suffer, would be on his knees in agony before starting to beg. *But who is it that'll force me? Is it Franklin…or Andy Hughes?*

Freeland reached over and took Phil's empty glass. He refilled it and passed it back before continuing.

"Mr Lotson, last year I was relieved that young Franklin was stopped. Now I wish he'd succeeded."

Phil frowned and sipped the sherry thoughtfully. *My God, it's as bad as that. Freeland wants other people's lives put at risk…*

But then, Freeland believed that members of the college were responsible for the murder of his mother. *Not some junkie smack-head in one of the least salubrious parts of London, no that was too far-fetched. Had to be the members of a Cambridge college, didn't it?* Jason Franklin's paranoia was contagious.

And yet…Jason he could understand to a point. The head porter's son had been tormented by inner demons since childhood, fair asylum fodder. James Freeland, on the other hand, was a respected academic with a PhD in anthropology and a string of academic books to his name. And he'd seemed such a well-balanced individual, according to all the accounts Phil had heard.

Guess this is what happens if you keep too-open a mind. Get too immersed in your work, let reality slip by… Phil swallowed thickly. The sherry tasted extra sour. He had the horrible feeling he was sharing a room and a conversation with his future self.

"Professor Freeland – "

"James, please."

"James – I want you to know that I'm very sceptical about Franklin's claims. It's just too fantastical, and…"

Freeland nodded. "Of course. No one can really believe, or understand. It wasn't until I took part in the ritual, consumed the flesh of the boar, that I truly believed."

Phil blinked.

"All will be clear when you read the files. Jason Franklin didn't lie to you." He indicated the large storage box underneath the PC desk. "Everything you need is in here." He eyed it with a shamed expression. "The proof Jason promised you…the guilt of the Fellows of All Souls. My guilt, my shame…the cross I bear." his voice trailed off.

Phil stared at it. It was a standard archive storage box, a foot long, in cardboard with a fake wood grain effect.

"It's heavy, about twenty kilos," Freeland said with a shudder. "A lot of history in there. A lot of suffering. Most of it was compiled by Jason Franklin."

Phil shook his head. Now he was being offered proof…and he wasn't sure he wanted it any more. But he'd come this far, he had to know…

"To fully understand it, you'll need some historical context. Your specialist period is the Early Modern period, is it not? Specifically, England in the seventeenth century…so I'm guessing you don't have much expertise in pre-medieval history."

Phil shook his head.

"Thought not." Freeland sighed and pointed to the hardback books on the shelf. "Most of those I've written. I've made a name for myself in the field of pre-Christian beliefs and societies. And it was the Celtic world that fascinated me the most. My books were serious works, focussing on the legacy the Celtic tradition left to the world, rather than the New Age self-help rubbish…" he laughed mirthlessly. "Ironic really. Even I had no idea of the true legacy left to us. But I must have come close, because it was my last book that attracted the attention of the Fellows of All Souls.

"An exploration of human sacrifice. An attempt to link the phenomenon from different societies, all over the world: to try to ask the question why humans create gods that demand killing."

"I remember it well, Professor. *Fear and Gods*…the title taken from the *Satyricon* by Petronius. 'It was fear that first brought Gods into the world.'"

"Very good, Mr Lotson. Not a very successful work, nothing new on the subject…or so I thought. But it was my section on Andraste and the Iceni that caught their attention."

"Boudicca's goddess, if I recall," Phil vaguely remembered the book. Again, he'd been too busy with his own research when *Fear and Gods* had come out. "Called upon to help defeat the Romans at Colchester."

"Yes," Freeland nodded grimly. "And the violence of her uprising is well recorded. She delighted in the savage killing of her defeated prisoners…because Andraste demanded it."

"I thought it was because the Romans raped her and her daughters? A personal violation as well as a smack in the face of the ruling power of the Iceni?"

"Yes, Boudicca knew this could not go unavenged…but it also had to be successful. The odds were stacked against her: despite the popular support she had it would not be enough. She needed help from beyond the world of men.

"You won't find much detail of Andraste in studies of Celtic mythology, because very little is known about her. To some historians she was similar to the goddess Badbh, or The Morrigan, the 'Phantom Queen' of battle who delighted in death and mutilation. Hence her appellation as a goddess of victory. But that's where the similarity ends." Freeland's face was grim. "What Boudicca invoked on the woods of Durolipons – the old, Roman name for what was to become Grantabridge, then Cambridge – was far more ferocious, more deadly than she could have expected. Andraste accompanied her, helped her destroy Colchester and Londinium…but Boudicca was defeated at Watling Street by the Roman Governor, Seuetonius Paulinus.

"Seventy thousand Britons lay dead for the loss of only four hundred Romans. Why was that, do you think?"

"That part's well known," Phil said. "She had a large following, but a lack of manoeuvrability and open field tactics… against the most ruthless, disciplined fighting machine the ancient world had ever seen. It was only a matter of time before the revolt was crushed."

"But she had Andraste on her side. *Why did she not help Boudicca at Watling Street?* It is rumoured that Andraste went back to the woods in Durolipons. What happened after that is anyone's guess – but it is certain she wasn't at the battle. Andraste lied to Boudicca, promised her a victory she had no hope of achieving…just as she lied to everyone who followed."

Phil took a breath. "What are you saying, professor? And what does this have to do with what's going on at All Souls?"

"Understand this, Mr Lotson. The Celts understood the world they lived in, far better than we do now. They had their own morality which we may consider barbaric – but they recognised that everything has a price. Human survival included…and that cost could sometimes only be paid in blood and pain. Their priests understood this better than anyone. The druids beseeched Boudicca not to invoke Andraste, because they knew the cost would be too great for humanity to bear. They knew that once she'd tasted blood on human soil…she would always hunger for it. She would return, unless appeased. Boudicca's invocation allowed her to secure a foothold on this plane, and she's had to be appeased ever since."

Phil stared at the archive storage box. He was where this was going.

"The ritual of appeasement has not changed, Mr Lotson. A man and a woman, every Midwinter's Eve…taken apart to sing to Andraste, to feed her and water her. Only this prevents her breaking through."

Phil was speechless.

"Destroyed in the Nemeton, upon which the chapel has been built. Twice-holy ground, Mr Lotson. Twice-defiled."

"You're joking." Now he remembered what the Master had told him about the college in the ancient woods surrounding what was now All Souls. The name given to it before the present college was founded. Nemeton.

"I wish I was. I wish I'd never written that section of the book, because that was when All Souls came to me. An Honorary Fellowship offered to me after I attended the Foundation Feast. To become a part of the oldest college in Cambridge, and entrusted with the task of writing its history."

Phil looked up.

"That's what they offered. But they had no intention of their history ever being recorded. Like the ancient druids, their history is an oral one, passed down from one college member to another, never to be shared with outsiders. Quite *literally* oral – once I had consumed the flesh of the boar...the secrets were made known to me. And I was trapped."

"Consumed the boar?" Phil stared hard at Freeland. "I don't understand. How can eating boar meat give you knowledge?"

"The wild boar was a very important animal to the old religions. To the Celts, it linked this world to the Otherworld...as well as its symbolism in war, the flesh of certain boar was considered magical. Food of the Gods, if you will." The professor's eyes were filled with self-loathing, and they moved back to the archive box.

"Supernatural beasts that could be hunted, but never caught. A common theme in ancient sagas. They disappeared into the Otherworld, and would only return when the time was right. For the beasts in All Souls, the time is around the winter solstice. That's when the Children of Andraste will make themselves known. When one will offer itself to be consumed...and its siblings guard the forest."

Phil thought back to the NO ENTRY sign on the West Gate of All Souls. Then he remembered the Master's reference to the boar and the Founding of the college.

On the day the foundation stone of All Souls was laid - the twenty-first of December, 1264 - a single boar was seen running through the woods. The first seen for hundreds of years. It was hunted, killed and eaten at the feast to mark the founding, and its remains buried in a patch of ground that was to become Old Court.

"Bloody hell," he whispered.

"Hell, indeed. I - I don't want you to read through these files here, Mr Lotson. Please take them away with you."

Phil's glare returned. "Why? Will I be so furious, so disgusted, that I'll physically attack you?"

"Maybe, maybe not...but I don't want to see the hatred and disgust in another's eyes anymore. I see enough of that when I look in the mirror each morning.

"Please understand me when I say that when I took part in these atrocities I really believed they were necessary. The rest of the Council...they still believe. That's why it still goes on. They had their doubts, but they listened to their predecessors, and learned to accept their duty."

"But *you* woke up!" Phil shouted. "You knew something was wrong, why don't the others? What changed your mind?"

"Jason Franklin...and The Elder. The Master may have told you that I left due to ill health, on the verge of mental collapse, and that much is true. If I'd stayed, participated in another of those...abominations, it would have destroyed me. What Jason told me, showed me in his artwork...that sealed it for me.

"Remember what I said about everything having a price – a price that includes blood, pain and suffering? This is where The Elder comes in. It's not just Andraste that demands sacrifice...The Elder is the only one who can stop her. But he requires blood also."

Phil's head was spinning. "No good guys or bad guys, then? If each needs human life, what's the bloody point of it all?"

"The Elder is different. He is a primal, terrible force of inhuman power, but he isn't evil. The sacrifice he demands is a willing one, to counter the unwilling sacrifices made to Andraste. I believe his role is one of guardianship rather than destruction.

"Jason Franklin was chosen to perform The Elder's task...not because of his unusual talent, but because he's closely related to one of the Fellows. Being the child – or descendant - of Andraste's followers gives you a certain power. A power that can vanquish her for good...if the bearer of that power lays down his life. Make no mistake: Jason Franklin was willing to die that night. If he seems disturbed to you, it's because that power has driven him mad."

"The son of Andraste's follower...but is the head porter part of the Council?"

Freeland closed his eyes. "Jason is not the son of the head porter."

"So who is he? And why has Franklin been made out to be his father?"

"Jason doesn't know. I suspect he's the son of one of the Council. One of the Fellows had a fling with a woman, wasn't careful...so when the child was born its death was faked and given to a trusted servant of All Souls to raise as his own.

"One of the conditions of joining the Fellowship is to remain unmarried, and more importantly *childless.* They believe, just as the druids believed, that having children weakens your devotion to your duty...takes some of your strength away."

"Makes you more human!" Phil spat, thinking of his own child, how he would die before anyone laid a finger on his head.

Freeland shrank. "The devotion to Andraste has to be total...if that weakens, *her* power weakens. Jason is proof of that. A child of a follower...becomes a threat."

"So how come it's taken so long for The Elder to find someone to stop the killings? Why did he only come close this year?"

"No, he came close quite a few times...the closest being the year 1799 when the Master of All Souls himself, Charles Harvey, converted to The Elder. That was when the meteor struck, setting fire to many of the college buildings."

"The Divine Judgment – another weapon of The Elder?"

"Maybe...but it wasn't enough. Charles Harvey tried to kill himself by throwing himself into the fire. He saw it as a sign that he had finally switched to the path of righteousness. I'd like to say he died contented, but the rest of the Council pulled him from the flames. To them, the meteor strike was proof of Andraste's anger – a punishment for their election of someone who converted to her enemy. So they made sure his suffering was terrible enough to appease her anger. That is why Searles is so afraid and unable to confide in those around him. He knows he weakened once last year – the propitiation was not completed in line with the full instruction last year, and the Fellows will not hesitate to revisit Harvey's fate upon him if he fails again."

"Jesus Christ," Phil whispered.

Freeland looked tired. "Christ can't help you. Read through the files, Mr Lotson. They'll give you the full details."

Phil leant over and pulled the archive storage box towards him. It was heavy. He rested a shaking hand on the lid.

"Details. I suppose the full extent of the ritual is described in here as well."

Freeland cringed, his once-powerful shoulders hunching inwards.

Phil took that as a yes. He tapped the lid. "If what I have here is proof that the Fellows of All Souls are engaged upon some act of systematic murder you'll have to face the music with the rest of them, give evidence at the trial…stand trial yourself." His eyes were cold.

Freeland didn't take his eyes off the floor. "I'll take that chance," he said in a hollow, far away voice.

Then it hit Phil. "My God. You don't expect it to get that far, do you? You…you think you'll die before it all comes to light?"

And now Freeland's eyes left the carpet, meeting Phil's with no hesitation. They were clear, calm and self-possessed.

"Mr Lotson, I don't know what the final outcome will be, but…I know I'll be dead before it happens." He raised himself from the sagging chair. His shoulders weren't so rounded anymore. He stood taller, straighter, a man who had made a decision…and been relieved of a terrible burden.

"You're a good man, Mr Lotson. You have a good heart and a strong mind… and you have family. I know you will do the right thing." Freeland's smile was a sad farewell.

"Professor…James. I really don't know what to say."

Freeland shook his hand. "Then don't say anything. Goodbye, Mr Lotson."

James Freeland felt the door close behind Lotson rather than hear it. He was alone again.

But…not really alone. Not for long, anyway. He picked up the framed photo of his graduation ceremony and tried to reconcile the smiling, jubilant young man with the broken, jaded and tainted old man he was now. He couldn't do it. The face staring back at him wasn't just from another life, it was from another world. But the face of his mother…now that was eternal.

He replaced the photo with a heavy sigh of contentment. It was over for him now. Philip Lotson carried his burden. The moment he saw the photos, he'd know.

And that would be when the danger would start for the Lotson family. Freeland regretted that, but there was no other way.

He walked to the window and pulled aside the curtain. Below, in the halogen lit courtyard the blue Rover Lotson climbed into looked like a toy. It all looked surreal, he mused. The slightly overweight figure, struggling into a toy car with proof of an evil thousands of years old and so cunning that it had deceived countless generations of good and intelligent men and made them into monsters, hardly looked like a sacred messenger. But who was he to question?

He shook his head as he inspected the window frame. Amazing. The Council should have replaced these frames years ago with ones that were impossible to open fully. How many suicides had there been in this area because of that?

Will one more make any difference? Will it change matters? Of course not, but that's not important now.

He felt a surge of guilt as he placed one slippered foot on the ledge. Cowardice. Surely he was obliged to stay and see how the matter ended? Small recompense for his crimes: but a gesture nonetheless. The blue Rover drove out of the pool of light and into the darkness. Freeland waited until the sound of its engine faded before swinging his other leg onto the ledge.

Because at the end of the day it was all about choice. He hadn't told Lotson that The Elder had chosen another to assist Jason. That *other* may well believe, but that didn't mean he would be strong enough to perform what was necessary. Far better to end it now, to take his chances with whatever judgment awaited him on the other side, than to remain and witness the full horror of Andraste's triumph.

The bitter wind whipped his trouser legs, the baggy corduroy material flapping like ship sails. He took a deep breath. The courtyard below him waited like a welcoming blanket.

"I hope you're stronger than I was…" the name he uttered after those words was snatched away by the wind. His grip loosened on the window frame.

The forecourt didn't rush at him with the speed of a bullet, as he'd expected. Rather it drifted slowly, leisurely up to him and allowed him to consider one more thing. The words his mother had said to him, growing up. It seemed cruel of his subconscious to remind him of it now – perhaps a final subliminal attempt to punish him.

Make your mark on the world, Jimmy!

The sodium vapour-lit concrete grew larger and Freeland smiled in anticipation. For a moment, he was sure the words were spoken now, whispered into his ear by his mother who eagerly awaited a reunion with her son. Or it may have been the wind again.

Make your mark on the world, son.

EIGHTEEN

In the Senior Combination Room David Searles looked steadily at the assembled Fellows. For once he felt calm and in control, with none of the fear or weakness usually associated with him in the eyes of the Council. They, on the other hand, all looked shaken. Pallid complexions and dark rings under their eyes. In spite of the liberal measures of port and brandy, very few of them would sleep well tonight. Or rather, this morning. The ornate wall clock told Searles it was half past midnight.

Fortunate indeed that the Senior Members of All Souls were obliged to maintain the ancient tradition of remaining single. No wives to make hurried excuses to, no children to reassure...

Apart from one. Searles dispelled the thought from his mind immediately. This was no time for weakness, for self-doubt. Andraste had commanded. They had to obey.

It was still an incredible sight for them all to behold. For the voice of Andraste to speak through the crucified…but that hadn't been the first time he'd witnessed it. He'd seen it last year. Just him and John Franklin, alone in the chapel. After the police had come and questioned all the members of the Council and dragged Jason away.

Dragged to safety. Andraste can't have him now.

That's what he'd thought when he left the SCR that night, to walk alone to the chapel. A sense of relief mingled with the shock of the evening's events. The taste of the boar flesh still in his mouth, rank and gamey. The liberal measures of brandy did nothing to take that away. He didn't know why he'd sought solace in the chapel. He had abandoned his Christianity years ago when he had Communed with Andraste, and saw the true nature of all things.

Now, he watched the Bursar drain his third brandy and narrowed his eyes. Simon Davies had been very disturbed recently, and it wasn't all due to the stress of his workload. His reaction to the animated Christ had been far more severe than theirs. Davies met his eyes and averted his gaze, and didn't see the Master's glare soften.

Yes, Bursar. I know what's shaken you. And I can't say I blame you. I remember all too well, when I saw it last year…

Staring at the physical image of Christ's Passion, he had felt a kindling in his soul. Perhaps God was trying to tell him something? He had stared into the agonised, despairing eyes, painted an impossible blue. A blue that seemed to glisten and shine, as though the eyes were welling up with tears.

And then John Franklin had entered, and sat down in the pew opposite, uninvited.

Does God weep, Franklin? Searles had asked, without taking his gaze from Christ's agonised, despairing eyes.

Not for us, Master. The tears shed are our own. Then it began.

The agonised expression of the crucified Christ turning to a mocking smile of triumph…the painted rivulets of blood trickling from the nail wounds becoming real, liquid rivers of crimson that dripped onto the floor and steamed in the cold night air…the burning eyes of the figure, blazing a hate filled accusation accompanied by harsh words spoken in that oh-so seductive female voice.

You are my Abraham. He is your Isaac. You have failed to give him unto me.

He had screamed then. Screamed and ran to the carving, beating it with his hands. He remembered the feeling of soft, emaciated flesh and hard bone beneath his feeble blows, and only Franklin had stopped him from trying to pull the crucifixion from its wall mountings.

You are my Abraham. He is your Isaac. You will give him unto me. Next year, Searles. I will have him then.

Even the head porter had looked shocked by the transformation from painted wood to animated, living, breathing flesh. The only time the Master had seen John Franklin scared. Searles often wondered what would have happened if Franklin hadn't had his hands full trying to restrain him. Would he have run in fear? Would he have broken down like he himself had done?

Searles would never know. The minute he had begun to compose himself the familiar cold, machine-like self control of the head porter had reasserted itself. As the blood faded from the floor and the heaving of the pierced torso slowed and froze to lifeless wood once more, Franklin sat silently in the pew, his eyes never leaving Searles.

He made it clear that this was Searles' fault. This was the result of disobeying Andraste. Franklin had exhaled noisily, an audible and visible sign of relief. And then explained that Andraste had been merciful. Had given them all –Searles in particular – a second chance.

But Searles had seen the visitation as a personal affront to him, Andraste mocking his once-cherished Catholicism. What was it Freeland had said? *She uses the things you hold so dear against you.*

Searles sipped his brandy, relishing the warmth burning down his throat. Now they had another problem. That man, Hughes – he'd obviously battled one of the Children of Andraste, and survived. He'd been sent to look for something, that much was obvious. He was a co-worker or friend of that Granta driver who was here yesterday, who was seen with the Selected in the bar. Perhaps he was looking for them.

At least Hughes hadn't made it into the cellars below the chapel. If the propitiation had been disrupted, Andraste's wrath would have been terrible to behold. And yet…as he watched Hughes run, pushing past Tom Ellis, through the porter's lodge and out onto Trinity Street he knew Hughes would be here again. Steps would have to be taken to prevent that. For that they would need Franklin.

Searles saw the door open behind him. Franklin entered, shaking fresh snow from his jacket. He nodded once to the Master and went to stand at the far corner of the room, next to the Senior Tutor. He saw Franklin whisper something into Nasen's ear. Nasen nodded slowly, and they both looked at the Master.

"Mr Franklin. I trust your trip was…successful?"

Franklin narrowed his eyes in response to Searles' dry words.

"Well enough, Master. Judith Cox has been dealt with."

"On the Senior Tutor's instruction," Searles snapped. "Not mine."

"There was no time - "

"Once again, I was not consulted!" Searles' eyes blazed as they swept the room. "I was not informed that the Bursar's secretary had a visitation …but I hold the Senior Tutor accountable for that. May I remind you, gentlemen, that you *all* have a duty to inform me of what is occurring. Twice now you have *all* failed to do so…I can only assume this Council is deliberately excluding me from matters relating to the increase of Andraste's power."

Hurried, guilty looks passed between the assembled Fellows. Franklin folded his arms tightly and glared at Searles.

"Nor is this the only thing that has been kept from me." Searles kept his voice calm, even. "It would appear the whisperings have no longer confined themselves to The Selected…*have they, Bursar?*'

Davies looked up in shock. His mouth gaped. He glanced angrily behind him. Nasen's face was impassive.

"Judith Cox told Franklin about your conversation earlier. That you have heard the whisperings also. A momentary weakness? No matter, others have heard it also.

No longer will we be able to pass this off as 'voices in the head' of the mentally disturbed, as we did with Jason Franklin and James Freeland."

"So Andraste's voice has grown more powerful, and is now heard by the Unselected. This is nothing to be overly concerned with, Master. It will cease when she has her offering." The Bursar straightened his tie with shaking fingers, his words an attempt to convince himself rather than the Master.

"Her power would not be as strong if she had been given the offering she demanded last year." Franklin's words cut like a knife.

The stunned silence in the SCR was a tangible, physical presence. Searles straightened and narrowed his eyes.

"You forget your place, Franklin."

"No Master, *you* forget *yours*." Franklin unfolded his arms and walked steadily towards the Master. His eyes remained fixed on Searles', neither Master nor servant looking away. A challenge.

"Jason should have been given last year, you know this. That is why Andraste mocks us. Her strength – and her anger - grows, Master, because the one she selected was not offered."

"You're wrong, Franklin." Searles forced himself to remain strong. To forget the exchange in the chapel last year.

You are my Abraham. He is your Isaac. You will give him unto me.

"Andraste has demanded another, and another will be given. That will secure her for another year, I am certain. We may not have time to fulfil the Communion with the third offering, but the soul will be enough.

"Andraste demanded something else, Franklin. You do not know because you were…occupied elsewhere." Disgust filled his words. The assembled members of the Council murmured amongst themselves, none of them able to forget what they'd seen and heard in the chapel this evening.

"Why is this man Hughes so alarming to her? Simple. The resemblance to Harvey is uncanny. Mr Franklin, I believe you told me earlier that fifteen years ago he looked vaguely similar, but now he is the same age as Harvey was when he succumbed to The Other there can be no doubt. He is walking, breathing proof that Woodcock's child survived. The blood of Harvey runs in his veins. And we know what Charles Harvey tried to do to All Souls."

Searles let that piece of information sink in. They suspected, they knew. Fifteen years ago, when Hughes had murdered those two men in the bar, it was not apparent. But that act had kept him away from All Souls, kept him from…

Fulfilling his destiny? Searles pondered. *Acting on the orders of The Other? And now he's here…and even Andraste is scared of him.*

Perhaps there was hope after all. But there was one other thing to tell them...

"You may not be aware that this Hughes character is friends with the writer Philip Lotson. Lotson is his former tutor." That caused a reaction. He saw their eyes narrow, faces grow hostile. *Because I invited him to an interview here without your approval.*

"Lotson went to see Jason Franklin this evening. How he managed that is immaterial. What is important is that he went to see James Freeland tonight. And Freeland killed himself less than an hour ago."

Stunned silence met his words. Only Franklin looked unsurprised by that. Searles leant back in the armchair, the green leather squeaking. He steepled his fingers and waited for the next member of the Council to speak.

"You're certain of this, Master?" Nasen said quietly.

"Beyond any doubt, Senior Tutor. I checked the London news just now. There have been unconfirmed reports of a suicide, a man who had jumped from a tower block. A tower block that Freeland lives – or rather, *lived* – in.

"Freeland knew Lotson was researching All Souls. He was in contact with Judith Cox but she never made her appointment. If Lotson spoke to Jason, Jason would have pointed him in Freeland's direction. And our erstwhile Council member would not have taken his own life had he not been confident that his message would be heard.

"We must therefore work on the assumption that Freeland had the proof he threatened to go public with. Franklin's attempt to ensure his silence by taking care of the man's mother last month has backfired spectacularly."

Franklin bristled, but he said nothing. Searles met his glare with a cold look.

"It would appear that you have all been listening to Franklin's advice a little too closely. A decision as drastic as the murder of Mrs Freeland and Ms Cox is one that should have been put to the Council...with the Master's presence. You forget that the Master of All Souls has the final decision. Was that the reason the decision was made without me? Did you feel that I would not have sanctioned what Franklin did?"

No answer but the shuffling of feet and down-turned faces, like guilty schoolboys caught murdering a school pet on the orders of an older boy. They glanced at Franklin, who at least had the good grace to look less smug and aggressive. Visibly surprised at Searles' newly found confidence.

"Would you have had the strength to order it, Master?" The Bursar asked quietly. "Or would you have weakened...*like you did last year?*"

Searles closed his eyes, and another memory of post-Feast drinks in the Senior Combination Room hit him. That was after his first Founders' Feast as Master and the discussion of what his true duties as Master were. It was years ago and yet it felt like only yesterday. He remembered how they had all looked coldly at him as he struggled to finish his portion of the boar flesh, the shared, silent exchanges that said *he hasn't the spirit to be Master of All Souls. His investiture is a big mistake.*

When he'd been instructed in the elaborate stages of the ritual his sanity had almost snapped. And yet they had seen it as weakness, ignored his protestations that what they were doing was contrary to every human feeling and value he held. They had done it for so long they had forgotten what it felt like for the first time.

And strangely, it was Franklin who had comforted him, Franklin who had put a strong, calming arm around his shuddering shoulders, guided his knife arm to where it had to go.

Although the head porter had never wielded the knives – not being a member of the Council he wasn't allowed to – he had been there at every ritual during his time at the college, guiding the previous Master's hand when it weakened. *It's okay to weaken, to have doubt. It proves you are human – and that's why we do this, why we* have *to do this. For the love of humanity.*

How strange to associate those words of comfort, understanding and empathy with a man who thought nothing of slicing an elderly woman to pieces on the steps of a London church, who thought nothing of sabotaging a car that would cause not just his intended victim's death but the deaths of others on the road.

Searles stared questioningly at the head porter. *What are you, Franklin? You talk of the love of humanity, and yet you enjoy the taking of life. Even - no, especially – when it seems unnecessary. What did you see at Goose Green and Tumbledown Mountain? What did you experience in the labyrinthine battlegrounds of the back streets of Belfast to make you this way? What did you have to do then, with automatic weapons and bayonets, to survive? What cost to your soul?*

Franklin stood straighter, an attempt to look taller and more imposing in the light of the Master's scrutiny. As if reading the thoughts running through Searles' mind, he said: "I think we should get back to the matter at hand. Time is running out, gentlemen. While we stand talking Lotson could be on his way to ruin everything. We can only rely on the loyalty of certain members of the police force. With your permission, Master."

Next time, Franklin, Searles decided. *Next time we'll discuss you. What makes you tick, what helps you help us to continue this terrible duty.*

"Franklin's right, Master," the Senior Tutor grunted. "Thank God someone remembers what we're here for."

Searles let that one go. "Well, Franklin, you seem to be the one with all the answers. What do you suggest?"

"Simple. And it'll resolve the problem of Hughes also."

Searles raised his eyebrows. "Interesting. In what way?"

Franklin turned to face the assembled Fellows with a smile of anticipation.

"Hughes had a relationship with Lotson's wife. Some time ago, but it was this that triggered his rampage fifteen years ago in the college bar. Some of you may well remember it…"

It was before Searles' time, but he had been informed. Lotson and his woman had been signed in as guests at the college bar. Two of All Souls' finest, rowers of the First VIII, proceeded to make improper advances on the woman Lotson was seeing. The woman who had recently ended her relationship with Hughes.

"Hughes saved her – I don't need to remind you *how*- but for some reason he held Lotson responsible. As the police dragged him out he was heard screaming that he'd kill Lotson for this…as if what he'd done to those two gentlemen wasn't enough."

Searles frowned. He could see where this was heading. "Rather tenuous, Franklin."

"Not at all, Master. Our friend Boyd has fed me some interesting information from his colleagues in the Thames Valley Police. Hughes was until last night employed as a bouncer for a nightclub in an Oxfordshire town. He did to a young man there what he did to Laws and Cartwright fifteen years ago. Someone pulled some strings, got him away."

"I'm sorry, I don't understand." Davies looked confused. "What has this to do with Freeland?"

"The gentleman in question died this morning. Andrew Hughes is looking at a murder charge. Detective Inspector Boyd asked me if I'd seen Hughes anywhere… needless to say, none of us have seen him." He smiled grimly at the Council.

"However, a man matching his physical description was seen leaving this college in…oh, say a few hours time? Seven a.m? Heading for Chesterton, to visit his former tutor. Who can say why?"

Relieved laughter from the Fellows. Even Searles smiled: a smile that was instantly wiped from his face with Franklin's next words.

"But Lotson must be dealt with, Master. If he has Freeland's proof, he will have read it by now. He doesn't drive, but his wife does. He will have read it on the car journey back, maybe out loud…"

Dear God, Searles thought. "Do they have children, Franklin?"

"One. A ten year old boy."

Searles shuddered. He then felt the gaze of the Council upon him, almost hear the thoughts they shared.

He's weakening once again. His advantage was slipping, and he was certain Franklin was smiling. Maybe at his weakness, maybe in anticipation of the killing. He made a decision, and then opened his eyes.

"Promise me one thing, Franklin."

"Master?"

"You make it quick, you make it painless. I want you to act with restraint, Franklin. Restraint you didn't see fit to utilise when you butchered Freeland's mother."

"Very well, Master." Franklin turned and left the SCR without a further word. Searles watched him step into the snow and couldn't help but feel a palpable sense of relief when the door closed. A sense of relief he suspected was shared by the other members of the Council – except Nasen.

"To other matters, gentlemen. The third offering has been named..."

"Hello Phil. How did you get on with Freeland?" Rob Benson crooked the handset between his shoulder and head to keep his joint-rolling hands free. After what they'd learned at the vicar's house, he needed one.

"I'd rather not say at the moment. Let's just say that...I've learned more than I wanted to learn."

Rob frowned as he held the Zippo to his spliff. Phil sounded nauseous, as though he was on the verge of throwing up. *Guess it's true after all, then. Jesus.*

"Well, we've learned a fair bit as well. That thing in my van? It came from All Souls." He exhaled green smoke. From the armchair across the room, Jasper raised an ear and sneezed.

"Wilkins reckons it's from the chapel when that bloody moon-rock hit it. Smashed right into the carving, stone fused with space rock, and it flew into Impington Com - "

"How's Andy?"

The interruption took Rob by surprise. "Okay, considering what he's been through. He's spark-o at the moment. God knows what he's dreaming about now."

"Rob. Freeland had proof...proof that everything Franklin said is true.

Rob gulped on the green smoke. "You're joking, right? Why don't you go to the Old Bill with it?"

"Kelly wants me to...I want to. But...Andy needs to see this first. Freeland insisted. And Freeland is now dead."

"Fucking *what?*"

"We've just heard on the radio. There's been an incident at the place I've just come back from. Someone's fallen from the twelfth floor. Suicide. It can only be Freeland."

"How far are you from home, Phil?"

"About half an hour."

"We're coming round." He prised himself free from the sofa and ran a shaking hand through his tousled hair. He climbed the stairs and knocked on the closed door.

"Andy? Wake up, man. Phil's on his way back."

No answer. He swallowed and twisted the doorknob.

"Jesus…"

Andy was sat on the edge of the bed, his arms wrapped tightly around his chest. He was shaking, pale and drenched in sweat.

"Andy?"

Andy glanced at him with glazed eyes. Then recognition filtered through. He took his hands from his sides and rubbed his face.

"Another bad dream?"

Andy nodded. He looked at Rob with bleary, bloodshot eyes. "What's happening?" he croaked.

"Phil just phoned. He's got Freeland's evidence…" Rob frowned. "He's shook up. Reckons Freeland killed himself just after they left."

Andy shivered and closed his eyes. Then he nodded slowly.

"Things are moving, then. Guess we should be as well." He reached down for his holdall and pulled out the bubble-wrapped firearm. Holding it in one hand he reached for his discarded sweatshirt. Rob's eyes widened.

"We taking that, as well?"

"We have to. Phil won't be safe now. And neither are we." He slapped Rob's shoulder and smiled grimly at his whitened face.

"Come on, Roberto. Let's go and exchange notes."

NINETEEN

Jason Franklin's visitors arrived at four a.m. Neither the driver of the refrigerated vehicle containing chilled meals for the patients nor his assistant had any idea of what awaited them beyond the locked door.

The two occupants of the Cambridge Catering Services delivery van had other things on their minds. Conrad 'Connie Boy' Teague, the forty-six year old driver, was eager to finish the run and get home early to hopefully catch his wife in bed with the security guard from the science park. An affair that had been whispered about among his drinking partners down the club for some time.

This way he'd have the perfect excuse to beat the guy to a pulp. Although he hadn't been in the boxing ring since his navy days, frequent fights with the rumourmongers down the social club proved that even twenty years later he'd not lost his touch. He was running to flab these days – hell, the early starts on this job never left much energy or time for the physical exercise he was used to, but there was solid muscle beneath the encroaching layers of fat. Muscle that made up in power and impact what it lacked in speed and grace. As Jim Simmons would find out later when Connie Boy burst through the door.

If I make it. Fancy giving me the spare vehicle today. This ancient bag of shit shouldn't even be on the road. Fuckin' management.

Paul Wright, on the other hand, looked like he just wanted to go back to bed and sleep off the rest of his hangover.

Looks like he's already started, Conrad thought sourly. Paul Wright had his feet planted on the dashboard, the white overall trousers creeping up above the calves of his skinny legs. His arms were folded tightly over his chest, and his head was twisted at an angle that Conrad would have thought made sleep impossible. His glasses were beginning to slide off his pointed nose, no doubt helped by the layer of grease. His mouth was wide open and snoring.

In spite of the fresh fall of snow that was already starting to freeze on the access road, Conrad braked harder than was necessary. The Luton swerved and Paul jerked forward, no seatbelt restraining him, and his head crashed onto his knee.

"Wakey, wakey." Conrad pulled the handbrake on and waited impatiently for his assistant to adjust his glasses.

"This is the Phoenix Unit. This is the one you don't take chances with."

Paul Wright nodded, slightly, not bothering to stifle a yawn. Conrad grimaced. *Bloody agency workers*, he snorted. *This little turd's already wiped out.*

"What time did you get to bed last night?"

Paul shrugged, yawned again and stuck a finger in his ear. "Dunno. Past midnight, I think. A lock-in at the White Swan."

Conrad shook his head in disgust. "So you've had less than four hours kip and you think you're fit to work, to drive a van?" he snorted angrily. This was an easy job if you could handle the early starts. 3.30 a.m. start times took getting used to, but you were usually finished by mid-morning. It had to be early because most of the cook-chill meals were perishable, to be consumed on the same date of delivery. Didn't look like this ex-student could handle it, though.

"Get the keys – and don't forget the temperature probe." *Like you did the last time.* More time added onto the run. *Bloody agency.*

Conrad Teague shivered at the sight of the Phoenix Unit. Ridiculous really, Jason Franklin was harmless now...so they said. Media hype, blown out of all proportion.

But he'd come across Franklin a few times and the kid creeped him out big time. Those weird green eyes: they always seemed to be looking through you, as though he was seeing to your very soul – or seeing something in its place...

He shook his head and stepped out of the van, leaving the engine running to keep the heater going. The fresh snowfall had frozen already. It crunched under his work boots like a spilled packet of crisps.

"Come on, Bamber!" he shouted to Paul. Paul shuffled behind him, head bowed, wincing at the cold. He raised his head and stared blearily at Conrad.

"Bamber? Who's Bamber?"

Conrad stared at him. His moustache bristled as he snorted in the fresh cold night air.

"Paul Gascoigne's dad. You got them keys?"

Paul nodded, wincing as his head moved too quickly. The clipboard with the temperature reading forms was held under his armpit, and the temperature probe's reader unit was stuffed in his rear pocket. Connie noted with annoyance that the probe itself dangled on its cable behind Paul like some sort of biomechanical tail.

"For Christ's sake, boy! That'll contaminate the readings!"

Paul twisted his head, and with a grunt of annoyance reached for the probe. In the light cast by the van's headlights he looked to Connie like some skeletal greyhound trying to scratch its arse.

Paul scowled as he pulled the cable and lifted the probe from the ground. Connie snatched the ward keys from off him, shoved them in his pocket and went to the rear of the van. He lowered the tail lift, pulled up the roller-shutter and dragged out the plastic crates containing the chilled meals for the Phoenix Unit. Fish pie and tinned tomatoes for tea tonight, he noted with a grimace as he stacked the trays on the dolly.

Paul pushed the stacked trays down the gritted slope, the castors on the dolly squeaking in protest. The temperature probe was balanced precariously on the topmost food container, threatening to drop off. Connie shook his head as he walked past the almost-comatose Paul.

He unlocked the Mortice lock then inserted the Chubb key. He swung the door open, stepped in and pressed the four digit code to deactivate the alarm. Then he hit the lights. The fluorescent strips stuttered into life.

He eyed the kitchen warily. Usually there were no problems: the inmates were fast asleep at this time, their meds wouldn't wear off until breakfast time when it was time for more. But Jason Franklin was different.

Always bright and alert. Whatever pills they were pumping him with, they didn't work. And sometimes he'd be in the kitchen, waiting to say hello. No threats, no violence…and that's what made him so scary.

Word got around. Sam Dawson had loosened his tongue in the social club a few weeks ago, about Franklin's 'unique' condition. Dawson was no bullshitter, and when he let on that even Longhurst was scared…well, that meant trouble was brewing. And today was the first anniversary of his attempt to burn down that college. He hoped Dawson and the Phoenix management were aware of this. Hoped they'd taken extra precautions…

He cocked an ear. No sounds from the hallway leading off to the kitchen.

Paul came to a halt, the castors on the stacked dolly screeching on the ramp. He glanced at the doorway, looking unimpressed.

"So this is where the famous Franklin's banged up."

"Banged up." Connie snorted. "That's the way they teach you to speak at Uni these days? Yeah, this is where he lives. This is the ward you don't take any chances with. Remember – he ain't the only dangerous one here."

"Woo." Paul smirked. "I'm bricking myself."

Connie had to resist the temptation to pick up the temperature probe and slam it in the smarmy little fucker's face.

"I ain't fucking around here, sunshine! Some of these nutters are smarter than they let on – and a hell of a lot more dangerous!" He slammed the door closed – and wished he hadn't. That could have woken someone up. "Just get them fuckin' trays in the fuckin' fridge."

"Yes'm boss," Paul saluted. He placed his hands on the stack and pushed it towards the refrigerator. He pushed too hard and the top tray flew off the stack. It hit the heavy steel door of the refrigerator and flipped over, scattering the sealed packages of food on the floor. The cellophane on two of the boxes split, and juice from the peeled tomatoes inside splattered on the floor. Paul grimaced at the red splatters on his overalls.

"You dozy, pissed up little *twat*!" Connie bellowed. "Pick 'em up, now!" Leaving the key bunch in the door, he turned, picked one of the packages – a six-portion pack of fish pie - from the crate and slammed it onto the drainer unit. He pierced the cellophane lid with the six inch steel point of the temperature probe and checked the temperature.

"Finished, Bamber? Right, stack 'em in the fridge."

"Can't," Paul mumbled. "Locked."

For fuck's sake. He'd forgotten about that. "The fridge key's on the bunch in the door. That'll fit it." He tapped the probe to stabilise the reading. Odd. It should read between one and three degrees Celsius above freezing. Instead the digital display was alternating, changing rapidly between 21 and 12. *Just like today's date*, he thought.

"Well done, Bamber," he growled. "You've knackered the probe."

"Well, just make the temperature up – oh, hello. Breakfast time, is it?"

Connie followed Paul's gaze, to the inner door leading to the dining room. The door that was now open and framed Jason Franklin's figure.

For a while Jason stood motionless. The shock of seeing two strange figures in white had frozen him, because he knew he had seen them before. Years ago.

He saw a man in his late forties, stocky and thick set, brandishing a sharp, pointed object at a younger man who knelt on the floor amid a pile of spilled food packages. Both were dressed identically in -

...white...

- white overalls, flimsy looking affairs that couldn't possibly keep out the cold, complimented by thin paper baker's caps. No, these were the delivery men from the cook-chill unit, on their rounds stocking the fridge up. Jason started to relax -

- white robes, spotted with blood. Blood from the offering...

- and the younger delivery man on the floor, thin to the point of lankiness, looking up at him curiously through his thick glasses. "Oh. Breakfast time, is it?" He had one of the cardboard cook-chill boxes in his hand. Something red and bulbous slithered under the plastic lid.

...red, slithering out of the offering's chest. Gathered up by the white-robed figures and reverentially placed in a box...

The younger man looked alarmed now. Jason's fear was replaced with black rage, making the younger man's eyes widen in fear, magnified by the thick glasses he wore. His gloved fingers involuntarily tightened on the box he held. The cellophane lid split along the side and the peeled plum tomatoes slithered onto the floor, the thick juice staining the cotton gloves scarlet. Jason Franklin sank to his knees, dug his fingernails into his thighs and shrieked.

...the box dropping to the floor, the steaming heart plopping onto the cold flagstones of the chapel's cellar...the white robed figures looking up from their work, eyes widening in alarm behind their masks. Eyes that narrowed, the realisation that this intruder had witnessed their grisly duty. Had to be silenced...

The younger man stood up in alarm and took a step backwards as his older companion advanced with the temperature probe. Jason's eyes focussed on the glinting steel point coming his way. His shriek became a scream that thundered around the tiled walls of the kitchen. A scream of fear, believing he was in danger; a scream of recognition, knowing that the scene playing out in front of him was the same now as it was then, years ago as a child, when he had stumbled upon the appeasers of Andraste.

...the knives point to him, steel edges glinting in the dim candlelight. A face appears above it, the frowning features of one he recognises creasing up in a mixture of relief and anger. Anger that their sacred duty has been witnessed: relief that it is only the eight year old who has witnessed them. "Go back to bed, Jason. Now. This is all just a bad dream. You'll wake up, everything will be gone. Go back to bed..."

Jason's eyes flutter. He almost falls under the calm, hypnotic tones of the Scotsman he calls father. But as his head dips, his glance falls onto the ravaged body of the offering. It's impossible to tell who it is, if it's a man or woman, or even human. No recognisable appendages to call arms or legs, the skin removed and folded reverentially on the side is coloured a mottled black-red from the heavy bruising. The neatly sawn stump of what he imagines to be a neck draws his gaze, refuses to let him go. He wonders whose head sat on top of that neck...

"Jason!" Louder, harsher tones. "This isn't happening. Back to bed, NOW!" Jason looks away from the body, stares at...

...the older delivery driver. "Back to bed, Jason! Now! Sam'll have your bollocks for breakfast if he knows you've been up and about."

Jason blinked. Sam? Who's Sam? He blinked again. For a moment, his father's face was replaced by another's, that of a stocky, florid faced man with wide, frightened eyes. But only for a moment. Jason knew that his father would never allow fear to show on his face. He looked down at the floor.

Strange, the flagstones seemed to have changed to some shiny ceramic material, green squares like tiles. But the blood spilled on them, the inverted box and its unspeakable contents…

Memory flashes of a small, frightened boy leaving the cellar in a daze, going back to bed and forgetting all that had occurred until years later. He shook his head frantically. No, that hadn't happened. That wouldn't happen. If he meekly turned his head away from the blood and organs on the floor, walked away with his father's orders booming in his ears, he would never be able to live with himself. He'd witnessed murder, for God' sake! How could he walk away from that?

If he stood his ground, showed the same strength of purpose and lack of fear as his father…who knew? Perhaps a sea change would occur. Perhaps he would find a new respect for his son. Perhaps the beatings and the intimidation would stop. All he had to do was stand his ground. Remember the exploded chest, the surgically tucked and folded stump of the neck. It was difficult, with the body gone, but if he shut his eyes firmly he could envision it.

"What the hell is he doing?"

Jason ignored the coarse words. Hardly fitting language for men who belonged to the country's oldest centre of learning. But then, mutilation and murder were hardly fitting subjects for a degree course, were they?

He had to stand up. The stench of plum tomatoes…no: not tomatoes, blood, was overpowering. He calmly got to his feet, eyes fixed on the white-overalled figure holding the weapon.

"No more father. *No more!*" With a cry that had been stifled in his soul for the last decade – only now allowed release – he lowered his head and charged.

Connie Teague fought to take in what was happening. It had all been so sudden. Jason Franklin appearing at the door like a ghost, uttering screams that only the seriously mentally disturbed could make, calling him father…*father*?…and now this. The event he had secretly feared ever since he had started to make food deliveries to the Phoenix Unit. Jason Franklin, Fulbourn's most celebrated and most feared guest, had finally lost it completely and was heading straight for him.

It was the realisation of his darkest fear that stilled him, made him forget the nimble footwork that had enabled him to out-manoeuvre his opponents in the ring. He even forgot about the temperature probe in his hand.

Jason's head struck him in the chest. Not hard enough to bring anything more than a slight grunt of pain to Connie's lips, but enough to make him lose his balance.

He fell backwards, his left arm clutching at the drawers of the kitchen unit, and he managed to stop himself falling to the floor. The temperature probe hit the floor.

Jason was carried forward by his own momentum. He overbalanced and stumbled into Paul, who was making small panicky noises and had by now completely sobered up. Jason landed heavily on the packages of food, the tomatoes squelching and bursting beneath him.

Connie forced his fear into a tight ball and swallowed it, imagined he was back in the ring; that the man in front of him wasn't a sectioned mental patient, just another unfortunate – or stupid, it came down to the same thing – challenger who thought he could take on Connie Boy.

"Come on, bastard!" He pushed himself away from the unit, angled himself towards Jason, fists clenched and formed into a defensive stance. Jason stared at the tomato juice running down the grouting in the tiled floor and shrieked.

Connie's fists lowered in surprise. *What the fuck is running through this kid's mind...and where the hell is Sam Dawson?*

"Paul! Get on the blower, tell them we've got a problem!" His eyes flicked back to Franklin. Jesus, he was just sitting there now! Slumped on the floor, legs spread wide, gazing stupefied at the liquid on the floor. Paul was immobile, standing motionless by the door. Like the bloody dummy he was.

In the single second it took for Connie's eyes to move from Jason to Paul and back again, Jason Franklin acted. A feral expression of pure hatred on his face, he slid over to Connie's feet where the temperature probe lay. In one fluid, graceful motion, he grabbed it and shot to his feet.

Connie had one brief image of a huge steel ball shooting towards him, as though someone had shot a ball bearing at his eye.

The force and momentum of the blow was so great that Jason Franklin found himself with his thumb stuck in the orbit of Connie's eyeball. The six inch steel probe, along with its plastic pommel, was buried deep inside the driver's skull. The body thrashed and writhed as though huge bolts of electricity were coursing through it. It jerked backwards, collapsing on the floor and tearing the probe from Jason's grip.

He stood watching the body judder and writhe for a moment. He cocked his head to one side, looking at the strange white box attached to the killing knife he had wrested from the other. He looked around him. The cellar of the chapel was deathly silent. The other Fellows seemed to have fled the scene. He couldn't blame them. They had seen him kill his own father, John Franklin, the feared head porter of All Souls. Frightened of the head porter, they would surely be more terrified of the man who had killed him. He looked at the now lifeless, still body and felt a surge of satisfaction. It was far from over, but it was a start. The Elder would be pleased.

Then he was aware of the presence of another. To his right, backing away to the doorway leading out of the cellar, he saw one of the white-clad murderers. He noticed the red stains on the robes and growled. He was glad to see fear in the retreating man's eyes.

"It ends here and now. No more killings for Andraste. Tell the College Council that. My father won't be able to get you the offerings anymore!" He kicked the lifeless body triumphantly.

The other stared back at him, bleary eyed and squinting. Of course, this one wore glasses, didn't he? He looked too young to be involved in this. In fact, too young to be a Senior Member of the college, almost his own age...

Jason shook his head. *No.*

The face was changing now: the lips forming mute pleas, bony hands raised to ward away the steel probe. Changing into the face of David Searles.

Here was the real focus of the evil. No matter that rumours circulated, telling of Searles' reluctance to assume the duties of the Council leader. He was Master of All Souls: he participated in and led the ritual. He was the leader. He was guilty.

Jason examined the sharp point of the probe. It was slimy with blood and optical fluid. It had bent slightly when he pulled it out of his father's eye socket, but not too badly. It was still straight enough to enter another eyeball.

Searles put up less resistance than his father. Lying on the floor, arms pulled over his head in a vain attempt to ward him off. Jason wondered if it was fear that paralysed Searles into defencelessness – or if the Master of All Souls secretly welcomed his imminent execution. A purging of his sins. It didn't matter.

What did matter was what Searles said to him just before the six-inch tip rocketed through his right eyeball and pierced his brain.

"Not me, Jason. *Not your father...*"

It was only when Jason extracted the probe that Searles' words sank in. Not your father.

The cellar walls lightened, changed texture. Heavy, rough stone turned to pristine white wall tiles, gleaming in the light from the fluorescent strips overhead. The bodies of the two white-clad Fellows remained where they lay, but their faces changed. No longer Franklin and Searles.

The offering they had been tearing to pieces was no longer there, and the offal they had been boxing up resumed its sweet aroma of peeled plum tomatoes.

To Jason Franklin, this smelled as bad as the coppery odour of freshly spilled blood pooling around the booted heels of the deliverymen. This was the gut-churning stench of realisation. Proof that he had been wrong.

Proof that he had murdered two men. The steel probe felt cold and slimy in his hands. He threw it away with revulsion and howled his agonised guilt to the open door.

Perhaps it was awareness of the cold seeping in through the open door, or the smell of exhaust fumes now mixing with the stench of blood. But now he knew the means of his deliverance was at hand. The Elder had not lied to him.

But what a way to go about it, he thought miserably. *To kill two guys who were only delivering food.*

But then…was it really his fault? The white overalls had triggered a deep-rooted memory within him, made him relive the sight of the propitiation room in the chapel of All Souls.

Yes, he told himself. That was the memory that had needed to surface, needed the right trigger. Longhurst had set it in motion with the word 'cellar' at their last meeting. And the two delivery men – wearing similar overalls to those worn by the Council when they appeased Andraste…and the words from the younger man, almost the same words he'd heard in the cellar…no wonder he'd thought he was back there.

The acrid smell of the van's fumes brought him back to the door. He hardened himself. *What's wrong with you? If you hadn't been given this opportunity these two would have died anyway, in less than twelve hours along with the rest of humanity! You've got a job to do, Jase.*

He cast one last, guilty look at the dead delivery men and opened the door. The van blazed its headlights at him in greeting.

It wasn't the grandest of getaway vehicles. A 1989 Ford Transit van with a Luton box conversion. Rust spread like ivy along the sills. The Hubbard chiller unit made a stuttering sound, and judging by the black smoke belching from the exhaust it looked like there was little life left in the van.

Still, beggars couldn't be choosers. He uttered a quick prayer of thanks to The Elder and pulled open the door.

He swung his lithe body into the cab and gingerly placed his bloodstained hands on the steering wheel. It had been a long time since he'd driven, and never anything as big as this.

The gearstick shuddered violently in its neutral setting, in time with the rattling of the poorly maintained engine.

He checked the fuel gauge, saw the needle pointing to FULL and smiled. His smile broadened when he saw the fuel card on the dashboard. Because not only did it mean the acquisition of all fuels and oils for this elderly van, the silver embossed words below read PETROL ONLY.

An old, old van. One that ran on unleaded.

That was great. Petrol would burn much easier than diesel.

TWENTY

The contents of the box were piled on the coffee table in the Lotson's living room. All except for the sheaf of colour photos scattered across the floor. The tree lights reflected off the glossy photographs, festive green and red light providing an incongruous illumination to the horror.

Andy's hands shook as he read the letter Freeland had written. Behind him, he could hear Phil's son playing with Jasper, the collie barking in delight as Nick flashed the torch around the carpeted floor of the hallway. Kelly and Rob were sitting at the breakfast bar, in the kitchen, their voices low.

Andy resisted the temptation to look in their direction. The last time he had seen Kelly look so terrified was fifteen years ago, when he'd saved her in the bar of All Souls. She'd seen the pictures, read what Phil had read. Andy closed the door.

Mr Lotson

If you have followed my wishes you will be sitting at home reading this. By which time I will be dead. I'm sorry, but I simply cannot live with the guilt any longer. I know what awaits me on the other side and I know I deserve it, and it is infinitely preferable to what will happen when December the 21st draws to a close. Because we will all be in Hell then, everyone of us. Guilty and innocent alike will suffer when Andraste breaks through.

"What's Andraste?" He could see why Freeland had insisted Phil get the box last night, though. It was just gone six in the morning. December the twenty-first had dawned. There were less than eighteen hours until midnight.

"Read on," Phil said in a shaking voice. He looked terrible, even worse than when he'd answered the door to Andy and Rob. He'd been up all night reading and examining the contents of Freeland's archive that he'd begun to read on the journey back from London. It wasn't just the black rings under his eyes or the grey, pallid complexion that disturbed Andy so much. It was the look in his eyes. That look spoke of the death of hope.

And that is the terrible irony of the whole matter. The Fellowship of All Souls have been carrying out the ritual for centuries, and before that the ritual was performed by another fellowship, a secret band whose existence history has never recorded. All with the same intention – to prevent Andraste returning. They were not evil men. Their intentions were honourable, but misguided. They have been deceived.

Because it is their adherence to the ritual that will guarantee the opposite. Far from appeasing Andraste, each soul given increases her strength. Each soul that is torn from the body feeds her, empowers her. Each year that passes shows signs of this increased power, because gods and humans are very alike in many ways. Just as a man given too much power will eventually be corrupted by it and use it for his own ends, mocking those he wields it against, so too with Andraste.

She grows smug with each year that passes. She becomes overconfident. She delights in mocking the faiths of those who hold their religions sacred, to make them believe that their gods are powerless against her. She also glories in forcing them to confront the dark aspect of their pasts, showing in full detail the horrors of their former years – as she did with the Bursar's Secretary, Judith Cox, in Old Court this evening.

For no other reason than that she can. It is a reminder of her terrible power, and, it is said, a mere foretaste of what will happen if she is not fed regularly.

Only a few have seen past that, to find strength and self belief in the face of Andraste's terrible mind games. To have faith in themselves and believe what they know is true in their hearts. Very few survive.

Jason Franklin knows her time is near. It will only take one or two more souls to give her the power to break through to this plane. His attempt to destroy the college last year was admirable, and I believe he will attempt to do so again. But that alone will not be enough. Jason is a part of the equation; but not the full solution.

There is another who will be called upon. One who may be known to you, one who has a darkness within him that even Andraste fears – and a shared inheritance with Jason. Without this individual, Andraste will have her final triumph. But it is not certain if he will have the strength to go through with the task. Even The Elder is uncertain.

All I can ask you to do is pass on this information to him. Show him what you have been shown. The rest is up to him.

One other thing. I said that Andraste mocks other faiths, to destroy belief, to destroy hope.

Well, I believe in God now. And I hope he will understand why I myself took part in those terrible rituals. I hope He understands that I was deceived like everyone else by an evil that is more intelligent than Man can ever be. I hope he understands that I am only human.

The Elder doesn't have all the answers. But it is clear that he is operating from some other authority, something ancient that precedes Andraste. I personally believe that it is God, because there is so much emphasis placed on individual, human choice. I may be wrong, that is the one thing for which I don't have proof.

But since when has faith needed proof?

I wish you well, Mr Lotson. May God – or The Elder – guide you. Pray for me.

J. Freeland.

Rob took out his tobacco tin and rummaged inside it, trying to find a ready-rolled spliff. Kelly looked at him with a half smile.

"Go on, then. But don't offer any to Nick." She pushed an empty coffee mug over for him to use as an ashtray. "Nick! Take the dog outside, will you?"

Nick lowered the torch and pouted. "It's freezing out there! You should make filthy-lungs here go out instead."

"Nick. Just do what you're *fucking well* told. Now!"

Rob blinked at the anger in her voice. Always a bossy cow, he'd thought, but the sort of woman that was good for Phil. Phil needed a good boot up the arse on occasion and there were plenty of those from Kelly Lotson. But this was different. The strain and tiredness, the irritability, that was one thing – but he'd never heard her swear in front of her boy before. This was fear.

The door slammed shut.

She waited for Rob to light his joint before speaking. She cast a nervous look over her shoulder, and Rob followed her eyes. They'd both heard Andy close the door.

"Hell of a night," she murmured. Rob exhaled, coughed, and passed the joint to her.

"You wouldn't believe the stuff that old vicar mate of Phil's came out with. He almost bricked himself when he saw the Green Man in my cab." He sighed. "Load of old bollocks. You don't believe this shit, do you?"

She took a small puff, coughed it out immediately. Then she took another drag, a longer one this time, and held her breath. Rob raised his eyebrows. Kelly had never been much of a smoker, even during her Uni days. *She obviously needs it now, though.*

"You saw those photos Phil brought back?" she said in a strained, high pitched voice. "This is good stuff, by the way."

Rob shuddered. "I had a quick glance at them. That's enough for me…"

"Do I believe in some bloodthirsty goddess trying to invade the planet? Of course I bloody don't. But I do believe in evil – human evil - and what Phil brought back with him is proof of that. People have been murdered…tortured to death." She shook her head. "I don't understand why this Freeland wanted Phil to speak to Andy about it, though. What the hell's it got to do with him?"

"Maybe nothing. Maybe everything." He told her what the vicar had said about Woodcock's bloodline, his child and relocation to Wallingford. The Green Man Jen had bought for him. He shuddered at that, and Kelly noticed. No way was he going to tell her what he thought he'd seen it do in his van. Burning his fingers off, speaking to him…bollocks. Just that extra strong skunk again. *Really should lay off it. But…later. When all this shit's over and done with.* He took the joint back from her and inhaled.

"Sounds bloody loopy to me. But…Andy coming up here, with that piece of rock. Seems too much of a coincidence, yeah?"

She nodded slowly. Reluctantly, he thought. *Really don't want him around here, do you?*

As if reading his thoughts, she sat back on the chair and looked at him steadily.

"He's got a part to play in this. I know that. But you've got to realise…I never wanted to see him again."

Rob frowned. "All due respect, Kelly... I could never understand this. He saved your life, didn't he?"

Kelly's eyes were distant, far away in the past. Rob knew she was reliving that night fifteen years ago.

"Yes…I won't deny that. But…he almost killed Phil. He blamed him for it, because he'd introduced us. How the hell was Phil to know what pills and powder they'd carried with them? My God, you don't expect two men who represented Cambridge at the Boat Race – world class athletes, no less – to be druggies, do you? The way Andy went on it was almost as though Phil had sold the stuff himself."

Like Kelly, Rob would never forget that night. Him and Phil following the screams of pain to the locked cubicle…Kelly with her skirt around her waist and trying to pull her underwear back up, sobbing hysterically…hearing the thudding of steel toecaps into human flesh, the cracking of teeth and bones…watching the red rivulets appear under the cubicle door, running towards them…

Rob shuddered. Phil had raced to Kelly's side, tried to comfort her.

Don't touch me, bastard! You should've been here…YOU should've protected me…

It was Rob who had broken down the door. Who had shouldered his way into the cubicle, determined to stop his friend before it was too late…

"I was unfair on Phil, I know." She sniffed. "Andy had strange views on what constitutes the 'protection of women' – right out of the Dark Ages, expected a man to stay at his woman's side at all times. It was bloody claustrophobic sometimes, y'know? Even if I wanted to go to the toilet he'd insist on waiting outside for me. There was a gap between me dumping him and seeing Phil. But when I started going out with him…Andy didn't take it well."

Rob said nothing. As Andy's former best friend he knew him better than anyone, knew what made him tick…but also knew how much of a strain he could be. Kelly was her own woman, wouldn't expect a bloke to hold doors for her or follow her around everywhere.

"I know. And that's when his work started slipping, spent more time working the security at the Anglia SU bar than in the library. There was no way he was going to finish his dissertation – God, even finishing the third year was out of the question. Hard when your personal tutor is knobbing your ex-girlfriend."

She snorted. "Thank you, Robert."

"Sorry."

"And that's the irony. Phil wasn't there and Andy was. Yes, he stopped them raping me, but…well, you saw what he did to them. Jesus."

Andy lowered the letter. "Seems like he got religion pretty damn quick."

Phil said nothing. Andy stepped over the photos, trying not to look at them. He sat on the sofa next to Phil and inspected the files stacked on the coffee table.

The first one was a heavy square-cut folder stuffed with yellowing newspaper cuttings that referred to missing persons. Andy scanned them quickly. There were also printed screenshots of reports taken from various news websites.

They were a mixed bag. Red top tabloids, twice folded cuttings from the broadsheets, and not confined to Britain or the English language. Some were in French, German, Italian…some in characters that were either Chinese or Japanese, he couldn't say which.

"Freeland told me that Andraste doesn't confine her choices to these shores," Phil said quietly. "He said they feel the call in far off lands, feel an irresistible urge to come to Cambridge. Secretly, impulsively. Not a word spoken to their loved ones. Some cover their tracks well, to make it look like they've pulled a disappearing act. Some fake their own deaths – yes, the call is that strong."

"And the final port of call is All Souls College." Andy tapped the date on one of the cuttings. There was no logical pattern to the timing of the vanishings. Neither was there a particular type. Men and women – no children, thank God – but all from varying age groups. Neither was there a particular psychological profile to those chosen by Andraste. Some were noted as being depressed, suicidal. Some had mental health problems or drink and drug issues. But only a few.

The only thing the reports had in common was the plea for information, and the anguished words of relatives or loved ones, begging them to contact them – or begging whoever had taken them to let them free.

"Quite a collection," Andy murmured. "But it doesn't really prove anything, does it?"

"The diary entries do." Phil waved a tired hand at the archive storage box sitting by the presents under the Christmas tree. Andy turned and saw the collection of black A4 hardbacked books within. "Freeland made notes of various physical properties which I'm sure will match up to the descriptions on police files. And then, of course, there're the pictures…"

Andy nodded grimly. Judging by their current location on the floor it was obvious that they'd been thrown away from where Phil was sitting in horror. Steeling himself he knelt down and picked them up. He winced at the pain in his abdomen, and then took a deep breath through gritted teeth at the sight before him.

High resolution, full colour but poorly lit. Freeland had used a good quality digital camera but he hadn't been able to use the flash. Only the candle flames illuminated the stone floor of the cellar and the victims.

Makes sense, Andy thought. *Can't be easy to take photos when the other Fellows are nearby. Freeland had guts, I'll give him that.*

A piece of white material – probably the sleeve of a robe – half-obscured the lens on the picture. Andy could only just make out make out the goose pimples on the skin of the victim. *Through terror or cold?* he wondered.

"Jesus Christ in Heaven," he hissed. Phil watched him, saying nothing.

The first picture showed a young Oriental looking woman, probably Japanese, in her early twenties. She was naked, her wrists and ankles tied to heavy iron rings set in the floor. Her eyes were wide, her mouth open in a silent scream that found voice in Andy's imagination. It rolled and echoed, a terrifying cry of despair and terror that would never leave him.

The next photo showed the same girl. He assumed it was the same girl, but it was difficult to tell. Too much of her had been removed.

Andy felt the photos slip from his loosened fingers. His head swum and bile rose in his throat. He sat back on the sofa and rubbed his eyes with the heels of his palms.

Phil stared at the dropped pictures. He made no attempt to pick them up.

"The operation is the same for each victim. And each victim looks exactly the same afterwards. When you remove the limbs, facial features and finally the skin I guess there isn't much difference between anyone. We're all the same underneath."

Andy took his palms away and Phil visibly flinched beneath his glare. "Freeland's words, not mine. And he wasn't joking either."

Andy looked with reddened eyes at the scattered photos on the floor. The two he'd dropped had fallen beside a photo of a male victim with a face that he recognised. The flabby bulk and pony tailed head of Geoff Michaels was unmistakeable. He closed his eyes. *Well, no surprise there.* He wondered if it was worth phoning Pearce yet to tell him.

"Freeland wrote down the precise stages of the ritual. It has, he said, never been put to paper before until now. The teaching was passed down through the centuries, continuing the oral teaching tradition of the original college that was here long before All Souls." Another typewritten page was passed to Andy from Freeland's archive of pain. He looked at it warily but was shaking too much to take it.

"The ritual goes under a very cute name," Phil said bitterly. "Freeland calls it 'The Song to Andraste'."

"The…song?" Andy spat the words out. "Like a fucking Christmas carol?"

"A song of pain. The philosophy behind it is that when the human body suffers unbearable agony it reaches a stage where the mind shuts down and blots out the messages sent from the pain receptors. However, if it is done slowly, gradually…this can be avoided."

"Jesus Christ…"

"He didn't even recognise me. Shit, I didn't recognise him. The blood on his face, even in his eyes…and none of it his. He looked like a fuckin' demon. And what he'd done to the second guy…you wouldn't think it possible."

Kelly rubbed her eyes tiredly. The skunk was powerful stuff, and Kelly wasn't used to it. But it had calmed her somewhat, numbed her. And that was what she had wanted. Needed.

"Had he ever been in touch with you since that night, Rob?"

Rob's throat was dry. He walked to the kitchen sink, swilled out his coffee mug then filled it with cold water. Gulping it down, he wiped condensation from the window and stared at the torch flashing in the dark garden. He saw patches of speckled white fur dance in the snow and heard the muffled sound of laughter and barking, two creatures enjoying a play.

"When he got out of prison he went back to his mum's in Wallingford. That was three years ago. I went down there, had a couple of drinks with him to celebrate his release…he doesn't have many friends, Kelly. But I think you know that."

She nodded. Her eyelids were heavy.

"He told me what he'd been up to when inside, some real horror stories there. But there was no friendship there anymore, that had died twelve years ago after that night. And if anything, the anger…well, it's not just anger, is it?"

She lifted her head. "No, it's not anger. It's rage…and darkness. You said he was like a demon…perfect description."

"Well, that darkness was even more pronounced. His old man died when he was inside, emphysema I think. And his mum was pretty frail by then, the cancer had come out of remission. He knew she didn't have long…he was raging against the world again.

"Anyway, I did the usual bollocks, promised to keep in touch and then fucked off back home as quick as I could. Kept in touch with the occasional email and Facebook post, but that was it. He met this Jennifer bird after that: she was doing the catering at one of those festivals he did the security for…and from what I saw on his profile she had a real good effect on him. Calmed him down somewhat. They moved into her place in Didcot."

Kelly nodded, somewhat wistfully. "I'm glad. Is he still seeing her?"

Rob hesitated. "I don't think so. She's staying with her parents in St Neots. He didn't go into details, though."

"No, he never does. Hang on…she's gone to her parents for Christmas? Without Andy?"

Rob nodded. "Doesn't look good, does it?"

Phil read aloud, his face contorting with fury and disgust with each word. He stumbled over certain passages where the detail was too great. When he had finished Andy took the paper from him and read it for himself. He had to. He had to see for himself, he had to know that another human being had physically written this down.

THE SONG TO ANDRASTE

The Fellows of All Souls have known for successive generations the true meaning of Andraste's power. Some have felt it for themselves. All know the cost of failing to bind it with the ritual of appeasement that has been named the 'Song to Andraste'.

It is a ritual that, we have been taught, requires the ultimate strength. The strength to inflict such pain and suffering on another human being that it can destroy your very grip on sanity. It calls the whole nature of humanity into question; that to save mankind inhuman torture and suffering – and then death – must be inflicted on a fellow human being. Only in this way can Andraste's power be held in check for one more year.

It is this that can destroy you. Knowing that the ritual must be performed yearly, without fail, for as long as mankind exists. You cannot help but have doubts; cannot help but weep for every offering.

The ritual takes place over two days. The first is the hardest part because this is the crucial forming of the Song. The five senses of the Offering are taken. The sense of touch goes first – fingers and toes are removed. Then the sense of smell – the nose is taken and the nasal passages burnt. Hearing is taken by slicing away the earlobes and driving needles deep into the ear canal to perforate the eardrums. Cutting out the tongue removes the fourth sense. The stump is cauterised to ensure the offering doesn't choke to death on his or her blood. Then, finally, the sense of sight is taken.

The offering lies for twelve hours, sustained by drugs and intravenous injections. The cruellest stage of the Song and not just because of the agony endured. When the human body loses one sense it compensates by sharpening the remaining four. The blind can hear more acutely, the deaf see with more clarity and focus. What then, for those who lose all five senses, all five methods by which we perceive and interact with the universe around us? What compensation can the body offer?

The only compensation can be full shut down of the brain, divorcing itself from the horrors inflicted on the body. That is when the power Andraste hungers for is revealed.

Little is known about the sixth sense, or why it is more powerful in some individuals. Many parapsychologists believe each human has it, that it lies dormant, unused in a plane of existence that relies so heavily on the other five levels of perception. But those that Andraste selects to sing for her have it in ways even they are not aware of. And when the other five senses are stripped away, the sixth shines like a beacon in the darkness.

A beacon that summons her. The sixth sense is our direct link to the other, hidden levels of existence that are denied to us. To the sources of power in the universe that engineer the whole of Creation. It is, to be blunt, our link to God. It is our soul.

It shines when we are close to death, when our senses have shut down and the body is ready to expire. It shines to God as a message, a plea for Him to take us to the next stage of existence.

But when it shines in the cellar beneath the chapel of All Souls, when its glory is corrupted by the manner of the ritual, it finds its way to Andraste rather than God. Because in that terrible, everlasting twelve hours the offering is still alive, in a state of agony and total sensory deprivation. The sixth sense cannot allow the mind to shut down and instead shows the Offering the hidden powers that work all of Creation, a sight that was not meant for mortal minds. All of this, with the Dark Whispering that speaks directly to the mind without need for aural communication.

The Dark Whispering is formed by the previous souls that Andraste has in her thrall, that come before her, announcing her coming much the same way a light show precedes a meteor before it alights and begins its devastating work. The Offering is in Hell and the voices of Andraste's Selected make it clear that this is only the beginning, that worse agonies await those who are forcibly denied access to the path of God.

The offering has sung to Andraste, and has brought her to them. But she cannot take them yet. The life is terminated by the severing of the head from the body, the skin is flayed to remove all traces of covering for the soul and the remains of the Offering are taken apart and prepared.

The song has been sung. Now Andraste must accept the Offering and agree to depart. This is done by Communion with her children.

Andy lowered the page. It was trembling in his hands. "Communion?"

Phil stared at him despairingly. "The physical remains of the offering, fed to the beasts of the wood. The children of Andraste are -"

"The same thing Rob hit with the van ." Andy frowned. "Fed to the boar…and then that boar is consumed at the Feast. Jesus. That means…"

"Yes, Andy. The offering is consumed three times. Eaten by the boar. Eaten by the Fellowship. And the soul is consumed by Andraste."

TWENTY ONE

"So what made Freeland realise that the ritual has the opposite effect?"

In answer to Andy's question Phil lifted a small padded envelope. He lifted the unsealed flap and removed a small black notebook.

"Careful," he said as he handed it to Andy. "It's over two hundred years old and it hasn't fared well. But it did its job."

Andy held the small book gingerly. The leather was faded and heavily creased. It smelled of dampness and rot. He turned the cover gently, wincing at the sound of splitting leather and crumbling binding.

The pages were yellow and stained almost sepia in parts, which made it even harder to decipher the spidery handwriting in faded black ink. He could just about make out the cover on the flyleaf. His breath left his lungs as quickly as if he'd punched in the gut.

"Charles Harvey."

Phil nodded grimly. "Wilkins told you, then. Charles Harvey, Elizabeth Woodcock, the Divine Judgement…and you."

"Hold on." Andy handed the diary back to him. Phil glanced at it but made no attempt to take it from him. "That vicar had no proof Woodcock had a kid from Harvey that moved to Wallingford. And even if he did…it's no proof that I'm related to her. To *him*."

"The Green Man is proof enough, surely."

"Come off it," Andy snapped, holding the book further out to Phil. "You're a historian. You of all people should know the importance of hard, documented evidence. A piece of moon rock in Rob's van that looks like the thing nutcase Franklin calls The Elder…what does that prove?"

"Think about it this way, Andy. The Fellows of All Souls are forbidden to have children, a condition of the covenant between them and Andraste. Freeland thinks it is forbidden because children of the Fellowship have a power that Andraste is scared of – a power they're not even aware they possess. It's a dark power, though – and it can destroy them, just as much as it can be used against her. Jason Franklin's madness is proof of that…and so is what you are capable of." *And what you've done*, his eyes added.

Andy took a stiff breath. Phil continued, unafraid.

"Whatever power passed on to the child of Harvey and Woodcock, it didn't die with them. It passed along that child's descendants, waiting for the one who would return it to Cambridge.

"Who knows, Andy? Fifteen years ago you might have done it…but the Green Man wasn't ready for you. Where it was at this time – and how it finally ended in Wallingford - is anyone's guess. But your…darkness got the better of you. I think the followers of Andraste were greatly relieved that you were out of the picture."

Andy's head was spinning. *Too much, can't take all this in*…he dropped the diary onto the gap between them.

"Jason is the son of the head porter though – and Franklin isn't a Fellow."

"No. Jason is the son of the Master, David Searles. Looks like Franklin pretended to adopt him, and would have made sure he was offered to Andraste when the time was right. Which should have been last year…but it seems Searles wasn't having any of it."

"They offered Geoff Michaels instead. And I guess Andraste isn't happy, is she?"

"More than that, Andy. She's frightened. Think about it. The only two children of the Fellowship are here in Cambridge at the time she feels strong enough to return. One she could cope with – but two?"

Andy shook his head. "I'm not buying this. It's bloody crazy. How come you're so convinced?"

Phil spoke quietly. "Because I've read the diary."

They heard footsteps coming from the hallway. The door was pushed open slowly and both men looked up.

Rob looked the worse for wear, Andy thought. The eyes were bloodshot and he was swaying on his feet. He hadn't had much sleep either, but…Andy narrowed his eyes at the smell of dope breathed into the room.

"Chaps. I gotta go now, some of us have work." He hiccupped.

"You're joking," Andy said flatly. "Work, now?"

Rob raised a hand. "No lectures, Andy. I know I'm not at my best -"

"I'm not talking about that!" Andy roared. "People are dying here, we have proof – "

"Spare it, Andy!" Rob looked angry now. "I've had it with this bullshit. You've all lost your fucking marbles. 'Specially you, Phil. Listening to mentalists like Freeland and Franklin rather than your missus."

Andy reached over the coffee table and picked up the photo of Geoff Michaels. "You think that's the product of a mentalist, do you?"

Rob didn't take his eyes off Phil as he replied.

"Matter of fact, yeah. Amazing what you can do with Photoshop these days."

"For God's *sake*, man!" The picture crumpled in Andy's clenched fist and Phil put his head in his hands.

"Get a grip, the pair of you! Freeland knocked those snaps up, pasted Geoff's face on it to make it all look real. And you've bought into it. You're going to look a right pair of twats when you go to the police with this."

Andy didn't reply. His burning eyes narrowed, searching Rob's. Rob held his glare, looked back angrily. And then Andy saw it.

"You don't want to believe, do you? Don't want to face the fact that your mate's dead…that Emma went the same way."

"Emma is *not* dead! She's got a mug on with me and ain't answering her phone… that's *all*!"

"Well, if that isn't denial I don't know what is." Andy glared. His burning glare followed Rob as he waited at the front door for Jasper. A thumping of paws on carpet followed with an excited yap, then the door closing. Andy sighed when he heard the Transit's engine start up. He shook his head and picked up the diary.

"Does this have all the answers, then?"

"I wish it did. But it does clear up certain things. What happened to Harvey, how The Elder showed him the way…and what he knew he had to do."

"Hang on. Harvey was killed in the fire that was caused by the meteor strike, yes?"

Phil shook his head. "There's more to it than that, Andy. Harvey wasn't killed by the black rock's fire. The Fellows offered him to Andraste, they tore him to pieces. But…he tried to kill himself before that."

"Now you've lost me. Say that again?"

"Just as the ritual, the song, brings Andraste closer to us and…feeds her, so another sacrifice will vanquish her. A self-sacrifice, just as the ancient priesthood enacted when Andraste was first known on this world. Jason Franklin drew a picture of it. That's why Harvey tried to immolate himself – and why Andraste is still here. The Fellows of All Souls stopped him in time."

Andy pondered this. Of course, the vicar had told him this last night but it sounded just as crazy coming from Phil's lips. The far from level-headed history lecturer, prone to getting carried away with his own enthusiasm for the past...he could see why Rob Benson wasn't convinced.

And I can't say I'm convinced either. The killings, yes, I'll accept that – even Pearce suspected this. But this bloodline thing, this connection to a college Master...no, that's bollocks.

Phil smiled grimly. "Just read the diary. Harvey's own words. Then tell me what you think."

Andy noticed the small piece of paper tucked into the back of the book like a marker. An address of an organic farm, supplying exotic meats, specialising in wild boar...he grimaced as he held it up to Phil.

"Did you check this out in the end? Find out it was all bollocks?"

Phil nodded.

"We know where they get their boar meat from now, don't we? Explains why they close off the West Gate entrance for the winter. Bet Roberto didn't think of that."

As Rob pulled away he frowned at the Toyota parked in front of Kelly's Rover. It looked familiar, somehow. He peered over the steering wheel, trying to see if there was anyone inside. Probably was, there was a hell of a lot of condensation inside.

*Ah, fuck it. I'll be seeing ghosts next...*he turned on the radio as he waited in the queue of traffic on the Elizabeth Way roundabout. He occasionally glanced at the Green Man, all too aware of the strange glances it was getting from oncoming motorists. He wound down the window and tossed the butt of a cigarette out, then promptly lit a fresh one. He coughed, hawked and spat something green onto the road.

A weather report on the radio. More heavy snow forecast tonight, possibly two or three inches. Then clear skies and sunshine. It would freeze again. The bookies had slashed the odds against having a white Christmas, but with all the accidents – including the horrific A14 snarl up yesterday – it seemed that people had had enough of the festive winter wonderland and were almost hoping for good old-fashioned British rain.

"Never happy, are we shitbag?"

Jasper yawned.

Rob tried to keep his mind blank as he got closer to the warehouse. All that 'evidence': the photos, the meetings with two mentally ill people...Christ, how could Phil be taken in by it all?

What about the boar, Rob? That wasn't make-believe, was it?

He shrugged his shoulders. Simple explanation, some student prank. The carcass stolen from the kitchen and put it in his van when he was trying it on with Emma.

You know that's bollocks. All the students went home. And what about that dent in the van?

That wasn't a human being you hit, it was one of the things in the wood – the same thing that attacked Andy!

"Bollocks. Pure and simple. Too much weed and absinthe. Nothing more." He closed his eyes and repeated the words over and over again. But with eyes closed darkness had him. And then he could see the black woods of the college and the creatures that chased his vehicle…the one that came charging towards him…the explosion of flesh and blood as it bounced over the bonnet.

He opened his eyes and repeated his mantra.

He checked his watch as he pulled alongside the closed door of Granta Office Supplies. Eight o'clock – normally open by now, but perhaps it was too cold for Jim.

He shivered as he shut the engine down. He looked warily at Jasper. Then at the Green Man. In the side mirror he could see a face appear in the upstairs window. A face that frowned and disappeared.

"Harrison…don't give me any grief today, sunshine. I ain't in the mood. C'mon, boy."

He dragged open the sliding door and beckoned for Jasper to enter. Jasper sniffed at the doorway and whined; he sat down and looked beseechingly at Rob.

"C'mon, shitbag. Get in there."

Jasper followed Rob in slowly, unwillingly. He waited by the door, as though ready to make a swift getaway. He sat with his tail beating feebly, disturbing the fine layer of black ash that coated the grey concrete slab of the warehouse floor. It eddied and whirled like dust clouds, and Rob could see now why Jim had kept the warehouse door shut. He turned and dragged the exterior door closed again.

At the far end of the warehouse, Higgins and Harrison stood, staring at him.

"Morning, gents," Rob nodded. "No Jim today?"

Harrison was trying, not very successfully, to hide his smirk. Higgins at least had the grace to look uncomfortable.

"He's upstairs. I asked him to leave us, so that we could have a word in private."

Rob noticed a small brown envelope in his hand. "What's that, Christmas card?"

"It's a card of a sort, Benson," Terry Harrison's grin was wider. "It's your card, and it's been marked."

"Fuckin' what?" Rob roared. "You sacking me? Why?"

"A formal complaint from the college of All Souls – from the Bursar, no less. Didn't like your attitude when you delivered the toner."

"Bursar? I didn't deliver that, And – " *oh, fuck. What did you do, Andy?*

"And what? As if that wasn't enough the desk delivered to the Master was broken – damaged in transit? Rubbish. I know deliberate damage when I see it." Higgins' cheeks were red. "I had to go out personally to help Terry pick it up. Then eat humble pie and promise the Master we'd get it replaced before the new term."

Rob was no longer listening. His eyes were fixed on the black ash on the floor. It was darker, no longer a powdery grey. It was a thick, almost viscous black – and it was moving.

"You've had enough warnings, Benson," Harrison said smugly. "I said that if you –"

Now he was aware of the black ash. All three men watched the streams of coarse powder flowing into the centre of the warehouse. From behind the returns cages, from underneath Jim Maskell's desk, from the charging generator of the forklift truck…the black ash was flowing rapidly into the area where the three men stood. Almost liquid in its movements, a black sea that was taking shape.

Harrison's rage diminished, fading into confusion as the ash flowed over his Oxfords. He yelped as though a snake had crawled over him and jumped backwards, banging his elbow on one of the returns cages. Rob stepped backwards and glanced briefly at Higgins. Higgins met his eyes and a look of fearful understanding passed between them. Because like Rob, he knew where this ash had come from.

It blew upwards, into the air, into their faces, swirling like a miniature desert storm. Rob coughed, feeling nauseous at the taste of cremated pork.

He felt even more nauseous as the cloud of ash settled: the particles less animated as they formed a shape in the air. Like one of those 'invisible man' films he remembered watching as a kid, where dust or sand is blown across an unseen intruder to give him a definite outline, the ash cloud formed the image of a pig-like creature, a sculpture made entirely of black sand. And then, as though the force behind it was intent on making its creation as realistic as possible, textures were added. Hollows and lighter patches, concave sections: a perfect three dimensional sculpture. Then the ash settled further, became darker, more dense. Rob blinked, and in that split second the ash was indistinguishable from the black bristles that raced along the animal's spine.

A few seconds passed, the only sound the terrified barking of Jasper, and then the ash was gone. Every part of the thing was now coated in glossy, thick fur that bristled as it took its first deep, shuddering breaths of air.

Black fur parted on two equidistant points on the beast's head, and Rob Benson found himself facing again those terrible black eyes of the boar he had run into in the woods of All Souls the night before.

"Hello? Pearce…wondered when you'd call." He looked at Phil meaningfully, and stood up. He wanted this conversation alone.

Walking through the hallway to the kitchen, the mobile clamped to his ear, he pulled open the kitchen door and stood out in the garden. Blood red sunlight reflected off the snowman that Nick had made at some stage.

"Yes, I know where Geoff Michaels is. He's where you suspected he is – or rather, his body is."

Silence followed.

"Nothing to say, Pearce? Yes, I've got proof…of a sort." He checked his watch. Eight thirty. He wondered if it was too early to phone Jen.

"Then you know how he died?"

"The same way the others did," Andy said dryly. "I can give your… 'interested party' a copy of the photo – if you're sure you want them to see it, of course."

"No, that won't be necessary. Thank you, Andy."

Andy frowned. This wasn't right. "Pearce, you seem very – well, blasé about all this. I said he died the way the others did – and you didn't question that?"

A sigh. *"I know what's been happening there. I just needed…unofficial confirmation."*

"So what next? Police involvement? Because that's the next step here."

Pearce chuckled darkly. *"Come on, Andy. You know very well these guys will have one of Cambridgeshire's Finest on their payroll. No way can they make all these bodies disappear without collusion."*

That, he'd suspected. "So what are you going to do?"

"Question is…what are YOU going to do?" And then he told Andy what was going to happen next.

The boar sniffed the air. Its nostrils twitched wetly: twin plumes of steam snorted into the air from its snout as it effortlessly released its first reborn breath. The flanks of the beast moved like a pair of bellows, contracting and expanding. Each breath that escaped the animal rumbled in its throat, each breath a warning. And then it stood.

Its bristling hide sounded like white noise in the silent warehouse. Its black, dead eyes scanned the warehouse slowly, contemplating its surroundings – or searching for prey. The unnatural white tusks gleamed like ivory in the glare of the ceiling lights.

The eyes narrowed as they fixed on the van - an almost human gesture, Rob thought, as though the beast recognised it and hated it.

And when the beast's head turned to regard the three men standing horrified and disbelieving behind it, the eyes narrowed again. Rob Benson knew then that the creature recognised him.

But what else did it remember? Why had it come back? Rob stared into the eyes of the boar. He backed away slowly, edging to the rear wall of the warehouse. The boar stood, motionless save for the heaving of its flanks, the steam pouring into the cold air – breath that reeked, stank of decomposing organs and rotten meat. The stench of death.

Now he knew why Jasper had been so fearful, so reluctant to enter the warehouse. He looked to the entrance, saw Jasper sitting by a gap in the double doors. His hackles had raised, lips pulled back from his teeth. Both ears were flat against his head.

The boar squealed as Rob tried to move past him, its wickedly sharp tusks rolling in his direction. He froze against the wall, remained still. The boar roared again, its message clear. *Remain where you are!*

Rob looked over to the forklift truck that they had used to pull the beast off the van yesterday.

No harm in trying, he thought. The boar was staring at Harrison and Higgins, both men frozen immobile in horror and fear. Its eyes were off Rob, now was the time –

It moved like lightning, tearing its bulk around to block his path to the forklift. It lowered its head and one of its tusks prodded his calf. He let out a sharp yelp of pain. Then another nod forward from the boar: another jabbing, sharp pain in his other calf. He fell to his knees, his face level with the boar's snout. He stared at it, saw its eyes gleam with anticipation. The tiny red pinpricks of its pupils dilated, scarlet holes of death widening to take him. Black saliva dripped from its gaping mouth, pooling on the floor like tar. It moved closer, its tusks brushing against his throat.

Hearing sobbing from Andy Hughes was one of the strangest sounds Phil Lotson had ever heard. It was a sound that just didn't fit with the man, not with the almost unnatural calm and self control he had displayed earlier. It chilled him more than the screaming of rage and hatred that Andy had thrown at him fifteen years ago. This meant the stakes weren't just higher than he'd thought – now they looked unreachable.

The sobbing ceased abruptly, as though Andy was aware that his self-control was slipping – or that he knew he was no longer alone in the garden.

"You knew what Jennifer was in line for. *You knew before you sent me here, you fucker!*"

Phil took a step backwards as Andy swung in his direction. The rising sun reflected in his eyes, blood red shining on cold gold-flecked emerald, and Phil had never seen rage like it before. This was far, far worse than fifteen years ago…

"Then I'll bury them all, Pearce. One way or another, it ends tonight. *And then I'll be coming for you!*"

His eyes blazed as he cut the connection. He didn't say a word to Phil, just pushed past him and stormed into the kitchen.

He stood over the knife block, his hand raised, and Phil's heart sank, his mind slinging him back to that terrible dream, that moment when Andy had wielded the knife.

Then Andy paused. His hand was rigid over the bread knife, as though frozen. Then he smiled.

A smile that chilled Phil far more than the subzero temperature of the shortest day of the year: a smile that was barely human, glorying in violent actions to come.

"Now why should I fuck around with a knife when I've got one of Santa's specials in Rob's van?"

The doorbell rang. A monotone version of Bing Crosby's *White Christmas* floated down the hallway. Phil and Andy looked at each other.

"Guess Rob had a change of heart," Andy said tightly. He looked visibly relieved – Phil knew then that Andy Hughes did not want to be on his own when he ventured into All Souls College. His hand left the bread knife and Phil let out a sigh of relief.

He heard a thundering sound from upstairs. Nick never did know how to walk down stairs quietly. The thought of playing with Jasper again had obviously excited him.

"Don't bother getting the door, Lotson," he heard Kelly call out. "You just stuff your fat arse with more buns."

Andy smiled. "Still a gobby cow, isn't she?" He then stared at his feet, his smile fading. He looked pained.

"She's been good to you, Phil. And for you." When he looked up Phil was stunned to see tears in his eyes.

"A great kid, too. You're a lucky man, Lotson. I'm so glad you have her…"

He heard Kelly curse as the door opened to let the winter chill in. Then a strange tone in her voice.

"Er…can I help you?"

Phil peered around the doorway to see who was at the door. A tall, heavy set man in a black suit and striped college tie stood calmly on the doormat, a briefcase in his left hand, his right hand buried deep in the inside breast pocket of his overcoat. His grey hair sparkled in the winter sun like glitter from the Christmas card Nick had made for them at school. The smile that broke under his steel grey moustache was far from festive.

"Yes, Mrs Lotson. I believe you can." John Franklin lifted his briefcase and shook it gently. Something metallic rattled inside. Phil let out a strangled cry as the head porter of All Souls walked into the hallway uninvited.

The hypnotic gaze was broken. The boar roared: black spittle flying in Rob's face as it was torn from its victim. Rob staggered backwards, watching in disbelief as the speckled black and white fur mingled with the black bristles, sharp canine fangs clashing with porcine tusks. Jasper's teeth sank into the beast's flank and tore away a piece of flesh that came away with a wet tearing sound. It was in his black-blood stained mouth for a brief moment and then his jaws bared once more. His throat was empty and Rob realised with horror that Jasper had swallowed it.

The roaring of the boar, scarcely noticing the wound in its flank, was matched in volume by Jasper's ferocious barking. Jasper didn't have a chance.

But he'd given his caretaker one. Rob wasted no time. In spite of the pain from his bleeding calves, he leapt to his feet and raced to the forklift. He leapt into the cab of the machine and twisted the key.

The machine hummed into life. Rob pressed his foot hard on the pedal and swung the wheel in a hard right lock. He looked behind him and saw the boar throw Jasper clear across the warehouse floor, right up to the gap in the doors. Jasper landed heavily on his back with a yelp, his paws scrabbling in the air.

Rob brought the forklift around, its tines scraping on the concrete with an ear piercing screech, to face the creature. But it wasn't hanging around. Having dealt with Jasper it turned to the nearest human.

Jasper's shattered ribcage made a sickening, clicking sound as he hauled himself along the warehouse floor, whining as he tried to escape the slaughterhouse. His hind legs dangled uselessly, nothing but dead weight now his backbone was broken. His nose twitched as it met the cold, clean air of the outside world.

Higgins let out a groan, his stomach bulging. The boar snorted wetly, shaking its head to dislodge its tusks from Higgins' belly – or rather, Rob realised, to enlarge the wound it had made. The tusks came free with a triumphant flourish and a sickening, squelching sound. The beast shook its head again, more vigorously, in an attempt to remove the garland of blue and red intestine that trailed around its tusks. Higgins screamed again as he saw his own internal organs pulled out and dropping to the floor.

Higgins sank to the floor like a split sack of potatoes. His legs gave way and he fell heavily to his knees before toppling into the glistening pile of blood and offal in front of him. The boar turned its head to the ground, raising a paw to rid itself of the lower intestine that crowned it, oblivious to the mechanical yellow monster speeding towards it.

Instead it turned its attention to the horrified Terry Harrison who stood to one side of the now-dead director of Granta Office Supplies. His feet slid in the red mess. The boar stood its ground, steam rising from its gaping maw, daring Harrison to move.

"I'm marking YOUR *card, motherfucker!"* Rob screamed, aiming the machine towards the beast. His words echoed around the warehouse, rolled through the partially-open doorway leading to the offices and the workers beyond. He pulled down on the lever that controlled the elevation of the mast. With a whine the forks moved upwards.

He saw Harrison break free, running towards him and the forklift truck. He took his foot off the pedal, realising that if he carried on he would impale Harrison and not the boar.

"KISS-ARSE!" he bellowed. *"SHIFT! Fucking MOVE!"* To get the speed was one thing, difficult enough in this limited space – but he needed to get the angle right. First time.

Harrison stumbled, slipping on the pool of blood from his boss. That was all the boar needed. Its right tusk tore into the back of his thigh and drove upwards at a sharp angle, up through his buttock and beyond.

Even over the noise of the electric motor Rob could hear the scrape of tusk against pelvic bone as it worked its way through Harrison's groin, bursting through in an explosion of blood and urine. The scream was barely human.

The boar continued its charge, a flick of its powerful neck muscles flipping the writhing sales rep over its head. Its tusk slid out with a sickening plopping sound, and Terry Harrison crumpled in a heap besides Mark Higgins, bleeding and weeping.

Now the boar was in Rob's sights. He made another, final adjustment on the elevation. Only when the tines were level with the softer grey fur of its belly did the beast seem aware of what was coming.

It tried to move sideways but wasn't fast enough. Its left flank was angled towards the speeding truck when the forks struck.

The left tine entered the creature's throat smoothly, passing out just below its right ear, while the right struck the ribcage with a jarring thud. The creature roared and thrashed on the impaling tines: the wheel spun in Rob's hands and he fought to control it, burning the skin of his palms in the process. The rubber wheels of the forklift painted black smears on the warehouse floor as Rob fought to keep the machine moving. He pulled down on the mast elevation, raising the beast to his eye level, and kept his foot on the pedal. The machine bumped, tilted to the left as it ran over something then came back down to the floor with a crash. He could smell the stench of acid escaping from the battery cells behind him.

Only when the red coated tines hit the far wall, crashing into the brickwork on the side of the entrance doors, was the truck halted. He pulled on the park brake and jumped out of the cab, sank to his knees, shuddering and watching the beast buck and writhe its agonised death on the forks. Black blood splattered and dripped on the floor along with chunks of masonry and clouds of brick dust. He shut his eyes against the beast's horrifying shriek of pain, an almost human cry. Coughing up brick dust, Rob heard more cries – more human than...

He opened his eyes and gasped.

The tines of the forklift had struck something else before they had entered the wall. The right had entered Mark Higgins' already gored belly like a final insult. The left…

Oh, dear God. The left…he stayed on his knees, clasping the sides of his head, moaning. He couldn't look up. He stared at the floor, gibbering.

He could see Higgins' entrails, crowned with an envelope that had been brown once, with his name written on it.

He heard voices from behind the closed door and stood up shakily, knowing he had to move. No one would believe him if he told them why he had run the forklift into the wall.

No, he decided as he ran blindly towards the exit, his eyes stung by the dissipating clouds of ash and black dust. *When the rest of the crew start work there's only one conclusion they're gonna draw.*

The boar had disappeared. All that remained of it was the black dust that seared Rob's throat and stung his eyes. No sign of the creature that he had run through with the forklift.

Just the impaled bodies of Mark Higgins and Terry Harrison: the latter's groin pierced and pinned not by the tusk of a creature that had no right to exist, but the steel of an industrial machine operated by a man.

Rob sobbed as he picked up the shattered body of Jasper, already going cold in the morning air. He was dimly aware of curious faces pressed against the windows of the office building opposite but concentrated more on opening the side door, getting Geoff Michael's dog into the van. His head rolled on the wooden partition, blood oozing from the gored holes in his body. Blood that soaked into the bubble wrapped shotgun that Andy had brought with him.

Rob slammed the door shut, sobbing uncontrollably, but this time with rage and grief rather than fear.

Now he believed.

TWENTY TWO

Phil Lotson's eyes were so rooted on the briefcase and its contents that he didn't notice Andy slip quietly away.

Franklin kicked shut the door behind him. Only when Kelly and Nick opened their mouths to scream did Phil realise that Franklin had withdrawn his hand from the inside pocket. He saw what Franklin was pointing at his family and he opened his mouth to scream.

The head porter lowered his briefcase, wiped his feet on the mat and walked forwards to Kelly. He grabbed her by the hair and pushed the barrel of the Browning Hi-Power handgun under her nose.

"Mr Lotson." Franklin spoke slowly and calmly, without looking into the kitchen. "In the living room, if you wouldn't mind. Take your boy with you. And tell him to keep quiet. No one's going to get hurt."

Phil blinked as the 9mm automatic swung in his direction. He froze. He looked at the mute, terrified face of his wife, shaking as Franklin pushed the silenced Browning into the small of her back. Nick began to cry.

Phil's reaction took him by as much surprise as it did Franklin. The vision of that summer day, that trip punting down the river of blood and the killing of his wife and son, flooded his mind while adrenaline flooded his body. Without even crying out he launched himself down the hallway, a cannonball aimed at the head porter.

A soft thud and his left leg gave way. He sank to the floor, his momentum carrying him forward, rolling along the carpet. Only when he came to a halt by Franklin's feet did the pain from his exploded kneecap make itself known. His scream was barely human, and brought fresh cries of terror from his family.

Franklin crouched down with a grin. He placed the Browning on the welcome mat, just out of reach. Not that Phil was going to reach for the gun anyway. He was twisting on the floor, hyperventilating, consciousness cruelly eluding him.

Franklin rose to his feet and reached for Nick and Kelly. He clamped a firm hand over each mouth. He pressed hard, his fingernails gouging into the flesh of their cheeks, making them struggle even more, and their muffled cries rose in pitch. Then he slammed their heads together.

They stood at the foot of the stairs, swaying like drunks.

Franklin worked fast. Turning back to the briefcase he flipped open the catches and raised the lid. The black and red mist of agony lifted slightly from Phil's vision, slightly, just enough to see what Franklin held in his hands.

Phil's cries were stifled by the five inch strip of ducting tape Franklin pressed against his mouth. The head porter rose to his feet.

"That's the trouble with these modern homes," he said. "The walls are so thin, and I can't count on both of your neighbours being out at work. Not this side of Christmas."

Phil found that not being able to scream made the pain in his obliterated knee even worse. He thrashed wildly on the floor: his face white, blood seeping into the carpet.

Franklin shook his head as he turned to Kelly and Nick. They were starting to make noises again.

He grabbed Nick by his sweatshirt and shoved him through the open doorway over Phil, into the living room. He crashed to the floor, falling besides the presents under the tree. Franklin was on him in an instant. Pressing his bended knees into Phil's belly he pulled Nick's hands behind his back and wrapped another length of tape around them. He was hauled to his feet, another piece of tape clamped over his mouth, and pushed back to the floor. Phil felt Nick's bound hands collide with his shattered leg and brilliant white light blinded him.

When his vision cleared and the pain became almost tolerable, he saw Franklin had repeated the process with Kelly. Kelly's wide eyes bore into Phil's piteously. Franklin looked down and nonchalantly kicked Phil just below the sternum.

Phil choked on the breath that tried to evacuate his winded abdomen, the gag too tight to allow it to exit from his mouth.

Heavy swishing, then darkness. Phil almost entertained the faint hope that it was an angel's wings sweeping down to take them away from this terrible nightmare but he knew that Franklin had just drawn the curtains.

The head porter went to the dining table at the far end of the room and pulled forward two of the heavy pine chairs. He pushed Kelly onto one, secured her shoulders to the backrest and tied her ankles to the legs. Then he did the same to Nick.

He went back to the coffee table, looked briefly at the photos on top of the folders and raised his eyebrows in genuine surprise.

"My, my. Freeland really took a chance, didn't he?. No David Bailey, but still…" he frowned. "The diary. Where is it?"

Phil stared at the red foil garlands on the ceiling, convulsed in pain. He heard the heavy footsteps of the head porter approach him.

The duct tape was savagely stripped away, taking strands of beard hair and pieces of skin with it. Phil's gasping, hyperventilating noises sounded alien even to him. He'd never heard any creature, let alone a human being, make noises like this.

Franklin stooped over Phil, his steady, normal breathing a mocking insult to Phil's own. When Phil's breathing approached something like normality, Franklin spoke.

"Mr Lotson…Phil." He smiled gently. "I must have that journal. Tell me where it is, please."

Phil heard muffled squeaks from Kelly. He heard Nick struggling in his chair, but couldn't bring himself to look at them.

"G- go f-fuck yourself," he gasped.

Franklin waved a disapproving finger. "Now, Phil. That's really not the attitude. You're in no position to be abusive. Give me the journal, or your family dies while you watch."

Phil's voice rose to a scream. *"You f-fucking maniac!"*

Franklin clamped a palm over Phil's mouth. Phil tried to bite down on it, but Franklin's grip was too tight. He tasted the sweaty leather of Franklin's black glove and wanted to retch.

"I told you to keep the noise down," Franklin said in a reasonable tone. "If you insist on screaming like a baby I'll cut out your tongue and you can write the location on the Christmas tablecloth with it."

The threat silenced Phil far more than the hand over his mouth. He knew Franklin meant it. Franklin removed his hand.

"Once again, Phil. Where is the journal of Charles Harvey?"

Phil remained silent. Franklin sighed theatrically.

"Very well." He placed a fresh strip of duct tape over Phil's bleeding lips and went to the hallway. Phil turned his head fearfully. His eyes widened as the head porter lifted a small metal case and waved it at him…and then Andy Hughes was on him.

Andy's silent momentum knocked Franklin off his feet and both went crashing into the front door with a heavy thud. Franklin cried out in surprise but not pain, even though the impact his head made on the door handle must have agonised and dazed him.

Must have, Phil thought.

Franklin whirled round, unfazed and in no visible pain. He dropped to his knees, a swift punch aimed at Andy's groin. His left hand went to the welcome mat to pick up the Browning. Went down and came back empty.

Andy grunted and staggered, but kept his grip on the silenced Browning. He staggered backwards, the gun raised and pointed directly at Franklin. Franklin grinned.

"Hughes! Didn't think we'd meet here…" he got to his feet slowly, his eyes shining in anticipation. "I see one of Andraste's Children had a go at you. Well done, laddie. Few escape them. So I'll finish what they started…"

Andy laughed mirthlessly. "Want the diary, Franklin? Did you think we'd be so stupid as to leave it here?"

Franklin's eyes narrowed and his voice was a hiss. *"Where is it?"*

Andy didn't move. "Not here." A small bead of sweat trickled down his ear. He'd seen the state Phil was in.

Phil let out a moan as fresh pain rode him. Andy glanced at him, just a glance, no more than a second –

But that was long enough for Franklin. The briefcase flew up in front of him, smashing into Andy's elbow. Andy grunted in pain, his finger clenched around the trigger as his arm shot up, but the gun didn't fire.

Safety catch, Phil thought dreamily as Franklin followed up his counter attack. The head porter's right fist powered into Andy's abdomen. Phil saw fresh blood spurt under the light brown T-shirt from the wounds the boar had inflicted last night, wounds that Franklin's devastating blow had opened up again. A dazed look passed Andy's face, he swayed on his feet, and the Browning clattered against the wall.

Franklin's left fist shot forward, as lightning fast and devastating as the right, into the centre of Andy's jaw. Andy's head snapped back and caught the corner of the wooden banister on the staircase. His eyes glazed and he sank to the floor, a thin trail of blood painting his descent on the wall.

Franklin stared impassively for a while before patting down Andy's body, flipping him over and searching the back pockets. He grunted as he saw the bread knife on the floor that Andy had dropped when he had attacked Franklin.

The head porter smiled as he examined the serrated edge of the blade. Then he picked up the small metal tin from his briefcase. The cranberry coloured lights of the Christmas tree reflected bloodily on it and Phil shrank back in terror. He knew what was coming.

Franklin crouched down in front of him and placed the bread knife on the floor. Then he opened the case like a book, extended towards Phil. He picked out the instrument with care, showing it to Phil's horrified gaze with the same pride as the cutlery salesman he had seen on one of the digital shopping channels recently. The salesman had been chopping up empty tomato cans to show the power of the blade, though - Franklin would not be.

"Say hello to Santa's Little Helper, Mr Lotson." Franklin said in a reverent tone. "Surgical scalpel. The tool of the professional – or the artist."

He lowered the blade, side by side with the bread knife from the kitchen. The same bread knife from Phil's dream.

Franklin looked at them both, chewing the nail of his thumb, brows creased, as though he was making a choice about which dessert to have after a fine meal.

"Tough choice, eh, Mr Lotson? Which do I use first on young Nicky's throat? The scalpel will open the jugular cleanly and instantly, like an overcooked pasta tube. But where's the fun in that? Perhaps the bread knife. Messy, but much more painful. Ah, decisions, decisions…" his eyes hardened. "Decisions, Mr Lotson. Your decision is the easiest one in the world. 'Do I tell Mr Franklin where the diary is or do I let him kill my boy and my lassie?' You needn't agonise over this one."

Phil couldn't take his eyes off the bread knife. He shrank into the carpet, curling into a ball. He saw Andy's unconscious body in the hallway, infrequent shallow breathing and blood trickling from the head wound. Tears stung his eyes.

Franklin glanced over his shoulder briefly and then back to Phil. He placed a hand under the man's head and pulled it up slightly.

"Now, I'm going to allow you to speak. If you try to scream for help – or even in pain – your wife loses a breast. Understand? Nod once if you do."

In the easy grip of the head porter, Phil quickly moved his head downwards, then up. It was all he could do. That and play for time…

The mental picture of Nicky's open throat spraying blood into the uplighter and the ceiling decorations, the image of Franklin holding Kelly immobile while he sawed into her with the blade she normally used to slice his hot cross buns blanked out his own pain completely.

For the second time the tape was stripped from his mouth. It didn't take as much beard or skin with it this time. Franklin stood over him, watching him sidle over to Kelly leaving a trail of black blood on the carpet. Then he moved.

Phil rolled over onto his back, staring at the uplighter to blot out the tortured look in his wife's widened eyes. He blinked away tears and heard the sound of a cotton blouse being torn open, then a muffled holler of terror from Kelly.

"In your own time, Mr Lotson," he heard Franklin say. "I've got all the time in the world."

Phil swallowed noisily and said to the uplighter: "It's not here."

He heard Franklin sigh. "Don't insult my intelligence."

"I promise you, I don't have it. I had it this morning and I…" he forced himself not to gabble. He forced himself not to look at Andy.

Because Andy had read the diary, after this he would believe. *Where did you put it, Andy?* He knew Franklin was going to kill them all, regardless of whether he was given the book or not. He just had to play for time, hope Andy came to, hope Rob came back…

Hope. It was nothing, but it was all he had.

"And you *what*? Where did you put it, Phillip?"

"I posted it… Parkside Police Station…"

A pause. "You're telling the truth? No lies?"

"Honest to God! It went last night, will be on their desks this morning - "

"This morning? Even though you only got back from Freeland's last night and spent this morning going through the files. And you decided to send them the book." He shook his head. His voice steadily rose in volume, in anger.

"Not the files with the more believable and verifiable truth - you gave them something that can be dismissed as the ramblings of an eighteenth century madman. Not photos and lists of those who could clear the Missing Persons files of several international police agencies. Look at me, Lotson. LOOK AT ME!"

Phil twisted his head around. He saw Franklin take the knife from Kelly's left breast, and position it under her right ear.

"In precisely ten seconds time I will have your wife smiling again, through her neck. Now, for the last time. *Where is the diary?*"

The point of the bread knife pressed into Kelly's neck. A small droplet of blood materialised and ran down her shoulder, identical to the plastic red berries from the table's centrepiece. Phil closed his eyes and opened his mouth to scream.

Then the blade was withdrawn. Franklin put a finger to his lips, making a hushing motion to Phil.

"Hughes. He's already read the diary, hasn't he?"

Phil's hunched shoulders slumped.

"I'll take that as a yes, then." Franklin sighed, and looked back to Kelly. "Well, I don't think he'll believe a word of it. But I'm not going to take any chances. Detective Inspector Boyd will find it when he gets here, I'm certain."

He dropped the bread knife into Kelly's lap. She recoiled as though a snake had landed there. It fell to the floor.

Franklin approached Phil slowly, smiling at his quizzical expression.

"Confused? Don't worry. I'll explain it all as I'm working." He gently wiped the blood from Phil's chin and shook the blood from his gloved fingers. Then he tore off a fresh piece of ducting tape and sealed Phil's mouth again.

Phil groaned, realising that Franklin had only wiped the blood away to ensure the adhesive on the tape stuck.

Franklin glanced at his watch and frowned. He glanced at the unconscious body of Andy, eyes narrowed for any signs of recovery. When he was satisfied he turned back to Phil and picked up the scalpel.

Andy Hughes stood in the archway dividing Old Court from Cloister Court. He squinted against the fierce glare from the fire raging through the Great Hall. One of the mullioned windows exploded under pressure from the superheated air within. Fragments of stained glass and lead framework shot across the snow covered lawns of Old Court, clattering on the stone of the ornamental fountain.

Another explosion, another window blossomed. This time a fireball carried the fragments of lead and glass, but Andy ignored this. His attention was focussed on what was coming past the porter's lodge, a sight which almost took his breath away.

White horses galloped through the narrow passageway into the Old Court, the same unearthly white horses that had haunted his dreams previously.

Only this time the location was different. Rather than pursuing him across country, over unfriendly moorland and foreboding valleys, they had now followed him to All Souls College.

Dozens of them, two abreast. Giant male beasts, the size of shire horses: their unmarked white coats glowing with some inner light. Eyes burned like the rubies in the boar's head in the Hall, eyes of fire. Lips snarled and black spittle flew onto the lawns, staining the white snow like drops of diesel oil. Their steel-shod hooves threw sparks from the cobbled walkways, sizzled on the snow as they thundered towards the screaming figures pouring out of the Great Hall's double doors.

Andy closed his eyes against the slaughter that followed, but the screams of those crushed underfoot, along with the wet crunching sounds of stampeded flesh and bone painted a stark visual image in his mind. He opened his eyes.

One of the horses halted and turned to him. Blood on its hooves glistened in the hellish light from the inferno raging through All Souls College. Its scarlet eyes rolled and it reared above him, front hooves clawing the air. Its blood-splattered mane bristled with a life of its own. The whinny that came from its lips was a cry of triumph, one that was immediately taken up by the other horses, over two hundred identical white stallions, a song of victory and death to compete with the Song to Andraste.

The flames licked and rolled over the stone of the college walls, and it was with streaming eyes, almost blinded by the heat and smoke, that Andy realised the fire was not affecting the horses. Their ethereal white coats remained unsullied by the billowing smoke, the flesh untouched by the high flames raging around them.

No, not around them, he realised. Raging *from* them. Andy let out a cry of fear and wonderment that was quickly swallowed by the raging thunder of the horses' stampede through the archway dividing Old Court and Cloister Court. Past him and onwards to the rear of the grounds.

To the woods and the creatures that waited for them.

Each stallion rolled its red-ember eyeballs as it thundered past, and the rush of air that followed in their wake brought the flames closer to him. The heat from the fire rolled over his skin and burned the air from his lungs but there was no pain. Instead he felt cleansed. Tears of joy and relief rolled down his cheeks, evaporating to steam in the heat. The last of the white chargers exited the archway and in their wake Andy saw the human bodies. Blood oozed and bubbled away to nothing from the wounds inflicted by those unearthly hooves, hoof prints that still glowed. Heads were shattered, faces mashed to an unrecognisable pulp. But the ceremonial robes and gowns left him in no doubt as to their identity.

The chapel and Great Hall exploded, adding to the rolling sea of fire that swept through Old Court and roaring over the remains of the Fellowship of All Souls and consuming them utterly, before reaching for Andy.

Just before they reached him the flames parted momentarily and allowed him to see the face within.

A face that retained its greenish hue in spite of the fire. A face that kept its halo of winter greenery, the oak, holly and mistletoe twisting triumphantly in the flames. A face that fixed on Andy with human eyes and allowed a broad smile of approval to break its stone visage.

And behind, in the far distance, escaping through the cobbled archway past the porter's lodge, out of the college and into Trinity Street – he saw Jennifer.

Alive. Free. And unharmed. She halted, turning to look over her shoulder. A look of sadness and gratitude in her blue eyes. She smiled and mouthed the words *I love you.*

That was when he woke, returned to consciousness with a cry of jubilation. For the first time since this whole affair began he felt hope.

A dream sent by the Green Man that offered hope: a resolution to the evil events. Victory and justice over the Fellowship, and the destruction of All Souls. The horses, terrifying and majestic at the same time, were a symbol. No horses like that had ever existed on the planet, he knew that. They looked as though they'd come from Hell itself, but the destruction they had wrought was not for evil ends.

And I beheld a pale horse, and upon it a pale rider…and death was his name…

"And all Hell followed with him," Andy whispered. Then his vision cleared, the headache descended, and he saw through the open doorway the blood on the carpet of the Lotsons' living room.

The smell hit him like the wall of fire in his dream. A sweet coppery odour combined with the stench of loosened sphincter muscles. The living room was dark but there was just enough light for him to see Phil Lotson and the pool of blood expanding underneath him. The scattered photos and notebooks from Freeland had gone.

Phil lay on his side, knees drawn up to his chest. His face was pale, whiter than the snow on the lawns of All Souls. His eyes contained a very faint spark of life, but also a look of such utter despair and horror that Andy momentarily forgot about the pounding in the back of his head and the ravaging agony in his belly.

He pushed himself through the doorway. He saw Phil's hands were taped behind his back, unable to reach the wooden handle of the thing that was buried in his stomach.

"Oh Jesus," Andy crouched down and raised a hand to the blood-stained, tearful cheeks of Phil Lotson.

There was a lethargic shuffling of feet, with no energy. The final movements of a dying man. Andy now saw huge gouges in the carpet, some so deep that the wood and concrete underneath would have been visible were it not for the blood that had welled up in deep pools there. Behind him there were cracks in the plaster on the lower wall where Phil's head had struck it repeatedly. Andy closed his eyes, felt the room spinning. He was amazed the Christmas tree was still standing.

Phil Lotson's body must have jerked, thrashed and writhed as though lethal charges of electricity rode it, wracked with agony. The duct tape sealing his mouth would not even have allowed him to scream properly.

Phil's eyes blinked slowly then turned in Andy's direction. A look of recognition: but no sense of relief or any lessening of the despair. If anything, it had increased. Andy was afraid to take the gag off.

Behind him Andy could hear a buzzing and sizzling sound, like a wasp caught by a fly zapper.

The tape came away with a thick wet sound as Phil coughed and then tried to scream.

All that came out was a rattling, wet sound. His mouth opened wide enough for Andy to see jagged stumps of broken teeth and clotted blood.

The wet rattle slowly transformed into sobbing. Andy knelt down in Phil's blood, positioned himself to hold his head and shoulders in his lap. He closed his eyes as Phil wept, rocking back and forth with Phil's sobbing head in his arms.

When Andy opened his eyes he kept them fixed firmly on the closed curtains, trying to ignore the smell coming behind him. He knew now why it was so dark. He'd caught a brief glance of the uplighter and heard the blood hissing against the light bulb. Arterial blood, which had shot up, splattered on the ceiling, and dripped into the uplighter.

"…dead…all dead…"

The words were badly formed because of Phil's shattered mouth, slurred speech that was barely audible.

"…oh God in Heaven, how they suffered. He wouldn't let me scream, wouldn't let me beg…"

Andy held Phil tighter. The words he heard hit him like a blow to the stomach.

"He – he held my head, forced my eyelids back so that I could watch them die."

Andy's stomach constricted further. He held Phil's head back slightly and looked down. His gaze met Phil's haunted eyes then travelled down to the bread knife embedded in Phil's stomach. He put a hand to it. Phil gasped.

"You – you shouldn't have done that, Andy…"

Andy loosened his grip instantly. "I'm sorry…I didn't mean – "

"No…no." A heavy, rattling sigh. "Fingers…fingerprints. He planned that. Police…"

Andy looked back into the hall. The phone. *Police? Fuck that. Ambulance first, surely.*

"Police…police coming. Fingerprints." Phil hung his head.

Then Andy realised why Franklin was no longer here. It didn't matter about the diary now, whether he'd read it or not. There would be no way he could act on the information received if he was being held by the police for the murder of the Lotson family.

Fingerprints. His fingerprints, on the bread knife that Franklin had left embedded in Phil's stomach. Sirens, in the distance, coming closer. Alerted by Franklin.

Andy could do nothing. His head slumped, his chin resting on Phil's crown. Phil's breaths were slower and shallow, until finally there was nothing at all.

Nothing but Andy's weeping and the screech of tyres on the road outside, the blue revolving light spilling through the gap in the curtains, sweeping across the blood-soaked carpet and the open necks of the dismembered bodies tied to the chairs in the dining room.

The open necks that smiled a welcome to the uniformed officers who entered the house.

TWENTY THREE

Jason Franklin's euphoria at his new found freedom was short-lived. Enjoyable though it was to be behind the wheel of a vehicle again after all those months, he knew it wouldn't last so he'd tried to put his foot down, make the most of his short time on the road.

That wasn't going to happen, though. He'd only had six driving lessons and the vehicle was hardly capable of head turning speeds. Every clumsy, inexperienced gear change led to thick black plumes of smoke belching from the exhaust and a petulant whine from the engine. The van was on its way out.

That wasn't important. At least he knew he'd give it a good send off. What worried him now was how long it would be before the pursuit began. Sam Dawson would be relieved at eight a.m – just as well he'd been working a double shift – but the cook-chill Luton was a well known sight around the hospitals of Cambridge and its deliveries were timed. The van's disappearance and the discovery of the drivers in a pool of blood in the kitchens of the Phoenix Unit would hasten its description and registration number being relayed to the police. He had little time.

A petrol station came into view. An empty forecourt, the cashier yawning widely in his booth. Jason hadn't intended to stop; there was more than enough fuel in the tank. But the sight of the neon red sign glowing in the night sky reminded him of something else he might need. Something that would have served him well at the Founder's Feast last year if he'd had the chance to use them.

Of course, a van loaded with unleaded fuel would be far more effective than a couple of petrol cans, but what the hell. *For old time's sake.*

Ten minutes later, with three plastic green petrol cans purchased with cash from Connie Teague's wallet and filled with fuel paid for by the van's fuel card, Jason Franklin felt complete for the first time in over a year. He bit into a Ginster's pasty as he drove off towards the centre of Cambridge.

He was concerned about entering the college too early. Daylight unmasked a multitude of sins, especially stolen three ton white metal ones – but he had no choice. He had to get the vehicle inside the college grounds as soon as possible. The woods – the Nemeton – would hide him and his vehicle. And The Elder would tell him what to do next, he was certain.

He pressed the channel buttons on the radio in an attempt to find something Christmassy.

As he finished the pasty he wondered idly if the 'other' mentioned by The Elder was on his way to the Nemeton – and what he was bringing to assist in the destruction of All Souls. He wondered if Phil Lotson had managed to speak to Freeland, if Freeland was still alive.

Well, no matter. Pointless worrying. Omelettes and broken eggs, Jase. Omelettes and broken eggs. Just wish I could remember what I'd done to Sam Dawson, though….

He turned the volume up and tried to sing along to The Waitresses' *Christmas Wrapping*. He couldn't remember all the words, so he made some up as he drove.

"Christmas magic…will bring this tale to a very happy ending…"

Christmas magic was the last thing on Rob Benson's mind as he drove down Jesus Lane, blinking away tears. Every time he came to a halt at traffic lights or pedestrian crossings he could hear the soft thump of a small furry body rolling up to the bulkhead.

Sorry, shit bag. I did my best. But at least I got that fucker…

The broad wintry expanse of Midsummer Common flew by on his right. If only I had wings, he thought. *Fly right over it, drop past the bridge and I'd already be there.*

It was only a matter of time before the bodies were discovered in the Granta warehouse. The Transit had been seen arriving – and leaving. They'd have heard his voice shouting in the warehouse as he drove the forklift straight towards the boar. They'd have heard him shout the name of Terry Harrison, and would remember the grudge the two of them had shared.

His fingerprints would be on the controls of the forklift and the bloodstained envelope containing his P45. His boss and his love rival impaled on the tines. Only one conclusion would be drawn. And only one person could help him.

"Yes, Andy. Yes, Phil, I fucking believe it now, okay?" he shouted at the windscreen as he rounded Mitcham's Corner. He just hoped they knew what to do now.

Because I'm fresh out of ideas. The Green Man was silent.

"What say you, old man? Still wanna go to…what is it, the Nemeton? Don't know what that is, but if it's at All Souls you're in luck. Because I bet Andy'll be going there soon…and he's going to need you."

And the shotgun in the van, he thought. Now he was glad Andy had brought it with him to Cambridge. At least they'd have something to fight with...

"Assuming the Old Bill don't stop me getting into the college," he muttered to the Victorian villas of DeFreville Avenue. The gothic turrets frowned down on him.

He passed the church and turned into Phil's street. Past Kelly's battered red Rover, he saw a space that had been filled earlier. He frowned as he swung the van into the space, trying to think what was there before. He shut the engine down.

A blue Toyota Celica, now gone...

He slammed his fist onto the dash. The Celica! For fuck's sake, of course he'd seen it before. Only now it was gone did his mind fill in the gaps. He had seen it in the tiny car park on the Trinity Street side of All Souls. It belonged to the head porter.

And now it was gone, which meant Franklin had done whatever he had come for.

A sick feeling rose in his guts, a feeling that turned to icy horror as he heard the sirens.

His shoulders slumped. He lowered his head onto the steering wheel, taking deep, shuddering breaths.

Christ, for it to come to this...what bloody hope did we have?

The icy slush of fear and despair churned again in his stomach, a physical pain this time. He clutched his stomach and sank to the floor of the cab, out of sight of the two uniformed police officers that ran out of the Vauxhall Astra patrol car.

There was a hammering of fists on wood, not metal. Only when the door to the Lotson's house crashed open did Rob realise they hadn't come for him.

He cautiously peered over the steering wheel, the slushing in his stomach forgotten. The door was open, the two uniforms already inside. Rob looked at the metallic green Mondeo that now pulled alongside the patrol car.

The officer climbing out of this car wasn't in uniform. He had a dark blue overcoat through which Rob could see the lapels of a non-descript grey suit jacket and blue tie.

He was young, late twenties with cropped, ginger hair and a neatly trimmed goatee. His face was pale with watery blue eyes and he had a slight frame that he carried with a strange mixture of arrogance and nervousness.

He entered the open door. Rob cautiously flicked the key in the ignition to allow the electrics to work. He lowered the window, and then twisted the key back to the off position.

Five minutes passed before the plain clothes officer returned, a mobile phone clenched to his ear, his face even paler than before.

Rob quickly sank beneath the line of sight again, crouching in the footwell. He listened to the detective's words.

"Sir? DI Boyd here. Hell of a job you did in there, Mr Franklin… Did you have to be so bloody thorough? The child as well? Yes, we've got Hughes: pinning this on him will be no problem…what happened to the Lotsons is the work of a psycho, so - "

Rob closed his eyes in despair. He fought back a sob.

"I'm sorry, Mr Franklin. I meant no disrespect." Rob heard the detective swallow nervously. "I meant that with Hughes' previous record of violence and his grievance with Lotson, his guilt will be beyond question... I see. Very well, sir." The call was ended.

Rob heard Boyd mutter something, then footsteps retreating back to the house. The door was left open.

Rob pulled himself back into the driver's seat. He stared at the closed door and saw the welcoming Christmas wreath was now on the floor. He swallowed. Phil, Kelly and Nick. Dead. *Killed by Franklin.*

Three deaths attributed to Andy Hughes. And what could he do? Any moment now the call would go out to Boyd's colleagues, with a full description and registration number of the van.

Within moments both he and Andy would be charged with murders they hadn't committed. Both out of the picture: allowing the Fellowship of All Souls to continue their obscene ritual.

"Wonder if we'll share the same cell, Andy?" Rob whispered hoarsely. He turned to look at the Green Man. The eyes were closed, the mouth frozen open. No help, no comfort, and no advice forthcoming.

"Who's going to take you to All Souls now?"

He stared through the rapidly steaming windscreen at the green Mondeo. Then at the patrol car, the blue lights still flashing.

Three coppers. And surely there'd be more on the way after the discovery of the bodies in the warehouse.

Okay, he thought, closing his eyes. *Down to me and me alone.*

He didn't have much time. Neither did he have anything to lose. He stepped out of the van, closed the door gently and walked to the back of the van. He opened the rear doors and looked inside.

He tried not to stare at Jasper's face, his brown eyes staring lifelessly at him, his black-blood stained mouth fixed open in a permanent rictus. There was a scorched smell of melting plastic. He blinked at the dark bulkhead. For a brief moment he thought he could see green shoots trailing and reaching for…

No. Can't be. Hallucinating already, Benson. Grief and wishful thinking.

He focussed on the bubble-wrapped firearm instead.

With the second kick to his bleeding stomach Andy Hughes almost blacked out. Pain flooded his entire body. With his hands cuffed behind his back he couldn't fight back or resist. He writhed on the carpet, his face burying into the pools of blood from Phil's body.

Blackness played at the corners of his eyes, promising him oblivion, and then cruelly denying it.

The uniformed officer's eyes were filled with loathing and disgust. His beard was similar to Phil's, Andy thought hazily: the same unkempt dark brown turning to grey. *Probably Phil's age as well. With a wife and kids, maybe a boy the same age as Nick. That'd explain the rage and the hatred.*

"Bastard! Murdering *bastard*!" Another kick thudded into his ribs. This time Andy screamed.

The door to the hallway opened. Cold air from outside accompanied Boyd. The uniform snapped his head back at the approach of his superior and lowered his foot.

"Willis. Where's Beasley?" Boyd asked in crisp, upper class tones. He seemed unconcerned with the kicking Andy Hughes was receiving. *Thinks I deserve it*, Andy thought with a grimace. The stabbing pain in his stomach lessened to a dull, throbbing ache, allowing him to breathe again.

"Throwing up in the kitchen. Can't say I blame him after what this…this *demon* has done here." Willis spat on Andy's face. "Murdering cunt…"

"All right, Willis, that'll do. Go and nursemaid Beasley. I want a chat with Mr Hughes."

Willis wiped the saliva that trickled from his beard. "Make it a physical one, sir."

"It'll be painful, don't worry about that. Now go."

Boyd watched the door to the hallway close with his watery blue eyes. He squatted down next to Andy. He bunched up the ends of his overcoat to ensure no blood stained it.

"I don't approve of Mr Franklin's methods, Hughes. But he's a necessary evil. People like you and Lotson…what you tried to do could end all human life on this planet, don't you realise that?"

Andy lifted his head from the floor and fixed Boyd with a contemptuous sneer.

"You an All Souls alumni, pal?"

Boyd's watery eyes hardened. "As a matter of fact, yes. I graduated from there eight years ago."

Andy coughed and spat. "Figures."

Boyd glanced behind Andy at the dead, bloodless bodies tied to the chairs. The sunlight was brighter, stronger, and had forced its way through the gap in the curtains. The drying blood was ruby coloured in the harsh light of day. His voice wavered.

"You've brought this on yourself, you know." His words lacked conviction, and Andy laughed grimly, knowing that Boyd was trying to convince himself, not his prisoner.

"Like I brought on what's going to happen to Jen?"

Boyd sighed. "Yes, Mr Franklin told me you'd find out about that. One of the reasons you must not be allowed anywhere near All Souls. I'm sorry, Hughes, I really am. Just take comfort from the fact she suffers for humanity – and that she won't have to visit you in prison."

Andy roared. Boyd sighed sympathetically. He cocked his head to the left, frowning as he heard a noise from the doorway.

He froze rigid at the touch of something cold and metallic pressed to his ear.

"No one's going inside, Boyd. Not Andy, and not me. Don't. Fucking. Move."

Andy raised his pounding head and stared in disbelief. Boyd was still crouched, holding the bottom of his overcoat in his hands to avoid staining – looking for all the world like he was going to take a shit.

Not far off the mark, Andy thought. Having the 20.3 inch barrel of a Franchi SPAS 12 combat shotgun thrust in your ear was one way of loosening your bowels.

Boyd's eyes bulged in terror as Andy spoke to him calmly.

"Do as he says…Boyd, is it? Yes, Boyd." He pushed himself up from the floor with his knees, wincing. But a damn sight happier than earlier. Now there was hope. He stood slowly, backing away from Boyd.

"No sudden movements, Boyd. Roberto has used one of those before." *Take it easy, Rob. Don't stare too long at the bodies*. Rob's grip on the shotgun was tight, but jittery. Andy could see sweat greased the pistol grip. Rob's trigger finger fluttered.

Boyd let out a little squeak of panic.

"Andy…what the fuck did that monster do to them?" Rob's voice shook as much as his grip on the shotgun. The Christmas tree lights glinted through the holes on the shotgun's folded metal stock.

"Roberto. Cool it. Keep your voice down. Boyd, call out to your men. Get them in here…but no warning."

Rob pulled back on the weapon, allowing Boyd to turn his head and call out. He walked behind the crouching detective, his face pale at the sight of Phil's body. Andy frowned at the blood on Rob's fleece. He didn't look wounded, but badly shaken.

What the fuck's he been up to? What happened in that warehouse? Whatever it was, it had been bad enough for him to believe that coming here was his only option.

"Beasley, Willis!" Boyd yelled. Rob pressed the shotgun into Boyd's right ear now. Boyd took the hint and lowered his voice. "In here now, please, lads."

"Better," muttered Rob. "No, don't get up. Stay on the floor. Crouch if you want, or sit. But don't fucking stand. And keep your hands where I can see 'em."

Andy nodded approvingly. Rob was thinking clearly. With Boyd on the floor he had a clear line of sight on the two uniforms hurrying through the doorway. Rob raised the weapon.

"You. Over to my mate, take his cuffs off. *Slowly.*" He glared as the bearded cop moved over to Andy, then turned his eyes to the younger one.

"Don't even think about it!" Rob roared. Even Andy was surprised by that. The younger cop had been reaching for his two-way radio. Now he raised his hands, palms upwards.

"On the floor, please." His grip on the SPAS 12 was more relaxed, less jittery. Andy tensed as he felt the cuffs twisting on his wrists. He felt the copper breathing nervously behind him as the key turned.

Three things happened then. Andy whirled round, the heel of his palm rising to meet the bridge of his captor's nose. A wet cracking sound followed and the bearded cop's eyes glazed. Blood bubbled from his nose and he fell to the floor, dead.

Rob's eyes widened in horror. The shock of the killing made him lower his arms. Boyd, aware that the shotgun was swinging away from him, took his chance. His hands released the bottoms of his overcoat, his right reaching inside, under the coat, into the jacket and the shoulder holster beneath.

The younger uniform lowered his palms and reached for his two-way. A harsh squawking sound from the black unit followed and he moved back into the hallway, kicking the door to the front room shut.

Andy followed the direction of the noise and reached for the door, pulled it open. He lunged for the cop, grabbed him and dragged him back into the front room. His back was to Boyd and Rob.

It was Rob who saw the Glock 17 in Boyd's hands, who saw Boyd get to his feet and pull back the slide on the handgun, pointed squarely at Andy Hughes' back. It was Rob who stopped him.

"Andy! Get down!" His finger moved of its own accord and snatched at the trigger.

He thought a bomb had exploded. The noise reverberated around the small room, the flare of the muzzle flash was blinding and there was agonising pain in his wrists as the recoil twisted the heavy weapon from his hands.

The Christmas tree toppled over and fell on him as he crashed backwards to the floor, the plastic and glass baubles bouncing on his face before falling into the blood pools from Phil's body.

He shakily got to his feet, pushing the tree away. The cranberry lights flickered once and died. The ringing in his ears was an almost physical presence, his skull housing a bell clapper that tolled for the dead.

He saw the prone figure of Detective Inspector Boyd, thrown by the force of the blast over Andy – who had ducked down immediately on hearing Rob's cry.

Andy pushed the body away from him, grimacing at the charred pieces of ribcage and smouldering, ravaged organs that fell from Boyd's body. His eyes fell on the Glock clasped in the dead grip of the detective. He reached for it, prising the fingers away. He stood, nodded briefly at Rob, and turned to the frozen uniform standing in the doorway. The front door was open.

In, Andy mouthed to the police man. He beckoned with the gun. The uniform took one look at the exploded torso of his superior and shook his head frantically. Andy sighed, reversed his grip on the gun and lashed out.

The ringing in Rob's ears slowly faded. This time he heard the body fall to the floor.

"Swap you," Andy barked, tossing the Glock to him. Rob caught it with shaking hands. It felt light as a feather compared to the heavy assault weapon he had brought into Phil's house.

"Don't worry, the safety's on now." Andy reached behind him and retrieved the SPAS 12. Smoke was still coming from the end of the barrel, and the stench of burnt cordite was almost as strong as the slaughterhouse stench of the living room.

Andy put the shotgun over his right shoulder, his finger resting on the trigger guard. The steel folded stock must have cut into him, the shotgun was that heavy, but Andy seemed oblivious. *Christ, it looks like it was made for him!*

"Rob." His eyes were hard, but full of concern. "You okay? What brought you back here?"

"That boar…don't ask me how, but – it came to life. Attacked me and Jas…"

Andy's eyes narrowed as Rob continued his story. He shook his head, smiled ruefully. "Looks like you're in the same boat as me, Roberto."

Rob couldn't look at the bodies of the Lotsons anymore. He'd never get over this, never. Everywhere he looked, he saw death. The prone bearded body of the first officer, the bones in the bridge of his nose driven upwards into his brain: the twitching figure of the younger uniform, blood pouring from his ears and coating his stab vest – *Christ, where did he hit him?* And the exploded body of the compromised Boyd. *Dead by me!*

He turned to the gap in the curtains, blinking in the warming rays of the winter sunlight that sliced into the room. Through the window he could see the rear doors of the Transit, where Jasper's dead body lay.

*Jesus, so much death…*he swallowed thickly against the rising bile. Andy rested his free hand on Rob's shoulder. His face was strained.

"Come on, pal. We can't hang around now. You don't know, but Jen's been taken."

Rob twisted his head round. His jaw dropped.

"Pearce told me – right after you left. She – she's singing to Andraste now. I've got to get her out."

Rob nodded slowly. He stared at the Glock in his palm. The SPAS 12 resting on Andy's shoulder.

"Need some help, pal?"

Andy's smile was warm and chilling at the same time.

"I'd greatly appreciate it, Roberto." He tossed a key fob to Rob who caught it with his free hand. He stared at it and smiled sadly.

"Boyd's gun *and* his motor? Sure you don't want me to take his fillings as well?"

An interested crowd had begun to form alongside the patrol car. It soon dispersed when the tall, bald man with the combat shotgun slung effortlessly over his shoulder reached the Transit.

Rob sighed as he slammed shut the door on the Lotsons house for the final time. He turned, saw the Transit speeding away.

Will that Green Man talk to you, Andy? Give you some help and advice?

He forced a smile to the people gathered on the kerb. A small boy in a Santa hat, no more than five or six years old, looked up at him with fear. Rob tried to smile reassuringly, but he knew it came out as a grimace.

And then the boy took the Santa hat from his head and passed it to him.

"Your nose is red, officer."

Rob took it with a smile, and wiped the blood from his face. He almost handed it back to the boy, but the look from his mother, hastily backing away with the pushchair containing her other offspring, told him it wasn't a good idea. He shrugged and dropped the Santa hat to the ground. Blood stained the snow. He climbed into the Mondeo, dumped the Glock onto the passenger seat and twisted the key. The crowd moved back as he drove the vehicle off the kerb. Suspicious faces glanced back to the door, as the penny finally dropped.

He reached into his fleece pocket and took out a much needed Mayfair. The little boy waved at him strangely as he drove past.

He exhaled, watching the cigarette smoke curl against the windscreen. It was already beginning to take away the sickly odour of the mulberry and clove air freshener that Boyd had dangling from the rearview mirror.

Rob put his foot down, tearing past the graveyard of St Andrews Church to catch up with the Transit.

Rob Benson forced himself not to look at the grave markers, tried not to think of the bodies he'd seen in the last hour. Bodies that earlier this morning had been awake and vital, full of life. In front of him, the brake lights of the Transit flared scarlet, like a promise of more spilled blood. Rob shuddered.

So much death, he thought grimly. *And more to come.*

TWENTY FOUR

The kitchens of All Souls College smelled like a slaughterhouse. As they should do, Mark Cassell told himself as he tied his apron. There was a faint smell of the disinfectant cleaner that signified the wash-down at the end of last night's duties, but other than that the only other smell was emanating from the dead boar on the steel worktop before him.

He flared his nostrils appreciatively, savouring the aroma. The animal's own nostrils, like its mouth, were wide open as if still struggling for breath – or trying to release something. Something black and wormlike. Cassell leant his huge bulk forward, frowning.

Now that was strange. The carcass had been bled fully before it had been hung; yet some blood had obviously remained hidden, as if waiting for the arrival of the head chef of All Souls before seeping out to greet him.

Well, well, he mused. Life was full of surprises, but death could still throw a few in your path as well. He dipped a chubby finger into the black, clotted liquid leaking from the left nostril, tracing a thick line down to the drainer. It had the thickness of sump oil but its smell was unique.

To other noses it would have been the stench of death, rotting body fluids and the corruption of flesh. To the head chef of All Souls College it was the heavenly scent of life itself. His skills with herbs and spices would not only transform the meat into something exquisite – a piece of art far superior to the garish dishes paraded on television by the celebrity chefs he despised – it would turn the dead animal into a giver of life. From corrupted flesh would come the promise of salvation.

Survival. The world and its peoples safe from the ravages of *Her*. For another year, at least.

The kitchens were silent and, save for him, deserted. It was something he insisted on every year. Apart from Peter Ford, one of the longer-serving kitchen workers who were fully trusted with the secrets of the Feast, the rest of the catering staff would come in later, just before noon, to begin work. That gave Cassell plenty of time alone with his work. The boar was his alone. His canvas.

Mark Cassell had been in professional catering for so long he couldn't remember doing anything else – and all within the kitchens of All Souls. He hadn't needed tuition from the recognised catering colleges, or any sabbaticals at the famous eating-houses of Britain and Europe. Everything he had learned was either self-taught or passed on from the head chef before him. Since graduation, over twenty five years had been spent here: learning every technique, every preparation. Every secret.

However, the last few years had been a trial, a new learning experience, as he and his team had taken on board the techniques required to cater for the higher end of the market – the conference and corporate hospitality market that the College had entered. With the lack of students the College had been forced to diversify, to open its doors to other means of income.

Feedback from the Catering Office had been favourable, but some of the clients had remarked on a 'lack of originality'. Cassell wasn't concerned with that. Like all of the College's most devoted servants, he was a creature of tradition. Traditionalists didn't concern themselves with innovation, originality. If they wanted that, Cassell ranted to the Bursar one day, they could bugger off to Heston Blumenthal's or Marco Pierre-White's. They were outsiders, anyway. How dare they presume to tell *him* what food should be served? The purpose of the kitchens of All Souls was the preparation of dishes that had remained true to the original recipe for hundreds of years. And in the case of the boar, thousands.

This dish had a sense of purpose, a gastronomic experience that went beyond satisfying taste buds and filling bellies. It wasn't just living history on a plate. It was life itself.

He raised his head from the worktop and stared out of the one window whose blind he hadn't pulled down. It looked out onto the woods behind Cloister Court. His puffy eyes narrowed as they swept over the tops of the snow-capped trees, searching for unwanted visitors. But the only intruder in the woods was the first ray of dawn sunlight.

Franklin's news of the intruder last night had unnerved him. No matter how much the head porter may try to play the matter down, it was obvious to all that something had gone badly wrong. Rumours amongst the kitchen staff had flown about the increasingly concerned meetings of the College Council. The Fellows had been seen leaving the pre-breakfast emergency meeting yesterday white-faced and in visible distress. David Searles, it was murmured, was on the verge of a nervous breakdown. Many wagged fingers, pointing to the Master and his wavering last year as the reason for the crisis All Souls was facing.

Only Mark Cassell had been entrusted by Franklin with the full story. Because only Mark Cassell could perform the necessary preparation work with the boar. He was left in no doubt as to the scale of the crisis facing them all.

But now, faced with his yearly and most cherished task, the crisis was forgotten. This was what mattered. It was this that was important. This was the task he had been born for, the reason he had been put on this planet. Some would feel it an onerous task, maybe an unbearable one. Not Mark Cassell. His duty may have dealt in death, but he saw it as a celebration of life itself. Preparing meat to be gorged upon and washed down with the ever flowing wine from the cellars of All Souls. Wine had replaced beer and mead in the last few centuries: an attempt at sophistication along with the use of cutlery and tablecloths, a civility that tried to distance the Feast from its more medieval and, arguably, more barbaric origins.

Arguably. Cassell chuckled softly as he sliced into the belly of the beast. Those individuals Franklin was so concerned about obviously considered the task the Fellowship of All Souls was performing to be worse than barbaric. What did they know? What could they know? Franklin was right, they couldn't be reasoned with. It was unfortunate that they had to be dealt with in the manner they had, but too much was at stake.

He was so engrossed with the slicing of the meat, the parting of furred skin and fatty dark flesh, that he didn't hear the footsteps shuffling through the snowbound courtyard outside. A sharp knocking on the locked doors jerked him out of his concentration and had him looking impatiently around.

"Mr Cassell." The unmistakeable Edinburgh brogue of Franklin's voice.

Cassell sighed and reluctantly put his knife down. Rinsing his bloodstained hands in the steel washbasin next to the worktop, he half-heartedly shook them dry, walked to the doors and unlocked them. His eyes widened in surprise when he saw that the head porter was not alone.

"Master!"

David Searles nodded in greeting. He looked tired. Worse than tired, Cassell decided. The rumours were obviously true, then.

He stepped aside to allow the Master of All Souls entry to the kitchens.

Searles didn't so much walk in as creep, the mark of a bowed, weary and, worryingly, *defeated* man. He had visibly aged since the Feast last December. The stress of the responsibility had taken its toll.

His grey, pallid face wrinkled in disgust at the sight of Cassell's handiwork. A thin, trembling hand covered his mouth and nose to block out what Cassell considered to be sweet perfume.

The head chef allowed himself a momentary pang of contempt for the Master. His weakness, his inability to lead the Fellowship in anything but the most trivial of administrative duties. This could all be forgiven if he rose to the one task for which he was appointed. But even that seemed beyond him. The unforgivable omission in the final act of communion last year could have doomed them all. It could still do, if the remedy this year was not accepted.

He caught Franklin's eye, noted with satisfaction that the head porter shared Cassell's contempt – as well as the frustration that the College Council felt for their inability to overturn Searles' decision.

The Master of All Souls seemed to be regaining his composure – or at least was aware of the unflattering scrutiny and was making an effort to appear that he was. He took his hand away from his face and turned to the head chef. Now there was contempt in *his* eyes. Contempt for the huge bulk of the head chef, sweating copiously even though the kitchens were cold enough for the breath of the three men to turn to mist. His nose wrinkled at the sour smell coming from Cassell's armpits, almost as overpowering as that emanating from the dead boar on the worktop.

"I'm sorry to disturb you, Cassell…"

Cassell shrugged his shoulders, a half-mocking smile on his greasy lips. "Quite all right, Master."

Searles coughed, looked as though he was going to vomit. "Doubtless Franklin has informed you of, ah, recent developments?"

"The Lotsons? Yes. Unfortunate I know, but – "

Searles raised a hand. "It didn't quite go to plan. Hughes was arrested, but he managed to escape before Detective Inspector Boyd could get him to Parkside."

Cassell's face darkened. "He *escaped*? How?"

Franklin answered. "It would appear he had assistance from a friend of Michaels."

"Michaels!" Cassell snorted. "Then that means…"

"Yes. We have to assume that Hughes knows Michaels met his end here." Searles stared at the open belly of the boar.

"That in itself is not really an issue," Franklin continued. "Hughes is hardly likely to go to the police with his accusations, not now he's been implicated in the…resolution, of Philip Lotson. And the killing of several police officers. What is an issue is the fact that Hughes has a girlfriend. She came here."

Cassell opened his mouth. Then shut it. Franklin nodded.

"Jennifer Callaby," Cassell sighed. "This is very awkward."

"Precisely, Cassell. Very awkward indeed. But Andrew Hughes is not the only unwelcome guest we can expect soon." Searles spoke with a waver in his voice. And, Cassell noted, guilt in his eyes.

"Go on," Cassell folded his arms and stared hard at the Master.

"Jason escaped from Phoenix this morning. He killed two deliverymen and stole their van."

"He's coming, Mark." Franklin used the head chef's first name in what felt like years. "He's coming back to finish the job."

Cassell chuckled softly. In the chilled emptiness of the kitchens it had an eerie quality. Eerie enough to make Searles shudder.

"He *thinks* he's going to finish the job." Cassell moved between Searles and Franklin, back to his porcine canvass. "The young man just can't take a hint, can he?" Chuckling again, he picked up the cleaver and stroked a finger lovingly down the blade.

"Sorry to disappoint you, Mark." Franklin took the blade from him. "I'll be taking care of young Jason."

Disappointment clouded the head chef's face. Searles opened his mouth to protest, but Franklin cut him off. "This is a sign from *Her*. A second chance."

"But the offerings have been prepared!" Searles protested. "There's no time for -"

"I don't think there'll be any need for prep-work on Jason," Franklin said firmly as he placed the cleaver on the worktop. The blade reflected the dull yellow tusks of the boar and the glare of the fluorescent strip lighting. "He'll be accepted as he is, I'm certain. She has been kept waiting too long for him. I don't think she'll be too… fussy." His eyes fixed upon Cassell.

"I need you to keep an eye out for Hughes and any friend he brings along. If he knows about Michaels he'll know what awaits Callaby. It is only a matter of time before he comes here." He tapped a finger on Cassell's tool. It rocked on the metal worktop, sending reflected flashes of light into the eyes of the Master and the head chef. "You just make sure that if they do find their way into the kitchens that they don't leave in anything less than several large pieces."

Cassell grinned. "Pieces, eh? Shame Callaby is spoken for. It would have been nice to reunite the lovers in death. Putting Hughes and Callaby together…it would make one hell of a jigsaw."

Searles' eyes blazed in disapproval of Cassell's gallows humour. "As you said, Cassell. Callaby is spoken for. You will leave her alone. Perhaps we should leave you to continue your duties in peace."

"Maybe you should, Master," Cassell smirked. "I know how squeamish you are."

Searles bristled. "Squeamish? That's the least of the insults I've had spoken about me. If I am visibly affected by the sight of what you do, it is because I haven't forgotten what it means to be human!"

Cassell took a step backwards, eyes widening. This was a side of the Master he hadn't seen before. Real fire in him, anger that was not in his nature. It meant he really was close to breaking point.

"No matter," Searles breathed. "I've already been through this matter with the Council. They can't understand so I don't expect a mere...*cook* will."

He nodded towards the boar, a finger raised and pointed to the gaping hole in its belly before sweeping out of the kitchen.

"Enjoy your work, Cassell."

Andy Hughes checked the side mirror. He'd lost sight of the green Mondeo down Trumpington Street and hadn't seen it since. That meant Rob had decided to go in via the Queen's Road access. Andy had been surprised by Rob's suggestion, especially as it meant he might be meeting one of the Children of Andraste again.

But there was no fear in Rob at this possibility. Instead there was a look of anticipation, even hope. A chance to avenge the poor little bastard in the back of the van.

King's Parade. King's College passed by: the façade of its chapel rather small and insignificant now. The beauty of holiness was shabby and inconsequential in light of the knowledge of the afterlife Andy Hughes had obtained. No keys to Heaven, no blissful rest in the kingdom of God. Just eternal suffering at the hands of Andraste.

All Souls came towards him. The traffic slowed and brought his van to a halt, but the college buildings seemed to still rush towards him, the blackened clunch walls eager to swallow him. He closed his eyes and took a deep breath. Lightheaded, he realised. He wondered how much blood he'd lost over the last twenty four hours.

He hadn't put the seatbelt on, knowing how much that would irritate his stomach wounds. He lifted his sweatshirt and grimaced at the fresh blood seeping through the bandages.

He looked up and saw the Green Man's reflection through a haze of red.

The eyes were open and staring straight ahead at the college. The pupils glowed a savage red as flames billowed from its open mouth.

Andy took a deep breath. He put a tentative hand near the carving's mouth and allowed the flames to lick at his fingertips.

Nothing. No pain, nor even any sensation of heat. He took his hand away and smiled.

"Well, well. You trying to tell me something, old man?"

The carving was silent. The unearthly glow from its eyes was its only answer. Blood, gleaming an unnatural scarlet, welling up before the eyelids blinked and the fluid ran down the carving's cheeks. Tears of blood.

Now he knew what was going to happen. Black rock from the Divine Judgement – split from the meteor that struck over two hundred years ago. And now, finally, coming back to be reunited. He didn't know how it was going to happen – it was welded solid to the bulkhead, it was only going to come free when it wanted to. And it had chosen him to take it.

He knew he wasn't alone. He knew that Jason Franklin would be in the grounds as well, that he had to do the same thing as Andy. Because now he understood the significance of what destroyed the college in his vision. Power horses.

Horsepower.

He turned the van into the gravelled driveway and noted grimly that the fiery reflection had gone. The carving was dead stone once more. The Elder's message had been sent and understood.

Just let me get Jen out before I do what I have to do, he silently pleaded. *Please let that part of the vision be true as well.*

A porter came to the van and indicated for him to wind down the window.

"What are you doing here?" The porter was young and looked edgy. Andy searched for a tell tale bulge of a concealed firearm under the man's armpit but couldn't see one. The porter stared at the Granta Office Supplies logo on the panel then back to Andy.

"We're not expecting any deliveries – my God!"

"You're expecting this one," Andy jerked a thumb over his shoulder, indicating the stone carving that caught the porter's widened gaze. "Tell Franklin Andy Hughes is here. Then tell him I want the girl. Alive and unharmed."

The porter took a step backwards, his eyes never leaving the carving. Andy grinned as the porter spoke into his two-way radio.

"…Hughes is here. Yes sir, you heard me! He's got…bloody hell, it looks like Charles Harvey!"

"The girl. Jennifer Callaby." Andy said tightly.

The porter spoke again into his radio, genuine bewilderment on his features. "He says he wants…Jennifer Callaby, whoever that is." His eyes shot to Andy's when he heard the answer.

"Stay here. Mr Franklin's on his way."

"I'm not going anywhere, son." Andy watched the porter shuffle back into the lodge. He threw off the jacket that covered the SPAS 12 and rested his hand on the pistol grip.

Jason Franklin licked his lips nervously and stared out of the windscreen of the cook-chill van. The shadows cast on the bodywork by the ancient white oaks were moving, dark skeletal veins crawling over the rusted panels.

He took a deep, shuddering breath and squeezed the steering wheel.

Relax. He'll come. The Elder won't abandon me now, surely. He'd done everything asked of him. For the fifteenth time he took one of the cherry-scented antibacterial wipes from the tub in the cup-holder and cleaned the steel prong of the temperature probe. He tossed the used rag to the floor with the rest. There wasn't a single trace of blood or grey matter on the weapon now.

He'd entered the West Gate of All Souls College just before eight o'clock. The gate had swung open automatically, the camera mounted on the railings inactive. He had driven the vehicle slowly up the gravelled pathway, expecting a porter to come rushing at him. Instead he had been allowed to drive into the woods unchallenged.

The van was now parked deep within the ancient grove, the snow covered oaks masking him from view. He had waited anxiously for over an hour for signs of life, a porter patrolling the woods coming across an unauthorised vehicle parked in a strictly forbidden zone, the call to the lodge, the inevitable wail of police sirens…

On the day of the Founder's Feast, as well. He couldn't believe it. Either the head porter had been sloppy with his security – not bloody likely – or perhaps his presence had been noted. Perhaps they were waiting for him to make the first move.

He wound down the window, shivering in the cold morning air, listening for sounds of activity. Nothing. Not even birdsong.

He opened the door and stepped out, the snow and frozen leaf litter crunching underfoot like the bones of a small animal. He couldn't even hear the distant hum of traffic from Queen's Road. And it was so bloody *cold.* He hugged himself, teeth chattering loudly.

If you are cold, come and warm yourself. Come to the fire.

He turned and saw the van had vanished. In its place stood a roaring fire that leapt up at the lower branches of the frozen oaks. The branches shrank back, as though afraid of the flames.

The Elder stood behind them, his green robe almost glowing in the light of the fire. The fire threw strange and wonderful shadows over the inscrutable, emotionless but oh-so-welcome face.

The Elder raised a hand, beckoning him to come closer. Jason Franklin obeyed, tears of joy and relief running down his cheeks. He wanted to kneel, to prostrate himself, to give thanks to –

The hand turned, palm outwards. A signal to halt.

The flames reared and retreated, a clear parting formed in the centre of the inferno that allowed The Elder to step forward, unharmed.

Welcome to the Nemeton, Jason. You have done well.

Jason couldn't speak. The smoke and heat made it difficult for him to even breathe – his emotions too overpowering for words to form. He stood still, feeling his tears evaporate from his cheeks.

It will not be long, Jason. Soon it will be over. The green eyes stared unblinking at him, the pupils boring into his with a crimson glow. With a sudden chill, Jason realised it was the same colour he had seen in the rising sun earlier.

The Other approaches. He brings with him my icon. He brings my Divine Judgement to the Fellowship. He brings death.

Jason could finally speak. "And me? What do I bring?"

Your own judgement – your awareness. You know now your identity was a lie, perpetuated by those close to you. Your own father denied you. You grew up believing yourself to be the son of another. You suspected for a long time – you knew this morning with my final message…

Anguish flooded Jason's body. Lips bared to the morning sky, he roared aloud, giving vent to his anger and the betrayal. It brought no relief. Instead, it seemed to him that the flames of the fire caught his agonised feelings and flung them back at him, burning intensely.

The Elder looked at him, a hint of sympathy in those green and crimson eyes. He waited for Jason to look back to him before continuing.

In your dungeon you came to know the strength of your fury, the potential of your rage. It is a weapon available only to those who are born of the bloodline of the Fellowship. Harness this rage, Jason. Unleash it against your father.

Jason Franklin suddenly felt weak. The strength the anger had bestowed upon him seemed to leak away. His shoulders slumped and he felt tears in his eyes. Not tears of joy at finding The Elder, but tears of self pity.

He wasn't meant to be. He was an accident, an unplanned pregnancy. A product of an indiscreet affair – or a one night stand – one that had been hushed up and denied.

He had no doubt that in an earlier age he would have been killed.

"So I'm a child of destiny then? Not an unwanted foetus but a product of fate. A weapon of justice. But a product first – a human being last, *if at all*."

He turned his head from the fire. He wanted those tears to flow, not to be whisked away and evaporated by The Elder's holy fire. He deserved that, at least.

"All I wanted…was a *father*!" The tears became a torrent, his wracking sobs louder than the roar of the flames. "For him to acknowledge me…love me…"

The Elder watched with annoyance as Jason continued his weeping. There was a harsher tone to his voice now.

This I cannot help you with, Jason. But remember this: your father's refusal to offer you to Andraste last year was out of guilt, not love. Eventually he would have been swayed by the Council and would have offered you this year by Andraste's command. He is a weak man. He would eventually give your body to the knives of the Fellowship and your soul unto Andraste.

You now have the chance to ensure this will not happen. You are not alone, nor are you unarmed. A faint smiled played at the corners of his mouth.

Jason wiped his nose on the sleeve of his sweatshirt. Not unarmed? Then he remembered the temperature probe and what it could do.

"And this…Other?"

He will also be armed. As will his associate – and it is his associate who will need aid. You must show him the kitchens. You must prevent Cassell preparing the meat.

"But The Other? You said he'll defeat Andraste for good. How? What makes him so special?" He was aware of the petulant, whining tone of his voice and hated himself for it. He knew it was wrong to feel jealous, to think: *Why him? Why can't I do it all?* It was the sort of thing a younger sibling would say when referring to a special honour bestowed upon an older brother. But who could blame him? He'd not exactly had a normal childhood, had he?

Dry your eyes, Jason. There was harshness in the voice now, the tone of an irritated father. Jason almost smiled at the thought.

The Other has been marked for this task by forces higher than I. It is not for me to question. He must defeat Andraste by offering himself to the One Power, the power to which I willingly bound myself. He will replace me…but only if he chooses to do so. And he can only make that choice with your help in defeating the Fellowship. Do this for me, Jason. Give your life meaning.

For the love of humanity.

Jason watched The Elder fade from sight with eyes bleary from weeping. The fire roared once, then faded and retreated into the remnants of its fuel. Embers glinted like the red pupils in the eyes of The Elder, faded to dust, and then memory.

Behind him the Luton awaited its driver. Jason sighed and pulled open the door. He twisted the key and the engine shuddered into something close to life. He flicked on the wipers to remove some of the snow that had fallen onto the windscreen from the trees.

He stared idly at the path leading back to the West Gate. He cocked his head. Sound at last. A motor vehicle. *Think I know who this is.*

He flashed the headlights in greeting. The driver of the Mondeo braked sharply, the wheels skidding and sending the car off the path. It bumped into one of the oaks with a soft thudding sound. Fresh snow clumps fell to the ground and rested on the dented wing.

Jason Franklin smiled as he took another antibacterial wipe from the drum and methodically squeezed it around the tip of the probe. He was still smiling when Rob Benson clambered out of the Mondeo and took aim with the Glock.

TWENTY FIVE

In the cellar beneath the chapel of All Souls David Searles stared at the naked, shivering girl with pity and horror. The pity was heartfelt, a genuine tearing in his heart.

But the horror was the stronger emotion. Horror that the first step in the ritual had begun, that other, worse tortures were to follow. Horror that he himself would soon take part in those tortures. Horror that this yearly ritual would never end: that he would perform it year after year until the day he was ready to die and handed over the position of Master to a newly elected Senior Member.

Each and every year, without fail. An unnatural part of the natural cycle of seasons, until the end of time.

For the love of humanity.

In the faint light cast by the candles nervous, watchful eyes peered out through the holes in wooden masks. They turned from the offering to the Master. Waiting for his first move. His first cut.

His palms were greasy with sweat beneath the heavy white robe. The sacrificial knife slithered in his grip like a venomous snake. He tightened his grip, thankful that the other members of the Council couldn't see his revulsion, his self-hatred, as he steeled himself to perform what they saw as his natural duty.

Dear God in Heaven, I can't do this. But what choice did he have? The Fellowship had made him fully aware that Andraste hadn't forgiven his trespass against her in refusing to offer Jason, that they couldn't fail her again. Judith Cox had been ample warning.

Strike now. Administer the first cut then the rest will be easier. One girl, for the sake of the whole human race. Was it really such a terrible price to pay?

Of course it is! Torture a girl to death – for what? To give the human race another twelve months to tear itself apart? Another year of war, violence and suffering? Is it really worth it? Why not just cast away the blade – use it on my fellow murderers if necessary – deny Andraste and let her take the planet? What can she really do that's worse than the evil mankind has already inflicted upon itself?

Impatient feet shuffled on the cold flagstones. Questioning looks burned through the eyeholes of the masks.

The girl muttered something inaudible. It might have been another plea to her mother. The Selected always did that. Always the mother: no matter how old the victim was, even if the mother of the offering had herself been in her grave for years, it was always the mother that would be screamed for.

He was assured that he would learn, eventually, to shut his ears to the screams and the pleas. That was what Franklin had told him, anyway. David Searles was as far from believing as he ever was.

She raised her battered face from the floor. At the sight of the knives she opened her mouth. Her scream was barely human.

Searles closed his eyes. God, if this was what she sounded like now, what noises would she utter when the pain began? A sudden thought: turn the knife on himself. A swift strike to the heart. Absolve himself of responsibility.

No, it wouldn't work that way. Andraste would be waiting for him on the other side. Besides, the task would be completed by the remaining council members. A new Master would be hurriedly elected and the ritual would continue. He was just a figurehead - important to the ritual, but not indispensable.

He bent down and extended his knife arm. He wanted so badly to ask God to forgive him for what he was about to do but he knew it would be a useless plea. God wasn't listening anymore. The exchanges in the chapel with the carved figure of Christ proved that. All he could do was complete the ritual, and hope that Andraste would have mercy on him.

On us all, he thought sadly. He raised the knife and began his task.

Her screams sliced through him like the blade that cut through her fingers.

He was about to slice off the fourth finger when the door at the top of the stone staircase was forced open. The rusty hinges shrieked, scraping on the stone. Searles looked up and saw the imposing figure of Franklin framed in the doorway.

The other Fellows took a step back into the shadows as the head porter quickly made his way down the stairs. Only Franklin would be allowed to interrupt the offering at such a crucial stage, because he would only do so if absolutely necessary.

"My apologies, Master. Hughes is here. He has the remainder of the Divine Judgement!"

Shocked gasps from the Fellows fluttered the candle flames. Searles almost fell backwards. He got to his feet shakily.

"You're certain of this, Franklin?"

"Positive. He's in his van, by the Lodge. The rock is embedded in the bulkhead, and it's carved in the likeness of Charles Harvey. There can be no mistake."

Searles took all this in, nodding thoughtfully.

"Well, Mr Franklin. We'd better bring him here, hadn't we?" He made a forceful effort to hide his relief at this sudden interruption, the excuse to withhold the torture. He threw away the mask and pulled the robe over his head, tossing it unceremoniously in a corner by the stone staircase.

"That's not necessary, Master," Franklin began. "I can deal with him -"

"Not without me, Franklin!" Searles snapped. He fixed the head porter with a withering glare that made Franklin take an involuntary step backwards and then turned it on the Fellows.

"Leave the girl for the moment. Do not touch her until I return."

The anger from the Fellowship was silent but palpable. They didn't trust him, but they couldn't disobey. Searles indicated the steps. Franklin reluctantly turned, with a glower, and took the lead.

The Master of All Souls wondered now if there was another force that had answered his unspoken prayer. Franklin had overestimated Boyd's abilities, that much was certain. But none of them had assumed that Hughes would make his way here so quickly. He obviously knew his girlfriend was singing to Andraste, so lying low to evade arrest was not going to be a viable option for him.

But who told him? How did he find out?

"The Divine Judgement? Why would he bring it here, Master?" Franklin fell into step alongside him as they made their way across the lawns of Old Court. The sky had darkened considerably. The sun was nothing more than a tarnished silver disc skulking behind the heavy steel-grey clouds.

"It's obvious, Franklin. Hughes probably thinks he can bargain with it. An exchange: the stone for his girl." *Or perhaps, join the carving with the stone in the Great Hall. And then it's all over.* But that was a false hope, he thought. No way could Hughes know about that.

But it was only when he and Franklin came across Hughes' van, hemmed in by the archway, and saw the thing that grinned at them from the bulkhead did he realise how badly the Fellowship of All Souls had underestimated the ex-prisoner. Franklin halted in mid-step, a sharp exhalation of breath misting in the morning air.

The head porter shook his head from side to side. "No. It can't be…"

Searles stepped past him, walking slowly towards the Transit. David Searles' mouth dropped when he saw the carving on the van's bulkhead. A carving with an open, gaping mouth and eyes that switched from a tortured, agonised expression to a direct glare of hatred, as if it had become suddenly aware of the two men approaching it – and aware of what they represented.

Hughes had turned in his seat and was facing it. And smiling.

"And what else do you have for us?" Searles asked in a whisper. A whisper that was somehow heard by the face in the leaves, even though there was a six foot gap between the Master and the crumpled bonnet of the van. The ivy and holly leaves rustled in its mouth and the lines around the eyes tightened, turning the open, burning glare into a narrow eyed, thoughtful appraisal.

It knows, Searles thought. *It hears, it senses…it knows.* And David Searles knew without any doubt that this was not only the second piece of the meteorite - the Divine Judgement that came so close to destroying the college over two centuries ago – it was the physical representation of the thing that had haunted Jason's days and nights. The face of what he called The Elder.

The psychiatrist Longhurst had said The Elder was only in Jason's mind. Searles knew now he was wrong. The Elder was in Jason's mind, yes…but in his heart also.

Spirit. He carried The Elder in his soul. And Hughes had brought the physical representation. If they should meet…

Franklin raised his two-way. Thumbing the talk button, he spoke quickly in crisp, clear tones.

"Tom. It's Franklin. You and Neil, check the clearing in the woods. I think Jason's here already." He paused. "Yes, go armed. It won't be just Jason in there."

Searles stroked his chin. "Well, Franklin, looks like we're having quite a few spectres at our Feast. First things first. Let's make our guest welcome."

They turned as one to the Transit, its driver and its mysterious cargo. From the corner of his eye Searles noted the wolfish grin of anticipation that broke out on Franklin's face.

Rob Benson's hands shook. This was the second time he had pointed a loaded weapon at another human being and it wasn't something he'd ever get used to.

But for fuck's sake – at least the Plod had had the courtesy to look scared when he was pointing the shotgun at them! This fucker was just grinning at him, wiping a piece of cloth that smelled of black cherries up and down some steel probe.

Jason Franklin. He recognised the face from the newspaper pictures last year. You didn't forget eyes like that. The eyes of the truly insane.

It was a look of both calm and fury. Peace and rage merged into one. Both emotions living uneasily together: each trying to displace the other and be the dominant force that determined the actions of Jason Franklin. And it looked like the rage had won. There was no peaceable way in which the cook-chill vehicle could have been taken from its drivers.

This was why he kept the gun raised. They would not have willingly handed it over to a mental patient who was hell bent on escaping and returning to his old college to burn the place down.

"Okay, Franklin. How did you get here?"

Jason paused in his cleaning. He leant out of the window and made admiring noises at the Mondeo.

"Same way you did. Disguised as a washer woman."

"Funny fucker. C'mon, spill the beans." Rob's hands shook, but Jason seemed unconcerned at the automatic pistol aimed less than six feet from his face.

"It was tinned tomatoes, actually. But never mind that." Jason's eyes hardened. "I know why you're here."

Rob took a step backwards as Jason Franklin opened the door of the van.

"Relax…Roberto, isn't it? Rob, sorry. My mistake." He smiled and held out his hand. "You know me. My name's Jason."

Rob backed away even further, raising the Glock higher. It wasn't his imagination. And it sure as fuck wasn't tinned tomato juice under Jason's fingernails. That was blood.

He stared at Jason Franklin's getaway vehicle. Black smoke from the exhaust billowed around the rusted bodywork, snaking around the skeletal oak trees like rags torn from a rotting burial shroud.

"A permanent loan from the Phoenix Unit. A farewell gift, you might say." Jason stared at his fingernails then shrugged.

"Come on, Rob. This is no time to be squeamish. You've spilt the blood of a man today, haven't you?" He glanced at the Mondeo. "That's a police car, and that gun you're holding is a third generation Glock 17. Not standard issue for the Cambridgeshire Constabulary, but I think Boyd had special status."

Rob swallowed. *News got out quick, then.*

Franklin shook his head. "No, not news. But I can't be bothered to explain how my…gift works. Not now. We've got other things to worry about."

Rob shook his head. The sun had hidden itself behind heavy black clouds and the woods were getting dark. Almost as though night was falling.

Yeah, the temperature was definitely dropping. *What the fuck's going on?*

"Tell me something, Franklin," Rob said. "How come the gates were open? I thought they'd have put extra security on or something."

Franklin folded his arms. He looked over Rob's shoulder. "My guess is that they were expecting us…or me, certainly. I don't think they want any more police involvement, not today of all days. They'll deal with us personally. Or at least, they'll try."

The smile that broke out on Jason's face was something that would stay with Rob Benson for a very long time.

Something was stirring in the woods. He heard the noise of a frozen twig snap far to his left. He spun round and squinted, trying to make out something other than the swaying and creaking of the ancient oaks. He remained still, listening intently.

"Look. Here they come now." Jason pointed with a disinterested finger at the figures moving in the woods, running towards them.

The grin on Franklin's face vanished when the black barrel of the SPAS 12 swung in his direction. Andy saw the head porter freeze when he worked the pump, feeding a shell. It was all he could do to prevent his finger tightening around the trigger, to blow that psychotic bastard's head off.

"Stay where you are!" he barked. "Franklin, Searles. You know why I'm here. I want Jen."

The Master and the head porter glanced at each other.

"Jen who?"

"Don't even go there, Franklin. I know you have her."

"Then you know *why* we have her," Searles said reasonably. "And why we can't let her go. Did Boyd tell you that before you killed him?"

Andy hesitated. The smell of discharge was still powerful, so it was no great leap of logic to assume that the shotgun had been used earlier.

"Boyd told me a lot of things," Andy smiled grimly. "Confession's good for the soul. Bring Jen to me."

"I'm afraid we can't do that Mr Hughes," Searles said tiredly. "Andraste has chosen her to sing. She must be given, for the love of humanity."

Andy's jaw tightened. He jabbed the barrel into Searles' stomach. Searles winced.

"Let me explain something to you, Searles. I've been implicated in the killing of my former tutor and his family. I've seen first-hand the work this murdering bastard is capable of, work he does for you and your fucking college. You really expect me to believe that anything connected to him is for the love of humanity?"

Franklin remained silent, his eyes burning into Andy with hatred.

"I've got nothing to lose by blowing both your heads off here and now. I know what you do, and I know where you do it." His words were a hiss. He tapped the trigger guard of the SPAS 12. "This is an eight round model. One shell opened Boyd up to the world. After you two I'll still have five shells left. Do we understand each other?"

"We do indeed, Mr Hughes." Searles smiled sadly. "Believe me, I would welcome death. You have no idea how onerous our duty is, no comprehension of the way it tears our souls apart."

"My heart bleeds," Andy growled. But he detected a weariness and sadness in the Master's voice. The prematurely lined face and the dull eyes spoke of someone who wrestled nightly with his conscience, agonised over a duty he was compelled to perform. *For the love of humanity*, he'd said, and he could almost believe him.

But that didn't explain Franklin, who took a sharp intake of breath at the Master's words.

"You really need convincing, Andrew?" Searles asked. "Let us show you what the black rock can do."

"Master?" Franklin looked incredulous. "You can't do this!"

"I believe we have no choice, Franklin." Searles raised his head and stared sadly at Andy. "You and Mr Lotson know it as the Divine Judgement. It is no such thing. To us, it is the Covenant between us and Andraste. It is through this that she reveals herself to us. Her wishes…her demands. Come and see for yourself."

"Later," Andy snapped, swinging the barrel to bear on Franklin's groin. "Franklin, if I see you reach for that walkie-talkie again I'll blow your balls through your arsehole, clear?" He turned back to the Master. A strange look passed between them, and Andy thought about what he'd said earlier, about death being a welcome. Franklin looked distinctly uneasy now, almost worried. And that could only be a good thing.

"You have my word that Jennifer will not be touched."

Andy stepped back and pointed to the doorway of the Great Hall. The Master of All Souls and the head porter turned, trudging slowly through the snow on the lawns towards the Hall.

Okay, Searles. Let's see what you're playing at.

TWENTY SIX

On entering the Great Hall of All Souls Andy Hughes froze. For one moment he forgot everything. The Master and the head porter, standing five feet away in front of him with raised hands: the heavy weight of the combat shotgun in his hands. The dire situation he was in. Even the danger facing Jen.

For one brief but seemingly endless moment he was immersed in the majesty of the Great Hall of All Souls and nothing else.

No pictures he'd seen could do justice to the sheer size of the Great Hall. The pitched roof added height to the already cavernous interior. Chandeliers and fiery cresset torches added rich, fluid light to the opulent furnishings and wall tapestries, dispelling any sense of oppressive darkness or gloom that could so easily have overcome visitors to the medieval dining hall. For a brief moment the twenty first century did not exist.

The thing atop the triangular portico on the wooden screen brought him back to reality, reminded him why he was here. A gilded carving of a boar's head: its ruby eyes as red as the pupils in the Green Man, blazed down on him. They seemed to move around the room, but surely that was only the dancing, flickering light from the candles and the cressets. Surely.

"Impressed, aren't you?" Franklin's words travelled across the room, the sardonic voice echoing from all points.

Andy's footsteps echoed on the cold white marble of the centre tiles, approaching High Table. The golden boar's head glared down at him with its baleful eyes.

Andy stared at the black rock embedded in the centre of the table beneath it. The candle light gave it a strange luminescence, the buttery yellow flames illuminating the thin traces of red and green minerals on the polished fusion crust. Andy rested the shotgun on it and heard Searles gasp. He listened for a hollow sound but couldn't hear anything. Whoever had mounted the rock in the table had done a good job. The broken side, the fracture, was well hidden. He turned back to the Master and grinned.

"The Covenant with Andraste, eh? You stupid, stupid bastards."

The Master sighed. "That rock has shown us the way. Each of us, all senior members of the college, past and present, have been given a glimpse of Andraste's terrible power through contact with it. Each of us has been shown the proof of her existence – and has reluctantly shouldered the burden placed upon us."

"What about Freeland? He threw off the burden. He took the view Jason Franklin did, not the Fellowship. He believed that this Andraste deceived you all, that each killing strengthens her rather than appeases her. Did you consider that?"

There it was again, that look in the Master's eyes he'd seen outside. Not just pain and anguish, but doubt. Doubt he had fought to keep hidden from the rest of the Fellowship. Andy decided to turn up the heat.

"So why do you think Freeland killed himself, Searles? He'd given Phil the proof that you were wrong, had been wrong, for thousands of years. He couldn't live with himself anymore, couldn't face the guilt."

"Not quite, Hughes." Franklin kept his distance from Andy and the High Table, but his words carried well. "Freeland killed himself because he was convinced Andraste was going to break through. Terrified of what he believed to be inevitable. That is proof indeed of the terrible prospect of Andraste returning – that men would rather kill themselves than face the prospect of being on the same planet as her."

"Jesus. The fairy stories I've heard in the last twenty four hours..." Andy shook his head. He tapped the black rock with the shotgun.

"But nothing matches *this* one. God's Divine Judgement – a message from the Almighty. As long as it stays here in the Hall, evil will never return. Kept the superstitious townsfolk reassured, I guess."

Franklin was walking slowly towards him. Andy shot him a withering glare, and the head porter paused in mid-step.

"But not all of it is here, is it? The meteor broke in two, the second part merging with the Green Man carving in the chapel before flying to Impington. Charles Harvey's suicide – or rather, his self sacrifice – was prevented. And that's why Andraste remained. So what if the pieces were joined?" Andy hefted the SPAS 12 over his shoulder. He turned and faced Franklin.

"What do you reckon, Searles? Worth a try, surely? Got to be better than what you fuckers are doing in the cellar of the chapel every year."

The response to that was silence. He'd been expecting that. But what was surprising was the contrast between the two men's expressions. Searles looked relieved at Andy's suggestion, almost relaxed. Franklin, on the other hand...

The head porter's hatred of Andy was palpable, an almost physical force that burned as brightly as the torches on the walls and the candles on the tables. The pent up rage was reaching breaking point.

Why? Why do you hate me so much? I'm no threat to you. Unless…

A smile broke out on his face. Now he saw what fuelled Franklin's hatred of him. It was well hidden, but it was there, revealed when he'd mentioned joining the two pieces together.

Fear. John Franklin was scared of him.

"I think, Mr Searles, that your head porter has been keeping a few things secret from you. Now's the time to come clean, Franklin." He took the shotgun from his shoulder and levelled it meaningfully at the head porter.

The fury and hatred in Franklin's face abated a little.

"I'm hiding nothing, Hughes," he said condescendingly. "I have been nothing less than a faithful servant of All Souls – and humanity. In fact, if it wasn't for me, certain members of the Fellowship would have weakened in their duty so much as to make Andraste's return inevitable."

Searles glowered but said nothing. Franklin continued.

"Our Master grudgingly understands that I have been forced to take somewhat extreme measures to ensure the continuance of our unhappy but necessary duty. After the fiasco of last year I have made certain that Andraste will not be displeased again this year. We cannot – *will* not – allow you to jeopardise the propitiation tonight. Too much is at stake."

Andy's grip on the shotgun tightened. "Extreme measures. Unhappy duty. *That why you laughed as you tore Phil's family to pieces?*"

"Mr Franklin has been rather heavy handed in his duties, there is no doubt."

Andy almost dropped the SPAS 12 in disbelief at Searles' softly spoken words.

"Heavy handed? Jesus wept!"

"But I can assure you, all other aspects of the propitiation to Andraste are essential. We have no choice. See it from our point of view, Andrew. Every year we have to offer up two innocents to her. Not just take their lives, but tear them to pieces. Torture them to death. Do you have any idea of the effect this has on us? Do you really not understand that we would rather kill ourselves than perform this horror, year after year after year? What do you think this does to our sanity?

"I can understand your anger that Jennifer has been chosen. But you must understand. Andraste chooses the offerings. Not us. Andraste commands, we obey. We have no choice."

"Crap. Everyone has a choice. You especially. You're the Master. Lead by example, make the choice. Join the stones."

Searles glanced at Franklin. The head porter nodded slightly. Searles gestured to the meteorite on High Table.

"Nothing I can say will convince you. So why don't you see for yourself?"

Andy followed Searles' trembling finger towards the meteorite. In any light that thing would look mysterious. It was older than the Earth itself and it had travelled distances inconceivable to the human mind. And by sheer chance it had landed at this particular spot.

But *was* it chance? Who was to say there wasn't some unearthly power behind it, guiding its course?

A judgement on human evil, a warning from God. Or, as the Fellowship believed, a grim gift and reminder from Andraste. A covenant between her and her appeasers. Proof from Andraste herself that they were doing the right thing. That they were not misguided and deceived murderers, they were saviours of mankind.

For the love of humanity.

"You're being given a very great honour, Hughes," Franklin growled. "Only Senior members of the College – those on the Council – are allowed to touch the rock, to commune with Andraste. The Master obviously thinks very highly of you to allow you near it." He stared impassively at Searles. "Perhaps he understands your pain."

Perhaps it's a trick. Franklin had edged closer than he had realised. Searles was to his right, a few metres away. The head porter had stealthily advanced and was mere inches away, his hand reaching open –

"Back off." The SPAS 12 was raised again.

"Do as he says, Franklin. Give him room."

Even Andy was surprised by that. Searles smiled sadly and said,

"The knowledge will only take a few seconds to enter your mind. But be warned – it will feel longer."

"*Master…*" Franklin shot Searles a glare. Searles glared back.

"It is only right that he be warned, Franklin. It's essential that he knows why we are doing this. Now do as he says… *and back off!*

"Lay your hand on the stone, Andrew. Share the secret. Know the truth."

Andy waited until Franklin had walked towards the great double doors of the Hall before he looked at the rock again. Even Searles stood backwards, waiting at the far right side of High Table for Andy Hughes to commune with Andraste.

The mineral traces glittered invitingly in the candle light. *Only a few seconds. That's all it'll take to prove they're all fucking loopy…*

He rested the shotgun over his left shoulder, his right hand free to touch the stone. No way was he going to have his back turned towards these two when he touched it.

His right hand hovered over the rock. His fingers outstretched…and then he hesitated.

What if?

What if they were right after all? What if he was wrong – that he was sharing Jason Franklin's delusion, even his madness? The Green Man in the van, identical to Jason's vision of The Elder – surely a sign of madness, a symptom of a fractured mind.

James Freeland – had he allowed his fear and doubt to get the better of him? He'd been traumatised by the murder of his mother. And Judith Cox? She'd been hospitalised in Fulbourn years back after a miscarriage and a breakdown.

Perhaps it was the strongest minds alone that could survive the duty to Andraste. Single minded, unquestioning, obedient.

But where's the humanity in that?

The candles flickered once more. A breeze rattled the windows as if demanding access.

Andy Hughes held his breath and then lowered his free hand firmly on the top part of the ancient stone.

It was cold, but not overly so. Certainly no colder than any piece of rock or stonework would be. The fusion crust was smooth. The mason who had dressed and polished this stone had done a good job. He pressed his palm harder onto the meteorite, and thought that it might have been the same mason who had carved the Green Man.

Nothing happened. No visions, no dark whispers, no hidden secrets. Nothing.

Andy stared across the empty expanse of the Great Hall towards the head porter. He smiled mockingly.

And then it happened.

Jason Franklin noticed that Rob Benson's hands shook on the Glock as he brought it to bear on the two figures running from the eastern side of the wood. Two bulky human figures that wore a matching uniform of black blazers with the All Souls crest upon the breast pocket. They broke back branches, crunching snow and frozen leaf litter underfoot as they advanced towards their prey.

Jason's lip curled. Not just porters, these were an unofficial private army, John Franklin's dishonour guard. Hired thugs who had terrorised and beaten him when he had discovered the secret in the cellars beneath the chapel. His hand tightened on the temperature probe.

The two men kicked up clods of snow as they thundered towards the vehicles. They either didn't see the gun Rob raised or were unconcerned by it. Jason glanced upwards, frowning.

Probably the former, he thought. The clouds were darkening, no longer the thick steel grey of snow clouds. Now it seemed that daylight was vanishing, the sun dying behind the clouds.

They didn't see it, but they sure as hell heard it. Jason Franklin stared at the driver of the Mondeo with new found respect. He was no stranger to firearms: that was certain – he was wincing at the effect of the recoil and the noise, but he knew what he was doing.

The first shot went wide and hit one of the branches of the oak nearest to the left porter. Snow flurries appeared in the air, sparkling in the glare of the muzzle flash from the Glock. The first porter threw himself to the ground, rolling to his right and into the shelter of the tree that had taken his bullet. The second carried on running, his eyes narrowed with purpose as he saw Rob Benson struggle with the physical effect of the recoil.

Jason tapped the fingers of his free hand on the steering wheel thoughtfully. In the glare of the van's headlights he could see all too clearly the murderous expression on the porter's face. His eyes were the cold grey of gun metal, his thick lips twisting into a snarl. His hand reached into his jacket pocket, reaching for what Jason Franklin knew would be a gun.

"Drop it, sunshine," the porter barked. His eyes bored into Rob's, his grip on the Browning steady and unwavering.

Jason knew this porter now. The gruff Yorkshire accent and the jowls were those of Tom Ellis, who'd served alongside John Franklin in the Falklands. Another psycho – and just as dangerous as the man who had claimed to be Jason's father.

His eyes were fixed on Rob, trying to psych him out. Rob's face was pale, his hands trembling. There was a gap of three metres and a barrier of green steel between them.

Jason dropped gently to the ground. He was all too aware of the second porter hiding behind the tree – that would be Neil Street, one of the younger porters. Jason couldn't remember too much about that one, but guessed he wasn't as experienced in the use of firearms as Ellis.

But he won't be running away, that's a dead cert. Jason knew he had to act fast. Ellis was the nearest, he was the most dangerous if Rob couldn't pull the trigger. But Street couldn't be ignored. It was only a matter of time before he brought reinforcements – maybe even the head porter himself.

Jason smiled in anticipation. The man he'd called father all his life…*oh, I'm going to enjoy watching you burn as well, Franklin! But, first things first...*

The standoff couldn't last indefinitely. Someone had to give way. He saw Rob Benson's eyes flick in his direction and cursed.

Don't fucking give me away, idiot! He dropped to the ground, hidden by the open door of the cook chill vehicle, but it was too late. Tom Ellis had seen him.

"Street!" he heard Ellis bark. "There's the other one. *Get him!*"

Rob fired. This time he didn't miss.

The Glock spat fire. Sparks flew as the slug passed through Ellis' knuckles and struck the trigger guard of the Browning. Ellis shrieked in agony and pulled the trigger.

Jason broke cover and ran towards him. He raised the temperature probe above his head, the digital display box slapping the side of his head as the glade exploded in noise and light, the cannon-like roar of the Browning Hi-Power, the screams of agony from Ellis leaving him unable to hear the howl of rage and hatred that left his own lips.

Left him unable to hear the thing that crashed through the frozen undergrowth behind him.

Ellis turned, the Hi-Power slipping from his shattered fingers and falling to the blood soaked snow. His eyes widened in horror, his agony briefly forgotten as he saw Jason running towards him – and brought crashing to the frozen ground by the thing that charged into him.

Rob Benson was momentarily blinded by the muzzle flash that angled skywards. The booming report of the Browning was deafening, but he felt no pain. He knew the armed porter had missed. He dropped below the safety of the Mondeo, blinking frantically, trying to dispel the orange smears clouding his vision. The ringing in his ears merged with screams and shouting beyond Boyd's car. His heart raced, adrenaline from the standoff coursing through his body, and he shook violently. With a nervous swallow he brought himself to a sitting position and wiped the cold, greasy sweat from the handgrip of the gun on his fleece. Then he twisted over, forcing himself to peer behind the shelter of the driver's door.

"Bloody hell…" he watched open mouthed as the former inmate of the Phoenix Unit nimbly spun away from the creature that towered over him, spinning his body through the hind legs of the beast and gracefully rising to a standing position behind it. Jason's breathing was rapid but measured: his stance firm but flexible, ready to adapt to any move the boar might make next.

The creature spun round, its jaws wide open, snarling and dripping something black and viscous. Jason watched it calmly, the steel temperature probe and its plastic readout hanging loosely in his hand.

The boar raised its head to the darkening sky and howled. It was a sound Rob Benson had never heard before – not even from the boar he had fought in the Granta warehouse – and hoped never to hear again. This was a cry that belonged to no earthly creature. It was a long wolf-like howl, directed to the forces that surrounded it and gave it life – and death. It was a howl of rage and pain, of grief for its unnatural existence. It was timeless. It was terrifying.

There was also a hunger in that cry. A desire for spilled blood and torn flesh. Even Jason hesitated in his advance. For a brief moment his eyes met Rob's and a look passed between them. Rob shuddered and almost shrank behind the shelter of the Mondeo. That look would remain with him for as long as he lived.

The co-existing fury and calm were still there. But there was also self-belief and reassurance. In that one brief glance, in spite of the events spinning wildly out of control, Jason Franklin was telling him that everything was going to be all right.

Crazy. Impossible. *I've killed three people today. Even if I get outta here alive I'm gonna be banged up for that. Not that that's gonna happen, anyway. Another fucking boar and a gunman to get past – and then Franklin and Searles. And here I am feeling comforted by an escaped lunatic…*

But that reassurance was a tangible thing, a physical force that flowed into his body from Jason's brief gaze. Rob Benson could finally see that this thing Jason called The Elder was indeed working through him.

But it was a last-ditch attempt. Andy's missus was going to be torn to pieces at any moment and then Andraste was going to break through. If they didn't get out of the clearing in the woods alive, Andy Hughes was on his own.

Rob Benson had the sickening realisation that despite the military cannon Andy carried, his chances of success were slim.

Turning his eyes back to the beast, Jason tensed, putting his body into a defensive crouch. The probe was raised and glinted in the halogen glare of the headlights. Rob saw the beast's solid black eyes narrow, almost human in its appraisal of its enemy. The ridge of bristles on its dorsal crest thickened, stiffening. Then it charged.

Jason angled his body to his right, feinted with the probe. The beast hurtled in the direction it sensed the human was going, its trotters thundering on the iced ground as it charged.

And then, when it was too late for the boar, Jason twisted to the left. The boar's tusks missed him by inches and the probe went straight through the creature's right eye, bursting it like a lightly-boiled egg. Jason withdrew it before the boar's momentum tore the weapon from his hand. He grabbed the ridge of bristles with his free hand and jumped onto the back of the boar.

Rob realised that the probe must have penetrated the creature's brain. Its movements were jerky and uncontrolled, its body lurching spasmodically. Its maw and tusks were coated in black blood and viscous optical fluid which splattered glutinously onto the churned mud of the wood floor. Jason drove his knees inwards, his weight and the weakness of the boar combining to bring the beast to its knees. Holding the probe in both hands he raised it above his head and then drove it downwards with devastating force.

The sound of the boar's skull cracking was like the sound the Glock had made when Rob fired it. He winced, and then remembered the gunman.

Rob jerked his head to the left, trying to locate the other man. There was the bloodstained Browning Hi-Power, kicked to one side by the charging front legs of the boar. Following the trail of dripping blood Rob saw that its owner had backed away, out of the clearing. He held his damaged hand to his chest, blood staining the white shirt beneath his blazer. There was a sickened and horrified expression on his face and when Rob turned back to see what Jason was doing he saw what had caused the porter's horror.

Rob had to physically turn away from what Jason was doing. The balance between calm and rage had shifted in favour of the latter. As if goaded by victory, his nostrils flared and a maniacal gleam was in his eyes as he wrenched the probe out and brought it down again, this time into the beast's right flank. Again, and again, at times grating on the ribs, most times effortlessly shooting in and sliding out again.

Then the left flank. The same relentless assault. Rob couldn't see it, but he could hear it. He saw the porter back away from the mutilation of the impossible beast.

Don't fucking blame you, pal. Then he saw the man's head turn and a strangled cry of terror passed his lips, now the only sound in the clearing as the squelching and tearing noises Jason was making ceased.

Perhaps his energy was spent, his hunger for violence temporarily sated.

Or perhaps he was aware of the sight that captivated the injured porter and now Rob Benson. He dismounted and stood up, not even bothering to wipe the black blood from his face.

The three men stared silently at the pack of four boars that had until now remained motionless, watching silently as their companion was hacked to pieces.

Jason's victim uttered one last blood-bubbled exhalation before the gleaming black light in its eyes dimmed, faded and died.

As one, the four boars attacked.

TWENTY SEVEN

A stomach churning lurch, a shift in the ground beneath him and the air around him, and Andy Hughes was no longer aware of the piece of rock beneath his hand. Neither was he aware of the opulent medieval surroundings of the Great Hall, nor of his two companions. He certainly didn't see the sly grin on the head porter's face, nor the sympathetic grimace from the Master.

He saw nothing, heard nothing, felt nothing. All five senses were dead, useless. He was in a complete state of nothingness, a limbo where he had neither bodily sensations nor any sensory connections to the world he knew.

Nothing but darkness. A blackness so complete, so total, it had a physical presence of its own. Rather than a mere absence of light the darkness embodied an invisible and unknowable force, a destructive entity that was aware of his presence.

Perhaps the sensory deprivation was a blessing. Andy realised that if he could smell this entity it would fill his nostrils and burn his nasal membranes with an unbearable stench of putrefaction, of boiled blood and incinerated flesh. Its touch would be arctic ice and desert sun encased in smooth silk and jagged steel, cutting and burning and freezing. The touch of death in a thousand and one guises, perfumed with the stench of ultimate decay. An evil that would need more than five earthly senses to comprehend it fully.

For a moment he thought he heard something, and instantly prayed to God that he hadn't. How could human ears possibly hear the voice of this entity without driving the owner insane?

Then lights. Tiny, far off pinpricks of weak light in the darkness around him.

It took him a long time to realise they were stars.

Now they rushed towards him, and then past him. Their speed increased, the stars blurring into thin white lines like strands of incandescent spaghetti as they raced past him – or rather, as he raced past them. Hurtled through the void.

Or pulled. Deeper into space, towards whatever awaited him.

A journey that crossed such distances it must have lasted for millennia ended as abruptly as it began. Freed from all earthly senses and perceptions, freed from the limitations imposed on the human body and mind, Andy Hughes had suffered none of the soul-grinding weariness or ennui that he would have associated with such journeys like those in the science fiction books of his childhood.

It didn't appear to be much of a destination. No swirling milky spirals of densely packed suns, no rainbow-hued clouds of cosmic gases, no explosions of new-born stars.

Just the same blackness as before, pinpricked with stars that were motionless.

No, he realised. Not quite the same as before. The stars here seemed faint: shining feebly with a weaker light, and there were far fewer of them.

They were dying. As though the blackness around them was a poison, slowly draining the light – and life – from each.

Rubbish, he told himself. But he wasn't sure which the most disturbing scenario was. The first option – that the darkness wasn't an absence of light but a very real, physical presence that contained an evil inconceivable to human perceptions.

Or the second option – that the stars here were dimmer, their glory fading as they died alone, because he was at the furthest flung outpost of the universe. That he was here at the very borders of the end of creation.

Beyond that, there could only be nothing. Less than nothing...

The blackness opened up before him, a horizontal line of deep, scarlet light that would have burned earthly eyes if he had been witnessing it through them.

He had no idea of how close to – or how far from – he was to this line. He couldn't see an end to either side of it – perhaps there was no end. It was beyond human measurements or perceptions of distance. He felt his mind crumble at the sheer effort of trying to perceive it…

Now it grew. The scarlet line became a wall, a barrier that blazed through the darkness.

The upper and lower boundaries were curved slightly, a meniscus, rolling away from something spherical.

In the centre of the light, as the black curtains rolled fully away, lay a pit of darkness, deeper and blacker than the empty void of space that had surrounded it earlier. A darkness that hungered for life.

At the very end of the universe, at the last outpost of creation, Andy Hughes found himself staring into an eye.

The incandescent, almost liquid quality of the scarlet light that had opened earlier formed the eye's sclera. No iris, just an unmoving pit of blackness sat in the centre of this orb of furious light like a malevolent black hole, greedily sucking in any trace of life that passed nearby.

This was more than some alien optic. It was the force that had pulled him across the galaxies at incomprehensible speed and distance. It had paused, allowed him to look upon its hideous, limitless glory to awe him with its power before resuming its pulling.

It seemed an age before the growing blackness overtook the entire scarlet sclera from his vision. A lifetime for him to anticipate what lay beyond this final exit from the universe, this grim doorway to another – *another what?* He asked himself. *Dimension, parallel universe – or Hell itself?*

The eye didn't blink as it drew him in. But the darkness disappeared instantly, as though he had passed through a heavy curtain of impenetrable blackness to view the terrible show on the stage behind.

A show of horrors that threatened to shatter his mind into pieces more numerous than the dwindling stars he had passed on his impossible journey. Andy knew that he was truly in Hell.

Now he saw the fate of those offered to Andraste. The physical tortures that had accompanied them in their last agonised hours should have ended with their lives. Not so. Freeland was correct.

He now had an idea of the sheer scale of Andraste's power in the number of victims that writhed and thrashed in the vacuum around him. Everywhere he could see, the offerings to Andraste screamed soundlessly, mouths stretched wide to give vent to the agonies they each suffered. Eyes rested on him briefly, awareness of one who was not like them. Pitiful, mute pleas for help that they knew would never come burned from their eye sockets before they turned away to concentrate on their own, individual suffering.

Limbs tore themselves from torsos: skin peeled itself away and burned to an instant crisp. Jaws were stretched wide, dislocated, and tongues wrenched free by the same invisible forces that tore the teeth away in fractured lumps from the gum. Blood welled up in earlobes and dribbled downwards. Eyes bubbled and popped in the faces of some of the offerings whilst in others the orbs were simply scooped away and snapped clean from the sockets.

It took some time for Andy to appreciate the sheer scale of the suffering in front of him, because each victim was torn to pieces in different ways, at different times, so that he didn't immediately take in the fact that the tortures were repeated on the victims as soon as they ended.

He recognised certain faces that he had seen moments before, now fully intact, only to be stripped of their defining features as the unseen forces of Andraste's pain machine tore them to shreds once more.

And through it all, the most horrifying, obscene aspect of this eternal, unrelenting blood-show, was that each of the victims was unaware that others suffered with them. Eyes that had registered the presence of Andy failed to recognise the existence of other victims that suffered equally.

Each was in their own, private Hell. Tortured to death, torn to pieces, dying in agony and reborn in pain, forever alone.

Andy closed his eyes and screamed. He screamed for all the souls suffering in front of him. For the dead who could not die, who found no release from their suffering after death. And most of all he screamed for Jennifer Callaby, who was fated to join the flocks of ravaged souls in this abomination of an afterlife. He screamed his defiance of Andraste, a vow that she would never have Jen.

A voice. A single voice in this deafened wilderness of suffering where even the screams of the damned were silenced. A whisper, barely perceptible at first. A female voice.

Jennifer will join my choir. You have no say in the matter.

"You'll never have her!" Andy screamed again.

Her path has already been chosen. She belongs to me.

"She belongs to no-one!"

She is mine. The propitiation has commenced. She will join my choir…

"SHE GOES NOWHERE! SHE COMES HOME WITH ME!"

You dare to defy me? You doubt my power?

The attack began the moment the light in the dead boar's eyes faded to black. There was no hesitation, no delay and if Rob didn't act quickly, no chance.

There was no way Jason was going to be able to repeat his success with four of the fuckers tearing towards them. They hurtled onwards with a chorus of guttural snarls and a thunder of trotters beating on frozen earth. A strange, maniacal roar of rage and savage glee that could only have come from Jason.

Jesus Christ, the mental bastard's actually enjoying this!

It was the armed porter that went down first. Rob Benson watched in horror as the Yorkshireman crashed to the ground. His left arm was trapped beneath a beast that was burrowing its tusks into his side. He scrabbled in the frozen mud for the Browning with his damaged hand, the desperate screams of the porter chilling him to the bone. The porter had only his damaged hand free, and his shattered knuckles would not allow him to grip the gun, let alone put a finger into the trigger guard.

At least it was keeping one of the beasts busy. There were only three to deal with.

Rob leant over the bonnet of the Mondeo and squeezed off two shots at the boar nearest to him. It went down, squealing and roaring at the same time. Black blood pumped slowly from the hole in its right flank like sump oil. Another round from the Glock and the top of its head came away.

Its companion continued its destruction of the porter, oblivious to everything except the warm innards and gushing, life-giving fluid that drenched its head.

The other two had turned to attack the grinning Jason. His arms were extended, beckoning each creature to strike first. They pawed the ground on either side of him, steam rising from their open maws. Their eyes glowed ebony in the light, matched by the intensity of the light that shone in Jason's eyes.

Rob shook his head disbelievingly as he brought the Glock up. *You ain't indestructible, young mentalist. You can't take both of them on.*

He waited for a moment, the gun trembling in his hands. He needed to wait, to see which one Jason would go for first…

Jason swung to his left. The probe described a silver arc in the headlights and slid effortlessly into an undead eye.

He's really got that thing down to a fine art, Rob thought as he aimed at the other beast. *Just as well he's on my side. For now…*

Right flank fully exposed. A clear shot. Rob fired.

The reports from the Glock were drowned out by the cries of the two boars. The squeals of pain and death were nightmarish, identical to the cries of the boar in the warehouse.

These were not the pitiful cries of creatures in pain. They were monstrous howls of rage and fury from creatures that knew death all too well. They had already experienced its dark embrace and had no fear of it for they knew that – for them, at least – it was purely temporary. That they would return.

He continued firing until the magazine was empty. Only when the beasts were silent did he hear the firing pin clicking on empty chambers. And knew that there was still one more boar to be taken down.

He glanced fearfully to his left and saw the beast retreating from the dead porter, pieces of torn intestine looped around its tusks like some grim Christmas garland. It snorted, blowing out thick red human blood from its nostrils, daring Rob to come towards it to retrieve the Browning.

It lay in the blood-stained snow and churned mud, shiny and enticing, like the best Christmas present he could ever hope for.

It was also just two inches from the dead porter's outstretched fingers.

Shit. Now what? He glanced back and saw that Jason had disappeared. Where he stood before there was nothing but congealing black blood from the boar's head.

"Cheers, pal…" then he saw the cab of the Luton was rocking back and forth. *What's he fucking doing in there?*

Jason emerged with something green and bulbous in his right hand. Only when he stepped over the dead boars and advanced fearlessly towards the front of the Mondeo did Rob Benson realise what it was.

The cap of the plastic petrol can was tossed contemptuously towards the remaining boar. Its nostrils twitched wetly, scenting the acrid aroma of unleaded.

"I'll wash. You dry."

What? Then Rob knew what Jason meant. The can was jerked sideways, its contents thrown over the boar's head. Washing the blood from its tusks. It sneezed, its eyes squeezing shut.

Rob felt in his fleece pockets with his left hand and found an empty packet of Mayfairs. Where was his fresh one? And where was that fucking lighter?

Another splash of liquid. The boar roared.

In the car, he realised. He stepped backwards, leaned into the driver's seat and saw the Clipper lying on the dashboard with the fresh pack of cigarettes. He tossed the spent Glock onto the passenger seat and picked up the lighter.

He exited the car and thumbed the wheel of the lighter. A buttery, golden flame leapt up to greet him. He held the empty cigarette pack over it, turning it to make sure flames engulfed it completely before throwing it at the petrol-soaked boar.

Hog roast from Hell, he thought darkly as the stench of the burning boar flesh reached his nostrils. He'd never eat bacon or pork again.

Jason smiled at the unearthly screams from the creature, his face glowing hellishly in the dancing flames of the burning beast. He flared his nostrils and closed his eyes, appreciating the stench.

"Oi, Bisto Kid!" Rob's eyes streamed from the heat and the black smoke.

Jason opened his eyes with a frown.

"We've washed and dried. Let's put the dishes away."

Jason grinned. "Now you're speaking my language."

He walked over to the burning pyre, picked up the Browning and tossed it to Rob.

Rob caught it with one hand: his streaming eyes never leaving the jerking, smouldering wreck of boar meat.

"What the fuck are those things?" He stared at the dead beasts behind Jason. It must have been a trick of the torch light. One was still twitching

He realised it was the first one that Jason had killed. It hadn't been moving for a good five minutes. Now it was stirring.

"I think," Rob said with forced calm "we should make a move."

Jason followed Rob's nervous gaze and nodded.

"Fine. But I wouldn't recommend walking. The porters might be waiting, and you've probably guessed that death is only temporary to our furry friends…" his eyes narrowed. "You've seen one of them before, haven't you?"

"Yeah. Accidentally… 'picked one up' night before last." He put a cigarette in his mouth and lit it. He inhaled, savouring the smoke that washed away the stench of unnatural blood and cremated boar flesh. "Came back this morning. Tore my mate's dog to pieces. Fucker."

Jason's eyes widened. "Where?"

Rob blew smoke. "My van. It's parked outside the porter's lodge at the moment. Why the interest?"

"I'll explain later. We'll take my vehicle."

Rob watched Jason climb into the driver's seat of the cook-chill vehicle. *Your vehicle, eh?* He shuddered to think how Jason had managed to make the previous owner part company with it. With a sigh he reached into the Mondeo and switched off the lights and the engine. He had a feeling he might need the car later, if he was still alive.

Jason opened the passenger door for him. Rob thrust the Browning into his pocket. He took one last look at the twitching corpses behind him, shuddered violently and climbed into the cab.

The scene changed. The floating pieces of corpses, the vapour clouds of blood, all vanished. The blackened area he was in began to change, a void that gradually acquired physical form.

He no longer floated in the limbo of Andraste's torture chamber. Gravity rooted him, held him solidly upright on frozen, black ground. He lowered his head, swallowing dryly. His throat was hoarse from screaming. How long had it lasted? How long was it possible to sustain a scream that had torn itself from the very bottom of his soul?

His head spun and he swayed on his feet. *Forget that,* he told himself. *Get your bearings. Where am I?*

He frowned. This wasn't the medieval cavern of the Great Hall. He wasn't even sure if he was back in Cambridge.

Night air surrounded him. Pale moonlight washed over the frozen, unploughed fields that stretched in all directions. To his right he could just make out the comforting glow of sodium vapour streetlights. Human company and the twenty first century were only a few miles away. He turned and headed for the light. The ground was firm underfoot, the unploughed earth of the field frozen and unyielding, but at least there was no snow.

Strangely, although his breath misted in front of him with every step, he didn't feel cold. He glanced up and saw the stars glinting coldly in the heavens that hid a Hell beyond human imagining. Something caught his eye, in his peripheral vision. A light that shone slightly brighter than the stars.

There it was. He narrowed his eyes, squinting at the pinprick of light that was moving. Growing.

Approaching.

It wasn't just Andy Hughes that had come down to Earth. Andraste had sent something back with him. Heading in the same direction that he was taking, but it was going to get there before him.

At first it resembled a shooting star. Beautiful in its own way: a spot of heavenly light that carried a clear line of stardust in its wake.

He remembered Elizabeth Woodcock, the shooting star that had made her horse throw her into the icy wastes of Impington Common and yet had also carried her salvation. A meteorite, a piece of rock that carried the spirit of The Elder.

It could have looked nothing like this. It was a hell of a lot bigger for a start, and he was reminded of the unearthly alien eye he had travelled through earlier.

As it tore through the night sky it lit up the darkness with scarlet incandescence that reflected off the distant buildings. Just before it struck Andy saw familiar land marks – the incinerator chimney of Addenbrooke's hospital, the red brick tower of the University Library –he knew he was in Cambridge now.

And then they were gone, the sodium vapour of the streetlights replaced with a blinding flare of crimson light, exactly the same light that filled the eye of Andraste at the end of the universe.

It was accompanied by heat, a searing blast that turned all in its endless path to flame, instantaneous, unrelenting and unstoppable. One that would travel far beyond the city it was destroying.

Even the air burned.

Andraste's voice made itself heard again, with peals of almost human laughter at the sight of the devastation that had begun.

You see at last. As the Covenant with me is broken, so too is your planet. Watch and despair…

Now Andy knew what Andraste meant. He knew why Searles, Franklin, and the members of All Souls believed what they did, did what they felt they had to do.

The conflagration of the Earth raged around him, below him…he felt himself lifted from the ground, heading upwards. The snow-dusted fields below became postage stamps of white and scarlet before the fire obliterated them. He saw towns and cities overwhelmed by the blanket of fire that raced over the ground with ferocity, speed and a sheer hunger that surpassed any earthly inferno.

A fire that now spread across the planet. Once, the Earth viewed from space was a precious jewel of oceanic blue and swirling, pristine white. Now it was a sickening parody, a malevolent globe of raging fire that burned in the heavens.

Andraste's promise of oblivion was delivered right before his eyes. Still the fires raged, though surely there could be nothing combustible left on the planet now. Surely…

"Oh Jesus…"

You see now. Is this not proof enough?

What he saw now wasn't a planet in flames. It wasn't a fire. Perhaps it never was.

In the mere seconds it had taken to overcome the Earth's surface, the destructive wave had possessed the characteristics of fast moving lava. And a shade of scarlet far deeper, far more luminescent than that found in the bowels of the Earth.

The same shade of scarlet as the eye of Andraste.

The scarlet wave was slowing now, thickening. Brightening. A second eye of Andraste had been created.

A second eye, countless billions of light years from its twin. And in between them, an immeasurable distance that stretched from this solar system to the end of the universe.

All of creation was within Andraste's eyes.

Now he knew for certain that All Souls had been taken in by lies and falsehoods. The belief that the Fellowship had taken as their creed was a false one. *But not even Freeland saw this.*

Andy doubted if anyone had seen the full extent of Andraste's desire. Whereas the doubters – Freeland and Jason Franklin – had seen the truth behind the lie, that the propitiation strengthened Andraste rather than appeased her, it was unlikely they had witnessed this.

Andraste didn't just want the Earth, she wanted everything. And so certain was she of her triumph she had become even more arrogant. She had shown Andy her true plan because she was certain he was powerless to prevent it. She wanted to feel his despair, savour his agony, knowing that not only was the love of his life to be sacrificed to an ancient evil, her soul was to be condemned to eternal agony. And all to complete Andraste's passport to the secrets of the universe.

This was far worse than a pointless sacrifice. This was an abomination. It couldn't happen. He couldn't *allow* it to happen.

You still believe you can make a difference? Her laughter rang in his head. *You enjoy fighting a battle that is already lost? What can you possibly do now?*

"Put me back in All Souls, bitch. You'll see what I can do." He kept his voice calm, filled it with a confidence he didn't feel. But he wasn't defeated just yet. The fact that Andraste was so keen to boast to him gave him hope. Her attitude was one of conceit and pride – human failings.

Human failings that could be exploited.

"Back to the Hall. Give me a chance to prove you wrong."

Your arrogance amuses me. You have no hope of convincing the Master of what you have seen. He has made his decision. He will not waver.

Still, it will please me for you to see with your earthbound eyes the ravages your lady undergoes. Franklin will be happy to show you…

Candlelight. His eyes were filled with dozens of burning candles. Each flame writhed in its wick and tallow prison as frantically as the lost souls in Andraste's limbo.

He could smell them as well. Melting wax. The burning of disturbed dust motes that fell in their path. The familiar odour of cold, ancient stone. He was back in the Great Hall of All Souls College.

He blinked. Flaring candlelight, displaced dust…that should have told him something. But what?

He looked down. His hand was still clasped firmly on the meteorite. It felt warm, and his palm was slick with sweat. The weight of the SPAS 12 was painful on his shoulder.

He jerked his hand from the stone, rubbing the palm with his fingers. He looked up. The candles danced again, energised by something. The air rushing past them as something – or someone – rushed behind the table, behind Andy…

He spun round. The shotgun flew from his grip, crashing to the floor with a clattering sound as the head porter smashed his two-way radio into Andy's bicep. A jab to the stomach followed.

Winded, fresh pain added to the wounds caused by the boar last night and the policeman's assault, Andy could only stare helplessly through a red mist of agony as Franklin kicked the shotgun away and lifted him up by the armpits, preventing him from sagging to the floor and raising him up to eye level.

"Hope you learned something, Hughes," he said coldly. He squeezed his fingers under Andy's armpits, bringing a fresh cry of pain. "Some lesson, eh laddie? That's just the start. Your real education starts here."

Franklin cocked his head and looked over Andy's shoulder.

"Well, Master? What d'you say? Do we let him see how little Jennie's going to save the world?"

The Master stared sadly at Andy's back. "I think he's earned the right to say goodbye to her properly. He can have that at least."

Franklin grinned. He picked the shotgun up from the floor, jabbed Andy in the gut with the barrel and spun him around.

"Okay, bastard," he whispered into Andy's ear. "Come and see just how sweetly your lady sings to Andraste."

The barrel of the SPAS 12 pressing into his spine, his stomach and upper arm on fire from Franklin's assault, Andy Hughes staggered, half pushed, half supported by the head porter, to the double doors of the Hall where the Master was heading. Outside, to the chapel, where Jennifer Callaby waited for Andraste.

TWENTY EIGHT

Jennifer Callaby had reached the point where she no longer knew if she was alive or dead. The darkness kept slipping over her eyes like a storm-tossed wave, so thick and heavy it felt solid. Reassuring, comforting, because it contained the promise of permanent oblivion.

And then the candles would punch bright holes in that blanket, light that reminded her of where she was and what she was going through. Then the pain would return. Waves of agony that spread throughout her body and had her curling up even tighter in her foetal position: rocking and shuddering on the cold stone of the cellar floor.

She didn't know how long she'd been here, or when the fingers on her left hand had been taken. She could still taste the blood that had slipped down her throat from her broken nose, sickly sweet and metallic, making her gag. She'd had enough presence of mind to angle her head forward to stop more of the blood slipping down her throat, but this instead made it flood her already blocked nasal passages, adding to the pressure of the clotted blood already there. It was the chef who had done that, she remembered. That bastard Cassell. On arriving at the porter's lodge she'd been directed to the kitchens, shown where to change into the overalls.

And the door had opened suddenly: the huge, sweaty bulk of the head chef bursting in on her and restraining her with one flabby but powerful arm before she had a chance to scream. Breaking her nose with the handle of the carving knife…

Candlelight reflected on something metallic nearby, a reddish glint in the corner of her eyes. She remembered seeing it before, wielded by the man who had taken the first of her digits. It was motionless now, lying on the thick, black cloth along with the other knives.

And here they still were, waiting to be used on her. *So why are they delaying? What are these bastards waiting for?*

She lifted her head from the floor, wincing at the fresh pain that hammered behind her eyes. She looked to the left, then to the right, her eyes streaming in the merciless glare of the candles. Nothing moved in the shadows beyond the candles. No one else's breath misted in the air apart from hers. She was alone.

Had they been interrupted by something? Or was this just one more part of the torture, to leave her alone with the instruments of her destruction, to imagine where they would cut, what parts of her would be sliced away next?

And all with no explanation. That was the worst part of it. She had no idea why they were doing this.

"No reason," she croaked. The nearest candle fluttered in the breath from her lips, and the light on the knives lengthened. Her blood pooling around the stumps at the end of the palm turned from scarlet to black and then scarlet again. She stifled a cry and looked back at the knives.

They almost seemed to glow with the stolen souls of their former victims. Jennifer Callaby knew that she was not the first victim to feed the knives. And she knew that the former victims had gone through exactly the same despair she was. They too were given no reason. They too were ravaged: cut piece by piece, howling for release, screaming *why*?

She wept then. She wept for herself and she wept for those who had gone before her. But most of all, she wept for those who would surely follow her.

The candle flames danced again, higher, burning brighter, and she felt a colder rush of air on her back. She heard footsteps on stone stairs. A torch beam played across the dripping stone of the back wall, the shadows rearing as if to strike. She turned her head and the beam shone directly into her face.

And then she heard a voice she thought she would never hear again.

"JENNIFER!"

It was the only time she could remember him raising his voice. The only time he had ever shouted.

She looked towards the open door. The despair lifted from her at the sight of Andy Hughes.

It lifted for a few seconds only. When she saw the horror on his face, the haunted look in his eyes and the shotgun levelled at his head by Franklin, the despair came crashing back.

So they had Andy as well.

Andy froze, struck motionless at what he saw illuminated by Franklin's flashlight. The head porter played the beam over the woman's body slowly, from head to toes and then back again. Forcing Andy to see what Jen had been reduced to.

For just a brief moment there was hope in her eyes, a light of recognition and love, but just for a moment. Her eyes took in the weapon held to his head and the man holding it, and then that light died. Her eyes closed and a despairing sob worked itself free. Her head sank to the bloodstained floor again.

The sight of her mutilated left hand triggered something inside Andy. It was confirmation of his final fears: not only could he lose Jen, he would lose her in the most painful, obscene manner possible.

All to perpetuate a lie as old as humanity. The black rage overwhelmed him, pure, dark fury coursed through his body faster than the adrenaline that followed.

Franklin was still behind him. He could feel the cold muzzle of the SPAS-12 pressed tightly into the back of his head. He also knew that Franklin's free hand was taken up with the flashlight.

Andy's left foot left the floor and the ankle of his boot scraped down Franklin's shin. Andy twisted his head away from the muzzle of the shotgun, whirled round, ducked and punched Franklin in the gut. Even in such a confined space Andy managed to impart enough force to dig his bunched knuckles right up and under the head porter's diaphragm.

The bellow of pain and surprise roared around the stone walls of the cellar. Light spun crazily as the flashlight fell from Franklin's grip and tipped over the ledge of the stone step. Before it fell to the floor and knocked over the candles nearest to Jen it lit the head porter's face in a leprous mask of pain and fury, yellowed teeth bared in a bestial snarl. Then it was gone, just an afterimage burned onto Andy's retinas.

In that split second Andy saw that Franklin had his index finger outside the trigger guard, not inside curling around the trigger.

He knew it wouldn't stay that way for long. He pulled his fist back, rose and lashed out at where he thought Franklin's face was, his left hand reaching for the SPAS 12.

His right fist was on target, but only just. Franklin must have jerked his head back because Andy's fist only scraped along his left cheek, his thumbnail gouging a large scratch. His left hand made brief contact with cold metal. Metal that fought back.

An explosion rocked the cellar, and everything within was briefly illuminated. But it was Franklin's face that dominated Andy's view, the blood welling from the cut in his cheek, soaking his moustache a bright crimson. The eyes shone with manic glee at the confrontation, no trace of pain in his features at all.

Over his left shoulder Andy could see the shocked, open-mouthed face of the Master, his hands coming up to his ears – too late to block out the deafening sound from the combat shotgun.

Then Andy smelled the smoke and cordite, the burning blood and flesh of a shotgun wound.

The room tilted, his whole body forced off balance. It was only when he fell backwards down the stairs, his head jarring on the edge of the last step and bringing instant blackness, that he realised that the burning blood and flesh was his own.

The hijacked cook-chill van went through the outskirts of the woods at a speed Rob Benson thought was unwise, given the lack of visibility and the deadly cargo onboard.

The Transit dipped suddenly, an unseen pothole in the frozen dirt track making the vehicle rock violently on its springs. He swallowed nervously as one of the full petrol cans rolled against his thigh with a thick sloshing sound. The cap hadn't been tightened properly and fluid spilled down the neck of the container.

There were four of them in total, five if he included the one emptied out on the last boar. The smell of petrol was strong in the cab, and for once he didn't feel like lighting up a cigarette.

"Careful, young mentalist," Rob snapped. He pushed the can back with the Browning Hi-Power nervously. "What the fuck are these for, anyway?"

Jason was hunched over the steering wheel. He grinned at Rob, then the side mirror. "I think you know, Roberto."

"Repeat performance of last year's fireworks. Jesus." Rob found himself shrinking back in the seat, edging towards the door. He glanced in his own mirror. The trees raced past in the gloom and he couldn't see anything following them.

Not yet, anyway. He should have felt safe in the van, an armoured shell against the creatures that lurked in the woods of All Souls College. But the driver of the van was probably just as dangerous.

"Those things out there – the wild boar? They are dead, aren't they?"

Jason shook his head, struggling with the steering wheel as he hit another pothole. "As I said, death is temporary to them. During the winter solstice, at least."

"So what the bloody hell are they? How come no-one's mentioned them before?"

"The college doesn't really want to draw attention to the Children of Andraste."

"The *what*?" Rob pushed away another moving petrol can. This one leaked more fuel than the other. He felt the remaining blood drain from his face.

"They're descendants of the wild boar that roamed here when everything was covered in forest. They made a permanent home here because of the food available in the Nemeton at this time of year." Jason glanced out of the window again.

"Food?"

"Whatever was left over from the propitiation. Given to the beasts of the forest." The tops of the Cloister Court buildings were now visible. "An exchange for one of their number submitting to the Feast."

Rob opened the window to release some of the overpowering petrol fumes. Jason changed up a gear as the track levelled out. He glanced at Rob and smiled.

"Yes, Roberto, they come from here. Live wild boar hasn't been on this ground since medieval times…but dead ones remain. They return on the shortest day of the year. One offered to the Fellowship, to complete the Communion. That's why its body is buried with full ceremonial honours afterwards. Andraste demands that everything about her is treated with respect – especially the burial of her Children."

Just when it couldn't get any more loopy. For fuck's sake.

"Earth to earth, dust to dust…and flesh to flesh. And that's the key, Roberto. Flesh. It's flesh that allows them to return each year. Flesh from the propitiation, from the victim offered to Andraste, has special powers of its own."

Special powers of its own…explains the boar in the warehouse, then. Jasper, you poor little fucker. Rob felt the comforting bulge of his cigarette pack in his fleece pocket. Perhaps it was the fumes from the leaking petrol cans that made his head spin. But there was something Jason had said earlier that had unsettled him.

"Hang on. You said whatever was *left over* from the propitiation. What did you mean by that?"

Jason smiled grimly. "Didn't James Freeland put that in his dossier? No? Oh well, he did have a lot on his mind in the last few months, poor man."

"Well, you helped compile that folder, didn't you?" Rob was tired now: tired of the smugness, the arrogance and the bizarre word games. "Just fuckin' tell me."

"Next stop's the kitchens. It's at this time that Cassell is prepping the boar meat… so you'll learn then."

The blackness didn't last long. Franklin had retrieved the rubber-cased flashlight and held it over the torn flesh. The torchlight spun furiously in Andy's eyes, as did the surviving candles and the head porter's grinning face. Behind him he could hear Jen moaning softly.

It was the sound of her pain that galvanised him, not his own agony. Despite the spinning cellar and the fire spreading from his left shoulder he forced himself up on his right elbow. Every shuddering breath he took fuelled the fire.

He fixed Franklin with a hate filled glare. Franklin just grinned back at him, circling the wound with the beam of the torch. The top of Andy's shoulder was a charred mass of blood, burnt cotton from his sweatshirt and ground meat.

"Aren't you the lucky one? Just grazed you. Never was very adept with combat shotguns. More of a rifleman, myself." Franklin stepped off the final step and crouched down. He shone the torch in Andy's face. Andy averted his head but kept his eyes open. A small act of defiance.

He ignored the porter's mocking words, knowing full well that he had deliberately missed. Franklin was playing with him, spinning out the game and the pain – for Jen as well as him.

"Lucky for *you*, cunt," Andy snarled. He shuddered at the pain these words cost him. Every breath was agony. Speaking was almost unbearable.

But I won't give this psychotic bastard the satisfaction of silence.

The head porter leant over him. A drop of blood from the scratch on his cheek ran down his jaw line and dripped onto Andy's nose. Andy closed his eyes and forced himself to take slow, calm breaths. *Gently. Focus on the breathing, not the pain, the breathing not the pain…*

An explosion ripped through Andy. A tunnel of fire bored down from his shoulder blade into his abdomen. Shotgun wound and goring injury met. His elbow gave way and he crashed to the floor, his screaming so loud it fluttered and extinguished two of the candles closest to him.

Franklin stopped patting Andy's ravaged shoulder and stood up.

"Not so lucky for *you*, Hughes. You'll wish that shell had gone through your throat by the time I've finished with you."

Franklin waited patiently for Andy to recover. When he was satisfied that Andy wasn't going to pass out, was fully conscious of his surroundings and situation, was on the verge of getting to his feet again, his foot lashed out and slammed into Andy's ribs.

Two voices spoke then, two voices ringing in Andy's ears as he doubled up. By then the pain was so great, so all-pervading, that they didn't register.

Only when the red screen lifted from his eyes did they filter into his consciousness. The first had come from Jen. A cry of anger and hatred, spitting out the name *"Franklin!"*

The second came from above. Lower in volume, but with just as much fury as Jennifer's.

The Master of All Souls stormed down the stairs, his footsteps echoing around the stone walls of the cellar. Franklin turned lazily and shone the torch in his face.

Searles' face was a mask of barely contained fury. Eyes widened, they didn't even blink in the harsh glare of the Krypton bulb.

"That's enough!" The Master's hand came down in a fast downwards strike, knocking the torch out of Franklin's hand. It hit the floor, spinning its harsh beam directly into Andy's face.

Andy sensed Searles crouch down by him, sensed Franklin move backwards, away from the fury of the Master of All Souls.

"This has gone on long enough, Franklin! For God's sake, just finish it. Now!" He grabbed the torch and thrust it at the porter. He turned his attention towards Andy. His expression softened.

"I'm sorry, Andrew. I truly am. I wanted you to see how necessary this all is before you died – that's why I wanted you to see through the eye of the stone, see what Andraste is capable of."

"And you think it's changed my mind?" Andy spat blood onto the concrete floor. "You really thought I'd die happy, just by seeing your fucking *proof*?"

He coughed again, spat another lump of blood. This one landed on Searles' left shoe. He wanted to rise again, at least get his head off the floor. But it wasn't happening.

"What d'you think I saw, Searles? What did *you* see? Let's compare notes."

Searles looked behind Andy for a moment, with guilt and self-loathing as he saw the girl.

"I saw Hell," he said quietly. "I travelled to a red globe at the far end of the universe. And in there I saw countless men and women torn to pieces in a silent void. Torn to pieces, coming back together: rebuilt, somehow – only to be ravaged again. Again, and again and again. Eternal, unceasing pain and despair. And the awareness that this awaited every man, woman and child on Earth unless she was properly appeased."

Andy moved his head against the stone floor. It was the closest he could come to a nod.

"Yeah. Pretty much what I saw. Except I didn't have this…*awareness* that that was the fate for all mankind if Andraste wasn't fed properly. Perhaps I missed something that you more enlightened guys picked up on. Didn't you ever have doubts?"

Searles' face came closer to Andy's. It had stopped spinning, but the pain still wracked his body. He was light-headed, and knew he was going into shock.

"Of course we had doubts, Andrew. The Fellowship always had doubts. From the date of our college's foundation, many of the Fellows believed they were doing the work of Satan by performing the propitiation. How many prayers were said to God for guidance on this matter, we'll never know."

Searles looked at him with sympathy. But Andy sensed a change in him now. He saw before him a man who had been undergoing a crisis of conscience for a very long time, and had finally come to a decision. The Master continued.

"If any good came out of our agonising, it was a reminder that we are all alone. That only we have the power to save the human race from extinction. It is up to us alone, and this we do for the love of humanity.

"We have been abandoned by God, as have the souls that Andraste has taken. Oh yes, Andrew, we know they suffer for all eternity. And where is God now? If He will not intervene on earthly matters, surely the last word on a human being's immortal soul belongs to Him? No. Further proof He cares nothing for his creatures."

"Assuming God exists, Master." Franklin's voice was low but taut. Andy craned his neck past Searles to stare at him, could feel the tension between the two men as much as the pain in his shoulder.

They've had this conversation before, he thought. *And they've disagreed on it, more than once...*

Perhaps that was it. That was Searles' crisis – one not just of conscience but of faith. Deep down he still had a shred of belief in God: one he had fought against and tried to deny.

An all too human desire, Andy thought. One he could exploit. *It's all I've got now. Nothing to lose...*

"For the love of humanity..." Andy spat more blood. He felt cold. "You're not saviours. Freeland was right. Jason Franklin was right. You've been lied to, right from the start. You think that just because you agonise over your task that that makes your continuance of it justifiable?

"I saw something else in the stone, Searles. Something that I don't think anyone else did. Your Andraste has grown cocky. I know what her plan is. She told me. You appease her one more time and she has the strength she needs to break through. To turn this planet into a world of blood and fire.

"Haven't you guessed yet? Do you know what you are? You're caretakers, that's all."

Searles frowned. "Caretakers? What do you mean?"

"Read your history, Searles. An old definition of a caretaker is a land maintainer. Someone put in charge of a farm after the tenant's been evicted.

"And that's what happened. Boudicca's little pet was evicted by the Romans, but Andraste still had a group of misguided idiots who looked after her farm. Watering it with blood: feeding the soil with pain – until she's strong enough to come back and take possession.

"For the love of humanity...no. For the service of Andraste. That's all."

Searles shook his head. "No. You're wrong..."

"Yeah? Think about this. There's another factor in this equation, something that Jason was put away for – and one that I'm now starting to believe for myself. The Elder may not be much of an ally – shit, an ally that sends you insane isn't much of a friend – but he's real. And he doesn't just appear in dreams."

Andy stared at the Master of All Souls. *Come on Searles. Face up to your doubts. Face the truth.*

The Master sighed heavily, and then his face hardened. Andy knew then that Searles had come to the end of his crisis. He had made his decision.

Andy had lost.

"This *thing* called The Elder is nothing more than an aberration created by the mind of a very sick young man." He cast a glance at Jennifer, his eyes impassive now, and then glared at Andy.

"It is that aberration that turned him against the college and his father, that almost destroyed the Fellowship and our college last year – and thus our efforts to appease mankind and safeguard humanity's future!" His voice rose. No longer a thin, tremulous voice, his words were now hammer blows that pounded the thick stone confines of the chamber of appeasement. This was worse than the violence meted out by Franklin. Andy Hughes' last hope had gone.

"I will hear no more of this 'Elder!' Freeland, Lotson, yourself – all taken in by this phantom. And you – to bring in a manufactured stone likeness of this...this delusion, and to bring it here on this of all nights, to make us question ourselves and our duty even more..." Searles closed his eyes, clenching his fists. He took a deep breath, a visible attempt to calm down.

Even Franklin looked surprised by this outburst. And then Andy knew.

"It's all about Jason, isn't it? Your son."

Searles' eyes were incandescent with rage. "I broke the rules. I had a son, in spite of what we were taught. Just as Charles Harvey did two centuries ago, I wandered from the path of duty. Andraste forgave my trespass, with the condition that I offered him to her before he reached adulthood. To do so, Jason had to be kept in college grounds, within site of the Fellowship and its servants at all times."

"So you made him adopt the head porter's name, made him believe he was Franklin's son. Not yours." Andy shook his head. "And then kept him here until the time of offering."

"Precisely." The Master's words were ice. "It was up to me to offer him, and I failed. I weakened. I denied Andraste, gave her an offering that was a poor substitute. We feel her power – and her anger – more this year than ever before, and it's *all my fault.* But I'll not fail in my duty again. I will offer unto Andraste everything she demands. Jason is in the grounds of the college. Andraste will have him before today has ended. And she'll have the other she demands… "

His eyes looked past Andy. There was no sound from Jen. Andy shuffled on the bloodstained floor, his eyes searching for signs of life in the woman he loved and would fight for. Would die for. She had passed out, but even in her unconscious state she shivered.

"You're – not – having her, *bastard*!" He shuffled forward, the nails of his right hand scratching the cold stone. His hand outstretched, trying to grasp her mutilated hand.

Andy heard him Franklin walk behind him. He tensed, expecting another kick, but he was still not going to let Jen go. His fingers brushed her hand and he heard Searles speak.

"I sympathise Mr Hughes, I really do. But you cannot expect us to share your delusion. I have already told you of the anguish we go through every year. We do not expect thanks or recognition for our painful duty. *We do not even ask you to believe in what we do.* We know what we are doing. We pay the price: we shoulder the burden, and we endure. And for the continued survival of mankind, for the love of humanity, we must not be stopped."

Jen's skin was so *cold.* Andy felt tears well in his eyes. The arm dropped from his grip and he watched the damaged hand fall to the floor of the chamber with the wet slap of dead meat. She didn't stir. Her eyes remained closed.

*Don't wake up, darling. Go now, before the knives return. Sleep, darling, sleep…*he didn't hear the exchange that followed.

"Franklin, I'm going to the SCR. The Council will reconvene for their task in precisely half an hour. Ensure the chamber is fit for the sacred duty. While this lady sings to Andraste you will find Jason and bring him here."

"Very well, Master. And Hughes?"

Searles' voice tightened, but it was strong with self-belief.

"He's had his chance to say goodbye. Finish him."

TWENTY NINE

"Here's what we'll do." Jason Franklin slowed the vehicle as the road changed from dirt track to gravel pathway. "I'll drop you off at the service area of the kitchens. You can't avoid being seen, so get in there as fast as you can. That cannon of yours should be enough to freak Cassell out. Wave it about a bit, fire once if you have to…but you probably won't need to."

"Why's that?"

"Because, Roberto, all hell will have broken loose on the other side of the Hall." Jason grinned and patted the nearest plastic fuel can. "And it'll be me doing the breaking. Don't ask for a signal, you'll know what it is the minute you hear it. Not sure how much time that'll give you to get your friends out – assuming there's anything left of them to save."

Rob swallowed nervously. *Cheers, pal.* Horror and fear filled his guts with ice water.

"But remember, you won't have long so don't hang about. Get them – and yourself – out as quick as you can."

"What about you? How're you getting out?" Rob almost regretted the question. Jason Franklin's eyes still had that spark of madness, but now combined with an animalistic look of anticipation. Hunger.

"In a puff of smoke. This is the end of the road for me, Roberto. I'm going to finish the job and the bastards behind it."

The van moved onwards and Rob almost wished they were back in the woods. Here, in the stone surroundings of Cloister Court, he felt they were helplessly exposed and all-too visible in the stolen van.

Exposed to what? He asked himself. *What can be worse than those things in the woods?*

He didn't know, couldn't think of an answer to such a ridiculous question. It just felt like there was no safe place in the college of All Souls. You left one hazardous hell-spot for another. Human beasts or unnatural, undead four-legged ones, there was no quarter from either.

And now, straight into the centre of the hell-hole driven by an insane man who relished the prospect of suicide and the chance of taking as many members of the college to hell with him…

The black clunch walls of Cloister Court enveloped them in cold, dead stone for a moment and then they were in New Court. Rob saw the service yard of the kitchens, the green wheelie bins and the pile of black refuse sacks. He remembered his last visit there, with Jasper, and the grief Cassell had given him. Christ, it felt like years ago.

He remembered where Jasper was now. Lying in state in the back of the Granta Office Supplies vehicle. *Poor fucker, never even had a chance to bury you properly, did I?* He knew now he never would.

Jason brought the vehicle to a halt. He gestured to the service yard.

"Well, mind how you go Roberto."

Rob exited the van on shaking legs, the Browning held nervously to his chest. He was more exposed and vulnerable now, about to enter a whole new world of shit – but he also felt massively relieved to be away from this suicidal fruitcake.

"Don't stop for any scraps from the table!" Jason added. "You won't know *what* you're eating!"

Rob slammed the door with such force rust patches flaked away from the sills. He stared daggers at the van as it drove away. *Good fucking riddance, mentalist.*

He turned to the kitchen entrance. One set of double doors, seemingly unlocked. Bright fluorescent light peeped through the square glass panels at the top, briefly blotted out as moving figures within passed in front of the lights.

Sounds of cutlery and crockery moving on metal surfaces, along with raised voices and muffled swearing – the sounds of a large kitchen preparing for an important function.

To the right of the doors, underneath a steel safety rail, a concrete ramp covered in gritting salt sloped downwards to the wheelie bins. Rob stepped up to the ramp and wrinkled his nostrils in disgust at the smell from the bins. The lids were firmly closed and were padlocked. He thought he heard the summery hum of flies buzzing around rotting meat, but not in these temperatures surely? The gunshots in the clearing earlier must have made his hearing fuzzy.

But his nose didn't lie. And he remembered the words Jason had said about their unearthly attackers as they sped away in the van. *Some of them made a permanent home here because of the food available…whatever was left over from the propitiation. Given to the beasts of the forest…*

"Jesus, no. It can't be…"

Emma. He had to know. Had to be sure. He took the butt of the Browning and smashed it down on the lock of the nearest bin. It fell in two pieces and was swallowed by the snow. The tensed plastic lid fluttered as it was released. He pulled the bin away from the wall to allow the lid to roll back fully.

More noises came from beyond the double doors. Closer now, but Rob didn't notice. His assault on the wheelie bin hid them, as did the cry that escaped his lips. A roar of anguish as he tore open the black bin bags and saw what had been responsible for the stench of decomposing meat.

Now he knew how the followers of Andraste disposed of the bodies. The wheelie bins were unmarked: they certainly would not be collected by the City Council for emptying. These would be sent to the beasts in the wood.

It seems that flesh ravaged by the followers of Andraste's ritual has special powers of its own...

Healing powers. The power to transcend death. To return from the grave – again and again and again.

But that wasn't the worst part. He broke open the padlock on the second bin, steeled himself for the grim discovery, for the heads, faces of his friends. Instead there was a second pair of legs, male by the look of them, and offal in the third.

But that didn't explain why there were only the arms and legs of Emma and Dan in the bins. Where were the heads? The torsos?

Whatever is left over from the propitiation. Cassell is prepping the boar meat, you'll know then.

"Oh, Jesus," he breathed. He tore himself away from the bin and its hideous contents, thundered up the ramp towards the double doors, his eyes streaming with tears of rage and grief.

The doors suddenly swung open. Rob cried out in alarm, swerving to avoid being hit in the face by the nearest door. His trainers skidded on the snow and he felt the world tipping sideways. His right arm shot out and inadvertently pulled on the trigger.

The kitchen worker was slammed into the door by the force of the gunshot, tearing it off its hinges. The muzzle-flash turned the sudden spray of blood into a glittering shower of rubies.

Rob's vision swam as his head made contact with the steel guard rail. He winced but somehow managed to grab onto the railing, stopping himself falling to the ramp. The Browning had dropped to the ground, wrenched free from his loose grip by the powerful recoil.

Rob then found himself battling a heavily bleeding body that fell from the broken doorway. He yelped in shock as the warm blood pumped onto him, retched as it reached his lips. The kitchen worker made strangled sobbing noises, clutching at Rob's shoulders, panic and terror in his eyes.

Eyes which glazed as each second passed. Rob closed his eyes, took a deep breath and twisted the body round and backwards.

The kitchen worker slumped over the safety railing, his arms dangling by his sides, head angled to the ground like a passed-out drunk. More fluid spattered onto the frozen concrete from the hole in his chest, warm blood turning the snow into crimson slush.

Rob almost giggled as he got to his feet. Another death, though this one had been an accident, and the result was absurd. The dead worker reminded him of himself: so many times when he'd had one too many, slumped over the nearest solid support as he heaved his guts out, feeling his whole life slipping away in a never-ending torrent of fluid.

He turned his attention to the kitchen. He heard cries of panic, of slamming doors and people running down corridors. The alarm would be raised at any moment.

With shaking hands he retrieved the Browning. He winced at the pain in his wrist. *Should be used to that by now*, Roberto, he told himself.

The air in the kitchen was rank with the smell of burnt cordite and gamey meat. Rob shook his head, told himself that it was just lingering in his nostrils from the encounter outside. That changed when he walked past the refrigerators and closer to the stainless steel worktops. That's when he saw the source of the smell.

At this distance it was more potent than the scent of gamey meat. This was the powerful stench of rotting, putrefying flesh. He wondered how long the boar had been dead. And would this one *stay* dead?

It lay on its right side on the central work surface. It was roughly the same size as the beasts he and Jason had battled against earlier. Even the complete removal of its pelt didn't reduce its size. Only the bristles on the head remained.

In between the trussed limbs Rob could see a clean, surgical cut in the beast's belly, running from the base of its neck to just above its genitals.

Rob moved closer, his free hand squeezing shut his nose against the stench. The beast's eyes were open. They were glazed, immobile and very, very dead. There was none of the liquid blackness and unholy red glinting pupils he had seen in the eyes of the others. Its thick tongue rested between its open jaws on the silvery surface of the worktop like a lump of rotting liver. Those tusks were identical to the others, though. Eight inches long, and unnaturally sharp.

There was something about the abdomen that puzzled him.The belly bulged.

Stuffed and prepped for cooking, he thought. *But what with?*

He placed the Browning on the adjacent work top and stretched trembling hands towards the belly of the boar. The cut was clean and surgical, a completely straight line. The sliced sides of the belly had been pressed back together but not stitched. In places the flaps of flesh had begun to part again, showing the yellow layers of fat beneath. His fingertips brushed it tentatively, as if expecting the hole to close around his hand and drag him in…

Stranger things have happened, he told himself grimly.

The skin was cool, the flesh beneath firm and slightly yielding. Just as dead meat should be. He pressed harder, straightened his fingers and prodded two inches below the slit.

The boar's belly flexed. Rob jumped back.

The flaps of flesh parted. The stench was even stronger now, but it had a slightly different tang to it.

Something pink and fleshy nestled within. The fluorescent strip lighting revealed just enough detail for Rob Benson to cry out in horror and twist himself away, clutching the stainless steel door handle of one of the refrigerators for support. He sank to his knees, gagging. Dry heaving, gagging on an empty stomach with nothing but the taste of bile for his efforts. Now he wished the hole in the boar's belly had closed around his hands and dragged him in. Anything but the cold reality of what had been done by human hands.

Glistening with the remnants of the boar's blood and intestinal juices was the dismembered torso of a human being.

A woman. The scorpion tattoo on the left breast was clearly visible.

Jason drove through the narrow gateway into Old Court. The headlights shone on the spray of water from the ornamental fountain in the centre of the lawn. Now Jason paused and took in his surroundings.

Was it only a year ago that he had last been here? It seemed so long ago. The fountain that had tripped him in the darkness as he ran from the Great Hall – for a brief moment it had run with blood as well as clear water, blood from the gash on his forehead caused by the head porter slamming his skull onto the marble edging.

The Great Hall was exactly as it had been before his attack on the building. The stained glass had been restored; the fire damage to the stonework had been fully cleaned. Inside it would no doubt be the same. All trace of his attempt to destroy the college wiped clean, cleared away and covered up. Given time, even the memories of those who were there on that night would fade.

In the passageway by the porter's lodge, he saw a parked Ford Transit. The door was open and the interior light was on, illuminating something dark and vaguely familiar on the bulkhead.

He opened the door and jumped out, noting that the snow was crisper underfoot. The air was colder, too. The temperature was dropping.

"Soon fix that," he whispered darkly. He went to the rear of the van and pulled open the flap that covered the tail lift controls.

Yes, looked pretty straightforward. He'd seen the cook-chill delivery men doing this time and again outside the Phoenix unit. And it really was as easy as it looked. Finger held on the centre red button, pull the lever down…with a protesting whine the tail lift folded out, fully horizontal, the inner edge flush with the rear doors of the box conversion. He stopped there. He didn't want to lower the lift to the floor. He was happy with it where it was.

A four-foot rectangular plate of heavy steel. Three foot above the ground. Just above waist height.

Although the outer edge was tapered, it wasn't overly sharp. But reversing – even slowly – it would be a considerable weapon. At the speed he would be going it would be lethal.

There was just one more thing to do before he climbed back into the van. He threw the fuel filler cap across the courtyard and took out the roll of bandages from the van's first aid kit.

When he finished he looked around the wintry scenery of the Court. So quiet, he thought. *Better make some noise – give Roberto a chance against Cassell.*

He spun the wheel into a full right lock and pressed down on the accelerator. The lowered tail lift clipped the top of the fountain as it passed by, a shriek of tortured stone filling the deserted Court. The headlights passed along the mullioned and transomed windows, twenty first century illumination invading fourteenth century darkness. Jason blasted the horn and kept his eyes on the double doors of the Great Hall.

Come on, come on. One of you, come out and ask what the noise is all about…

He saw the doors vibrate slightly, a sign that they were being opened. Jason grinned. He swung the vehicle round so that the rear was facing the entrance to the Great Hall. He put the handbrake on, engaged reverse then revved the engine.

The doors opened outwards. Jason pressed down harder on the accelerator, sending black plumes of smoke into the darkening air. He kept his eyes fixed on the reflected image of the opening door in the side mirror. He didn't wait long.

Two figures emerged, their gowned shadows cast by the fires within preceding them. They stood facing each other: the bulky one pointing nervously to the van, the other standing immobile, arms folded. They spoke to each other quickly then they walked to the vehicle, warily.

Jason saw their reflections grow in the side mirror. He took the temperature probe from the dashboard and wound down the window. Now they were coming into the field of light spread by the lamppost he could see their faces clearly. Davies and Nasen. The Bursar and the Senior Tutor.

The two Council members separated. Davies stood by the rear of the van, staring in bewilderment at the lowered tail lift. Nasen came up to the driver's door.

"Well, well," he spoke loudly over the roar of the engine. His silver cropped hair gleamed silver in the lamp light, his features creased into an arrogant, disdainful smirk. He stared at the petrol cans on the passenger seat.

"Back to finish what you started, young Jason?"

Jason felt a chill. The mocking smirk on the Senior Tutor's face, the arrogance of his stance – just as it had been last year when the head porter had knocked him down and held him immobile, waiting for the police to arrive.

With a now almost instinctive movement of his right arm the needle point of the temperature probe shot through the opened window and into the Senior Tutor's eye – right or left, Jason didn't know or care. He heard the plopping sound of a freshly punctured eyeball, felt his shoulder jar as the probe struck the back of the skull. That was all he needed to know. *Job done.*

"Yes, Senior Tutor. Back for good." He pulled the probe back, out of Nasen's skull. Little effort was required as the body was already falling to the snow. Gravity did most of the work for him.

The Bursar let out a strangled cry of horror. Jason popped the handbrake and sent the van hurtling backwards, acrid exhaust fumes filling the cab. Davies pulled his bulk to the right, but not fast enough to prevent the edge of the tail lift striking his raised left elbow.

Even over the mistiming roar of the engine Jason could hear the crack of bone snapping. He saw a huddled, black-clad ball of screaming agony shooting past him. He slammed the brakes on, surprised to feel the wheels skid on the grass beneath. The temperature was dropping even faster than he'd realised.

Davies looked up, his mouth open in agony. His bearded jowls wobbled.

Jason grinned at him. He leant over the steering wheel, gave a thumbs-up signal and then threw the thumb backwards, indicating the Great Hall.

Davies glanced at the Hall and swiftly got to his feet. He looked back once at Jason with widened, terrified eyes before shuffling his way to the double doors of the Hall, whimpering.

Looks almost grateful, Jason thought. *Won't be for long, though…*

Jason put the van in first gear and stepped on the accelerator. The engine roared and the van shot forwards, sliding again on the frozen ground beneath and straight over the bleeding corpse of the Senior Tutor. The steering wheel spun and the vehicle tilted to the left. The remaining petrol cans knocked against each other, one falling and hitting the hand holding the gearstick, making Jason tut in annoyance.

More annoyingly, it had a galvanising effect on the would-be diners. Cries of horror filled the air, joined with the squelching and cracking noises from underneath his wheels. It was enough to make them move.

Panic was inevitable, but he had thought the Fellows would remain in the Hall, retreating fearfully behind the false security of the medieval walls, thinking that a maniac with a lowered tail lift could not get at them. That was what he wanted. The more people inside the building the better. More fuel for the fire.

The Bursar had reached halfway across the lawns, onto the pathway that bisected the lawns of Old Court. He glanced fearfully over his shoulder at the glare of the reversing lights and the smoke billowing from the van's exhaust. His arm dangled uselessly by his side as he turned back.

Jason checked both side mirrors. In each he could see the opened doors of the Great Hall. He couldn't see the retreating, whimpering figure of the Bursar so he knew Davies was roughly in the centre of his path.

A bonus, he thought. This time let in the clutch slowly, pressed gently on the accelerator. The vehicle reversed, painting a perfectly straight line of black, lumpy blood on the lawns of Old Court. Satisfied the vehicle wasn't going to skid, he pressed harder on the accelerator.

The reflected images of the double doors bounced up and down in the side mirrors. He saw the panicked faces of gowned figures within, horrified expressions on their faces as they realised what the driver of the Luton was going to do. Slowly, the doors began to close.

The van's engine roared, black fumes enveloping the Bursar as he banged his good fist on the closing doors, screaming in terror.

Jason caught sight of Davies' flailing fingers in the nearside mirror before they disappeared and the van slammed to a violent halt. Jason's head slammed against the headrest and then the bulkhead. He cried out in pain, feeling the straining of neck muscles and the jarring thud of his skull hitting steel and wood.

His pain blotted out the shriek of buckling metal, the groan of medieval doors protesting against the steel intruder – and the barely human screams from the Bursar.

Jason's head slumped forwards. He stared dizzily at the red battery light on the dashboard, wondering why it looked so familiar. He closed his eyes, but the red light remained with him. The red light of sunrise.

Life fluid of ancient gods, he told himself. Now he remembered. He opened his eyes, glanced in the side mirror. The tail lift had driven a wedge right into the left hand door. Beyond he could see a glimpse of fluttering candles and cressets, the light of the Great Hall banishing winter darkness.

"Banished by spilling blood," he muttered. His vision cleared and now he saw the splatters of blood marking the ancient oak timber.

Then he stared at the figure advancing across the lawns. Illuminated by the head-lights of the Luton, striding purposefully across the lawn from the chapel, was the unmistakeable figure of David Searles. The Master of All Souls.

His father.

THIRTY

Jennifer Callaby's eyelids slowly opened. Andy saw how large and black her pupils were, and he told himself that it was nothing more than pupil dilation, caused by the dim light. All the same, they looked like two black pits of despair.

She blinked a few times. Her lips parted slowly, a dry tongue attempted to moisten her lips.

"Andy? Is that you?" The words were barely audible. She reached her hands to his face, a frown crossing her features as she saw the unrecognisable meat of her left hand. Then realisation – and the pain – returned.

Her howl of despair tore Andy's soul apart. His head slumped onto the cold flagstones, his teeth clenched together.

"Don't look at it, darling. Don't look…" he forced his head up, held her head in both hands and brought her lips close to him. Her eyes bored into his. Loving, pitying. Despairing.

"Why, Andy? Why are they doing this?" Tears dripped from her eyelids and ran down Andy's knuckles. Then she saw his wounded shoulder… and how much pain it caused him to hold her head in both hands.

"Oh, Andy…"

"Don't, Jen. Just look into my eyes. Just look at me." *Be strong, darling. Be strong.* He saw some of the despair leaving those black liquid pools. Hope was a far cry from replacing them, but it was a start.

"It ends now, Jen. They're not going to do any more to you, I promise."

A sound from behind them made her look over his ravaged shoulder. Her eyes widened in terror.

"Touching, Hughes. Very touching. But the Council have only just started on your woman. *And you're in no position to make false promises!*"

The back of Andy's head exploded. Stars spun crazily around the whitened face of Jen. A scarlet curtain twitched on either side of his vision and for a brief moment

Andy Hughes thought he was back in the Great Hall, witnessing the domain of Andraste. Then his right ear was grabbed and pulled savagely down.

Jen's face was replaced with the inverted, grinning visage of Franklin, then a blinding white light as the torch came crashing down on him.

He heard Jen scream, heard Franklin laugh, and heard the muted sound of his own teeth splintering. The torch was raised again, the light showing all too clearly the pieces of dental enamel buried in the rubber casing of the torch, and then it was brought crashing down on the bridge of his nose.

The pain in his face now eclipsed the agony of his shoulder, compounded by his inability to breathe. His mouth was filled with a gritty syrup of crushed teeth and his nasal passages were blocked with gushing blood, blood that fell back down his throat, forcing him to swallow, choking on the fragments of his teeth.

"You've caused me no end of grief, Hughes. Boyd should have had you banged up by now - but you and your alcoholic friend have fucked that all up. I owe you for that."

Andy didn't see the booted foot of the head porter swing back. But he felt it when it landed in his ribs, felt the splinters of bone break through the hard muscle of his abdomen. He blacked out.

It was the sound of Jen's shouting that brought him round. Not screaming, not pleading, he realised as he leant over and vomited black blood onto the stone floor. Shouting.

Through a haze of black and red he saw the head porter, with his back toward him. He was stood over Jen, his arms folded, his head cocked to one side. The stance of a man gently amused by the defiance of a small child.

Jen was climbing to her feet, her face contorted with hatred and rage. Never had he seen a look like that cross her features. Jennifer Callaby, the woman who didn't have a bad word to say about anyone or anything. It was the face of someone who, for the first time in her life, wanted to kill. Perhaps that was why Franklin was so amused.

He turned and laughed at the sight of Andy crawling towards them. He raised a hand to Jen, who had failed in her attempt to get to her feet. She stumbled, falling back to the floor with a cry of rage and frustration.

"I'll tell you in a minute, Ms Callaby." Franklin knelt down and retrieved the shotgun. Hefting it over his shoulder, he glanced down at Andy.

"Well, Mr Hughes, you've missed all the fun. Your young lassie has quite a sharp tongue on her. Andraste will enjoy tearing that out, I'm sure.

"Yes, I've told her what her role is, what's expected of her. What awaits her."

Andy crawled forwards, his nails scraping on the stone floor, every movement fresh agony. But the look of defiance and hatred in Jen's eyes steeled him. It gave him hope.

"Bastard," Andy hissed through the remains of his teeth. "Murdering bastard…"

Franklin's eyes widened at the sight of the battered, bleeding man crawling his way across the cold stone floor of the sacrificial chamber. He nodded in approval and genuine respect.

"I'm impressed, Hughes. I really am. But save it. It won't do you any good." He glanced at Jen's mutilated hand, then at Andy's intact one.

"Neither of you have much time left. The Fellowship will be returning shortly to complete the sacred task, so enjoy your brief time together."

Franklin stepped backwards and allowed the lovers to find their way together. He stared hard at Jen's left hand.

"No ring, Hughes? Shame on you. A good woman like this, you should have made a commitment a long time ago." He lowered the SPAS 12 from his shoulder. He examined the gaping hole of the muzzle then stared at the pistol grip. He looked back at Andy's left hand, the fingers splayed outwards, reaching for Jen's unmarked right hand.

"What's the point, though?" Franklin said ruefully. "What would you do? Share your life with her, share the household bills, raising of children, so forth…none of that's available to you now. But there is one thing you can share with her." Franklin raised the SPAS 12.

"Share her pain." He brought the butt crashing downwards onto the knuckles of Andy's left hand with enough force to crush them into a pulp, sever three fingers and strike sparks on the stone floor underneath.

Searles walked forward calmly, his gowned arms outstretched. Not a placating or conciliatory gesture but one of purpose. Secure in self-belief – a recent change, Jason realised. There was no trace of the Master's former weakness or self-doubt in that walk. Not even horror at what his son had just done – or fear.

He remembered the words the Senior Tutor had said to Franklin last year, just before unconsciousness claimed him.

Like father, like son, eh Franklin? At that time he'd thought it was a private joke or a strange insult aimed at the head porter. But watching the Master of All Souls advance towards him he knew now what Nasen had meant.

The desire for the end of Andraste, the destruction of the Fellowship of All Souls. The one thing Jason and David Searles had held in common. But it seemed now they didn't even have that in common. Searles smiled grimly, his eyes full of purpose and…

Duty, Jason thought suddenly. *The awareness of – and acceptance of- an onerous but sacred responsibility. He's come to accept the duty of Master just as I've come to free him from it!*

He opened the door and stepped out of the cab. He smiled. Running in thick rivulets underneath the van was the blood of the Bursar, pooling around his trainers.

But where was the body? He frowned, forgetting the approaching figure of his father for one moment. He turned and stared at the damage he had caused.

The right door was hung precariously off the top hinges. The bottom one had sheared away completely. The door rocked back and forth in time with the wind. And even though both hinges on the left hand door had sheared away the door was still standing - but only because the tail lift had driven into it by a full two feet.

He stared in wonderment. The blood on the raised anti-slip surface made a strange pattern, but not quite as strange as the severed top half of the Bursar that had fallen to his side, hands raised. The fingers were twitching, as were the grey and yellowish tubes spilling from below the Bursar's broken ribcage.

"Jason."

He turned to face the speaker. David Searles was four feet away from the open driver's door. Jason's eyes narrowed.

He reached into the cab and withdrew one of the petrol cans. Hefting it in his right hand he advanced towards his father.

"You don't seem too concerned to see me, Master. *Daddy!*" Jason spat the last word out and Searles halted. He lowered his hands and sighed.

"So you know, then. What do you want me to say, Jason?" His eyes were hard. No trace of weakness anymore, no regret – and no guilt. That was the hardest thing for Jason to accept.

"Apologise? Beg your forgiveness for giving you life? That was my sin, my weakness, and I've suffered for it." The Master's eyes were chips of slate. "And the world almost suffered for it. You should never have been born, Jason. You were an accident, the result of my lust. A symbol of my failure, nothing more."

Jason felt the rage build in him at the cold, impersonal brush-off from the man who now finally admitted to being his father. He remembered the words of The Elder. *Harness this rage, Jason. Unleash it against your father.* His hand tightened on the petrol can.

Searles glanced at it, a flicker of concern in his hazel eyes. But not fear. He saw the other fuel cans on the passenger seats and saw the blood-stained temperature probe on the dash. He shook his head slowly.

"It would appear that you're much better equipped this year, Jason." He looked back to the petrol can in Jason's hand and raised a pointed, steady finger at it.

"But to finish what you started? Forget it. You're too late. The propitiation is being prepared to sing as we speak. Andraste will be appeased in spite of your attempts to disrupt our sacred duty. It is only a matter of time before the police make their way here to apprehend you…but that will be the least of your concerns. You really haven't planned this properly, have you? As my son, I don't know if I should be relieved or disappointed."

"Neither. Be prepared." Jason's fury coursed through him now, ice cold and red hot. As cold as the snow that froze the unhallowed stones of the buildings of All Souls, as hot as the furnace that Andraste would turn the world into. An unnatural rage: that could only have come from one born of the bloodline of the Fellowship of All Souls.

"Prepared," Searles nodded, his eyes flicking from the petrol can to the severed body of the Bursar. "For what, exactly?"

Jason said nothing.

"Justice, retribution? Divine Judgement?" Searles took a step forwards.

Jason became aware of movement, a noise behind him. One he had been expecting. He turned smoothly, the petrol can striking the advancing porter in the face. The porter staggered backwards, blood gushing from the shattered ruin of his nose. The neatly trimmed blonde goatee, now turning crimson, told him this was Street, the head porter's younger deputy.

Street swayed violently, hands clenched over the pumping fountain in his face. Jason raised the petrol can high over his head and brought it down, hard on Street's crown.

The impact sent jarring shockwaves up his arm. The crack of plastic and bone was followed by fluid splashing on his sleeve.

He looked down in surprise. It wasn't Street's blood – that was spreading on the snowy flagstones of the path underneath the dead porter. He raised the can again to the light from the van's headlights, and saw that the moulding seam had split.

"Shit."

Now that he was alone Searles looked alarmed. He saw the fluid trickling down Jason's arm, soaking the navy sweatshirt, saw the body of Franklin's assistant twitching in its death throes on the steps of the Great Hall.

"Shoddy piece of kit," Jason muttered as he examined the split in the plastic. "Still, nothing lasts forever, does it, father?"

Searles couldn't reply. He opened his mouth to speak, only to have it filled with sharp, acrid liquid. He coughed, gagging as the petrol slipped down his throat.

Jason walked around the black gowned figure, splashing more fuel from the damaged petrol can onto him, eager to get as much on his father as he could before it was lost to the ground.

"Nothing lasts forever, dad. Twenty-first century plastic and fourteenth century stone – and all within – they all go in the end. Consumed by fire."

Jason threw the empty canister away. It hit the flagstones and made a hollow noise that echoed around the confines of Old Court. He watched Searles flapping in panic and genuine fear, a complete contrast to the arrogance and new-found contempt that had been displayed before.

The Master rubbed his eyes with the sleeves of the gown, blinking furiously. The coughing subsided. Now he looked ready to run. His eyes searched Jason, watching for his next movement.

Jason now stood by the near side of the Luton. He pulled the flap marked UNLEADED ONLY and pointed to the missing filler cap – and the rag stuffed there. He reached into his pocket and retrieved the lighter.

Searles' shoulders stiffened. He let out a long hiss of terror and backed away, his hands raised in supplication. Jason advanced, waving the lighter.

"Come on, daddy! How about a big hug for your number one son? Just got time before we all go up in smoke!"

Searles had moved behind the driver's door. Jason shook his head.

"No point hiding, daddy." His thumb rubbed up and down the wheel. It made soft, threatening clicking noises. He spread his arms wide, grinning in triumph and anticipation.

Then he saw what was tearing from the open door of the Transit parked outside the porter's lodge. His arms dropped and his smile froze.

What the bloody HELL?

Within a second, Searles was on him.

It had been human once. It had been skinned, gutted and deboned, but it could only have come from a human being. Whether or not it was male or female – Dan or Emma – he couldn't be sure. He didn't want to be sure.

Rob Benson's hands trembled on the steel worktop. His nails scraped along the steel surface, and the rocking motion caused the Browning to rattle.

He closed his eyes and tilted his head back. His breath came out in ragged bursts of mist in the freezing cold air. Now he knew what the Communion was. Why the boar was ritually buried. It wasn't enough for the victim of Andraste's choosing to be ceremonially tortured to death, for his or her soul to be eternally torn to pieces.

The final insult, the ultimate horror. And the remainder given to the beasts of the forest…

He swayed on his feet, felt the black and white tiles rearing up to meet him. He glanced around the empty kitchen. The fluorescent lights shone coldly on the catering utensils and shining white serving plates. He heard only the steady humming of the refrigerator units, the roaring of the fan ovens, a door opening to his left.

Rob turned around, saw the door marked CATERING OFFICE closing behind the huge bulk of the head chef who walked slowly towards him. Even from this distance Cassell reeked of sour sweat and halitosis. His greasy, fat lips were parted in surprise and anger, a pink slug-like tongue poking between them. His overalls were stained with crimson patches and brownish yellow stains.

"You again, boy? Come to get some scraps for your little doggie, have you?"

The wheezy laughter of the head chef echoed around the whitewashed walls of the kitchen. Rob's stomach lurched when he saw Cassell stretch out a hand to the knife rack to the right of the Catering Office doorway. Cassell didn't even look at the selection. His sweaty fingers closed immediately around the largest blade, a carving knife that Rob thought wouldn't have looked out of place on a Russian whaling ship.

*Fuck him! He's got a blade, but I've got a shooter…*he stretched his hand behind, feeling for the spot he was certain he'd put the gun. They met the cold dead meat of the boar's stomach contents. Rob's hand jerked away as if he'd touched a live electrical wire. His stomach flipped and he started to gag.

"Found out our little secret, white van man? Good for you!" He raised the carving knife. The reflecting strip-lighting turned the four inch wide blade into liquid silver.

Rob turned around, saw the Browning lay on the adjacent table – and lunged for it.

His fingers closed around the pistol grip just as a heavy industrial saucepan flew past his ear and struck his hand with unerring accuracy. Rob howled in pain and the pistol spun away from his hand, falling to the floor where it fractured one of the tiles.

A wet, clammy hand clamped onto his right shoulder and spun him round. Rob Benson felt rather than saw the tip of the carving knife placed under his left eye. All he saw were the eyes of Cassell boring into him; a cruel smile plastered on the sweating, pockmarked face.

"Bringing guns into my workshop, boy? Not even Franklin would dare do that!" The point of the knife jabbed forwards, bringing a small drop of blood to the surface. Rob cried out in alarm and tried tilting his head further back, but Cassell's fingers dug

dug into his shoulder and held him firm. The head chef brought his chin to the level of his knuckles, his eyes inches away from Rob's. He chuckled.

"I'm guessing you're friends with this Hughes man I was warned about." Spittle flecked from his fat lips as he spoke. "Yes, you know who I mean. Let me tell you something.

"This isn't just a kitchen, delivery boy. Not even a 'catering unit' as them that runs the accounts and tries to sell the food to posh nobs would like to call it. Every year, this becomes my studio. This is where I practices my art, see?"

In spite of the fear that held him frozen, Rob laughed.

"Art? *Art*? Cutting people up and stuffing them inside a pig – that's art? Fuck you, fat man!"

Cassell took his hand from Rob's shoulder and patted his cheek gently. The knife remained where it was.

"It's not an art you suffer for, is it Cassell? For fuck's sake, why? Isn't it enough that those poor fuckers are tortured to death – do you have to eat them as well?"

"That's the nature of the Communion, boyo. Andraste demands. Flesh of the offering binding to the flesh of one of her Children. The Fellowship consumes the flesh as Andraste consumes the soul." He laughed again. "But to merge the two meats – it's an art form, boy. One I wouldn't expect you to understand."

"That why you got so pissed off yesterday?" Rob snapped. The fear was fading, despite the cold steel under his eyeball. Rage and disgust replaced fear. "Me and Jasper almost spoiled your canvas, didn't we?"

Cassell's face darkened.

"Far worse than that, delivery boy. Your drunken little visit last night was *far* worse. Running over one of the Children of Andraste and taking its hallowed corpse away from the Nemeton – that's never been done before!"

"First time for everything…boy." Rob risked a sarcastic grin. "Don't worry; he's resting in peace now."

Now Cassell looked worried. His grip returned to Rob's shoulder and he dug his fingers in again.

"Where is it?" There was urgency in the head chef's voice. "Where is the boar?"

"Last time I saw him he was nothing more than a pile of cremated ash in my warehouse – until he came back to life and attacked me." Rob gritted his teeth. "Your mate Jasper saved me this time…but you'll be pleased to know he won't be pissing in your kitchens anymore."

Cassell stared wide eyed at him. Then he smiled.

"Now you know the true power of Andraste's children. How special those beasts are…and what an honour it is to be allowed to consume their flesh."

Knowing how much the boar had stunk when they'd forked it off the Transit yesterday Rob couldn't agree less.

"I'll take your word for that, pal." He wondered if Jasper had enjoyed the honour before he died. He must have swallowed a fair chunk of the beast's blood and flesh when he savaged it in the warehouse.

"You'll have to. It's an honour that won't be extended to you." He glanced behind him, to the open service doors leading to the dead catering worker hanging over the rail.

"Now, I've got work to do. You've left me a little short staffed today. I've got enough work cut out for me as it is."

He took the blade from Rob's face and extended his left arm as far as he could.

Then he lowered the knife and drove it into Rob's stomach.

THIRTY ONE

The pain was so great Andy couldn't even scream. He rolled on the floor, knocking over the last of the candles. He held the ravaged ruin of his hand to his chest and then tried to thrust it away, as though the more distance he could put between it and him the less agony he'd feel.

He couldn't breathe. Vomit and broken teeth filled his throat once more. He spun round on the floor and became vaguely aware of a booted foot prodding him in the broken ribs. He didn't hear the mocking words of the head porter.

"Three each. Well done, Hughes. You've shared some of her pain." Franklin lowered the combat shotgun to the floor and retrieved the flashlight. He shone it around the twisting, thrashing bulk of Hughes. In the light from the Krypton bulb the blood spraying from Andy's injuries gleamed unnaturally.

"Not as much pain as I'd like to give you, of course. But time's pressing on."

He crouched down, resting on his haunches, and relit some of the candles. He took care to keep the candlesticks away from Andy's thrashing legs.

He remained immobile for some time – long enough for Andy's agonised writhing to slow. He glanced towards the prone body of Jennifer Callaby and then back to Andy.

"You're a tough bastard, Hughes. I'll give you that." He spat on the floor. "And a dangerous one. I knew this fifteen years ago when you first set foot in the college. I saw the resemblance to Charles Harvey, I knew history was being repeated…I knew it was only a matter of time before you'd come and break the Fellowship and bring ruin upon us all."

Franklin crouched down, his knees inches from Andy's severed, still twitching fingers. He picked one up and held it to the nearest candle.

"Your rage marked you out as one of the blood. You had to be dealt with…and it was my idea to make you turn that rage against yourself. Didn't think you'd come back, though."

In spite of the spiral of pain in which Andy was lost, Franklin's words struck a chord. With dazed, barely comprehending eyes he lifted his head from the floor and stared at the head porter.

So Franklin had arranged for Kelly to be raped by the two All Souls students. Pumped them full of drugs – or had they taken the coke themselves to give them courage? Either way, it didn't matter. Franklin had engineered the whole thing. This was the man responsible for the attempted rape of Kelly. This was the man responsible for his fifteen years inside prison. And all because he was seen as a threat?

Andy coughed blood and spat on the floor. A reddish clump sat alongside Franklin's plug of yellowish phlegm. Franklin laughed and dropped the finger. It landed, nail first, into Andy's bloody spittle. The crushed bone glinted in the candle light. Andy stared at it, hardly believing that this piece of meat was once a moving, living part of his body.

Then he remembered the same thing had happened to Jen. He looked despairingly at her slumped, motionless body. Even unconsciousness had not brought a temporary respite to her suffering. Her face was still creased in agony, her eyeballs rapidly moving behind squeezed shut eyelids.

"You're wrong, Franklin," Andy's words were barely audible, even to himself. "Can't you even fucking see this? Or has your...*devotion* to your duty blinded you to what's good and what's evil?"

"Good and evil. Who are *you* to lecture me on the nature of evil?" Andy could hear genuine anger in Franklin's voice.

"I've seen and performed things that would turn your mind inside out, Hughes. I've killed and tortured in the name of Queen and Country – in the name of duty. Yes, it came easy to me. In that respect I'm blessed."

"Blessed?" Andy laughed bitterly. "Able to leave your humanity outside the door like a shit-stained pair of shoes? That's a blessing?"

"It's a gift, Hughes," Franklin growled. "One that came in very useful when I was working for Intel. Dirty tricks, cover-ups...you have no idea what I had to do in Belfast, Iraq and the Falklands. All necessary, just so that you lot can sleep peacefully in your beds at night. And we never asked for any thanks, any appreciation...we knew it was our duty and accepted it accordingly."

"And we're all eternally grateful," Andy spat.

Jen's eyes opened. From this angle, only Andy could see her smile and wink slowly at him.

"That's just it." Franklin's eyes blazed in anger and hatred. "You're not. Duty is a word your generation knows nothing about. All so quick to march on a protest against a war…because you have the luxury of choice. How quickly would you lay down your life for a cause?

"Even the older generation weakens, fails to step up to the mark when duty calls. Look at our so-called Master! A man who could have brought destruction upon us all by failing his duty. He won't weaken this year. I've steeled him -"

For the second time an explosion rocked the stone walls of the cellar. Jen moved with a speed that took even Andy by surprise, her arm moving to the trigger of the SPAS 12 laying between her and Franklin.

The recoil powered the combat shotgun backwards, spinning on the floor. Jen cried out in pain as the sharp edges of the folded metal stock slammed into her elbow.

Franklin staggered, his hands clamped to his ears – too late to muffle the sound from the shotgun. Andy saw him stagger, swaying on the blood-soaked flags like a drunkard, a dazed expression on his harsh features.

There was fresh blood on the floor. Andy realised why Franklin was staggering across the cellar. The head porter's right foot was a mangled pulp of meat, shredded black leather and shattered bone that dangled by several thin strands of flesh and tendon to the ankle.

Franklin's body rocked backwards and forwards. He put his weight down on the remnants of his foot, confused when it wouldn't support him. With a wet, tearing sound the last pieces of flesh and tendon ripped away.

He fell to his right, crashing to the floor with enough force to send the relit candles spinning away to the corners of the cellar. The flashlight remained clenched in his hand, and he shone it fearfully on his legs.

Andy blinked at the harsh glare of the Krypton bulb bouncing off the stone walls. It illuminated Jen's face briefly, and her grim smile of satisfaction. The beam moved elsewhere and her face was plunged into candlelit gloom once again.

"Andy?"

Her voice was drowned out by the inhuman sounds coming from the crippled head porter. Andy began to crawl over to her, his hands raised. Blood dripped steadily from the three stumps on his left hand.

Dripped onto her cheek, her parted lips. And in return he felt her ravaged hand make contact with his right cheek. He felt the gap between her thumb and little finger and felt a resurgence of the rage.

"Hey, tough guy. Supposed to be rescuing me, remember? Not the other way round…" Her words were shaky, trembling with shock and terror, but the strength in her voice – her very spirit – was undeniable. At that moment he loved her more than he had ever done before.

Strength in the face of overwhelming evil. Black humour and an indomitable spirit that had refused to succumb to despair – this was Jennifer Callaby. This was his love.

This was humanity, and a love worth dying for.

And killing for, he told the black rage building within. He lowered Jennifer's hands and kissed her deeply. She returned the kiss, the tears of relief and love mingling with the blood on his face. She tried to part his lips, but he shook his head gently. She hadn't seen the damage Franklin had done to his teeth.

Franklin...he released her hands and turned to stare at the head porter. The flashlight was transferred to his left hand now.

Franklin had overcome the shock of losing his foot alarmingly quickly. Even though he must have seen numerous comrades lose limbs on countless fields of battle, there was something unnatural, inhuman, about the way he blanked the reality of it from his mind and concentrated on the immediate task at hand.

It wasn't about survival – a tactical withdrawal; getting away from the combat scene as soon as possible was the last thing on Franklin's mind. Instead, his features were set in a determined grimace, his bleeding body forced onwards by the desire to face down the enemy and defeat it.

The cat-like mewling sound had diminished, a grunt of satisfaction replacing it as his goal came into view. Even now his right hand was outstretched, his fingers brushing the sight blade on the smoking barrel of the SPAS 12.

Andy shuffled forwards, each movement of his shattered ribcage a piercing agony. He leaned over and with his good hand dragged the shotgun from Franklin's fingers.

The mewling sound returned, softer, lower. The sound of a defeated man. The mewling became a wail when Andy took the flashlight from him.

Andy heard Jen getting to her knees behind him. He felt her hand on his neck, heard her gasp at the full sight of the raw meat that was once his shoulder. He lifted the shotgun and struggled to his feet.

"Jen. Take the flashlight. Shine it on this bastard, will you?"

He ignored the racking agony of his cracked ribs, the ravaged shoulder and the mutilated hand. He focussed all his attention on Franklin's increasingly concerned face, brightly illuminated in the shaking beam of light held in Jen's trembling hands.

Trembling because she knows what I'm going to do, Andy thought grimly.

"Hughes. Think about what you're doing. You kill me – if you deny Andraste – you're condemning the world to a future of blood and pain. *Think about it*."

Andy stood fully erect. He towered over the defeated head porter, the shotgun raised. Franklin's eyes flicked from the muzzle to Andy's cold, hard glare and back again.

His mouth dropped open, a gasp of disbelief escaping his lips. Andy Hughes had his ruined left hand under the pump of the shotgun. Squeezing his palm closed, ignoring the searing agony that punched shockwaves down his arm, with his thumb and little finger he pulled the pump back and slid it forward. A fresh shell was ready to be unleashed.

"Blood and pain, Franklin?" Andy's words echoed around the room despite the low voice he used. "I told you: that's what you and your fellow caretakers have been watering Andraste's farm with."

He shoved the barrel into Franklin's face. The sight blade cut a deep groove in Franklin's upper lip and twisted it up into a leer. The barrel was forced into Franklin's mouth before he had a chance to close it.

"No more blood and pain for the greedy bitch…except for *yours*, Franklin. Take care of this."

For the third and final time, the Franchi SPAS 12 combat shotgun exploded in the cellar and the top half of Franklin's head disappeared in a shower of red and grey confetti.

Jennifer screamed and dropped the flashlight just as the contents of Franklin's skull painted themselves on the stone steps leading out of the cellar.

Andy threw the shotgun at the still-swaying body of Franklin. The folded metal stock made contact with the teeth of Franklin's exposed lower jaw before it clattered to the blood-soaked floor. Then the body of the head porter of All Souls slumped forwards, falling to the ground and covering the weapon used to kill him.

Andy turned to Jen. Even in the darkness he saw her eyes gleaming in horror. He took her arm, frowning at the cold clammy flesh, and knew she was going to go into shock. He had to get her out.

He guided her past the dead body of Franklin, her arm around his waist and her head nestled in between his neck and right shoulder. They mounted the first of the steps and Jen cried out in horror. Her bare feet had made contact with the shattered bone fragments and warm, splattered brains that coated the stone.

Andy closed his eyes, waited for her shuddering to ease, and then led them both up the steps again, out of the cellar and into the warmth of Old Court.

Andy blinked in the glare of the harsh light, struggling to get his bearings as he searched for the source of the heat and light.

"Oh, Jesus…"

Jen looked up from his shoulder and followed his eyes. Her mouth dropped in disbelief. They both stared, silent and frozen rigid by the incredible scene in front of them.

When he was eight years old, his mother had made Rob Benson a trifle in the shape of a rabbit for his birthday party. It was his first taste of jelly and blancmange and it had made him sick. Now the memory of that wobbling, gelatinous lump of blackcurrant jelly and pink blancmange, freshly sliced from the midriff of the rabbit and passed to him on a cardboard plate came back to him. He was slumped on the tiled floor of the kitchen of All Souls, staring at the blancmange and jelly in his hands and wondering why it had come from his body.

"Bunny rabbit…come from *bunny*…" his slurred words sounded far away and not his own voice at all. He looked up, dazed, and saw a huge, fat man in stained kitchen overalls. He was grinning and waving a knife at him. That knife looked *huge.*

And it was covered in cherry sauce. God, why did mum insist on putting that on the trifle? What was wrong with cream or custard?

The knife waved in his direction. Droplets of the cherry sauce fell on his face, making him blink. One fell into his open, slack jawed mouth.

Then he knew where he was, knew what was happening and the pain hit him.

His howl of agony reverberated across the gleaming metal work surfaces, the shining utensils and knifes hanging on the racks, the glittering silver serving platters that would be used to serve the meat.

Cassell rocked backwards on his feet, momentarily surprised by the intensity of the scream. He winced, shook his head and then slowly grinned.

Rob's scream died slowly, but the pain remained. He was dimly aware of Cassell looming over him, the knife drawing back for a final blow. He didn't care anymore. Everything else that had led up to this moment was forgotten. The arrival of Andy Hughes, the disappearance of Emma, the murder of Phillip Lotson and his family, the death of Jasper and his bosses, the attack in the woods by the boar, the rediscovery of Emma…none of it mattered. Only the pain mattered now. A pain that was so great he didn't want to live anymore.

And the smiling, towering bulk of the white-clad figure promised an end to that. Rob Benson almost smiled in gratitude.

The expression on Cassell's face darkened, changing to one of confusion. The temperature dropped once more and an icy blast of fresh air came whistling in through the open service door.

The service door was nudged open by the nose of something very familiar. Something that now stood in the passage with bared fangs and a low, threatening growl escaping its throat.

Rob Benson accepted it. He was dying, he knew that. All sorts of weird hallucinations come to you when your life slips away.

First the rabbit trifle and now Jasper. Well, why not? No crazier than a tunnel of light or a beardy bloke in white robes…

But, strangely enough, the head chef of All Souls shared his delusion. Cassell's jaw dropped, a strangled cry of horror coming from his greasy fat lips.

Fat fucker's scared of shitbag. Why? Jasper won't hurt a …

The pain lessened slightly at the memory of what Jasper had done to the boar in the Granta warehouse. The ferocity, the lack of fear: the strength and fury that had driven him to save his caretaker from the impossible boar.

It was all here now. Jasper's lips were drawn back from his teeth, a snarl that until this morning was totally unknown to the dog. The growling increased, now a low rumble of thunder that threatened to break into a storm. And Cassell knew it. He backed away from Rob and the open door, moving slowly backwards through the well of the kitchen, past the other work surfaces. His hand was raised and the carving knife trembled in his grip.

Jasper's head turned to follow Cassell's progress. His eyes were no longer that warm, soppy shade of brown that Geoff and Rob had known and loved so well. Now they were gleaming black orbs with no trace of white sclera – and a red pinprick that could only have been a pupil. Eyes just like those of the boar that had attacked him in the warehouse.

His hackles were raised, his whole body tensed – even the torn muscles around the broken ribcage, through which Rob could see organs pulsing. A beating heart and working lungs, fuelling the body…a body that now powered itself forwards, tearing after the retreating head chef, leaping and landing with sharpened claws digging into the flabby gut.

Rob sank to the floor and closed his eyes. He no longer felt cold. The pain lessened, slowly replaced by a feeling of euphoria…he smiled in bliss. Cassell's screams of terror and howls of pain were a sweet lullaby.

Great way to go, he thought happily. *At least in a death-dream there's some sort of justice…*

But he couldn't sleep. Something wet was nudging him in the ear. He frowned and tried to turn over, wondering where his pillow was.

A low whine. Another nudge of a warm, wet nose. This time he relented. He sighed, knowing he'd be late for work. Good of Jasper to wake him…

He blinked, wondering why Jasper was licking his stomach. Then he felt the sticky crimson fluid on his cheek. Saw the ruined, steaming corpse of the head chef lying outside the door of the catering office, his innards exploded from his chest and scattered across the tiled floor like Christmas decorations torn down from the ceiling after a heavy office party.

Now he knew why Jasper's nose was so warm and wet.

Cassell's blood.

Oddly, there was no pain from the dog's tongue actions on his torn abdomen. If anything, the pain lessened. His head began to clear.

After a few more moments he was aware his breathing had returned to something approaching normal. No longer deep, shuddering breaths of agony that made his uncovered organs flop from the gaping hole in his stomach. And the pain was…

He stared down at the wound in his stomach. Revulsion would have been his first impression – revulsion that his dog was licking the torn flesh and fat of his stomach – if the wound wasn't healing.

The parted yellow fat of his belly was rejoining. Melting and merging back together with each lick from Jasper's dry and ice cold tongue. He could no longer see the sliced blackcurrant jelly and pink blancmange of the rabbit trifle.

He stared in bewilderment, his head shaking. He did the only thing he could think of. As ridiculous as it felt, it was the only thing he *could* do.

"Good boy," he said, patting Jasper's cold head firmly. "Good boy…"

Jasper's tail wagged, just as rapidly as it had done when he was alive. The tongue continued its work, and feeling returned to Rob's stomach, it tickled.

He fought the urge to laugh. He also fought the urge to take a closer inspection of his rapidly-healing belly. He'd wait; wait until all trace of damage had gone. That way he could pretend that he'd never had the stomach wound to begin with. That was the only way he'd cope with this. He thought back to his discovery of the contents of the wheelie bins outside the kitchen, the realisation that had struck him.

It seems that flesh ravaged by the followers of Andraste's ritual has special powers of its own…

Healing powers. The power to transcend death. Flesh ravaged by the followers of Andraste…fed to the boar, the boar that Jasper had fought, bit into. Swallowed the flesh and blood of the creature that had consumed the offering to Andraste.

That was why Cassell had been so alarmed. That was why he had panicked, demanding to know where the boar was.

The meat was too powerful to be consumed without the addition of human flesh.

"Good boy," he said in a quavering voice. He continued patting the undead dog and wondered if he really was on the side of good.

Again, he fought the urge to laugh. If he broke into giggles now he'd never stop, not until they came to take him away and bang him up in Fulbourn or Broadmoor.

No point questioning this, he told himself. *Just be thankful. And get the fuck out of here and find Andy and Jen.*

Jasper had finished. He looked up from the now-healed and blemish free belly of his caretaker and barked once. Rob shrank back. There was no blood on Jasper's tongue, but there was a foul stench of putrefying flesh coming from within him. And Rob Benson knew now that the gaping wound in Jasper's own belly was healing.

Rob stared into the glistening black orbs of the collie and tried not to focus on the small red pinpricks of crimson light in the centre. He shivered.

"Not the same, are you boy?" he said sadly. Jasper whined in answer.

Rob got to his feet, wincing. Incredibly, the pain in his stomach was now no worse than that delivered by a hefty punch in the gut. He grabbed the legs of the steel work-top and hauled himself up. The dead eyes of the boar met his own once more.

Rob turned around and stared at the corpse of the head chef. He wondered if Jasper's killing would be permanent, or if Cassell's wounds would slowly heal.

Not going to take that chance, he thought grimly. *Jason Franklin had the right idea after all…*

He stepped away from Cassell's canvas and walked over to the ancient looking gas cooking range in the far corner.

There were four cooking rings. Gas powered, not electric. He twisted the knobs on full, then reached over for a heavy wok. He balanced it on top of the dials. The weight of the wok kept the knobs depressed, and the gas flooding out.

Jasper waited patiently by the service door as Rob returned to the work top and pulled it forward. Its badly oiled castors squeaked and the boar's carcass and its unholy filling rocked on the platter. He ignored it.

He bent over and retrieved the Browning Hi-Power. He checked the magazine and sighed. Empty. Not even a live round left in the chamber. He threw it at the prone body of the head chef. Cassell's head jerked to the left as the Browning hit his face. Rob turned back to Jasper

"Okay, shitbag. Time to go. I *really* need a cigarette."

The Mayfair was in his mouth by the time they left the kitchens. Rob stared dispassionately at the slumped body of the catering worker on the safety rail. Then he slammed the door shut. Give the gas plenty of time to build up before he returned…

He stared at the open side door of the Transit van; saw the trail of congealed black blood and yellowish smears that Jasper had painted in the snow on his way to the kitchens. Then the green tendrils, fresh shoots retracting from the ground and disappearing into the van.

Eternal life in stone…he looked at Jasper and saw a shimmering green light in his eyes. It vanished as the shoots of green vegetation disappeared into the van.

As he stepped out of the cover of the kitchen building he saw the hijacked cook-chill Luton. His jaw dropped and the Mayfair dangled vertically from his mouth, held to his lower lip by nothing more than a trace of saliva.

He saw the broken double doors and the dancing candle and cresset flames within. On the crumpled, blood-spattered tail lift he saw the bisected body of a fat, gowned and bearded man that he recognised as the Bursar, Simon Davies. In front of the glaring headlights he saw the motionless figure of the porter who had run from the battle in the wood, soaked in an oily, clear fluid. The broken petrol can near his head told Rob all he needed to know about that.

And then he saw the battling figures of David Searles and Jason Franklin – *no, not Franklin*, he told himself. *Searles, Jason Searle*s – on the nearside of the van. Saw the open flap on the fuel filler; saw the dirty rag stuffed in where the cap should be. Saw the temperature probe grasped in the Master's hand, the point racing towards Jason's chest. Saw the lighter in Jason's hand.

The Mayfair finally disconnected from his dry lips. It hit the floor at the same time as the temperature probe slid under the Reebok logo on Jason's sweatshirt. The same time as Jason's thumb pressed down on the wheel of the Clipper and ignited the fuel-soaked rag.

THIRTY TWO

David Searles had seen Jason's eyes widen at the sight of what was coming from the kitchen. That was all he needed to race across, over the motionless body of Street, past the blinding headlights of the van, and thrust the steel point of the temperature probe into his son's chest.

The probe had easily pierced the Reebok logo and passed through the heavy cotton of Jason's sweatshirt. It travelled through the thin layer of flesh and muscle and then ground to a halt, scraping on the bone of his ribcage. Searles snarled in frustration, pulled back on the probe and angled it downwards. Then he pushed again. This time there was no obstacle to Jason's heart.

Jason's eyes widened further, in agony. He opened his mouth and screamed to the darkening sky; his body juddering and jerking as though lethal bolts of electricity coursed through it. Searles forced the probe deeper, his free hand reaching for the object clenched in his son's right hand.

Then he saw the thumb jerking involuntarily on the wheel of the Clipper lighter. Pressing down, moving back. Sparks flared and the gas ignited. A flame sprouted from Jason's fingers.

The hand dropped to the fuel-soaked rag that acted as a temporary filler cap. The flame grew.

A shining, blinding sword of light that became an expanding star of incandescence and searing heat. A star that became the centre of David Searles' universe.

All he could see, all he could feel, was the power of the fireball that consumed him. He was only dimly aware of his clothes and skin vaporising, the flesh stripping away from his bones. The paltry reserves of fat beneath his skin melted away to nothingness and his freshly exposed bones began to blacken and char.

He felt no pain, heard nothing but the screams of his son and the roar of the fireball. And even as his eyes, no longer shielded by the feeble protection of lids, popped and bubbled he was aware that he could still see.

Abraham…

It was a different kind of sight. A vision that owed more to what he saw in the meteorite embedded in High Table in the Great Hall than the human method of observing with two eyes.

In this bodiless manner he observed the scene outside the Great Hall. Next to the blazing white inferno of the Luton van he saw the charred collection of sticks that could only have been the blackened skeletal remains of himself and his son.

Isaac…

The light changed. The flames darkened, imbibed with an angry crimson colour. They moved differently, more fluid. They licked at the charred remnants of his bones, and David Searles knew now he was not alone.

You are my Abraham. He is your Isaac.

Alongside the chilling female voice he heard something else. He heard the screams of his son.

Finally, you have given him unto me.

The screams faded slowly and David Searles knew then that his son had departed to join the other choristers of Andraste. He knew then that he had been so utterly, utterly wrong: that his recent resurgence of faith in his duty was a terrible mistake. Knew that James Freeland and Charles Harvey had been right after all.

Knew then that he, like so many others before him, had been deceived. But in addition, he had the awful realisation that what was to come was his fault.

He had killed his son, given him to Andraste – and thus had given her the strength to break through at last.

The girl in the cellar was not necessary. But it was too late for her now. It was too late for any of them.

The flames were no longer angry, darting tongues of red and gold fire. They moved languidly over the charred remains of his earthly body, covering it from view with the flowing, liquid action of a running river.

A river of blood. Pouring from the centre of High Table; flowing rapidly from the glistening scarlet orb embedded in the blackened wood of the table.

Blood from Andraste's conduit: the blood of the thousands of slaughtered souls who had been offered unto her. Blood that signified her rebirth.

Your reward shall be great. You shall join your son, and you will both sing such hymns of suffering that the very stars shall tremble in the firmament.

Andy Hughes and Jennifer Callaby silently watched the flames leap into the sky, melting the falling snow before it had a chance to land on the slate roofs and pinnacles of the college buildings. They saw the wrecked Luton in the doorway of the Great Hall, its tyres nothing more than smouldering pools of liquid black rubber. The windows and windscreen lay in jagged fragments on the melting snow, glinting sharply in the light cast from the roaring fire that coated the bodywork and the underside of the box wagon.

The bonnet was missing and the exposed engine was a gleaming, white hot furnace. Behind the vehicle both of the wooden doors had been blasted off their hinges and thrust into the bowels of the Great Hall.

Andy's eyes streamed with tears from the heat but he kept them open, focussed on the two smouldering clumps of blackened bone lying by the nearside of the Luton.

Searles and Jason. Jesus, he finally did it. And he instinctively knew now that the Master had killed Jason *before* the fire began. Andraste had at last been given the soul she craved.

"Greedy bitch," he breathed. His words were accompanied by a shattering of glass; fragments of stained glass burst from the panes that held them and scattered on the ground. There was a loud groaning sound from the Hall, a sound more like the growling of a beast than the complaint of medieval brickwork and ancient timber.

"Andy, look!"

He followed Jen's pointed finger, and saw Rob Benson and the dog Jasper walking slowly towards them. Rob was eyeing the dented lump of blackened metal that had been the Luton's bonnet. Judging from the melting snow surrounding it, the bonnet had only just landed and avoided hitting him.

Rob's eyes brightened in recognition and relief at the sight of Andy and Jen – relief that soon faded when he saw the state Andy was in.

Andy raised a hand in greeting, and then stared hard at the dog. Jasper wagged his tail and barked in greeting.

"Fuck me, Andy! What happened to you?"

"Had a debate on the definition of the word 'caretaker' with Franklin. He lost." Andy turned his attention to the rest of Old Court. The whitened buildings reflected the dancing flames and the snow on the lawns was melting in the heat from the fire. He saw the motionless body of the Senior Tutor, the fresh fall of snow on his academic gown turning to slush. His cropped grey hair was splattered with blood and optical fluid, his remaining eye staring accusingly in Andy's direction.

"Looks like he's not the only one," Rob said. "Jason's been busy."

He whipped off his fleece and passed it to Jennifer. While she put it on, Andy gave Rob a hard look. He saw how pale Rob was, but the same could be said for all of them after what they'd been through. The strange thing, though, was the large vertical gash in Rob's bloodstained T shirt – and he noticed the same gash and bloodstain on the fleece Jen shrugged herself into. Rob Benson had obviously been wounded, yet showed no trace of pain or injury.

"And you? Had a run-in with Cassell again, did you?"

"More like a run-through," Rob said with a weak smile. And then Andy saw what looked like a newly-healed wound in Jasper's left flank – and the strange red pinprick of light in each black eyeball.

Andy shot him a quizzical look, the look that said *shouldn't this dog by lying in state in the back of the Transit? What the hell happened in there?*

"Don't ask me, Andy. I've given up looking for logic to all this." Rob shivered, staring at Jennifer with pained eyes. Eyes that moistened with tears.

"I'm glad you got her out, man. I – I know what happened to Emma. What would have happened to…" Rob's voice cracked. He wiped his nose on the back of his hand. "Well, tell you later. Let's get out of here. You still got the key to the van?"

Andy thought for a moment. He remembered putting the key in his back pocket when he followed Franklin and Searles into the Great Hall. Wincing, he slowly fished for the key. He held the warm piece of plastic and metal in his hand, about to hand it over to Rob, when the groaning sound from the burning Hall returned. Louder this time and higher pitched. Almost like a…

Andy looked back at the burning Hall. The pain racking his body, threatening to overcome him once more, was put on hold. Something wasn't right.

"Andy?" Jen asked, her hand on his tensing bicep. "What's wrong?"

His eyes widened in disbelief at what was taking form in front of them. Jen and Rob followed his eyes and Jasper began to growl.

Andy's fist clenched over the Transit key, snapping the blue plastic housing as his body tensed. No snow fell to the ground now. It melted, and then evaporated instantly. The snow on the ground was rapidly melting also. The lawns of Old Court began to reveal themselves in great, uneven patches that steamed as the melt water evaporated. The neatly trimmed grass didn't remain green for long.

Andy's breaths no longer misted in front of him with every exhalation, as the air temperature was rapidly rising. At first it was the pleasant warmth of a balmy day in late summer, complimented by the parched, sepia tint of the dying grass; then it was the uncomfortable, stifling heat of a furnace that tore the air from his lungs.

And all the while, the crimson light from the focal point of the Great Hall grew brighter, shining through the inferno of the Luton, dazzling and blinding them all. Accompanied by the roar of the beast that was breaking through.

A roar of shrieking, protesting steel and crashing masonry. Of splintering, fragmenting timber and shattering slate roof tiles. There was a howling noise that filled his ears like a gale, and Andy realised with horror it was the sound of air rushing past them, around them, and heading for the thing forming in the doorway of the Great Hall of All Souls College.

Air: from the lungs of those unfortunate enough to survive and witness the triumph of Andraste. Fire: from the petrol tank of the incinerated van. Stone: from the clunch that the medieval masons had used to build the walls of the college. Wood, from the heavy timber used to create the doors. Iron: from the steel bodywork and engine components of the vehicle.

And lastly, water from the blood of the innocents. Six elements conjoined. Six elements that were fusing: binding together with the assistance of an unnatural heat, a fire that was not of this Earth. A fire created by the final sacrifice, the touchstone that allowed this being from beyond the stars to work its power. A heat that transformed these six elements into something new, something unholy: something that had not been on this planet since Boudicca had, in desperation, invoked a being that she foolishly believed she could control, could use to win her battles and defeat her enemy for her.

A being that had deceived her. A being that was a far greater enemy than the Roman war machine ever had been.

The ground trembled beneath Andy's feet. The last trace of greenery had vanished, replaced with the dull, malevolent brown of baked earth. Earth that cracked into wide fissures running the length of the Court. The ornamental fountain shuddered, wavering as though floating on a moving ocean rather than mounted on solid earth.

Earth...

Earth that was no longer solid. The fountain disappeared from view; fell into a chasm that matched the length and depth of the grave dug to bury the body of the boar that would have been consumed tonight. The fissures increased in number, a multitude of cracks that now reached his feet, but Andy had no thought of running for safety. He had no thought of anything but the horror of what was coming for them.

He felt Jennifer's hand clench his, her fingers squeezing tightly, adding to the pressure he inflicted on the van key. He was dimly aware of fresh blood pooling from a new cut caused by the steel. Blood that trickled to the ground...

Blood...

He stared, despairingly, into her eyes...

She tried to scream something in his ear, but the air torn from her lungs sounded like a horse's whinny.

Horse...

He stared back at the thing forming in the Great Hall, and realised that its power wasn't unassailable.

...power.

He tried to shout the word into Jen's ear, but it was torn from him the moment it left his lips. She frowned, her mouth opened to form a questioning, silent what?

He mouthed the word to her. *Horsepower.* He smiled at her confused expression. Smiled reassuringly. Sadly.

Because he knew now what he had to do. Knew that the Green Man in the Transit was waiting for him, and why it had imprisoned itself on the van's bulkhead.

The link between himself and Jason was stronger than any of them realised. It went beyond the same colour eyes and the black rage. The Elder had spoken to both of them. Summoned them both – but demanded nothing.

Because it was all about choice. Jason had known it, and was happy to lay down his life – but it seemed his father had got there first. Jason's life had been taken, not offered. An unwilling sacrifice, and one greedily taken by Andraste.

And me? Am I happy to lay down my life? Andy Hughes looked at the Transit. In the red glare reflecting off the windscreen it should have been hard to make out the carving of the Green Man on the bulkhead. But the eyes shone brightly, twin orbs of green penetrating the red glare of Andraste's presence. That light illuminated the face, and the centre of the windscreen was an oasis of greenery.

He thought back to the war memorial he had seen the previous morning. Remembered feeling the same emotion then as he had done fifteen years ago, the first time he set foot in Cambridge. What had he said? *The idea of sacrificing yourself for a higher purpose...it's humbling, Rob. It really is.*

He smiled grimly. He saw the leaves writhing in the mouth of the carving as the lips parted wider, opening into a smile. A smile of approval at the choice Andy Hughes had made.

He walked slowly towards the Transit and The Elder. The pain of his broken ribs, mutilated hand and ravaged shoulder kept him company each agonising step of the way, but didn't hinder him.

He wouldn't let it. The choice was made and he would carry it through. He was aware that Jen, Rob and the resurrected Jasper were following him. He could imagine the confused expressions on their faces, slowly turning to horror as they realised his intention.

He would combine the horsepower of the vehicles, as hinted in the dream-vision The Elder had given him. In this way the two pieces of the meteorite would also be reunited. The Divine Judgement would be whole once more. Sealed with his own blood.

For the love of humanity. The door swung open easily. He blinked in the glare of the enveloping green light from the carving. The black pupils of the eyes swung and focussed on him. The lips moved, the vegetation twisting as words were uttered. Words that he heard clearly over the deafening roar of the storm.

You have made your choice. For that I thank you…but hurry. Andraste's triumph is at hand…

Andy turned to Jen and Rob. In the stormy crimson light spilling from the Great Hall, Jen's hair was a whipping mass of red snakes, but her eyes shone clear and blue. Glistening with tears of sorrow and love. She walked forwards, the borrowed fleece billowing in the gale. She put her hands on his cheeks and pulled him close. Her palms were dry and hot, and the congealed blood from her missing fingers had dried to a hardened crust. Her lips were dry and cracked, but they were the most wonderful things he had ever felt.

He closed his eyes, overwhelmed by the passion of their final kiss. For a brief, shining moment, the pain racking his body disappeared as she pressed hers closer to him. Nothing else mattered. Everything was forgotten. The horror of what he had experienced and fought against; the disgust he had felt at her treatment by the caretakers; and the soul crushing awareness of what he had to do now, the task that would ensure her survival – but would also ensure he would never see her again. All forgotten, for an all too brief moment.

The triumphant roar of Andraste put an end to that, a bellowing shriek that sounded like nothing on Earth.

Something that just shouldn't fucking be here, Andy thought. He raised his head and stared in hatred at the creature being formed from the six elements. He pressed Jen's head to his chest, thankful that she was spared the horrific sight. He felt her tremble against him, felt her sobbing, felt her tears evaporating on his sweatshirt.

"You know, then." Andy said. *"I'm sorry, Jen. It has to be this way."*

He glanced to Rob, frozen rigid at the sight of the transformation of the Great Hall and the Luton van. Beside him, Jasper was calmly sat, his impossible eyes staring thoughtfully at the cab of the Transit. Eyes that had a shimmer of green within them.

"Rob!" Andy had to call the name twice before his friend dragged his horrified eyes away. Even then he didn't look at Andy. Now he was staring at the Green Man. His jaw dropped even lower.

"Take Jen. Get yourselves out of here, now!"

Andy took himself away from Jen and gently pushed her in Rob's direction. Her hand reached out to his lips as they parted.

It was the last time he ever felt her touch. Her fingertips left his dry lips and she and Rob ran from Old Court, to the archway by the porter's lodge. Through the archway and out onto Trinity Street, heading for safety. Away from the nightmare, gone forever.

Gone from me. Stay beautiful, Jen. I love you.

The last sight he had of her was as she looked back in his direction, her lips forming the words *I love you* before his own tears blurred the image. He lowered his head and squeezed the rapidly drying tears from his burning eyes. He took deep, shuddering breaths, fighting to control the anguish. The loss.

The anger. The black rage.

Do not suppress it. Channel it…you know the strength of your fury, the potential of your rage. It is a weapon available only to those who are born of the bloodline of the Fellowship. Harness this rage…and then unleash it.

Andy Hughes felt the words of The Elder pound into his battered mind. A harsh goad, a spur to perform the task he had been appointed to.

The one I've been born for, he thought bitterly. He turned and stared at The Elder.

"Now I know how Jason felt," he said. He didn't hear the words he spoke over the roar of the storm, but he knew they were heard. "Did either of us ever have a chance? Was this all we were born for?"

The eyes of the Green Man softened sympathetically.

I do not know. All of this has been ordained by a higher power. There are rules that even I must follow, that even I do not understand.

"Higher power," Andy muttered as he twisted the key in the ignition. He couldn't hear the engine roar into life. He pressed on the accelerator, watching the rev counter needle jerk spasmodically. The air conditioning was on full blast and he gratefully gulped in the ice cold air blasting from the vents.

It was pointless looking at the Green Man now. The Elder didn't have any more answers.

In a way Andy Hughes was relieved to have that carving behind him. Now all he had to gaze upon was the immediate task at hand.

Through the smeared windscreen of Rob Benson's Transit, the final transporter of the Divine Judgement, Andy Hughes stared impassively at the thing that called itself Andraste. Through a shifting, liquid curtain of crimson fire, the entity took shape.

The Luton was no longer recognisable as a van. The white heat had melted the steel bodywork of the box conversion. The paint and the primer beneath had gone, scorched away by the heat of the unearthly fire. The steel had blackened and the van folded in on itself, becoming a huge, spherical object that pulsated organically behind the still-transforming cab.

The headlights of the van were still active, but no halogen bulbs powered the light that blazed from the twin housings. No earthly force was capable of producing the light that glared at the slowly approaching Transit.

Light that blazed a darker, more malevolent crimson than the light surrounding the Great Hall. Now the very stones of the hall glowed. Blackened clunch suddenly afire with a heat source so intense the lead panes of the empty window frames melted; thick pools of molten liquid dribbling down the scorching stones like black snakes, writhing and twisting in the heat.

They weren't the only things moving. With a grinding sound like something slithering over shingle, loud enough to overcome the gale that howled through the open window of Andy's van, he saw the stones themselves were moving. Each one pulsated, making the walls of the Hall sway like a Crusader castle seen through a desert mirage. He blinked.

The walls of the Great Hall buckled and writhed, each piece of masonry alive with an unearthly life-force. The thing that was once a vehicle reared upwards, the twin orbs of its eyes adding brilliant flashes of crimson to the white glow of the stones. A roar of crashing masonry followed.

There was no fear in Andy Hughes now. Jen was gone. She was safe. All he had to do now was make sure she stayed that way.

And the only way to do that is to send this bitch packing, he snarled to himself. *Let the genie come out to play...*

He felt the black rage course through him, allowed the raw power of pure, unadulterated fury to possess him once more.

This time there was purity in it, a sense of righteousness that had not been there previously. It had not been there fifteen years ago when he had killed the two students in the college bar. It had not been there when he had kicked the rapist to near-death in the nightclub in Didcot the night before last.

It was here now. He thought he heard a sigh of relief from the Green Man carving behind him, but couldn't be certain. He engaged first gear with a hand that no longer felt pain; released the handbrake. Let in the clutch and stomped on the accelerator.

The Transit bucked and swayed, rocking violently on its springs as it shot across the broken, ravaged wasteland of Old Court. He knew he wasn't going to be able to build up as much as speed as he wanted...

Certainly not as much speed as the meteorite had when it first visited All Souls, he thought wryly. *But it should be enough to bring it back home...*

The tyres were beginning to melt. He could smell the stench of melting rubber, almost as powerful as the smell of burning earth and baking hot stone. But something else overpowered them all.

A stench of death and decay, one that transcended mere putrefying flesh and boiling blood. An ancient stench, one his primitive ancestors would have huddled in their cave from, terrified in the knowledge that this was the foul perfume of the thing that called itself Andraste.

He felt the steering wheel judder violently in his right hand as the speed increased and the wheels protested. The sickly black underbelly of the creature rearing up to embrace the living stones of the Hall filled the windscreen. Thin traces of green and red had appeared, shot through the membranous surface of the beast. Alien blood vessels, reminding him of the tracery of minerals contained within the stone of the Green Man.

Blood and stone. Hell of a mix was the last thought that went through Andy Hughes' mind as the Transit came to a shuddering collision with the thing called Andraste.

Explosive sounds filled the cab. The sound of twisting metal, of shattering windscreen…

The cry of a human being in agony, his broken ribcage damaged even further, crushed between the steering column and the bulkhead that tore through the padded seat…

The explosion of a piece of stone that tore itself free from the moulded plastic that had imprisoned it, smashing though the thin glass barrier of the windscreen…

The unearthly cry of an ancient, otherworldly being that felt itself penetrated by a fragment of rock even older than itself. A rock that tore through the rapidly-forming, diamond-hard matter of Andraste's physical presence as though it were tissue paper, no barrier to its final destination…

And lastly, the scream of triumph that emanated from the lips of the stone carving as it sliced through Andraste and struck its severed partner, the meteorite mounted on the smouldering, blood-encrusted High Table, knocking it cleanly through the mounting of the table. It hit the smouldering floor, rolling like a cannonball over the now-welded face of The Elder.

Even as fresh waves of agony coursed through Andy Hughes' dying body his eyes were riveted to the sight of the Divine Judgement being made whole at last. The merging of the two pieces of rock was a blinding, incandescent explosion of all shades of green. The lime green of freshly unfurling shoots in the spring to the deeper emerald of tropical rainforests. The darker, earth-hued green of pine needles buried in winter snow. The bright green of moss freshly dug from tree bark. The majestic green of tropical oceans.

The Elder, the spiritual embodiment of the planet and its fearless defender, had finally merged with the power of the heavens, embodied within the rock that fell from the skies over two hundred years ago.

Andy suddenly realised he felt cold. That shouldn't be – Andraste's return had turned this patch of ground to a fiery wasteland, a fitting Hell on Earth. *Should feel hot, not cold…*

Then he saw the blood, gushing from a wound just above the steering wheel that had pinned him to the bulkhead. He tried to swallow, but instead only choked on the blood spouting from a rent in his jugular vein, a rent caused by a fragment of stained glass that had somehow not been fused to the stone by the heat of Andraste's return. He lifted his shaking right hand to the glass and pulled it free. The blood spurted even more powerfully, painting the crumpled bonnet of the van in a scarlet fluid that bubbled and boiled away on the hot metal.

He stared at the glittering fragment of coloured glass in his cut, bleeding fingers. The pigments sparkled like jewels in the light cast from the merging pieces of the Divine Judgement, imparting a perfect clarity to the Old Testament image of a tearful, bearded old man holding a sacrificial knife over the bound body of a younger man. Behind him, a bolt of lightning had set fire to a bush, revealing the horned face of what looked like a ram.

The image had some sort of significance, but Andy wasn't sure what it was. He wished he had the fire that was burning the bush, though, looked nice and warm.

He shuddered, frowning at the wheezing sound coming from below his chin. Felt dry, too. No fluid…

The smell of putrefaction was fading, he noted. Smelled like gas now…

He allowed himself a smile. Above the furious screeching cry of a defeated Andraste he heard the noise of groaning timber. The rafters of the Great Hall were falling, wrenched from their joists by the living stone. Timber rafters, coated in flame.

The green light from the Divine Judgement flared once more, before fading to nothing more than a soft glow. He could see the last of his rapidly drying and congealing blood trickling towards it.

Blood offered by him and him alone: the cement that would ensure the fusion of the two pieces and banish Andraste forever.

What Charles Harvey had attempted in February 1799 had now finally been accomplished by a distant relation, a descendant who had been blessed – or cursed – with the power of the bloodline of the Fellowship. As his eyes glazed and his sight faded to darkness Andy Hughes thought he saw a final image within the meteorite. The face of The Elder: a smile of thanks on his lips and tears of gratitude in his eyes. Eyes that were no longer green, but a warm shade of brown. Human eyes.

You're welcome, Charles, Andy said. His sight failed just as the LPG ignited, followed by the unleaded petrol. He heard the roar of the explosion, felt his body tear itself to thousands of pieces. Melting, burning. Vaporising.

He hoped his smile of satisfaction was the last thing that Andraste saw before her corporeal presence was destroyed and her evil spirit banished to the end of the universe where it belonged.

And as the stones finally settled on the grave of Andy Hughes, as the sirens of the emergency services replaced the howls of supernatural fury and destruction, the winter heavens opened once more. This time, there was no snow.

Now it rained.

EPILOGUE

"Looks like we'll not be having a white Christmas after all," the tall figure said. Standing with his back towards her hospital bed he pulled the blind back and shook his head sadly at the scene before them. A sunless, grey sky. Heavy rain soaking the overfilled car park of Addenbrooke's Hospital three storeys below, rain which had not ceased since the explosion that tore the college of All Souls apart three days ago.

"Strange to think..."

Jennifer Callaby blinked and raised her head from the pillow. She pushed her hair back from her eyes and winced at the fresh pain from the bandaged stumps of her fingers. She let out a cry. The man turned suddenly and let the blind slide back.

It was a cry of anguish rather than agony. The physical pain was a reminder not just of her mutilation, but also her loss. Five nights ago she had been in her two-bedroomed house in the Ladygrove Estate in Didcot, ready to leave Andy.

Now he was gone. Instead, the man who had summoned her boyfriend to Cambridge – and was therefore, in her eyes, responsible for his death - was her first Christmas visitor.

Her parents had been allowed to see her the morning after the incident but only after the police investigators were satisfied she had no more information to impart. The police would be back, she knew it. As soon as she was discharged, they'd be waiting for her – either at her Didcot home or at St Neots. Too many questions were left unanswered for their liking.

Too many for mine, as well. Like: what the fuck are you doing here, Pearce?

She took a deep breath and stared balefully at him. He smiled weakly and dropped his eyes. It may have been from guilt, but she suspected otherwise.

"I'm sorry to arrive unannounced, Jennifer. And I hope you'll allow me to explain a few matters."

She looked at the white ceiling. The cracks were growing, she was certain. The painkillers and the sedatives she'd been given had at first made them move violently, twisting like snakes on dirty snow. That had made her scream even more, making them give her more liquid oblivion. She had been in no fit state to explain that they reminded her of the appendages that had burst from the abomination forming from the combined burning Luton and ruins of the Great Hall.

The last thing she had seen before the explosion knocked both her and Rob Benson off their feet was the multitude of writhing, snake-like tentacles that had burst from the belly…the belly that Andy Hughes had driven the Transit straight into.

Gone now. This thing called Andraste that psycho bastard porter Franklin had so lovingly described. Never to return, thanks to Andy…

Pearce raised his eyebrows at her snarl of anger. He sighed.

"You blame me for Andy's death. That's understandable, I supp -"

"Of course I fucking blame you!" The venom in her reply surprised even her. It made her echoed words bounce around the special, private ward like ricocheting bullets. "That fucking shotgun I found in my home? Yours!"

"Belonged to an associate, actually, but I take your point."

She knew her teeth were still bared. She knew she was holding Pearce to account for all of the events. Although Andy had taken his own life, and had done so for a reason, that didn't stop her hating the man standing apologetically in his dripping black raincoat in front of her. The man who had brought her world crashing down in ruins.

Listening to what Rob Benson had told her in the ambulance on the way to A&E had kept her from slipping into unconsciousness. The surreal, nightmarish occurrences, the unrelenting horror of the chain of events that had began the moment Andy Hughes had stepped off the train in Cambridge station – she'd listened to it all with no response.

In her mind, she knew she needed a target. A human, recognisable one at that. Andraste - an otherworldly presence from beyond the stars that pretended to be a Celtic goddess? A secret Fellowship of a Cambridge College, ritual murderers sworn to appease that deity by a yearly sacrifice?

No, she'd slurred as the gurney rushed her down brightly lit, surgically clean corridors.

Pearce, she'd whispered as uniformed officers handcuffed Rob Benson and dragged him away from her.

It had to be Graham Pearce. If he hadn't supplied the shotgun to Andy to 'look after', she knew she wouldn't have been freaked out so much by the phone call from Didcot police station the night Andy had gone berserk in the night club. She wouldn't have left to go to her parents – and he would not have followed her.

Because that was the reason Andy had accepted Pearce's mission. The only, reason, surely?

"He wouldn't have come to Cambridge if it hadn't been for you, Pearce," she spat. "He's dead because of it."

"No, Jennifer." There was steel in his voice, a hard look in the grey eyes that rose from the polished tiles of the floor to bore into hers.

"He died because he chose to. And if he hadn't, we wouldn't be speaking now. We wouldn't even be breathing." His eyes flicked past her, to the closed door.

She'd been aware of something black and furry squatting in the periphery of her vision ever since the nurse had closed the door on her visitor, but she had told herself to ignore it. To concentrate on the man in front of her, and she wasn't going to weaken now.

All the same, it was hard to ignore the smell. Not just the warm, comforting aromas of a pet dog come in to a warm room from a drenching downpour of cold winter rain. This had the aroma of death and putrefying flesh.

"Andrew suspected that I was withholding information from him about the job. That isn't strictly true…I received very little information myself."

Jennifer sighed. Pearce held his hands up, his eyes beseeching. She remembered all too well what Andy had said about the gangster's mannerisms, how well it masked the violent and murderous qualities of the man. And yet…

"Pass me some water." She pointed to the plastic carafe on her bedside cabinet and pushed herself up to a sitting position.

"Of course." He hastened to obey, his hands shaking as he filled the plastic tumbler. She took it with her good hand, sipped it and eyed him thoughtfully.

"I wasn't acting on behalf of a client. I was acting on…well, this isn't easy for me to say. I could never have told Andrew this, but I was acting on the instructions received from dreams."

She almost choked on the water.

"Dreams like young Jason Franklin had," he added, almost apologetically. "Yes, The Elder spoke to me as well."

He drew up the small plastic chair next to her bed and sat down. The legs squeaked on the polished tiles.

"Very vague instructions, I have to admit. Not the sort of mission statement I'm accustomed to. But when The Elder speaks…" he shuddered and went pale. Jennifer Callaby suspected this was the first time anyone had seen Graham Pearce look unsettled. She didn't feel honoured.

"…well, suffice to say that you feel compelled to listen."

Jennifer took another sip of water. It was harder to swallow now.

"Compelled to listen?" she sneered. "Or obey?"

Pearce lowered his eyes again before answering.

"No, Jennifer, not obey. The Elder doesn't command…he believes in choice. But choices are not easy to make unless you have the full knowledge of the events that need your assistance."

She thought about this. She heard scratching sounds from the black and white mass sitting by the door. She kept her eyes fixed on Pearce.

"Why couldn't this…Elder tell Andy himself? Why did he have to go through you?"

Pearce shrugged his shoulders helplessly. Droplets of cold rain landed on her bedspread, reminding her of the droplets of blood that splattered her face from the injuries Franklin inflicted on Andy in the cellar beneath the chapel of All Souls.

"I really don't know, Jennifer. In truth, even The Elder doesn't have the full facts. 'There are rules that even I must follow' he told me on more than one occasion. But I had to ensure Andrew came to Cambridge."

"To All Souls," she said flatly. "To…to do what he did."

"There was no guarantee that he would, Jennifer. If you hadn't been involved… who knows if he would have made the same choice? I don't believe he would have done. He did this for you."

And I only got 'involved' here because I left him. Nowhere else to go to but mum's. Can't blame Pearce for that. Ain't fate a funny thing?

She smiled wanly. The smile froze when she saw Pearce reach into his top pocket.

"It would be rather bad taste to wish you a Merry Christmas. But I'd like to give you a gift." He held out the package. It was wrapped in green tissue paper and Sellotape.

"Not so much as a gift as a memento…" he said. "It seems the guardianship has been passed to Andy."

The object was cold and heavy. It felt like stone.

Her fingers played across the tissue wrapping. The corners had worked their way through the flimsy paper.

She heard a low whine from the creature in the corner. Pearce turned to face him. He smiled.

"If you'll excuse me, Jennifer. I have a new friend to look after. I don't think our friends in power will let Rob Benson see the light of day for a very long time… so it would seem that I'm Jasper's appointed caretaker for the immediate future." He stood up and gently patted her knee under the coverlet. She was too preoccupied with the package in her hands to flinch, or to notice the door open.

"I can't allow the authorities to take both of them."

With trembling fingers and a dry mouth, she tore the rest of the wrapping paper away.

It was a stone carving. A Green Man. The face in the leaves, the spirit of the earth: imprisoned forever in stone. Vegetation writhed in its gaping mouth, spreading around the face to form a green halo. Yet the face didn't appear to be in pain. If anything, those lips were spread in a smile. The nose was thin and angular, and all too familiar.

The eyes were wide open. Green eyes, a shade of green flecked with gold that she had seen before. In the eyes of her boyfriend; eyes she thought she would never see again.

The same eyes that smiled up at her.

"I found it in Impington Common of all places," Pearce said from the doorway. "This very morning. Not sure how it got there, the blast radius wasn't that large, but still…"

She turned to look at him through tear-blurred tears. He smiled awkwardly. Then he patted Jasper's head and beckoned him to follow. She saw that no leash was attached.

"Guard it well, Jennifer. I don't think we'll hear from Andraste again, but you never know."

He said something else and then she was alone. The door closed and she stared at the carving again. Tears ran down her cheeks and dripped onto the eyes of the Green Man. They sparkled, gleamed a beautiful, iridescent green. They smiled.

And as the sound of Pearce's footsteps – and the clicking of Jasper's claws – faded, she knew she wasn't alone. Pearce's last words stayed in her mind.

Take care of each other.

AUTHOR'S NOTE

I've played around with the geography and history of the city of Cambridge, but Elizabeth Woodcock was a real person. Most of the events described in chapter sixteen actually happened, but her romantic involvement with the Master of a Cambridge College - and the consequences - is pure fiction.

The Phoenix Unit is a product of my imagination. Needless to say, there is no All Souls College in Cambridge, and the academic institution in this book is not to be taken as a representation of any Oxbridge College.

None that I'm aware of, anyway...

-A.C.

Adrian Chamberlin was born in Wales in the early 1970s. His works have appeared in magazines, ezines and anthologies on both sides of the Atlantic.

He's a founding member of Dark Continents Publishing and *The Caretakers* is his first novel. He is now working on his second, a Lovecraftian thriller entitled *Fairlight*, as well as co-writing the third volume of the *Snareville* saga with D M Youngquist.

Jethro was born and raised in New Zealand and had a natural predisposition for creating darkly themed art. After many years of development and experimentation he is now producing his images by means of digital painting. He currently lives in the United Kingdom and is continually inspired by its diverse history and produces illustrations of speculative fiction. His work can currently be viewed at: Jlentle.blogspot.com

Lightning Source UK Ltd.
Milton Keynes UK
178701UK00001B/8/P

9 780983 160359